Michael Frayn was born in London in 1933 and began his career as a journalist on the *Guardian* and the *Observer*. His eight previous novels include *Towards the End of the Morning*, *The Trick of It* and *A Landing on the Sun*. His thirteen plays range from *Noises Off* to *Copenhagen*, and he has translated a number of works, mostly from the Russian. He is married to the biographer and critic Claire Tomalin.

Praise for *Headlong*:

'Frayn masterfully manipulates events . . . As you're dragged into this headlong race for fame and riches, you never know what will happen next.' Blake Morrison, *Independent on Sunday*

'For those who like their fictional confectionery dark and hard-edged (though not bitter), Michael Frayn is outstanding.' Caroline Moore, *Sunday Telegraph*

'It's brilliant . . . I loved it.' Penelope Lively, *Independent*

'Michael Frayn is the most philosophical comic writer – and the most comic philosophical writer – of our time.' Michael Arditti, *Daily Mail*

'Frayn keeps history and comedy in exquisite balance . . . Only after clapping *Headlong* shut does its full complexity dawn.' Anthony Quinn, *Mail on Sunday*

HEADLONG

Michael Frayn

faber and faber

First published in 1999
by Faber and Faber Limited
3 Queen Square London WC1N 3AU
Open market edition first published in 1999
This paperback edition first published in 2000

Typeset by Faber and Faber Ltd
Printed in England by Mackays of Chatham plc, Chatham, Kent

A CIP record for this book
is available from the British Library

ISBN 0–571–20147–4

2 4 6 8 10 9 7 5 3 1

Aims and Approaches

I have a discovery to report. Many of the world's great treasures are known to have been lost over the centuries. I believe I may have found one of them. What follows is the evidence for my claim.

I'm in a difficult position, though. If my claim is not accepted by scholars I shall look a fool. If it *is* . . . then I shall be in a worse position. The circumstances of the discovery are such that I shall emerge not only as a fool but as an object of outrage and horror.

I could say nothing, and no one would ever know. But if I have any pretensions to be a scholar – even to be a normally civilized human being – then I have an obligation to put my findings on record, so that my colleagues and successors, now and down the years, can evaluate them. And I must describe the tangled circumstances of this discovery of mine as fully and honestly as I can, because to arrive at a judgement they will need to examine them in the minutest detail.

Well, perhaps it's better to be known as a fool or a rogue than not to be known at all.

It's a painful prospect, though. Before I get to the end of this deposition I shall have to explain some shameful things. The anguish I feel about them is hard to endure. Even worse, though, is the anguish of my uncertainty about what exactly I have done.

Now, where do I start?

The obvious way would be to say what I think this treasure is. And at once a difficulty arises, because it doesn't have a name. I could simply describe it, and in due course I shall, but it wouldn't mean very much if I tried to now, because it's never been described before, and no one has ever had the slightest idea of what it looked like.

I think that the only way I can come at it, the only way I can bear to try, is to give up all attempt at a retrospective account. I shall have to go back in time to the very beginning, and relive what happened as it happened, from one moment to the next, explaining exactly what I thought as I thought it, when all the puzzles were actually in front of me, and what I was trying to do at each moment, given the possibilities that seemed open to me then, without the distortions of hindsight.

This has its disadvantages. My tone's going to sound inappropriately light minded at times. But that's the way it was. The tone of most of the things we do in life is probably going to turn out to have been painfully unsuitable in the light of what happens later.

So, from the beginning.

We're back in last year. Last year is now. It's early spring. A particularly appropriate jumping-off point, as will become apparent.

What's the first sign that something unusual's starting to happen?

I suppose it's a length of frayed twine.

The same length of twine, it occurs to me, that will bring the story to its end.

The Prospect Presented

Early spring, yes. It's one of those cautiously hopeful days at the beginning of April, after the clocks have made their great leap forward but before the weather or the more suspicious trees have quite had the courage to follow them, and Kate and I are travelling north in a car crammed with food and books and old saucepans and spare pieces of furniture. We're on our way to the country.

Where *is* the country? Good question. *I* privately think it begins around Edgware and goes on until Cape Wrath, but then I don't know much about it. Kate's rather a connoisseur of the stuff, though, and it's not the country for her, not the *real* country, until we've driven for at least a couple of hours, and turned off the motorway, and got on to the Lavenage road. Even here she's cautious, and I can see what she means. It's all a bit neat and organized still, as if it were merely a representation of the country in an exhibition. The hedges are machined smooth. There are too many stables and riding schools. We get impressive whiffs of decaying vegetable and animal waste from time to time, but we keep passing the wrong sort of houses – the sort of houses you might find around Edgware – and the people don't look right. There aren't many people to be seen, in fact, except in passing cars, like us. A lot of the cars are designed for rural life, it's true – specially squarish vehicles very high off the ground, made to keep their occupants well clear of foot-and-mouth disease. But the people inside them look disconcertingly urban. And on the few occasions when we've got close enough to any of their occupants to smell them – when we've stopped for petrol at Cold Kinver, for instance, or organic vegetables at Castle Quendon – they haven't smelt of earth or dung or mouldy turnips. They've smelt of nothing at all, just like us and the people we know in London. I share Kate's unease about this. We don't want to drive a hundred miles out of London only to meet people who have driven a hundred miles out of London to avoid meeting people like us.

The country, what *we* call the country, begins after we've turned off the Lavenage road down the unmarked lane just past Busy Bee Honey. After a mile or two the lane begins to fall away into a little forgotten fold in the landscape. The county council have evidently not investigated the state of the hedges here for some time. There's a half-mile squish of mud and shit under the tyres where a herd of live cows goes regularly back and forth between meadow and milking shed. Beyond the undergrowth on the left at one point is a scattering of bricks and broken tiles, growing a mixed crop of nettles and ancient leaky enamelware. Rusty corrugated iron flaps loose on ramshackle empty structures abandoned in the corners of tussocky fields. Lichen-covered five-bar gates lean at drunken angles on broken hinges, secured with rusty barbed wire. We begin to relax our guard; this is the real stuff all right. This is what we pay a second lot of bills for.

We're both silent as we get closer to our destination. It's not the authenticity of our surroundings that's worrying us now. We've started to think about what we're going to find when we arrive. This is our first visit of the year. How damp will the bed be? How cold the kitchen? Will the saucepans have been stolen? How much will the mice have eaten? Will they have scoffed crucial parts of the bedding again? Will they have started on the electrical insulation?

This isn't like any of our former visits. This time we're coming not for the weekend, or even the odd week. We're here for two months at least, possibly three or even four. Shall we be able to stand so much reality for so long?

There's another unsettling novelty about this visit, too – the long box jammed among all the junk on the back seat and held carefully in its place with two seat belts. Faint sounds are beginning to emerge from it. Kate twists round and gazes at the contents.

'You did put the nappy-rash cream in?' she asks.

'We should have woken her up before. You'll have to feed her before we've even got the fire alight.'

Yes, what will Tilda feel about the country? How will she and the mice get along? Will she find the cold and damp as bracing as we do? Will she appreciate the reality of everything?

I stop the car in the lake that collects in the dip by the wood where we found the dead tramp.

'Perhaps we should turn round?' I say. 'Go back home?'

Kate looks at me. I remember, too late, that this will count as yet another example of what she sees as my infirmity of purpose, my alleged sudden shifts from one project to another. But all she says this time is: 'I'll feed her in the car while you unpack. We'll leave the engine running.'

So we drive on, and the proposal to abandon the expedition is never put to the vote. And now here we are. There's no sign to announce us, just a little track opening off to the left, and a certain unsurprised sensation of having arrived, that *we* recognize, even if visitors wouldn't. Since we don't know anyone round here who might want to visit us, though, this isn't really a problem.

We bump slowly up the track. But when we make the

turn beyond the elders, from which this summer we're hoping to get around to making elderflower wine, it's not our familiar green front door that confronts us. It's a length of fraying baler twine.

There's a lot of baler twine in real country. One of the ways you can tell this is real country is by how much of it's held together with the stuff. Not just bales. Perhaps not bales at all – I've never seen bales of anything tied up with it. Bales of what, anyway? Everything else, though – black plastic sheeting, bright blue plastic bags, gates, trousers, agricultural machinery – everything that used to be secured with string or rusty barbed wire before baler twine was invented. It kinks and unravels, but no one ever throws it away, and it's made of plastic, so it never degrades. Some of it's pink and some of it's orange, so it shows up well against the rural greens and browns. This particular piece is pink, and it's tied across the rear of an ancient Land-Rover to hold its tailgate shut.

No question about the authenticity of this vehicle. It's as rural as a turnip.

Kate and I look at each other. A visitor! And not some friend from London – a real countryperson. Perhaps, after only two years, local society is putting out friendly feelers.

I get out to investigate, still in the wrong shoes, still not in country mode, balancing delicately from island to island in the mud. There's a huge barking, and two dogs the size of full-grown sheep come bounding round the side of the cottage. I'm a little taken aback to be kept off my own property by guard dogs – no, not a little taken aback, quite substantially taken aback, smack into the mud I've been avoiding. I'm wrong about the dogs, though; they're not keeping me out – they're welcoming me to the country, enthusiastically thrusting their wet snouts into my groin, and wiping their paws confidingly down the front of my sweater. By the time their owner appears round the side of the cottage as well, I look almost as real a part of the scenery as he does. And a more real countryman than him neither Kate nor I have yet set eyes on.

'Heel!' he says, in an effortlessly landowning kind of voice, and the dogs become instantly subservient. I'm tempted to lie at his feet myself, but find the ground a little too muddy, at any rate until I've got my country trousers on, and instead take the hand he's holding out.

'Tony Churt,' he says. 'One of your neighbours.'

He has the grip of a man who's used to wringing the necks of wounded game birds. He's taller than me, and as I raise my eyes to meet his I have plenty of time to take in mud-splashed boots, then mud-coloured corduroy trousers, and a mud-coloured check jacket. There are holes in his mud-coloured jersey, and any hint of garishness suggested by the triangle of muddy green flannel shirt above it is counter-acted by his muddy brown tie. He even has a gun, properly broken, in the crook of his arm. His long face, stretching away above me towards a mud-coloured flat cap, is the only feature that doesn't quite fit the prevailing colour scheme. It's simultaneously raw and bluish-grey, with little over-looked dribbles of dried blood where the razor's nicked it.

'Thought you might be round the back,' he says. 'Skelton said you were coming down.'

Mr Skelton, as Kate and I call him, is the man who fixes the local pumps and septic tanks. We phoned ahead to book his services. I introduce Kate. Tony Churt raises the mud-coloured cap, and reveals a brief glimpse of receding mud-coloured hair.

'Glad to meet you at last,' he says. 'I've heard so much about you both.'

'From Mr Skelton?' asks Kate. Though why not? A man who understands your sewerage might have a lot he could tell about you.

'From everyone.' Everyone? The woman in the paper shop, who knows which papers we take? Charlie Till, who knows what size of free-range eggs we prefer? 'We're all so pleased to have you down here. Great bonus.'

The country is taking us to its muddy bosom, at last. And Tony Churt has a faint smell that I find instantly and reassuringly authentic. It's the sign that we've always missed in the few other people we've got near enough to sniff, though exactly what it is I find difficult to say. There's dog in the mixture, certainly, and the tarry trace of oiled waterproofs. Also the harshness that goes with a certain kind of rugged woollen cloth. Something else, too. Something stiff and morally bracing. Carbolic soap and cold water, perhaps.

'Laura and I wondered if you might like to come over one evening,' he says. 'Dinner, why not?'

'How kind of you.'

'Nothing special. Say hello. Tell you the local gossip. Get you to tell us what's going on in the great world out there. We get a bit out of touch down here. Monday week? Tuesday? When would suit you?'

I mention Tilda.

'Bring her. Of course. Wonderful. Plenty of rooms to park her in. Upwood. Know where it is? So we'll say Monday week then? Eightish? That fit in with feeding times? We might possibly ask you to help us with a little advice while we're about it, if we may.'

A little advice. Of course. As I reverse to let him out, an alarm goes off inside the car with shattering loudness. Our clever little daughter is trying to warn us that someone is breaking into our lives.

Do we know where Upwood is? Yes, even we know where Upwood is. It's the big rambling house half-hidden in the trees at the head of our private valley. And now of course we know who Tony Churt is as well. He owns the valley.

Well, not all the valley. Not the patch of land around our cottage, for instance. Our property, as the urban owners of odd half-acres in the country like to tell you humorously in such circumstances, marches with his. The march isn't long enough to make either property very footsore, it's true, but it gives us a bond. We're fellow landowners. Neighbouring proprietors. Brother magnates.

By the time I've got three fan heaters whirring and a great log crackling in the hearth, with Tilda full of her mother's milk asleep in front of it, and four assorted oil stoves scenting the rest of the cottage with the cosy stink of paraffin, we're in curiously high spirits. There are fresh patches of damp in the bedroom, it's true, and strange efflorescences on several walls. The mice have eaten the towels and left droppings inside the refrigerator. Other, more surprising changes have come to light, too. I put on a pair of country trousers that I find hanging in the bedroom cupboard and can't get them done up round the waist. They've shrunk in the damp. Or is it me that's expanded? Am I catching largeness off Kate? I look at her moving slowly and bulkily about, stacking supplies of nappies on shelves. Three months after the birth and she's still enor-

mous. She rolls a little as she walks. She does – she rolls! I
laugh at her. She smiles at my laughter, and frowns to know
the cause of it. I don't say anything, but when she sits down
on the long stool in front of the fire to gaze at Tilda, as the
grey spring evening outside the windows deepens into
night and the three of us fill our little world, I come up
behind her, lean over her, take two fat handfuls of face and
tilt it up to kiss, obscurely pleased that there's so much of
her to love. Nor am I absolutely displeased that there's a little more of me now to love her.

'So,' I say, sitting down beside her, 'we're in with the gentry. All our vaguely leftish prejudices down the drain.
Instant corruption.'

'We could say Tilda was ill.'

'You don't want to go?'

'Do you?'

Do I? Yes! Why not? Social adventure. Human contact.
Life.

'We shan't enjoy it,' says Kate.

'Of course not. It'll be terrible.'

She says nothing, which is a sign of disagreement. That
is, she agrees it'll be terrible, but she knows I mean it'll be
wonderfully terrible, a source of amusement, and this is not
how she sees life at all. Also, she knows that my mind's
made up. For once. And that although it sometimes
unmakes itself of its own accord, it's unlikely to be discom-
posed by external pressure.

'Come on,' I say. 'He was charming. He raised his cap to
you.'

'I don't understand why he's asking us.'

'He said – he wants our advice.'

'Yes.'

'Well, you don't have to give it.'

Because what sort of advice does he want from us? Not, I imagine, our moral advice. Nor our advice about agriculture or animal husbandry. Is some small but vexing question of etiquette or precedence bothering him? Should the Lord Lieutenant take the divorced wife of the Queen's second cousin into dinner? Do I think it would be all right for him to wear a cummerbund to the Hunt Ball?

Or could it be my professional advice that he wants? My opinions as a philosopher on some epistemological question that's come to haunt him? Can he ever truly know that his tenants have feelings? Is everything around him – his estate, his brown check jacket, his Land-Rover – really a dream?

No, Kate and I both know what sort of advice he wants. It's Kate's professional opinion. He has a painting that's always been rumoured in the family to be a Constable, a Tintoretto, a Rembrandt, etc. A vase, a jug, a china dog, a porcelain shepherdess, which he of course doesn't suppose for a moment is of any interest or value, but which he'd be grateful if she'd just cast an eye over, if only to set his mind at rest, etc etc.

'I'll do all the talking,' I assure her.

Silence. She means I always do. *I* mean I'll explain to him that she's on holiday, she's on maternity leave, she can't be asked to identify things. And that even if she weren't on holiday, even if there were no small baby in the forefront of her thoughts, even if she were sitting in her office at the Hamlish, being paid to think about art, she doesn't think about art like that. She doesn't identify things. She's not that sort of art historian, whatever the woman in the newspaper shop or the man who fixes the septic tank may have told him.

More silence. I know what she's thinking. She's thinking that perhaps it's *my* views on art he wants. Perhaps, she's suggesting ironically, the Churt family have some painting which they've always believed to be by the Master of the Embroidered Foliage, an artist whose name opens up delicate ground between us. I shan't rise to this. I shall remain as silent as she is. But it's a little unkind of her to bring the subject up now, however wordlessly. I've given her no recent cause for recrimination. In fact I've just suddenly and surprisingly kissed her, which she loves my doing. But I shan't say a word. I shan't even *not* say a word. I shall simply nudge her fat shoulder and laugh her out of it.

'Come on,' I say. 'Just tell him it's a Constable and maybe he'll invite me to go shooting with him.'

And as soon as I say it, and the silence sets in again, I realize that even joking about the possibility of my finding alternatives to writing my book while I'm down here is going to stir her suspicions. She was uneasy enough about my sudden pounce sideways out of philosophy into something more like art, or at any rate the philosophy of art, as if I were trespassing on her territory. She was uneasier still when I decided to take a year off to launch my new career by writing a book about the impact of nominalism on Netherlandish art of the fifteenth century; openly alarmed when, seven months into my sabbatical, I suddenly put the book aside to write an extended essay on one particular artist of the period who'd come to seem to me grossly underrated; and not relieved, but even more alarmed, when I decided, two months later, that the Master of the Embroidered Foliage, far from being underrated, had no virtues that I could now perceive; when I abandoned this extramarital fling as suddenly as I'd begun it and returned to the lawful embrace of nominalism, with now only five months left to finish the book before I'm due back in my department. Eight of my fourteen months of freedom have gone. She suspects that considerably less than eight-fourteenths of the book that is going to launch my new career have yet been written. She fears that, come September, I'll turn out to have jumped off philosophy and fallen short of art. She thinks that I've lost my way in life. That while her reputation in comparative Christian iconography slowly and methodically grows from year to year, like the standard work of reference that she's writing on the subject, I've embarrassingly fallen off the back of the cart. This is why we've come down to the country – to get away from any friends or acquaintances, libraries or galleries which might put some bright new idea into my head. We shall cook, look after Tilda and write. There'll be nothing to tempt us out of the house, because there'll be nothing to do out there except fall down in the mud, and no one to speak to but sheep and cows. And now, within hours of arriving, I'm humorously contemplating another sudden relaunch as country gentleman. No wonder she's saying nothing.

I nudge her shoulder again, reassuringly, and announce a change of subject. 'The iconography of sports jackets. Why does Tony Churt's brown check sports jacket make it clear that he's a country landowner, while my grey pepper-and-salt sports jacket announces me as an urban intellectual? Why does the seediness of my jacket suggest high-mindedness and poverty, while the seediness of his indicates limited intelligence and wealth?'

Kate says nothing. But says it much more companionably now. Her moment of panic and distrust is over.

'In fact,' I say, 'the iconography of the entire estate is quite interesting. The battered Land-Rover – the broken gates – they're all expressions of a certain style of ironic understatement. They all shout money. We could do a joint paper on the iconic significance of frayed pink baler twine.'

'*Does* he have money?' says Kate.

'Of course he does.'

We go on gazing into the fire together.

'His name's probably another irony. Tony Churt. He's really Sir Tony. He's Lord Churt.'

'Is he, in fact?'

'No idea. I'm going to go on thinking of him as Tony.'

Tilda stirs, then settles again. We gaze at her instead of the fire. She's lovely.

'You're getting as fat as me,' says Kate, still looking at Tilda but I think meaning me, an ambiguity I find curiously touching.

I say nothing. So I'm getting fat, like her and Tilda. All right. It suits me. I've a fat, phlegmatic, cheerful disposition. We all three of us do. I'm going to finish my book, whatever Kate thinks. Everything's going to be all right. I *know* that. How do I know it? Well, how do I know that the sun's warm and oranges are orange and Tilda's lovely? There's a simple but philosophically rather profound answer to all these questions:

I just do.

The ironic understatement of the Churts' iconography at Upwood begins as soon as you reach the end of their drive. The first touch of it is in the announcement of the house's identity to the world at large. It's as modest as our own: *no* announcement. The Churts feel, presumably, that everyone they might conceivably wish to see already knows where their house is and what it's called, and they're too modest to boast about it to anyone else. The message for the rest of the world, which appears on a flaking board glimpsed in our headlights through the rain as we turn off the road, is simple: Private Property. Keep Out.

The style's continued in the string of potholes and lakes on the drive, over and through which our ill-prepared little car thumps and swims with considerable alarm. Kate puts a steadying hand on the precious box on the back seat. 'Did you put our boots in?' she asks.

'We shan't need them inside the house,' I assure her. 'Shall we?'

The house itself, when we reach it, consists phenomenologically speaking of a single lamp in the darkness and what the light from it falls on – a front door vast enough to keep the Peasants' Revolt at bay, with the barking of dogs on the other side of it, and the wetness of the rain on my head, reinforced by the spray from a spout of water falling from the gutters somewhere in the night overhead into another lake in the gravel underfoot.

Then the door's open, and we're in the middle of a genial battle to squeeze past a lunging, tangled, slavering, amiable mass of dog. We're simultaneously patting its snorting, sneezing, endlessly moving heads, holding our small human cargo out of its reach, and shaking hands with its roaring master. 'Oh, what bloody fools you are!' he shouts at either the dogs or us. 'Come on, come on, don't hang about out there, we'll all freeze to death . . .! Don't wipe your filthy noses on her . . .! Never mind these half-wits, just shove your way through . . .! That's not your dinner they're holding, you great apes!'

I was a little apprehensive that Tony Churt – or Tony, as I would call him now I've met him if he were anybody else – or Mr Churt, since he's at least fifteen years older than me, or Sir Tony, or Lord Churt – no, Tony Churt, why not? – that Tony Churt might have put on a suit for the occasion. Or a velvet smoking jacket, or even a black tie, because who knows what the conventions are here? But all he's changed since we last met, so far as I can tell, unless some of the shades of brown are subtly different, is his boots, which have been replaced by brown carpet slippers, though possibly he's nicked his face in slightly different places. I'm privately a little relieved, since I've defiantly come exactly as I was before, in my corduroys and Donegal tweed jacket. Actually, it was either that or pyjamas – I haven't brought anything else to the country with me. Tony Churt – no, come on, Tony, Tony – is wearing a tie, it's true – and in a festive shade of burnt ochre, now that I look more closely, which means he must have dressed up a little, because I'm pretty sure it was more like burnt sienna before – whereas my collar is as defiantly open as Shelley's. Well, that's me. Take it or leave it. I'm not going to change my ways for Tony, for Tony Churt, for Tony. Also, I've forgotten to bring either of my two ties down from London.

They offer us the nursery for Tilda, but it's a mile away, and long unoccupied, because Tony's two sons are grown up and gone. So she takes up residence in the library, where Laura's turned the heating on specially, or so Tony tells us, though I can see Kate feels hypothermia still threatens. Her box is installed on the great desk, watched over by ranks of silver-framed Churts and members of the house of Windsor, some of the latter modestly half-concealed behind autograph inscriptions. I sneak a quick look at the books on the shelves. There's abundant leather-bound evidence of the voracious appetite possessed by earlier generations of Churts for genealogy and local curiosities. But by the time the leather bindings cease, literary intake seems to have declined first to travel diaries and sporting memoirs, then to a few paperback thrillers and spy stories, then in the last thirty or forty years, so far as I can see, to nothing at all. Our new friend's obviously not a literary man.

We plug in Tilda's alarm and withdraw to a big room where small pools of light in the gloom show up little islands of heavy furniture and threadbare carpet. Kate and I perch at opposite ends of a long sofa, which I think a second-hand furniture salesman might describe as comfortably worn. In fact the upholstery seems to have been largely deconstructed by the dogs to tone in with the rest of the furnishings. The dogs settle themselves warmly over our feet, while their master pours us unidentified drinks out of a decanter. We sip them appreciatively. They taste . . . how do they taste? They taste worn. They taste brown.

'Don't ask me what it is,' says Tony. 'Some muck Laura got at the cash and carry on the ring road. I tell her to buy booze in Sainsbury's, then you know what you're getting, you know they haven't stuck the labels on a consignment of battery acid. But she never takes a blind bit of notice. Frozen food? Same place. Know where I mean? Used to be a factory. Made slug repellent. Poor pet. Half a hundred-weight of this, half a hundredweight of that, wholesale prices, breaks her back carting it all into the house. Well, what should we do without them?'

I hope he means cash and carries. I suspect he means women. I avoid Kate's eye.

'God knows what's holding her up.' He looks at his watch. 'She's not doing dinner for twenty.'

'Nothing we can do to . . .?'

'No, no. She'll have to get used to it. Did have a woman from the village who came in. Took umbrage, though. Also took twenty quid out of Laura's bag. Twenty quid *and* umbrage. Bit much, don't you think?'

To take my mind off the disturbing picture of poor Laura, stumbling broken-backed about the kitchen, struggling with unfamiliar saws and cleavers to hack off chunks of complete frozen sheep for our dinner, I have a quiet look round the room, trying to guess what it is he wants Kate to give an opinion on. A vaguely ancestral-looking portrait hangs over the fireplace, discreetly blackened by the smoke of centuries. In the gloom around the outer edges of the room I can just make out prints of racehorses and hunting scenes, of the sort that brewers hang in the grill-rooms of suburban hotels, though reassuringly more mottled and fly spotted. A few modern still lifes and landscapes hang in an alcove. They were paint-ed, I should guess – in the unlikely event of anyone wanting *my* expert opinion – by someone in the local Women's Insti-tute. It seems to me that the Churts may have very slightly overdone the irony of the iconography. I glance at Kate. She's also sizing up the artwork. She glances at me, and quickly looks away. She evidently feels much the same. The Churts' tasteful avoidance of ostentation verges on the garish.

A door opens in the gloom behind us. Tony looks up, and his humorous country gentleman's character changes somewhat. His voice takes on a slightly sharper edge.

'Problems?' he inquires. The dogs and I jump politely to our respective feet. 'What's that thing round your hand?'

'What does it look like?' says Laura. 'We'll have to get Skelton back to fix that bloody stove.'

She advances into the light around the fireplace, and I get rather a surprise. I'd been expecting, if not a broken old crone, then at least another comfortably worn accessory, like the sofa or Tony himself. But she's entirely out of keeping with the iconography. Not much more than half his age, for a start – a lot younger than me, younger than Kate even. She's thin and dark, and she's dressed not in brown but in scarlet – a loose scarlet sweater that rises high around her neck and comes halfway down over dark velvet trousers. She smiles at us, but doesn't offer her hand, possibly because it's wrapped in kitchen paper. 'How super,' she says. 'What a treat. So sweet of you to come.' She makes her point: she's not at all pleased to see us.

She looks suspiciously at the glass that Tony hands her. 'What's this?' she says. 'Not that home-made muck that Skelton sold you?'

'I thought it was the stuff you got from that foul place in Lavenage?'

'What did it say on the label?'

'Nothing. No label. That's why I shoved it in the decanter.'

I tuck my glass discreetly behind one of the perhaps priceless china ornaments. I hadn't realised that Skelton bottled aperitifs as well as emptying septic tanks. I nod politely at Laura's parcelled hand. 'You haven't . . .?'

'Don't worry about *her*,' says Tony. 'She's always in the

wars. If she's not putting her hand on the hotplate she's falling down the stairs. If she's not falling down the stairs she's falling down in the middle of the floor, either because there's no carpet and there ought to be carpet or there *is* carpet and she's got her toe under the edge of it.'

He watches her as he speaks. He's a watchful man, it occurs to me. He was watching us earlier, I realize, to see how we were taking his buffoonery. He's watching Laura now because he's irritated by her, and he wants to see whether he's managing to irritate her back.

'Or through the middle of it,' she says, giving us a little taut smile. He's succeeding.

'That's right,' he says. 'Stoves, stairs, rugs, everything in the house – something wrong with all of them. All conspiring against her. Poor sweetheart.'

And he's anxious about her. Poor sweetheart her, certainly, but poor sweetheart him, too. He's afraid she's going to run off with someone. Me, perhaps, I think suddenly. I see the whole story unrolling in front of us. It's only too plausible. Impotent ageing husband; discontented young wife. Now this comical egghead appears in the district. Someone strangely different. Grey tweed jacket instead of brown. And closer to her own age – someone she can talk to. 'A philosopher?' I imagine her breathing. 'I've never met a philosopher before . . .'

Whereupon some great tragic saga commences. Which might at least save me from writing the book. And there's something unsettling about her, I have to admit. The looseness of that scarlet sweater challenges the imagination, for a start.

I glance at Kate, and make a tiny subliminal face that means I'm trying not to smile. She subliminally suppresses a smile back.

Laura holds up a packet of cigarettes. 'You don't mind?'

'Of course they mind,' says Tony.

And of course we do. 'Of course not,' I say.

'If you didn't drop so much ash on the carpets there wouldn't be so many holes in them,' says Tony.

'Most of the holes in these carpets were there before cigarettes were invented,' says Laura. 'So you're some great art whizz, are you?'

I realize that she's looking at me through the smoke screen she's laying down, belatedly demonstrating a little polite interest in her guests. I nod at Kate. 'Not me. Her.'

Laura switches her gaze to Kate. 'Oh, wonderful,' she says. Kate, of course, says nothing; merely looks as if she's been caught out in some slightly disreputable piece of behaviour.

'She's at the Hamlish,' I explain, God knows why, except that I feel some obscure need to validate our lives in these alien surroundings. 'In the Ecclesiology Department. Comparative Christian iconography.'

'Wow,' says Laura. 'Do you know the little man round here?'

Kate looks startled. So, I imagine, do I. There's a local iconographer? A little man who pops round to decipher your mysterious griddles, keys and lions?

'He's rather a sweetie,' says Laura. I deduce from this, as obscurely as Laura was prompted to think of it, that she means not the local iconographer but the local Christian – the little man in the rectory. She's given up on Kate, though, and turned back to me. 'So what are you, then?'

'He's a philosopher,' says Kate.

'My God,' says Laura. 'I've never met a philosopher before.'

You see? It's all starting to happen. Though somehow I hadn't imagined the conversation taking place through a

– 23 –

haze of cigarette smoke. Or my end of it being conducted for me by my wife.

'But he's moving into art,' Kate tells Laura, amazingly loquacious now the subject is me instead of her. 'He's writing a book about the impact of nominalism on Netherlandish art in the fifteenth century.'

Laura gazes at me, immensely impressed. 'Where's everyone's glass?' says Tony impatiently, holding out the decanter. But she's not to be distracted. 'The impact of . . .?'

'Nominalism,' I repeat, and even as I say the word the meaning seems to drain out of it. I make an effort to stop the leak, if only to reassure myself. 'Nominalism's the view that there are no universals.'

I have her full attention. Nominalism is what she's been waiting all these years to know about. There seems no choice but to give her a complete tutorial.

'The view that the individuals making up a class do so merely because they have the same name, not because they share some common essence. That class membership's established by particular resemblances between members. That things are what they are because that's how we see them, because that's what we decide they are. It's essentially a rejection of scholasticism . . . Of Platonism. It's historically important because it's a step in Europe's emergence from the mediaeval world. It originated with William of Occam. In the fourteenth century.'

She releases the smoke she's been raptly retaining. 'Wow,' she says. I'm not sure, though, that dawning adoration is quite what I read in her eyes. I hadn't envisaged her unfulfilled longing for philosophical enlightenment taking us into technicalities quite so soon.

'Don't waste your breath,' says Tony. 'She doesn't understand a word you're saying.'

'Of course I do,' says Laura. 'I'm fascinated. And it had a tremendous impact, did it? All this . . .'

'Nominalism. Yes – it had a remarkably large impact, all over Europe. Including on Netherlandish art. Or so I believe.' And am ceasing to believe moment by moment as I expound it and she gazes at me. 'If you look at Rogier van der Weyden, for instance, or Hugo van der Goes, you see this tremendous concentration upon individual, ungeneralized objects, on things that offer themselves not as indications of abstract ideas, but as themselves, as nothing more nor less than what they are . . .'

I'm not certain, from the expression on her face, that she's heard of Hugo van der Goes. Perhaps not even of Rogier van der Weyden.

'Or look at Jan van Eyck,' I try. 'The famous mirror. The lamp, the clogs . . . In the Arnolfini Double Portrait . . . In the National Gallery . . .'

I'm not *absolutely* certain she's heard of the National Gallery.

'But he hadn't got very far with the book', pursues Kate, quite unnecessarily, 'when he was slightly side-tracked by the Master of the Embroidered Foliage.'

Laura looks first at Kate, and then at me.

'Because Friedländer is so ridiculously dismissive of him,' I insanely feel obliged to explain.

Laura turns from me to Kate and back to me.

'Max Friedländer,' I have to tell her. 'The great authority on all the early Netherlandish stuff.'

'But then', says Kate, 'he decided Friedländer was right after all.'

Laura turns back to Kate. 'So nice, your husband taking up your line of work.'

'Well . . .' says Kate, glancing at me. This is all a very

delicate area. I move quickly to head Laura off.

'Kate's strictly concerned with the iconography of art,' I explain.

'Whereas Martin's only interested in the iconology.'

Laura's head twists back and forth as she follows this rally, her eyebrows higher and higher.

'She doesn't think iconology's a real discipline.'

'He thinks mere iconography's beneath him.'

Laura glances at Tony, the way I glance at Kate, to see if he's savouring the conversation to the full. But he's gazing into his aperitif, lost in his own thoughts. 'Are we ready to eat?' he says.

I wonder whether to attempt to explain to Laura the difference between iconography and iconology. Iconography, I could tell her, informs us that a worn sofa and a vehicle held together with twine represent poverty. Iconology teaches us that the plain iconography has to be read in conjunction with a wider conception of style and artistic intention – that its real meaning is the opposite of what it appears to be. Iconography, I might go on, tells us that the look she's wearing on her face is one conventionally adopted to represent the expression of interest. Iconology, on the other hand, involves understanding that in this particular context what this conventional expression of interest actually conveys is mockery.

But all I say is: 'It's a distinction drawn by Panofsky.'

There's something about the helpless look she gives me that moves me to offer a little more assistance.

'Erwin Panofsky,' I tell her.

But with this I've gone two syllables too far. Her display of polite interest collapses like a soap bubble. 'Excuse me,' she says, and hurries out of the room, coughing on her smoke.

'Oh, my God,' says Tony, 'you've driven her back to the kitchen again.'

We settle down to another wait, another look at the race-horses. Wow, as Laura would say. This is going to be one of the great evenings. I make the mistake of catching Kate's eye, and at that moment I feel the hysterical laughter rising irresistibly out of the depths of me. I jump up as hurriedly as someone with the runs.

'I'll check Tilda,' I mumble.

'I'll do it,' says Kate, jumping to her feet as well, galva-nized no doubt by the same agonising spasm, but a fraction of a second too late, because I'm already half-way out of the door and merciless in my need. I rush for some room, any room, that will serve as a hospice for a man dying of laughter. But before I can find one I'm stopped by a sound from behind the half-open kitchen door.

Sobbing.

My laughter dies instantly. My iconology was totally wrong, I realize; I've completely misread the iconography. Laura's a lonely young woman shut up in this remote pile with her brutally insensitive husband. She turns to one of their rare visitors for a moment of human contact, a passing glimpse of the great sunlit world outside, and what hap-pens? The visitor talks about things that he knows she in her simplicity won't understand. He rebuffs and scorns her. This is why she ran out of the room so abruptly. She was in tears.

I suppose I should pretend not to have heard. But tact is overcome by ordinary human sympathy. I raise my hand to tap on the door and announce my presence when the sob-bing bursts out with a new and uncontrollable wildness.

I stay my hand just in time. Because it's not sobbing, I realize, now that I hear the paroxysm from the start.

It's hysterical laughter, just like mine.

I don't know what the problem in the kitchen could have been. There's nothing wrong with the pheasant casserole, or nothing that won't be right by the time they have it again tomorrow, reheated, after they've got Mr Skelton to fix the stove. And although the dining-room's large enough to accommodate all the Churts there ever were since there were Churts at Upwood, the temperature's by no means unbearable, if you edge your chair a little towards one of the fan heaters and get your feet under one of the dogs. And I suppose the cigarettes that Laura lights between courses must warm the air a little.

She's long since recovered her composure. So have Kate and I. In fact, we two have ceased to make much contribution to the evening; our conversational resources seem to have been exhausted by our exposition of nominalism and Panofsky. Not that this matters greatly, because now that they've got the initial polite interrogation of the guests out of the way the Churts seem perfectly happy to do all the talking themselves. After a few glasses of wine they've both become more expansive, in their different ways. The only thing they remain unforthcoming about is why they invited us. It can scarcely be anything to do with the pictures in the dining-room, which by now we've had considerable opportunity to assess, and which are mostly flyblown cross-sections of ancient square-rigged sailing ships.

They may simply have had the kind intention of disabusing us of any naïvely romantic view of the countryside. They distribute snippets of bad news alternately to Kate and me on opposite sides of the table, moving in and out of agreement with each other like two motors going in and out of phase, while Kate and I, in the stands now like Laura before dinner, revolve more or less mutely back and forth to follow the game.

'You two come cruising down from town', says Tony, 'and you think you've arrived in some kind of Shangri-La.'

'In fact you've walked into the middle of a battlefield!' cries Laura.

'Put your head outside that door – somebody'll blow it off!'

'The people round here! They're all lunatics!'

'Preservation-mad!' says Tony. 'That's the problem.'

'Yes, because you drive them to it!' shouts Laura. 'You're the biggest lunatic of the lot!'

'Not at all. No one could be keener on preservation than me. But what people round here do not understand, what they cannot get through their thick skulls, is that to preserve you have to change. You can't go backwards – you can't stand still. You must go forwards. Forwards, forwards! That is the law of life! The remorseless law of life! But this my good neighbours cannot begin to grasp!'

'They're trying to stop him building a scramble track.'

'A scramble track?' says Kate, surprised at last into breaking the rhythm of the conversation. 'You mean . . .?'

'Yes!' cries Laura. 'Yobs on motor bikes roaring about in the mud on Sunday afternoon!'

'Two thousand pounds a quarter for the lease, my pet!'

'Money, money! It's all he thinks about!'

'*Someone's* got to think about it!'

'He's already got the whole estate crawling with pheasants! You can't walk down the drive without them flapping out under your feet and squawking at you! Roast pheasant, boiled pheasant, fried pheasant, frozen pheasant – we'll be flapping around and squawking ourselves soon!'

'What do you *want* to eat? Barbecued sparrow?'

'I think it's absolutely disgusting, breeding creatures just so that you can kill them.'

'It's not for *my* benefit, poppet!'

'No – jeeploads of Japanese businessmen banging away all over the place! We might as well live in the middle of a firework display!'

'Two hundred pounds per gun per day! Say ten guns, when we really get going. Say a hundred bird-days per year . . .'

'Why don't you just sell the whole estate, and have done with it?' shouts Laura.

At this Tony becomes suddenly silent.

'This scramble track . . .' begins Kate. But Tony is moving towards a major statement of his beliefs.

'I happen to own this estate,' he says slowly. 'I didn't ask to own it. I just found myself with it, in exactly the same way as people find themselves landed with a big brain, or a weak heart, or nice tits. All right, *I've* got the estate – *she's* got the tits – *you* two have got the brains. As it happens. But it could just as well be Laura with the brain, and you two with the estate, and me with the tits. Since it's not, though, I'm the one who has to do something about it. Because I propose to go on owning it. Owning this estate is what I was put into the world to do. Nothing wrong in that. Every-thing has to be owned. That's what gives it life, that's what makes it mean something, having a human face attached to it. If we've learnt nothing else from the Communists we've surely learnt *that*.'

He turns to me. 'You're the philosopher. Isn't that so?'

'Well,' I begin, 'there's certainly something of interest at issue here . . .'

I've lost him already. 'Anyway,' he says, 'whether it's so or whether it isn't, I'm certainly not going to sit on my backside and watch it all go down the Swanee.'

'But down the Swanee is exactly where it all goes!' cries Laura. She turns to me. 'He has a spectacular ability for finding crack-brained schemes to invest his money in.'

'What do you mean? I'm one of the few people we know who survived Lloyds!'

'You weren't *in* Lloyds! They chucked you out of the syndicate!'

'I walked out on my own two feet, thank you very much.'

'What about that offshore thing?'

'I don't know what you're talking about. Remember the Arab thing, though. That came up.'

'No, it didn't – it went down, like everything else. They all ended up in jail!'

'I was out of it by then.'

It's beginning to occur to me that my iconology really *is* wrong. Totally wrong. I've entirely misread all the symbolism of the estate, from the baler twine to the holes in the carpet. Really no ology's needed – a little of Kate's straightforward ography's all that's required. The symbolism isn't ironic. It's literal. The Churts have no money. All they own is a bottomless, money-eating swamp and an equally bottomless incompetence.

Laura has schemes of her own, it turns out. 'I think he should try to get some pop promoter involved,' she says. 'Have some great festival thing here. Some New Age thing. Make a few crop circles. Ten thousand people – ten quid a head. All you need is a sound system and Portaloos. They'd bring their own sleeping-bags.'

'So where's all this happening?' says Tony. 'On the lawn?'

'No, away from the house. In that great empty bit.'

'Which great empty bit?'

'The other side of the woods. Where the barn fell down. There's no one round there.'

'You mean the field at the back of us?' asks Kate.

'Oh yes,' says Laura. 'Well, you could stay up in London that weekend.'

I can see that Kate's quietly resolving to join the local Preservation Society. But I can't say I feel too much alarm. I think the field will remain in its present charmingly neglected state for a long time yet. The whole estate will. Pop festivals, scramble tracks – none of their great ideas is ever going to materialize.

Actually, I feel a slight twinge of sympathy for them, even gratitude. It's their straitened circumstances, their fecklessness, which are preserving the reality of this little pocket of real country for us. Still, there's nothing we can do about it. I look at my watch, and begin to make the usual ritual regretful noises.

'Well, that was delightful,' I say. 'But Tilda's going to be waking up any moment. Also, we were up half the night last night. And we've got an early day tomorrow . . .'

Why does one always have one excuse too many? Still, by now Kate and I are on our feet.

'Has he shown you the picture yet?' says Laura.

Ah. Here we go.

At least we haven't sat through all this delightfulness for nothing.

It's in the breakfast-room. No, this scarcely does justice to its majestic presence. It entirely fills the breakfast-room.

This, at any rate, is my first impression, because the breakfast-room's relatively modest, designed to accommodate no more than a handful of Churts at any one time as they straggle down in the morning to their cornflakes and devilled kidneys, while the picture's entirely immodest. It lours down enormously from its elaborate gilt frame over the screened-off fireplace in the freezing room, occupying most of the wall between mantle and ceiling. Inside the frame . . . well . . . The four of us and the dogs, who have accompanied us to the viewing, all gaze at it respectfully but with difficulty, because we're far too close to it. It's leaning out from the wall, as if it expected to be at the head of a great sweep of stairs, with us approaching it from below. In its present position it seems to be angled for the benefit of the dogs. I lean back and sag at the knees, trying to get close to their eyeline.

Tony and Laura turn to look at me. My respectful cringe has established me as the authority.

'What do you reckon?' says Tony.

What do I reckon? Nothing, really. No thought comes into my head. 'Seventeenth century?' I venture cautiously.

'Right,' says Tony. '1691.'

'Italian, presumably.'

'Giordano. It's the Upwood Giordano.'

'Ah, yes,' I say wisely, as if I'd been about to say it myself. I'm not trying to claim false credit for my own percipience – I'm politely giving false credit to the fame of the painter and the picture. And actually I think I *have* heard of Giordano, if not the Upwood Giordano, in some context or other.

'What do you think, though?' says Tony.

I look at Kate, to pass the question on to her, but without much hope. She shrugs. 'Not my period,' she says.

Not mine either, of course. One of the dogs yawns and settles to sleep; not *his*, apparently. The other one sneezes thoughtfully. I privately agree with this assessment. But the scholarly fastidiousness of Kate and our two critical friends on the floor leaves me with the task of offering some more extended appreciation.

So, all right, what do I think? Well . . . Let's look at this systematically, in the way that an art historian would, since an art historian I am in my own small way trying to become. What do we have here?

We have some kind of mythological scene. There are many figures. It's taking place at night. The period, to judge by the costumes, is classical.

What's the subject? A number of armed men are hurling instructions and imprecations over their shoulders, some to the left, some to the right, none of them apparently listening to what anyone else is saying. They're supporting what seems, from the strain on their muscles, to be a substantial burden – a stoutish lady whose clothes have been disarranged to reveal her left knee and her right breast. There are flames in the darkness, and the night sky is full of chimeras. Waves are breaking around the men's legs, oarsmen are straining at oars. Yes, what the armed men are struggling to do is to place the stout party in a boat. She's the wife of a Greek shipowner, off on a Mediterranean

– 34 –

cruise. No – concentrate on the iconography. The figure hovering in the air above their heads, pointing out to sea, is Cupid. There's plainly some love interest involved. I believe Cupid is pointing in the direction of Troy.

'The abduction of Helen?' I hazard.

'The rape of Helen,' corrects Tony.

'Rape?' says Laura. 'It doesn't look much like rape to me.'

'*Ratto di Elena*,' says Tony firmly. 'Written on the back. Rape of Helen.'

'She's not exactly pressing her little alarm thing,' says Laura. 'She's not exactly squirting her little gas thing in their eyes.'

'Rape,' says Tony. 'That's what we've always called it.'

I don't think the Giordano shifting dimly about in the depths of my memory is a painter. Didn't he write operas? Perhaps it's the same one, though. Perhaps the picture's a kind of solidified opera. They're not shouting at each other – they're singing. This would explain why they're not listening to each other. People can't listen to each other if they're all singing in counterpoint together. Now we know what's going on we can guess, even without surtitles, that there's some dispute among the tenors about the correct bearing for Troy, perhaps a cautious suggestion from the baritone about going back to pick up some life-jackets.

'Rather splendid piece,' says Tony. He sounds not boastful, but humble at finding himself called by fate to serve as its guardian.

'Wonderful,' I murmur, continuing to gaze respectfully at the great work so as not to see the expression on Kate's face. Sometimes, I have to say, she carries honesty to unacceptable extremes.

'They really knew how to do it in those days,' says Tony.

'Real drama. Real feeling. They weren't afraid to let rip.'

Rip Signor Giordano has certainly let. But I'm not sure about the feeling, in the case of the soprano at any rate. Helen's not singing. Laura's right; she's remaining remarkably cool and collected. She seems to be neither pleased nor displeased by the turn of events – not even surprised. You can't help feeling that strange chaps are always carting her off in the middle of the night and starting major wars over her. Her right hand's upraised, it's true, which suggests she's mildly concerned about *something*. Perhaps she has a delicate chest. One more breast exposed to the freezing air of the Churts' breakfast-room, she thinks, and she may be spending her first night of illicit passion under the Trojan stars with a hacking cough and a streaming nose.

'So,' says Tony, 'what do you think?'

'Wonderful,' I say. 'Very . . . very . . .' Very something, certainly. But exactly what eludes me. Very unlike the Master of the Embroidered Foliage, at least. And very funny. In fact the more I struggle to think very what it is precisely, the funnier it seems. In every sense. Everything about it, starting with the way it's hung, with its elbows resting on the mantelpiece as if it were a bartender in a slack period leaning across the counter for a chat. It plainly doesn't belong here – the proudest possession of the Churts of Upwood is hanging on hooks put up for a picture at least a foot shorter. Don't they have a staircase here to hang it on? What's it doing in the breakfast-room of all places? It's not the kind of thing you'd want to come face to face with after a heavy night on some of Mr Skelton's by-products.

'It's certainly a very striking backdrop to cornflakes and boiled eggs,' I venture at last.

Tony gazes at me, baffled, out of his depth in the critical vocabulary.

'Breakfast,' I explain. 'I thought you said this was the breakfast-room?'

'We have breakfast in the kitchen,' says Laura. The idea of using a breakfast-room to eat breakfast in is obviously a naïve solecism. 'This is one of the rooms we keep shut up.' She shivers. Kate shivers. I shiver. The room's damp as well as cold. So they sit in the living-room looking at sporting prints, and keep the mighty Upwood Giordano shut away in the damp and dark to collect mildew unseen? What a lovable pair of eccentrics they are.

But apparently a critical assessment isn't what Tony was after.

'I mean,' he says, 'how much? What would it fetch? Current state of the market?'

'I've not the slightest idea. Why, are you selling it?'

'Might. If I could get the right price. Breaks my heart to see it go out of the family after all these years, but one has to make hard choices.'

'Not doing much good in here,' says Laura.

'So what do you reckon?'

I glance at Kate. 'I'll go and fetch Tilda,' she says, and leaves me to struggle on alone.

'Why don't you ring up Sotheby's or Christie's?' I say. 'Get them to come down and take a look?'

'Because he doesn't trust them,' says Laura.

'Of course I trust them! I trust them to take ten per cent off me, and another ten per off the poor mutt who buys it, and VAT off both of us! Don't tell me Sotheby's. I sold the Strozzi at Sotheby's. Christie's? Gave them the Tiepolo.'

Tiepolo? They had a *Tiepolo*? Good God.

'And don't say go to a dealer.'

'He certainly doesn't trust *dealers*!' says Laura.

'Been had once too often.'

'What, with that Guardi? Yes, because you went to some crook in a back street!'

And a Guardi! What else has run through their fingers?

Tony turns back to me. 'Anyway, off the top of your head. Ball-park figure.'

No wonder he gets ripped off, if he goes round asking for valuations from people like me. Let's make a guess, all the same. Start from first principles. I imagine that pictures of this sort have a value as interior decorators' properties. They'll be sold by acreage, like so much arable or grazing. How much per square foot for basic period oil on canvas? It can scarcely be less than £100. So what are we looking at here? It's about as tall as I am, and a foot or so longer. Say six foot by seven foot. Forty-two square feet. What's that? Over £4,000! This is ridiculous.

All right, knock off a thousand for plausibility. But then the frame must be worth a few hundred. And probably the bare breast increases its saleability. Perhaps even the naked knee's an attraction. Add a tenner for the inimitable expression on her face. Another couple of thousand out of politeness to my hosts. A thousand off again as a sop to honesty . . . Where have we got to?

'No idea,' I finally conclude. 'Fifteenth-century Netherlandish I might just conceivably be able to help you with. Seventeenth-century Italian – you might as well ask me about pheasant breeding.'

'Netherlandish?' says Laura. 'You mean Dutch?'

'Well, the Netherlands in the fifteenth century included Flanders and Brabant.' I can hear the pedantry in my voice again, the Erwin in the Erwin Panofsky. But this time it's Tony who laughs.

'What, Belgium?' he says. 'Chocolates and beer – that's all that ever came out of Belgium.'

– 38 –

So much for my little fling with the Master of the Embroidered Foliage. So much, for that matter, for the Master of the St Lucy Legend. Also for van Eyck, van der Weyden, van der Goes, Memling, Massys, Gerard David, Dirck Bouts . . .

'But *that's* one of your Dutchmen,' says Tony. 'Skaters and whatnot?'

I turn round. Propped up against the serving hatch is a little winter landscape. It looks like the lid of a rather large box of chocolates, though it's certainly not Belgian, and there's an odd chocolatey tone to everything about it, from the frozen polder to the plangently sunshot winter clouds. It's rather nice.

'Dutch, yes, certainly,' I assure him. 'Very attractive. Way out of my period, though. Seventeenth-century again. Who's the painter?'

He picks it up and turns it round. 'Doesn't say. So what do you think? Couple of thousand?'

'Very possibly.'

'Three? Four?'

'Who knows?' I say. Who knows, for that matter, why it's propped against the serving hatch instead of hanging on the wall? The hanging policy in this house is certainly difficult to understand. Who knows why there's another, rather smaller picture beside the skating scene lying flat on its back? Tents and flags in this one, with three men on horseback, and a girl pouring them drinks from a pitcher, with more horsemen dashing about in the smoke in the background. The name Philips Wouwerman comes to mind. Another seventeenth-century Dutchman. Good. Fine. Not my kind of thing, though.

'Label on that one,' says Tony. I turn it over. I was right – I should have spoken out and got the credit. 'Wouwerman: Cavalrymen Taking Refreshment near a Battlefield.'

Tony waits expectantly.

'Sorry,' I say. 'I still can't help. Anyway, it depends what they mean by "Wouwerman". Whether it's School of, or Circle of, or Follower of, or Style of, or nothing much at all.'

'Too much to hope that "Wouwerman" might mean Wouwerman?'

'That's the one thing it doesn't mean,' I explain. 'This label was written long before the Description of Goods Act. If it just says "Wouwerman" and not "Philips Wouwerman", the one person in the entire world you know they're certain it's *not* by is Wouwerman.'

'Perhaps it's a Rembrandt,' says Laura.

'Well, possibly. But if you really want my considered advice – ring Sotheby's or Christie's. Pay them their premiums. I think it would be worth it.'

Kate reappears with the carry-cot. 'I thought we were going?'

'Yes,' says Laura, 'let's get out of here. We're all going to have tuberculosis by tomorrow, like the sheep.'

I move thankfully towards the door.

'Sorry we couldn't be of any assistance,' I say. 'Delightful evening, though . . .'

But Tony's stopped.

'Just a moment,' he says. 'Where's the other one?'

'What other one?' says Laura.

'There were three of these Dutch buggers.'

'Oh,' says Laura. She goes over and reaches behind the fire screen that hides the empty hearth beneath the Giordano. 'Sorry, but it just fitted. Those bloody birds in the chimney keep bringing the soot down.'

She struggles to shift a large, unframed wooden board.

'It weighs a ton,' she says. I move to help her. 'Wait,' she says, 'you'll get your hands filthy.'

She finds an old newspaper under the empty coal box and scrubs at the board as best she can. Then between us we hoist it out of the fireplace and balance it on the table.

So it's there, in the freezing breakfast-room, among the indifferent chairs, with Laura still holding the filthy newspaper she's just been scrubbing away with, and Tony looking over my shoulder, still hoping for a valuation, and Kate in the doorway, still patiently rocking the carry-cot back and forth, that I first set eyes on it. On my fate. On my triumph and torment and downfall.

I recognize it instantly.

I say I recognize it. I've never seen it before. I've never seen even a description of it. No description of it, so far as I know, has ever been given. No one knows for sure who, if anyone – apart from the artist himself – has ever seen it.

And I say instantly. The picture's uncleaned, and for a few seconds all I can see, until my eye adjusts to the gloom, is the pall of dirt and discoloured varnish. Then again, how long is an instant? The human eye sees very little at any one moment. All it can distinguish with any clarity is what falls on the fovea, the pit no bigger than a pinhead in the centre of the retina where the packed receptors are closest to the surface. If I'm holding it at arm's length, as I am, to keep it upright, what I'm seeing at any one moment, really seeing, is a patch of paint about an inch in diameter. I'm seeing one tiny detail.

What is that detail? The first one I see? I don't know. Perhaps the highlights on the new green leaves where they lie in the track of the sun. Perhaps the figure caught for all eternity just off-balance, with his foot ridiculously raised to stamp the ground. Perhaps just the foot itself. But already my eye's doing what the human eye always has to do to take in the world in front of it. It's flickering and jumping in indescribably complex patterns, back and forth, up and down, round and round, moving fifty, sixty, seventy times a second, assembling patch after patch into a first approximation of a whole; amending the approximation; amending it again. For a picture this size, some four feet high by five feet long, even the most cursory scan must take a matter of seconds.

Already, even as I look at it in those first few instants, what I'm contemplating is not the picture but my accumulated recollection of it.

And already, somewhere in those first few instants, something has begun to stir inside me. In my head, in the pit of my stomach. It's as if the sun's emerging from the clouds, and the world's changing in front of my eyes, from grey to golden. I can feel the warmth of the sunlight spreading over my skin, passing like a wave of beneficence through my entire body.

How do I know what it is that I'm seeing? As with the orange of oranges once again, as with the loveliness of Tilda, I just do. Friedländer, the great Max Friedländer, is very good on this. 'Correct attributions', he says, 'generally appear spontaneously and "prima vista". We recognize a friend without ever having determined wherein his particular qualities lie and that with a certainty that not even the most detailed description can give.' Friedländer, of course, had spent his life among these friends of his. I've spent only whatever time I could manage over the last five years or so. And in any case, I'm still way out of my period with this one. All the same, I know. It's a friend. No, it's the long-lost brother of a friend. A long-mourned child walking back into our lives the way the dead do in our dreams.

Here's what I see through the grimy pane of time:

I'm looking down from wooded hills into a valley. The valley runs diagonally from near the bottom left of the picture, with a river that meanders through it, past a village, past a castle crowning a bluff, to a distant town at the edge of the sea, close to the high horizon. Running along the left-hand side of the valley are mountains, with jagged crags sticking up like broken teeth, and snow still lying in the high side valleys. It's spring. On the woods below the snowline, and tumbling away in front of me from where I'm standing, there's the first shimmer of April green. The high valley air's still cold, but as you move down into the valley the chill dies away. The colours change, from cool brilliant greens to deeper and deeper blues. The season seems to shift in front of you from April into May as you travel south into the eye of the sun.

Among the trees just below me is a group of clumsy figures, some of them breaking branches of white blossom from the trees, some caught awkwardly in the middle of a heavy clumping dance. A bagpiper sits on a stump; you can almost hear the harsh, pentatonic drone. People are dancing because it's spring again, and they're alive to see it.

Far away in the mountains a herd is being moved up the familiar muddy scars towards its summer pasture.

Just in front of me again, half-hidden in the raw spring undergrowth, watched only by a bird on a tree, a little thickset man holding two small wild daffodils is expressionlessly touching his comically pouted lips to the comically pouted lips of a little thickset woman.

And away the eye goes once more, and the heart with it, out into the vast atmospheric depths of the picture, into deeper and deeper blue, to the blue sea and the blue sky above it. The last clouds are just clearing in the warm westerly. A ship's setting sail, bound for the hot south.

But by now I can't see the picture any more – I'm ceasing to take it in. My eye's flickering back and forth too fast in its excitement, and my mind's clouded with anguish. Because it's all too obvious. It's so blindingly evident what this picture is that it can't be so, or someone else would have recognized it already. Yes, who else has seen it? How can even these two fools not know what it is?

I daren't think the name of its creator to myself, because it simply cannot be so.

'Very nice,' I say politely, laying it down on the table. 'Most attractive. Now, I've got a coat somewhere . . .'

Because now my mind's moving over the situation as fast as my eye did over the picture. I mustn't go on looking at it. I've grasped that first essential (and how long have I been looking at it already?). I mustn't make any sudden movement with the muscles of my face, mustn't let my voice shake – mustn't speak any unnecessary words. How do I manage to maintain this iron self-control? Everything inside me is urging me to shout out in astonishment – to let everyone know the joyful news, to claim the credit for my discovery. But I can't even wordlessly bring Kate across the room to look at it, because she'd recognize it even faster than I did, and in her guileless, straightforward way she'd simply announce it to the world.

I mustn't so much as think – no, I must stop thinking, in case it shows on my face. I must just get out of the house and sort things out where no one's looking at me. But Tony's reluctant to let it go. He stands the picture up again and inspects it ruefully. 'What, another dud?'

'They're none of them duds,' I hear myself saying, in a voice which even manages a hint of impatience in its hypocrisy. 'They're all interesting pictures.'

'Hasn't even got a signature,' says Tony. No, there's no signature. If there were, he wouldn't have his hand on the picture like that, because the alarms would have gone off and the security guards would have come running.

Laura bends down to look at the back of it. 'There's a label,' she says hopefully.

I hadn't even thought to look. I can scarcely bear to now; I don't want to know what it says. I shrink from seeing this sacred object insulted by misattribution. I shrink even more sharply from the hideous possibility that my great flash of intuition has been anticipated. It's not a possibility, of course. Not even these two clowns would be using it to stop the soot falling into the breakfast-room if they had the faintest inkling of what it was.

But I suppose I have to know what the label's telling the world.

'Martin,' says Kate, with the suggestion of an exclamation mark, as I squat concessively down to look. This is about as overtly reproachful as she ever gets; I realize how urgently she longs to be out of this terrible house.

The label's a piece of yellowing paper, almost as dirty as the picture itself. The only thing on it is a single typed line, followed by a handwritten parenthesis.

'*Vrancz: Pretmakers in een Berglandschap (um 1600 gemalt).*'

Wrong! Wonderfully wrong! Painter and date, certainly. Whether the title's wrong as well it's impossible to say, since no one knows what its title is.

'Double Dutch to me,' says Tony.

Yes. *Pretmakers* in a mountain landscape . . . What are *pretmakers*?

'1600,' he says. 'Bit closer to your period?'

'Still about a century out.'

'Very difficult to please you chaps. So you don't know anything about Mr Vrancz?'

'Not much.'

'Though if it doesn't say "*Charlie* Vrancz" . . .'

'Sebastian, I think.'

'. . . it's not by him anyway.'

'Unlikely, I agree,' I say regretfully. But truthfully, because it *is* unlikely – the probability of its being by Sebastian Vrancz is about the same as for the green cheese theory of lunar geology. My truthful reply's part of an outline policy that's already begun to form in my head. I'm thinking: I'm not going to lie, but I'm not going to tell any unnecessary truths . . . Mustn't think, though, mustn't think! But I *am* thinking, of course. In another long instant – long enough for the dogs to have got to their feet, and for all of us to have followed Kate and Tilda out into the hall at last – I've replanned my entire life.

I'm going to have the picture off him. This is my great project. I don't know how I'm going to do it, but do it I shall. On that central point I'm already absolutely clear.

'Another Rembrandt, perhaps,' says Laura, as she fetches my coat.

'Hope you didn't mind us showing you the family snaps,' says Tony, as he helps me into it.

'Not at all. Most intriguing. I only wish we could have been more helpful.'

'You can't imagine what it's like', he says, 'trying to sell something when you know bugger all about it. All you know is that every man's hand's against you. You're the loneliest soul on earth.'

He opens the great front door, and the dogs go bounding and barking away into the night. I look at him as we turn on the doorstep to make our farewells, and I suddenly feel sorry for him. There's a note of defeat in his voice. The water's still trickling softly from the broken gutter over-head, and the white paint on the door has been worn back to the bare oak over the years by the scratchings of the dogs. The wife beside him is in spirit away off into the night already, like the dogs. His world's disintegrating around him, beyond recall or understanding.

'He thought you might know someone,' says Laura. 'Some expert on Giordano. Or even someone who might want to buy it privately. He always goes about things in some ridiculous back-to-front way.'

The loneliest soul on earth is what he is. And he's just about to watch another of his possessions slip out of his grasp. If I can possibly contrive it. Because the second loneliest soul on earth at this moment is me. We're alone together in the arena, the two of us, and I'm going to take him.

I feel a flash of pure savagery. I'm going to have his property off him. He can't make good his claim to it. It's written in a language he can't read, because the only language he can read in his necessity is money. If he knew what it was, he'd hold the world to ransom. And if the ransom wasn't forthcoming he'd sell it to any money that presented itself – to a Swiss bank, an American investment trust, a Japanese gangster. It would vanish even deeper into the darkness, even further from the light of common day.

If fuel prices rose high enough, he'd sell it for firewood.

In any case, he owns it no more than I do. No one can own a work of art. You can own the oak, you can own the paint. You can't own the shimmer of the green, the comicality of the pouted lips, the departure of the ship.

So I'm going to have it off him. I'm not going to do it by deceit. I'm not going to stoop to the kind of methods he might use himself. I'm going to do it by boldness and skill, in full accordance with the rules of war.

I know how he despises me, and all the skills and connections of mine that he was hoping to make use of. I'm going to play the hand in what he regards as his strongest suit. I'm going to give him a lesson in the gentlemanly attributes of ruthlessness and style.

Change, as he so sententiously informed us, is the law of

life. That, he's going to discover, includes change of owner-ship. It includes the fall of one class, and the rise of another.

And immediately I'm terrified at the prospect of what I've committed myself to. I know I'm out of my depth. I can feel the waters closing above me.

I'm even more terrified, though, by his parting polite-ness, as he begins to shut the great door.

'I'll take your advice about the old girl,' he says humbly. 'I'll give Sotheby's a buzz.'

I'd forgotten my appallingly sensible suggestion. In another lightning cascade of thought I see the man from Sotheby's as he concludes his inspection of *Helen* and turns away – then turns back as his eye falls on the boarded-up fireplace beneath it . . . And I find I've the first glimmerings of a plan of action in my mind, and on my tongue.

'Hang on for a couple of days first,' I say, with a little smile. 'You're right – you'll be in a stronger position if you find out what the alternatives are. I might just possibly know someone who'd take a look at it for you.'

We pick our way through the puddles to our car. The rain has stopped, and the first true night of spring has hung the thinly clad branches of the trees with brilliant silver stars.

In a few seconds from now I'm at last going to be able to speak to Kate. Like a lover first breathing the name of his beloved, I'm going to release the secret burning with such sweet fire inside me.

But I don't. I don't say anything. We sit in silence as the car lurches and splashes down the drive.

The fact is that I'm still thinking fast. And what I'm thinking now is that I *can't* simply burst out with the amazing news. Not even to Kate. Least of all to her. She won't believe it. No one would. Not the most credulous of art lovers, not the most trusting of wives. And Kate's not the most credulous of art lovers or the most trusting of wives. As a specialist in the subject, she's committed to caution; as a wife, she's already sceptical of what she sees as my propensity to sudden wild enthusiasms. Her first thought will be that this is merely another of my fugues, another of my excuses for postponing work on the book. I'm going to have to be almost as circumspect with her as I was with Tony Churt. At the moment I'm relying on memory, on a fortuitous interest in something well outside the tiny smallholding of knowledge that I've begun to cultivate. Before I say a word to her I'm going to have to do some careful research. I'm going to have to prepare a very fully documented case.

But why is *she* so silent? Is it just the awfulness of the evening we've sat through, transformed now for me in retrospect, but not of course for her? Is she irritated at my slowness in leaving? Wary of my embarrassingly excessive forthcomingness to Laura? Hurt that the Churts and I were exchanging fatuities over yet another second-rate painting instead of tweedling appreciatively over the extraordinary and beautiful child she was rocking on the other side of the room?

Or has she sensed something suspiciously noisy about my silence? I make haste to bring it to an end.

'Wow,' I remark. 'As our gracious hostess might say.'

'What?' says Kate. Yes, something's eating at her; choosing not to understand is a bad sign.

'Them,' I explain, though it's entirely unnecessary. 'The house. The evening.'

'What about them?'

'Wow. No?'

Silence again. Heartbreaking, at a moment when we should be more united than ever in our identical reaction to the common enemy. Maddening, when I'm feeling so full of myself. Then, suddenly:

'What's all this about knowing someone who might look at the Giordano?'

Ah. So that's the problem.

'Nothing. Just trying to be neighbourly.'

'But you don't know anyone who knows about Giordano!'

'Don't I?'

'You'd never even heard of him before tonight.'

I thought I *had*, of course. But then I also thought he was the composer of *Andrea Chénier*, so I hold my peace.

'Then how's that being neighbourly?' she persists. 'Telling them you know someone when you don't?'

'I might look around a bit. See if I can find them someone.'

'Look around where?'

'The woodshed?' I suggest. 'Behind the cooker?'

But she's not to be jollied out of her dissatisfaction. She knows there's something up. I might be able to conceal it from the Churts, but not from her. In any case, I can't keep down the rising tide of excitement inside myself. I have to provoke her curiosity with further maddening hints and feints. The mystery of the missing Giordano specialist serves as a metaphor of the real mystery.

'Actually,' I say, 'I think I may be on the right track. I *might* find a possible candidate knocking around the cottage somewhere.'

I mean, of course – as I understand but she doesn't – that *I* shall be in the cottage, that I'm thinking of constituting myself as the helpful authority. This is the plan that I began to formulate on the Churts' doorstep. I haven't the slightest idea how I'm going to do it. An hour or two with a standard work of reference, obviously. But then? False beard? Dark glasses and foreign accent? Or could I somehow take the picture away for my supposed contact to examine in private? I explain that he's someone who doesn't want his identity known. It's true – he doesn't! But why not? What reason do I give Tony Churt?

Because he's a mystery *purchaser.* Yes. Everyone's heard of mystery purchasers. A purchaser is after all what Tony Churt had been hoping I might supply, and he won't be surprised if I find one who's a little shy of publicity. With good reason, perhaps. He's a king of the underworld, a *capo* with a taste for the corrupt grandiosities of the *seicento*. Something at any rate dodgy, even if not downright crooked. That should appeal to Tony Churt's fatal weakness for the devious. Particularly if this shady figure's offering top whack, cash down.

Kate refuses to investigate the mystery I've dangled in front of her. When we get home she feeds Tilda in a marked manner, mother and daughter cocooned together in a silent physical communion to which I can never be admitted. The subject hangs in the air until Tilda's asleep again and we're getting undressed in front of the fan heater.

'I know you like to be nice to everyone,' she says conces-

sively, hushed and perhaps softened by the presence of
Tilda in her box beside the bed, 'even if it doesn't always
mean very much in practice. But if you're not careful they'll
invite us again.'

Exactly. But all I say is: 'I've put both hot water bottles on
your side of the bed.'

An even more disagreeable interpretation strikes her, even
so. 'You're not suggesting that we have to invite them back?'

'Good God, no,' I say. This will be quite unnecessary. I
hope. I want to be in and out of *their* house, not ours, the
trusted local expert who deals with unwanted works of art
in much the same way that Skelton deals with the septic
tank and the aperitifs, or the wonderful little man at the
rectory with beating the bounds and comfort for the dying.
Yes, I shall become another of their local little men. 'I think
I can get my drug baron to go a shade higher on *Helen*,' I
hear myself saying confidentially, not too many weeks
from now. 'You want him to take a look at your Double
Dutchmen as well while I'm about it . . .?'

But there's a lot of work to be done before we reach that
stage. *Pretmakers* first of all. This is easy, because I keep a
Dutch dictionary in the kitchen with my other Flemish reference books . . . *Pretmaker, pretmakerij*: Merrymaker, merrymaking. So that's what those solemn clumping figures on
the hillside are up to! I can't help doing a little merrymaking myself at the thought.

The next stage is going to be more difficult, though. I have
to find out everything there is to be found out about my
merry folk and their creator. I have to be able to make an
objective case that will convince Kate. We've brought with
us all the research materials that either of us thought we
could possibly need, but neither of us foresaw our work
taking in this particular artist or this particular period. I

– 53 –

have to get to libraries and bookshops. There are no libraries and bookshops in the middle of these muddy fields and dank woods. I have to return to the city that we've just abandoned for three months. I nerve myself. Things have got to get worse between us before they can get better.

I wait until my hand is on the switch of the bedside light.

'Will you drive me to the station in the morning?' I say. 'A few odds and ends I've got to check. I'll be back in time to make dinner.'

I wait just long enough for her to see the innocent straightforwardness in my expression. Then click – blackness – before the answering disappointment appears in hers. Silence. She turns away from me. She knows I've another bee in my bonnet, another excuse for backsliding.

It suddenly occurs to me for the first time that she perhaps thinks my new love is *Helen*. I laugh silently to myself in the darkness. Then I start to think of *pretmakers*, and the four of us this evening performing our own ponderous merrymaking on the local hillsides. I laugh again. But not even the unexplained shaking of the bed provokes her to investigate further.

I lie for half the night listening to the faint sounds from Tilda's cot, as she rises restlessly close to the surface of sleep, then sinks away into the depths again. I rise and sink myself, moving back and forth between nightmarishly confused excitement and horribly clear-headed second thoughts. By the time Tilda's fully awake and demanding her three o'clock feed, I'm not quite as certain as I was about my identification. I'm not certain about anything.

One dark and uninterpreted formulation recurs: *the prologue is finished*. The prologue to what? I don't know. To my new venture. To our marriage. To life itself. The *pretmakerij* is over. Now comes the serious part.

What Are We Looking At?

There are some paintings in the history of art that break free, just as some human beings do, from the confines of the particular little world into which they were born. They leave home – they escape from the tradition in which they were formed, and which seemed at first to give them significance. They step out of their own time and place, and find some kind of universal and enduring fame. They become part of the common currency of names and images and stories that a whole culture takes for granted.

It happens for good reason and for bad, and for no discernible reason at all. It's always happened, even before the age of the rotary press and colour photography. It happened with one faintly smiling Tuscan woman, one greatly amused Dutchman. It happened with a vase of Provençal sunflowers and a couple tenderly embraced in a marble kiss. It was happening already in classical antiquity, with a statue by Praxiteles of the Aphrodite of Cnidus. But now that images can be reproduced so easily and so accurately, now that mass tourism and universal education have filled the great galleries of the world with holidaymakers and schoolchildren, now that you can buy a painting and send your greetings home on the back of it for the price of the stamp you stick on it, some of these images have become even more pervasive.

One of the most familiar of all is a landscape by Bruegel, sometimes known as *The Return of the Hunters*, more usually as *The Hunters in the Snow*. There they go again, those weary men with their gaunt dogs, on the walls of hospital waiting-rooms and students' lodgings, on your mantel-piece Christmas after Christmas, trudging away from us off the winter hills behind our backs, down into the snow-bound valley beneath. Their heads are lowered, their spoils are meagre. Three hunters, with thirteen dogs to feed and nothing but a single fox to show for their labours. There's no great rejoicing at their return; the women making a fire, outside the inn with the sign that's hanging half off its hooks, don't give them a glance, any more than the ploughman looks up to see Icarus vanishing into the sea in that earlier painting of Bruegel's that Auden made almost as famous as the *Hunters*. What takes the eye is the land-scape that opens away at the foot of the hill we are on: the village turned in upon itself by the cold, the tiny figures on the unfamiliar ice, the sky leaden above the white flood plain around the frozen river, a planing magpie black against the whiteness, leading the eye on to the broken teeth of the mountains on the other side of the valley, and the distant town at the end of it beside the winter sea.

You realize, from all this remembered detail, what an impression the painting has made on me. But I don't really remember all that much of the detail. What I remember is the wintriness. I can body it out like this because I'm sitting in the café of the National Gallery, looking at reproductions of it in the various illustrated books on Bruegel I've man-aged to buy in the bookshop here and in various other shops I went to on the way from St Pancras. There's one thing about the picture, though, that the reproductions fail to represent: the haunting *presence* that the original has when you stand in front of it.

It's in the Kunsthistorisches Museum in Vienna, a solemn

palace erected in the most grandiloquent years of nine-teenth-century Austria-Hungary to enshrine the imperial picture collection. The paintings are on the *piano nobile*, and you humbly climb to present yourself to them by way of a staircase huge enough to fetch you almost to your knees by the time you get to the top. The size of the *Hunters* matches its setting. The reproductions I've bought lie propped on the table in front of me, inches wide by inches high, and I look down upon them as I would upon specimens in a lab-oratory. The original hangs at eye-level and above, nearly four feet high by over five feet across, the size of a window, so that you're looking out into a complete world beyond the wall. You're drawn out of yourself, out of the warm and comfortable world you inhabit, and you're taken into a harsh cold place in a more precarious time, where the warmth of the domestic hearth, and the store of food saved from the harvest, are intimately precious. You're enfolded in the great stillness of that snowbound valley; surrounded by the strange muffled quietness of the day; brought before the throne of winter.

And it has a context. When you find yourself at last before the *Hunters*, as I did on a hot summer's afternoon seven years ago, having another of my life-changing *coups de foudre*, you're not looking at this one work alone. Turn your head, and there are Bruegels on every wall; you're in a room which contains about a third of all his known paintings, a room in which every gilt frame is a window looking out on to a different aspect of his world. On the end wall to your left are views almost as familiar as the one in front of you. Out-side one gilt window is the great Tower of Babel, its head in the clouds, listing like the Tower of Pisa as its foundations sink under the weight of its galleried masonry. Beyond the next window the eager crowds stream out of a little walled

Flemish town on a brisk spring day, on their way to Calvary to watch what promises to be a highly enjoyable triple crucifixion, turning with wide-eyed fascination as they realize that the principal performers are travelling alongside them, the two thieves gratifyingly white faced with terror in the tumbril, Christ on foot, piquantly collapsing beneath the weight of his cross. From the windows behind and to the right you can see the familiar, brutally charmless little brats at their *Children's Games*; the familiar cross-section of rural society celebrating *The Wedding Banquet*; the familiar peasants guzzling and wagering and clumping at their al fresco *Dance*; the familiar squadron of armed horsemen waiting in a forest of raised pikes as their colleagues rampage through the snowbound Flemish village at Herod's paranoiac command, slaughtering all the male children.

Now turn back to the *Hunters*. On the same wall are two more landscapes of almost exactly the same size, but slightly less familiar. Immediately to the left of the *Hunters* is another river valley, not the same one but evidently in the same part of the world, once again seen from the high ground above it, once again lined with mountain crags, but caught this time on a serene day in autumn, with the leaves russet on the trees and the grapes in the vineyards ready for harvesting. Going away down the hillside in front of us this time are not hunters but herdsmen, driving cows fat from their summer pasturage in the mountains back to the valley for the harsh winter predicted by the *Hunters*. Then to the left of *The Return of the Herd* is a third river valley in this same mountain kingdom, still seen from above, still overlooked by sheer rockfalls. Now we're in different weather – a blustery day at the very beginning of spring, with torn dark clouds racing across the sky and ships in trouble on the wide estuary. The peasants immediately in front of us this time are pollarding the trees before the first spring growth appears. The hillside beneath them, and the streets of the little village straggling up it, have been turned into raw mud slides by the late winter rains. A little mudhole of a place, in fact, in spite of the wide views, particularly (as the title tells us) on *The Gloomy Day* when we happen to visit it.

The three pictures are plainly related to each other, and there are two more in the same series which have become separated from them. If you go to the National Gallery in Prague – or turn over the page of your Bruegel book, as I'm doing now – you find yourself looking down on a fourth river and up to a fourth lot of precipitous cliffs. This time it's a brilliant summer's day, and we're further back from the valley, on more level ground, watching the *Haymaking*. Away from us once again, back to the village below, go peasants weighed down with baskets full of the produce of high summer, cherries and beans. And if you turn over once again, or go to the Metropolitan Museum next time you're in New York, you're looking out over a fifth valley. The country here is gentler, the weather hotter. There are no high mountains, and only a flash of the river as it joins the calm and busy sea. You're in *The Corn Harvest*, at noon on a day in the great heat of summer, when the men are laying the ripe wheat to sheaves and stooks, or sprawled asleep in the shade of a tree, and the women are cutting great loaves for the midday break.

Each of these five pictures (with the exception of *Haymaking*, which seems to be missing three or four centimetres at the bottom) is signed and dated. They were painted in the space of a single year, 1565, and a single year passes in the course of them. They show the four seasons, each characterized by its ever-returning round of rural labours and weathers. *The Gloomy Day* is plainly set in spring, *The*

Return of the Herd in autumn, and *The Hunters in the Snow* in winter. But between spring and autumn an oddity creeps into the scheme: we have not one but two pictures, *Haymaking* and *The Corn Harvest*, that represent summer.

Four seasons – five pictures.

Well, why not? It's not unreasonable to have two different scenes from the pleasantest time of year. But even within this lopsided framework the pictures are oddly distributed. *The Hunters*, to judge by the weather, shows us the deepest point of deep midwinter, perhaps some time in January. By the time of *The Gloomy Day* we've moved forwards only to the first days of spring – the tail-end of winter, really, before any of the conventional signs of spring have appeared. Early March, perhaps – only a month or so later than the preceding scene – and leaving a gap of nearly three months before the first of the two summer pictures, since they can't possibly be haymaking before June at the earliest.

What this odd bunching suggests is that there are not too many pictures but too few. There seems to be something missing.

My fate in life now turns out to hang upon exactly what it is.

Although the pictures appear to show four different seasons, and although the series is often referred to as *The Seasons*, there's no evidence that they were intended in that way at all. The only documentary hint we have about their origins is a reference in 1566, the year after they were painted, when they're listed among the pictures owned by an Antwerp merchant called Nicolaes Jongelinck. They appear under a collective heading, without further differentiation, not as *The Seasons*, but as *De Twelff maenden – The Twelve Months*. If this is right, though, and the five pictures represent not four subjects but twelve, then there's even *more* missing.

How much more? According to the list, Jongelinck owned sixteen paintings by Bruegel, of which, apart from *De Twelff maenden*, only two are named, *The Tower of Babel* and *The Procession to Calvary*. So the list includes fourteen unnamed pictures. At least five of these, the five we still have, must be part of the *Twelve Months* series; perhaps all fourteen are, or any number in between. Fourteen pictures to illustrate twelve months seems an even stranger anomaly than we started with, and most of the other intervening possibilities aren't any better. The most plausible division of the list, on the face of it, is two unspecified paintings and twelve paintings illustrating one month each.

In that case no fewer than seven of the series have been lost, which by Lady Bracknell's standards might seem like quite egregious carelessness. But it's perfectly possible. The

Netherlands were in turmoil by the end of Bruegel's life as they subsided into eighty years of war fought to throw off Spanish domination. Only forty-five authenticated paintings by Bruegel are extant, and we know that there must have been others because we have the copies and engravings that his followers made of them.

But whether there really are seven paintings missing from the series, or nine, or six, or five, or four, no one seems to know. I'm sitting now in the Reading Room of the London Library, my back firmly turned upon the green haze on the trees in St James's Square outside the window, speed-reading the seven standard authorities on Bruegel that I've assembled on my table, before I rush back to St Pancras to keep my pledge to make dinner for Kate. The more I read, the more uncertain everything about him seems to become. The uncertainty fills me with a terrible anguish. I need to know exactly what's missing. I really do.

Scarcely anything about him has survived, I discover, apart from some unknown proportion of the pictures themselves and a handful of dates from official records. He was admitted to the Antwerp painters' guild in 1551. From 1552 to 1554 he was on his travels to Italy. In 1563 he moved to Brussels and married the daughter of his former master. In 1569 he died. How old he was when this cryptic story ended no one knows, because no one knows when it started. Scholars have found various scraps of evidence that suggest he was born some time between 1525 and 1530, but can't exclude 1522, or even 1520.

There are two engraved portraits of him, according to the inscriptions on them, one by Lampsonius, the other by Sadeler. But no letters, and no certain firsthand recollections. Almost the only source of biographical information about him is an extraordinary work called the *Schilder-*

Boeck, the Book of Painters. The author was a painter himself, Karel van Mander, and the book is a *Brief Lives* of European artists from antiquity onwards, modelled on Pliny and Vasari. The most interesting section, though, is the one devoted to German and Netherlandish painters. The entry on Bruegel is brisk and anecdotal. 'He was a very quiet and thoughtful man, not fond of talking, but ready with jokes when in the company of others.' He used to go to fairs and weddings, with a merchant friend called Hans Franckert for whom he often worked, 'dressed in peasant's costume, and they gave presents just like the others, pretending to be family or acquaintances of the bride or the bridegroom. Here Bruegel entertained himself observing the nature of the peasants – in eating, drinking, dancing, leaping, love-making and other amusements . . .'

What else? Not much. He liked to frighten people with 'all kinds of spooks and uncanny noises'. When he was in Antwerp he lived with a servant girl, abandoned her because she was a terrible liar, and moved to Brussels to get away from her at his mother-in-law's insistence when he married. He left his wife one of his pictures and ordered her to destroy others.

Van Mander's book was published in 1604, thirty-five years after Bruegel's death, and since he spent most of Bruegel's working lifetime in other cities it seems unlikely that he knew him personally. So a question mark hangs over both the description and these odd few anecdotes.

Even Bruegel's name opens up fresh mysteries. Van Mander says that he took it from the village where he was born, Brueghel, near Breda in North Brabant, which is now part of Holland. But according to Friedrich Grossmann, one of the authorities I have open on the desk in front of me, there are two villages with the name of 'Brueghel' or

'Brogel', and neither is near Breda. One is thirty-four miles to the east of it, the other forty-four miles to the south-east, near the town of Brée, which in the sixteenth century was Breede, Brida or – in Latin – Breda. But if this was Bruegel's birthplace, then he was not proto-Dutch but proto-Belgian, and if Tony Churt's sensitive assessment is right, his works are either chocolate or beer, or beneath notice.

But then the mere spelling of the name is a puzzle in itself. The *Massacre of the Innocents* that faces *The Hunters in the Snow* in the Kunsthistorisches Museum is not in fact the one by Pieter Bruegel, which is at Hampton Court; it's a copy of it by Pieter Brueghel with an 'h' in the middle of his surname. Pieter Brueghel with an 'h' is not the same painter as Pieter Bruegel without an 'h', nor for that matter is he someone totally unrelated who confusingly happens to have almost the same name. He is, even more confusingly, our man's *son*, and of course is usually called Pieter Brueghel the Younger, to make the distinction from Bruegel the Elder a little clearer – though possibly not the distinction from Brueghel the Elder *with* an 'h', who is *Jan* Brueghel, our man's elder son, but called the Elder to set him apart from *his* son, Jan Brueghel the Younger. Not to mention Abraham Brueghel, the son of Jan Brueghel the Younger, and Ambrosius Brueghel, another son of Jan Brueghel the Elder – making a round total of five painters called Brueghel, all with h's, but all sprung from our man's mysterious and potent seed.

The one certain way of distinguishing between our man and all his descendants is that his name is spelt without an 'h'. Except that Wilhelm Glück, one of the most notable of all Bruegel scholars, I see from his great work on the table in front of me, spells him *with* an 'h'. But then so almost always did Bruegel himself, until 1559. Then, at the age of twenty-nine, or thirty, or thirty-four, or thirty-seven, or thirty-nine, when his reputation was already thoroughly established under the Brueghel trademark, he ceased to sign his pictures Brueghel and almost always signed them Bruegel. Why? Nobody knows.

Why not, though? It makes it easier to spell, it uses up a spot less paint. But then at once another mystery arises. If he liked the new version better, why didn't he give it to his sons when they were born in the following decade? Why did he condemn all his descendants to the 'h' that he didn't want himself?

Nobody knows.

Something, somewhere, in that great cycle of the year is missing. On this point almost all the authorities agree.

But what? That depends on what the five surviving pictures represent, and on this the authorities sharply differ.

I struggled with my mountain of accumulated scholarship all the way northwards in the train, frustrated by the difficulty of cross-referencing between a dozen different books with nowhere but my lap to put them. Exhilarated too, though, because they've one other single point of agreement: that the solution to the problem lies in the *iconography*. Bruegel (they all concur) didn't choose the seasonal labours and activities in these five pictures on the basis of his personal knowledge or observation of country life, in spite of all the espionage recorded by van Mander. He used symbolic ones. They're the labours and activities traditionally shown associated with particular times of the year in the calendar that formed part of a Book of Hours. 'A placid, bucolic, unchanging world', says Wieck in his study of this best-selling mediaeval title, 'in which there seldom penetrates any of the hard work and harsh poverty that was the reality of this life.'

So Kate and I can work on the problem together. She knows at least as much about the iconography of a Book of Hours as any of the authors I was balancing on my knees. The Book of Hours, in all its various manifestations, is as familiar to her as the works of Occam are to me. It was in a way through a Book of Hours that I met her – on a flight to Munich, when she was on her way to study the manuscripts in various south German archives and monasteries, including the celebrated *Calendrier flamand* preserved in the Bavarian State Library. Not for the first time I bless Lufthansa, and my admirable quickness and recklessness in pressing my refresher, paper napkin and even my handkerchief on her when the old-fashioned fountain pen she was using leaked over her; and the happy morning that followed two months, one week and three days later, when she used her fountain pen once again, and let me use it as well because I'd forgotten to bring anything to write with, in a room embowered in plastic flowers at Camden Town Hall.

In fact it will kill two birds with one stone, because her involvement in solving the iconography might also help to solve the problem I have of breaking the news to her, which seems to be more difficult the more I think about it. Any sudden dramatic announcement, I realize, even when I've fully mastered my accompanying brief, is going to risk her resistance. Much better to let her guide me through the undergrowth with no knowledge of where we're heading, so that she's led gently, step by step, to discover my discovery for herself.

Difficult, though, to find the right moment to broach the matter. Not, obviously, when I came out of the station and found her walking up and down trying to quiet Tilda. Not while she was driving me back to the cottage; not while we were eating dinner (which she, of course, had already made, in spite of my repeated assurances); not while she was telling me about exactly when Tilda had slept and woken, and how much she'd taken at her feed, and what Mr Skelton had said about the septic tank; not while she was being so careful not to ask me what I'd been doing in

London, or what the arm-breaking contents of my two plastic carrier bags were.

So now the following morning Kate's working at one end of the kitchen table and I've got all my books concealed as best I can behind my open laptop at the other end, stacked almost as awkwardly as they were on my lap on the train, because I'm trying not to let her see their titles, or any telltale illustrations. And what she's doing is trying not to look, because she has a pretty good idea that whatever I'm working on, it's not nominalism or its impact on Netherlandish art, and she doesn't want to know for sure and confirm her disappointment in me.

Am I frightened that she might not share my opinion? Not frightened, exactly – anxious to avoid the reciprocal disappointment in her that I should feel if she didn't. I'm as reluctant to lose the remembered brightness of the sky beyond her head in the window of seat 25A on flight LH4565 as she is to lose the remembered boldness of my smile as I offered her my accumulated airline tissues.

No, I'm frightened. I'm going to need her moral support in the next few weeks, including her agreement to let me back my judgement by borrowing rather a lot of money from the bank, and if she doesn't accept my identification when the moment comes I don't know how I'm going to manage.

I certainly wish I had her practical help right now. Because it's not iconology that's at issue here – it's straightforward iconography. The range of possible interpretations, and the various permutations of them, are bewildering. On the table in front of me I have Friedländer (of course), Glück, Grossmann, Tolnay, Stechow, Genaille and Bianconi. They quote each other freely, together with various other authors not available in the London Library – Hulin de Loo, Michel, Romdahl, Stridbeck and Dvořák – and they refer to the often mutually contradictory iconography used in two breviaries illuminated by Simon Bening of Bruges in the second and third decades of the sixteenth century, the Hours of Hennessy and the Hours of Costa; in the Grimani Breviary, also done, a little earlier, by Simon Bening and his father Alexander Bening, although the calendar itself is attributed to Gerard Horenbout; and in our own dear *Calendrier flamand*, as I think of it, in the Bavarian State Library.

Which month, for a start, does *The Hunters in the Snow* represent? According to Hulin de Loo, a snowy landscape is characteristic for February. Tolnay dissents; in the Da Costa Hours the snowy landscape illustrates December, and in Hennessy it goes with January, in which month Hennessy also places hunters, though for hares rather than foxes, which seems to be Bruegel's own variation on the theme. Glück agrees with the idea of January. But what are those women roasting over the fire they're tending in the snow outside the village inn? Glück believes it's corn, which reinforces his diagnosis of January. Tolnay thinks that it's not corn but pork, which both the Hours of Hennessy and the Hours of Costa show for the month of December.

So the *Hunters* might show any one of the three winter months. *The Gloomy Day* turns out to be just as indeterminable. Among the peasants pollarding the trees in the foreground are three who are not labouring at all. One of them's eating something flat and rectangular, like a matzoh or a slice of pizza, and holding a piece of it up in the air – perhaps to keep it out of the reach of a child wearing a paper crown and carrying a lantern. Tolnay sees the food as a waffle, which together with the lantern suggests that the allusion's to Carnival, in February, and Romdahl agrees. This, of course, overlaps with Hulin de Loo's placing of the *Hunters*, but de Loo, having set the *Hunters* in February, believes that the paper crown identifies the child as the Bean King, whose celebration is at the beginning of January – *before* the *Hunters*; Michel accepts this. But Glück places the scene in March, and Stechow agrees that in Hennessy (though not in other calendars) March is the month indicated by tree pruning.

So the possibilities for *The Gloomy Day* also range over three months – and the two pictures may even be in reverse order. *Haymaking* is a little more tightly confined, within a range of only two possible readings. For Hulin de Loo, Michel and Glück it's June, the month clearly established by the baskets full of beans and cherries being carried down towards the valley by the peasant women in the foreground. But in Hennessy and Grimani haymaking itself, the activity which occupies all the middle ground of the picture, is the main theme of July; as Stechow points out, the Netherlandish word for July is *Hooimaand*, Hay Moon. For Michel and Glück, though, July is the month of *The Corn Harvest*. But Stechow reminds us that *Oegtmaand*, Harvest Moon, is August – the month for which Tolnay says harvesting, the peasants' repast and siesta are all themes in the calendars; though he opens the possibility of a third month here as well when he warns that what appears to be a game of *boules* in the middle ground could be alluding to September.

Which leaves *The Return of the Herd*. This is apparently not a theme that figures in the calendars, but Tolnay believes it's Bruegel's adaptation of the return from the hunt, which the *Calendrier flamand* offers for November. Michel and Glück concur, and Hulin de Loo notes the bareness of the trees, and can somehow feel a cold wind blowing in the picture, both of which also suggest November. But then Tolnay draws attention to the ripe vineyards and nets in the valley below, and points out that both the wine harvest and the netting of birds are traditional for October. Stechow is likewise in two minds here, though at any rate not three.

So which months do the five extant pictures show? According to the iconography, so far as I can disentangle it, they may show any or all of them.

Except two. There are two months, and only two months, that are not identified in any of the various schemes, however many pictures are missing.

April and May.

For the first time since I set eyes on it, I allow myself to think about . . . about *it*, yes, about the unknown substance, the object for identification. *The Merrymakers*, as the label on the back names it. About my picture, as it's going to become. About the mud underfoot, the flush of green spreading through the bare brown woods, the little town in the distance, where people must already be sitting outside in squares and on street corners in the fresh warmth of the sun.

It's too late in the year for March, too early for June. So, yes, it must be either April or May. And once again I feel the uncontainable tide of excitement rising inside me, the insupportable anguish.

I have either April or May; it all fits. The only question is which.

Well, does it matter? One would be as good as the other, and to have found either is a miracle.

But there's one possibility that would be more miraculous still, so miraculous that for the moment I daren't even think about it. I need to know one simple thing first: April? Or May?

I cast my mind back to the weather in the picture. It's ambiguous. It feels like April where we're standing; it looks like May that we're heading towards.

What can we glean from the iconography?

'In the calendar,' I suddenly find I've said. Kate looks up.

'The calendar in a Book of Hours. What are the signs for April and May?'

She frowns. Is she going to ask me why I want to know? If she does I'll tell her. The same principle applies, I decide in that instant, with her as with Tony Churt: no lies, no unnecessary truths. But she's maintaining *her* policy, too: no questions that might provoke either.

How do we get into these ridiculous situations with the people we love?

'I don't know much about the calendar,' she says warily. 'I've only really looked at the devotional sections.'

I wait for the cautionary academic smoke screen of disclaimers to clear.

'The signs for April and May?' she repeats finally. 'You mean Taurus? Gemini?'

'Not the zodiacal signs . . . Why, do they have zodiacal signs?'

'In some calendars.'

I'm trying to remember, now she's suggested it: are there any bulls or twins lurking in the depths of the *Merrymakers*?

'I mean, what are the traditional labours?'

She frowns again. I don't think she needs to frown for very long to remember something that must be almost as rudimentary to her as the letters of the alphabet. I think she's trying to work out, without asking me, what I'm up to. She's guessed that it's something to do with that last picture at the Churts, the one she didn't see. Like me, she's trying to identify it – but at one further remove, with nothing to go on but what I let fall about it. She may manage it, too – may have managed it already, I think in a moment of mixed panic and relief.

'Well,' she says, 'for April you sometimes get planting and sowing.'

I can't recall any planting or sowing. 'What about May?'

'Sheep going to pasture. Cows being milked.'

'How about cows going to pasture?' I'm thinking of that tiny herd in the distance, that will come down again past us in the foreground in October or November.

'Possibly, though I can't think of an example offhand.'

But now she's warming to the work. I recognise the old awkward, diffident eagerness in the way she moves her head as she talks.

'Actually April and May tend to be rather a special case, because they're often illustrated not by labours but by pastimes. It's quite striking. All year round the peasants toil – and then when it gets to be spring the gentry suddenly put in an appearance. They own the entire countryside, of course, and now the weather's more agreeable they come outdoors and start enjoying it for a bit.'

'Like us,' I say, warming to her warmth.

'Yes, though I can't immediately think of a calendar where they get the septic tank repaired.'

'Poor souls. So what else is there for them to do?'

'In April they go hawking.'

'*Not* like us.'

'No, but then they also pick flowers.'

'We've picked the odd flower in our time.'

She looks away. 'The other thing they quite often do is flirt.'

'I seem to recall something of that sort,' I say softly, but what I'm actually remembering is the comic couple in my picture, with their two gallant little daffodils and their expectantly protruded lips. 'All this is in April? I don't like to think what they've moved on to by May.'

'Riding. Maying. Hawking again sometimes. And courting still. Making music.'

'Which reminds me – the mice have eaten through one of

the speaker leads,' I say, but what I'm hearing is the drone of the bagpipes and the heavy pounding of the dancing feet, and what I'm smelling is the choking scent of the mayflowers that the people beyond the dancers are pulling down.

'There's a lovely one for May by Simon Bening, in the Da Costa Hours,' she says. 'Two couples boating on the Bruges canals. One of the men rowing, one playing a pipe, and one of the women accompanying him on the lute. They're bringing home the branches of may they've picked, and they've a bottle of wine hung over the side of the boat to cool.'

Yes, now I think about it there was water somewhere in the middle distance. A millpool, I think, with more merrymakers beside it engaged in some kind of rural sports. I'm still not clear, though, whether the iconography indicates April or May. It seems to be as ambiguous as the iconography in all the others. But then my clumping *pretmakers* aren't gentry.

'What about the peasants?' I ask. 'Are *they* playing lutes and floating about in boats? Or are they doing their courting in more peasant-like ways?'

'The peasants?' She frowns again. 'I don't think any of the calendars show peasants courting. It would be against the whole social ethos. Peasants don't have fun – it's the gentry who have fun. Peasants labour.'

We retire into our respective piles of books again. This slight anomaly doesn't seem to me of any great significance. But as I read on I realize that something's changed. The pages in front of me have lost their urgency. The bright light of conviction inside my head has begun to fade a little. I have to read each paragraph twice, because what my mind keeps coming back to is these two jarring propositions: all the pictures in the series, as every authority agrees, are based upon the iconography of the Book of Hours – my picture shows activities that have no place in that iconography.

It's a trivial point. There could be a dozen explanations. I put it out of my mind.

It comes back. I begin to feel an old familiar feeling, of a stone growing heavy in my heart. Could it be that I've allowed myself to be carried away once again? One of the possible explanations for the discrepancy, it occurs to me, is a painfully simple one: that my picture isn't part of a series by Bruegel based on the Book of Hours. It's a scene of Merrymakers in a Mountainous Landscape, just as the label says, and it's by a follower of Sebastian Vrancz.

The fact that this explanation is simple doesn't for a moment mean it's true. But the balance of probabilities has shifted. I can't think now why I ever jumped to the conclusion that it was a Bruegel. Not a single objective reason comes to mind. It was just another sudden rush of blood to the head.

And I say *my* picture. But it's not. It's Tony Churt's picture.

Yes, at least sobriety has returned before any irretrievable damage was done. Kate's given me the chance to think again while there's still time. She's offering me a way out from the vertiginous enterprise I've got myself into; perhaps all the time I've been unconsciously looking for one. I bless Lufthansa yet again. Or at any rate I *should*. But somehow, totally unjustifiably, I find I'm feeling a little sour about Lufthansa. Next time I go to Munich I'll fly on some other airline.

I realize that she's watching me with another of her little frowns. 'What's the matter?' she says.

'What do you mean?' I reply shortly. 'Nothing's the matter. Why should anything be the matter?'

But I know from the way she's looking at me that she's still trying to work out, with the help of the extra evidence provided by my sudden change of manner, what I could have seen when I looked at that last picture. I suppose that now I could simply tell her.

I say nothing, though. I can't bring myself to let her know what a fool I've made of myself.

I slide Grossmann, Glück and the rest of them to one side, and press *Open File* on the laptop. 'C:\nominalism,' I type.

A short-lived setback. The truth, the simple underlying truth, comes to me in the middle of the night, somewhere in the dark hours before the six o'clock feed. It's the time when one tends to wake and find all one's previous certainties and satisfactions replaced by doubts and dismay. The corollary, I discover, is that if you go to bed filled with doubts and dismay, there's a chance that the metamorphoses of the night may change them into certainties and satisfactions.

This is the simple conviction that wakes me: that whatever my picture is, it's not by an anonymous follower of a painter no one's heard of!

It's not by the school of Vrancz, or the circle of Vrancz, or an imitator of Vrancz. It's not by Vrancz himself. I know this absolutely, even though I know nothing whatever about Vrancz or his school, circle, and imitators. Here's the simple reasoning that's worked itself out in my sleeping brain: if that amazing picture *were* by Vrancz, or anyone connected with him, then I *should* know about him, because so would everyone in the entire Western world, down to the parties of excursioning schoolchildren and the American tourists doing seven cultural capitals in seven days.

Remember Friedländer and his words of wisdom about how we recognize a friend, and with what certainty. The flash of recognition is the primary perception. It's not to be replaced or devalued by anomalous details – the false beard, the dark glasses, the foreign accent. All these little mysteries we can inquire into later, after we've thrown our arms around his neck and wept for joy.

In fact, now I see it the other way round: everything that seems to cast doubt on my identification really supports it. The question's not if it can really be my old friend in that red wig, waving his arms about and speaking broken English. The question is who else it could be *but* my always astonishing old chum. Who else in the world would have had the notion of behaving like that?

Look at it this way. Let's suppose that Sebastian Vrancz, or I, or anyone else you can think of, had set to work to paint the changing aspect of the year in a series of pictures based on the iconography of the Book of Hours. When we reached April and May, why yes, certainly, we'd have shown either peasants ploughing and milking, or ladies and gentlemen flirting and courting. But this is precisely why there isn't an entire gallery in the Kunsthistorisches Museum, or a whole row of books in the London Library, devoted to Sebastian Vrancz or me, and why there is to Pieter Bruegel. Because only Bruegel had the originality and boldness to diverge from the model where it suited him, and freely adapt it to his own ideas. It's an absolutely characteristic transformation, entirely congruent with his transformation of the traditional winter hare hunters into fox hunters – and unsuccessful ones to boot – and of the traditional autumn return of the hunt into the return of the herd.

Now I come to think of it, he shows peasants having fun in two of the other pictures in the cycle! In the snowbound village to which the hunters are returning, the local people are skating and sliding on the ice. In midsummer, in the village beyond the cornfields, they're swimming, and playing either *boules* or a rather more savage game called cock-throwing, where people throw sticks at a cockerel or a goose, and win it as a prize if they can grab it before it gets up on its feet again. So letting them enjoy a dance and kiss in spring is all part of the same pattern of adaptation.

Kate and I *are* working on this together, in a way, because she's unwittingly confirmed my intuitive identification. It's Bruegel, there's no longer a shadow of doubt in my mind.

Which brings me back to the same problem as before. April? Or May?

I turn on to my left side; it's April. I turn on to my right; it's May.

'I can't help you', says Kate quietly in the darkness, 'if you don't tell me what this is all about.'

'Nothing,' I whisper back. 'Just work. Just thinking about something. Anyway, you have. You have helped.'

Another clue for her to be working on, if she can't sleep either. I force myself to lie still. We'll have Tilda awake as well if I'm not careful, and I shan't be able to explain to her either. April . . . May . . . At once I feel I shall go mad if I don't turn back on to my left side . . . my right . . . If only I could be on my left side and my right side simultaneously I could get back to sleep!

I carefully get out of bed, and feel in the darkness for a sweater to pull over my pyjamas. I hear Kate's head turn enquiringly towards me on the pillow.

'Just looking something up,' I whisper.

In the cold kitchen I turn on the fan heater and slide my pile of books back towards me.

Where are we? Yes, *De Twelff maenden* in the list of Jongelinck's sixteen Bruegels. The list was compiled because in 1566 Jongelinck offered them as part of the security for a debt. The money was owed not by Jongelinck himself, but by someone called Daniel de Bruyne – 16,000 guilders to the City of Antwerp for unpaid tax on wine. Did de Bruyne ever repay the money? Was the security recovered? There's no record. But now I begin to move on in history. In 1594, twenty-eight years later, long after Bruegel had died, the City made a dutiful presentation to the Governor of the Netherlands, Archduke Ernst von Habsburg, which included 6 *Taffeln von den 12 monats Zeiten*. Could these six pictures of the twelve months be part of Jongelinck's security? It seems they could, because the inventory made of the Archduke's estate after his death the following year lists what must be the same six pictures, now described as *Sechs Taffell, von 12 Monathenn des Jars von Bruegel*.

So at this point, a quarter of a century after Bruegel's death, there were *six* pictures of the twelve months extant. Six remaining out of twelve, with half of the total already lost? Or could it be six remaining out of six, because there never *were* twelve?

I'm not the first person to have had this idea. Tolnay hit upon it in 1935. 'Everything becomes plain', he says, 'if one sets them beside the miniatures that inspired them, when one notices that Bruegel has put together in each picture scenes which illustrate two successive months.'

Six pictures, each representing not one month but two – this is what all the apparent ambiguities of his iconography demonstrate, according to Tolnay. I allow myself to dwell on this idea for a moment. Six pictures: three in Vienna, one in Prague, one in New York and one shortly to be occupying most of the end wall of this very room for a precious day or two, before moving on to take its rightful place in the National Gallery in London. To have found one of seven missing links in Bruegel's great chain would be a glorious discovery, that would light up the rest of my days on this earth. But to have found the one single one that completes it . . . !

This is what I've had at the back of my mind all through my struggles with the iconography. It's the conclusion I leapt to, in my simplicity, I have to confess, in the Churts' breakfast-room. It's what I thought I remembered from Vienna: that there was only one picture missing. The trouble is that none of the others, except Bianconi, agrees with Tolnay. I hunt through the remaining volumes, the pages clumsy beneath my impatient fingers. Glück, writing two years after Tolnay, with all the majesty implied by the royal plural, insists that 'we share the opinion of most scholars' in staying with twelve. Stechow, in 1970, believes that 'it is becoming more and more probable' that there were twelve. Grossmann, on whom Stechow based himself, is still agreeing with Glück in 1973. Friedländer, my beloved Max, even in the 1976 edition of *Early Netherlandish Painting*, still accepts twelve without question or discussion. But then Bruegel is right at the end of his period, tacked on in Volume 14, already out of the range suggested by the title.

Genaille goes in the opposite direction. He's troubled by the fact that only five were being listed in a Vienna inventory by 1653, which for some reason seems to suggest to him that there may never have been more than five in the first place. Glück, disturbingly, appears to agree that the series of twelve was 'probably never completed', though how many Bruegel actually did paint he doesn't suggest. Grossmann, even more disturbingly, reports the discovery of a later inventory of pictures in Brussels, which suggests that even a century after the event, when there were at least five and possibly six of the paintings known to be in Vienna, there were still six in Brussels.

Twelve, or six? Seven missing, or one? One-seventh of the deficit about to be brought to light? Or all of it? I sit at the kitchen table, consumed by this terrible new anguish that seems to have taken root in my life.

When my eye first fell on that picture at the Churts, I have to confess, everything seemed so simple because I thought I knew for certain exactly how many pictures in the series were missing. It was absolutely clear and simple, and the figure wasn't seven. Or nine, or six, or five, or four. It was one.

Why was I so sure? What did I see on that bright summer's day in Vienna seven years ago that put this idea so firmly in my head? The museum catalogue, presumably. Or perhaps one of those brief explanatory panels that galleries put up on the wall. This was, after all, before my serious interest in art began. Indeed, that hour in the Bruegel room, now I look back, may have been the very beginning of it, and the future course of my life turns out to depend upon reconstructing its details. But, as with so many things at the back of your mind that seem clear and simple until you turn to look at them directly, all the clarity and simplicity are vanishing moment by moment as I read.

I need to fly to Vienna and take another look at the panel. Or else find a copy of the catalogue. Where will they have one in this country? Not in the organic farm-produce shop at Castle Quendon, that's for sure. Not in the mini-market by the petrol station at Cold Kinver.

The door opens. Kate stands in the doorway, blinking in the light, watching me more uneasily than ever, waiting for me to explain.

But all I say is: 'Will you drive me to the station again in the morning?'

By quarter past eleven I have it in front of me. I'm in the National Art Library, inside the V & A, sitting at a serious and scholarly leather-topped desk surrounded by PhD candidates doing their theses on Escher and Cimabue and railway advertising, by art dealers trying to track down provenances and attributions for their purchases.

It takes me most of the day to puzzle it out, because my halting German is such an inadequate guide to the amazing convolutions of Austrian academic style. The case made out by Demus, Klauner and Schütz, the editors of the Kunsthistorisches catalogue, is complex, and depends heavily upon a word by word re-examination of the text of the documents, mostly in an archaic German which is even further out of my reach. One of Grossmann's arguments they counter by replacing a missing 'and'; one of Glück's by putting an 'of' in place of an erroneous 'with'. They demonstrate that the French version of a letter written from Vienna in 1660, nearly a century after the paintings were done, which gives an account of seeing *six pièces de l'ancien Bruegel, qui représentent la diversité des douze Mois de l'Année*, and a Spanish version of it which also mentions twelve months, must be anterior to, and more reliable than, the Latin and Flemish texts, which refer to six pictures representing only six months, with the implication that the other six months (and six pictures) are missing. The inventory cited by Grossmann showing six still in Brussels at the

– 85 –

same period they dismiss as a mistake. After this 'as we believe permanent repair of the weak points of the record,' they consider that the identity of Jongelinck's *twelff maenden* with the six pictures in Vienna described as showing the twelve months of the year is definitely established.

By the end of the afternoon I've also found a no less magisterial survey of the problem by Buchanan, in the *Burlington Magazine*, who concurs. Grossmann and Stechow seem to be holding out for twelve, but by 1953, I discover, even Glück, in a later book on Bruegel, has come round to six, because he thinks it impossible that the City of Antwerp would have presented the Archduke with an incomplete set.

The tide's turned, no doubt about it, though the iconography still won't work out smoothly. Tolnay makes his six pairs possible by beginning the year with December/January. But Demus, Klauner and Schütz, in the catalogue, point out that the traditional beginning of the year was in March. Glück agrees that the Netherlandish year began at Easter, but this leads him now to identify *The Gloomy Day* as March/April, and *Haymaking* as May/June – so in his view there's no gap in April and May, and he expects the missing picture to show November/December. Buchanan, however, cites a drawing by Pieter Stevens, freely based on *The Gloomy Day*, which is inscribed by the artist with the words Februarius and Mert. Demus, Klauner and Schütz believe that the difficulties can be resolved by accepting that the cycle breaks the year up in a less formal way than is permitted by the schema of months or pairs of months. They cite an old tradition according to which the year was divided into six parts, and they believe that Genaille is right in thinking that each picture catches 'the characteristic moment' of what Novotny suggests is Early Spring, Early Summer, High Summer, Autumn and Midwinter.

Which once again leaves Spring. High Spring. And this is what I have; there's no doubt whatever left in my mind, if ever there seriously was. It's something else, too. The old Julian year, which was still the basis of the calendar until Pope Gregory reformed it in 1582, seventeen years after the series was painted, began just after the vernal equinox, on 25 March. So my two months, if one had to be precise, are 25 March to 25 May. In other words, the missing picture, the picture I've found, is not just *one* of the series. It's the first. It's the point of departure for the whole enterprise.

Before I leave the library I stop at the shelves where the various records of sale-room prices are ranged. Not that I'm thinking about money, but it's impossible not to be curious. Difficult to find any point of reference, of course. No major painting by Bruegel has come on to the market since *The Corn Harvest* was acquired in Paris by the Metropolitan in 1919. In 1955 a small, very early work, *Landscape with Christ appearing to His Disciples at the Sea of Galilee*, emerged from the castle of the unnamed family that had owned it for the previous century and a half, was identified by Tolnay, and in 1989 was sold at Sotheby's for £780,000. In New York in 1990 a copy by Pieter Brueghel the Younger of one of his father's major works, *The Census at Bethlehem*, fetched £1,200,000.

Over a million pounds for a *copy*. So for an original . . . An original that opens and completes the great cycle of the year . . .

But I'm not thinking about the money. I'm truly not.

The Business Plan

'Am I driving you to the station again?' asks Kate neutrally over breakfast next morning, not looking at me.

'No, no,' I reassure her. Not that she gives any sign of being reassured, which is perhaps just as well, because my plans for today still don't involve doing what she thinks I should be doing. 'I thought I might go out for a walk. If that's all right?'

She doesn't comment. Doesn't ask where I'm going, or offer to come with me. Never mind – all will be made clear soon enough. When I get back from my walk, even, if all goes well.

In any case, she probably knows where I'm going. I thought I'd walk there over the fields, rather than drive, to make it seem more offhand. It's like the difficulty of contriving an accidental meeting with the woman one's pursuing. In so far as I remember that phase of my life. Rushing over to the Churts in the car and crashing all the way up their drive to announce that I've found someone who's interested in their *Helen* might suggest a suspiciously eager interest. Everything in this business, I imagine, depends upon all those little details of behaviour and manner that suggest dull, unsurprising normality. Everything in *what* business? Confidence trickery, I suppose, if one has to name it. No, that's ridiculous. What I'm doing is what a painter does – what Bruegel's doing in the cycle of the year; I'm constructing a plausible scenario. The scene will simply look easier and more natural if I start it by happening to drop in when I'm passing on one of my walks. I'll appear out of the woods round the back somewhere. There'll be mud on my boots – a sympathetic touch. And that means I'll have to take them off at the door, and talk to him in my socks. An amusing little genre scene. I might even bump into him, countryman to countryman, as I wander absent-mindedly along brooding on nominalism, and he strolls about his estate with a gun in the crook of his arm, cogitating upon the life expectancy of pheasants and how to lower it.

I trudge up from the valley bottom, through the great field where Laura wants to put her New Age festival. Where have we got to in the cycle of the present year? The first raw, blustering advances of Early Spring have exhausted themselves in a rather spectacular sequence of rainstorms, cold snaps, thunder and sudden snow showers, and we've not yet reached the great transformation scene in the next picture. We're in an unillustrated no man's land between the two, a raggedy come-and-go weather of patchy blue and white over patchy green and brown. The iconography's not much help, either – it's even more difficult to make sense of than Bruegel's. In fact, I find it difficult to locate any iconography at all. There are no peasants to be seen at their labours, no gentry at their pleasures. The only visible creatures of any sort are cows, who lift their heads mournfully as I pass, mumbling dull, soundless monologues about the bovine condition, then carry on with the one traditional labour that characterizes this and every other month of the year – the production of cowpat.

It's real country all right, our valley, and I've grown rather fond of it in the two years we've been coming down here. But it's a dull place compared with the kind of valleys they have in the Netherlands. Almost every valley there, if

Bruegel's to be believed, is overlooked by soaring crags, and has a river that winds past a village and a high-perched castle, with a distant view of the sea. Their springs are more springlike than ours. But of course Bruegel isn't to be believed, not literally. He's doing what I'm doing in my dealings with Tony Churt: constructing a fiction. Gross-mann agrees with Novotny that the pictures in the cycle of the year are what he calls *Mischlandschaften*, composite landscapes, built up from elements either invented or observed separately in different places. All those crags are the souvenirs of Bruegel's great trip to Italy. 'When he trav-elled through the Alps,' says van Mander, 'he swallowed all the mountains and rocks, and spat them out again, after his return, on to his canvases and panels . . .'

I stop as I reach the high ground at the edge of the woods, and turn back to look at the undramatic landscape I'm living in. No castles, no crags. Just gently sloping woods and fields. All the same, a landscape is what I see it as. It's given form and identity by all the painted land-scapes I've seen over the years. Which painter first saw landscape as landscape, and painted it for its own sake? Bruegel, according to Novotny, in the great cycle of the year, where for the first time in Western art landscape is given the rank of an independent subject.

It had begun as the background to religious events. You can see two distant valleys, with crags and castles, and a river winding towards the sea, framing the *Scenes from the Life of the Virgin and of Christ* that Hans Memling painted in 1480. In the early part of the sixteenth century Joachim Patinir brought the landscape closer, and shrank the saints he showed living in it. It was Patinir who first established the characteristics of this wonderful land, with its dream-like combination of Alpine crags and Flemish settlement, its valleys seen from the high ground, winding up through receding planes of blue to the sea and a horizon near the top of the canvas. What Bruegel did was to leave out the saints.

Before Patinir and Bruegel this valley I'm standing in would have had no artistic *use*, even less than it now has economic use. Rough pasturage for a few cows now, it would then have been merely the low-rent location for a miracle or martyrdom, perhaps with Tony Churt as proprietor kneeling importantly in the foreground.

I Patinirize it as I look at it, I Bruegelize it. A little practice for my project. I ennoble it with a line of crags. A river, a village, a castle. I paint in figures engaged in the appropriate labours. In the middle distance two boys got cheap from the local comprehensive on work experience are filling hoppers with pheasant feed. In the foreground a couple of investment bankers and the chairman of the local planning committee are shooting the pheasants the boys have raised. Through the window of the castle you can just see Tony Churt, putting in his application to the planning committee for a scramble track.

But those six pictures of Bruegel's aren't simply an image of the revolving wheel of the here and now to which we're bound; they're offers of an escape from it. They're travelogues, *invitations au voyage*, that lead us out of the flat lands of the north, out of the cold and wet, out of the mud, out of the dull daily round, to distant shores where the sun shines and things are different. So is the picture that I'm painting. I arrange the great diagonals that lead the eye out and up into the distance. I indicate the last bare branches of winter with the bitumen and carbonized walrus ivory that Netherlandish painters used for browns and blacks, then clothe them in the distilled verdigris and malachite with which they captured the elusive green tones, and touch in the sunstruck highlights with whitelead. I set the spring flowers blossoming with complex combinations of red mercuric sulphide and Zealand red madder, of poisonous yellow arsenic sulphide and the sweet yellow juices of broom, saffron, weld, aloes and dyer's oak. I grind the crystals of copper carbonate, the azurite or verditer, the famous mountain blue for the receding planes of aerial perspective, and paint my way, blue by blue, up to the distant sea, where my ship lies waiting.

I follow my own leisurely progress plane by plane up into the sunlit lands that lie before me, as I carry my picture off to hand over to the fictitious collector I've found to buy it, then, as I artlessly explain to Tony Churt, hang it on my own wall to enjoy it myself for a few days in transit; find myself falling in love with it; humbly raise several thousand pounds I can't afford to buy my purchaser out and keep it for myself; become curious enough about it to take it to be examined by experts; am stunned to find that I've made one of the most important artistic discoveries of the century; behave with characteristic modesty as I receive public and professional recognition in equal measure; look with innocent amazement and heroic equanimity at the huge sums of money dangled in front of me; regretfully decide that I must let the picture go out of my possession to some institution where it can be properly looked after and seen by a wider public; nobly insist that it must remain in the country, even though this means accepting a considerable financial sacrifice; contribute a remarkably generous proportion of the proceeds to help good causes in the arts; perhaps even make a small but entirely uncalled-for donation to Tony Churt himself . . .

Blue after blue. Grinding the azurite coarse for the deep blues, grinding it fine and mixing it with whitelead for the paler tones near the horizon . . .

Back to the foreground, though. What I have to concentrate on first is disposing of the Giordano. In any case, the true Jerusalem to which my ship's sailing is not the money or the fame, or any of the other ports at which it may touch en route – it's the chance to repay my share of the debt we all have to the world that gave us birth by restoring to it one of its lost wonders . . .

No! Put the azurite back on the palette! First a few murky brown shadows for *Helen* to disappear into.

I don't bump into Tony Churt as I climb through the woods below his house. One or two of his hand-raised cock pheasants, yes, to our considerable mutual surprise; but not their proprietor. The carefully crafted scenario of my walk goes wrong, in any case, when I discover that the path has been closed by rusty barbed wire and another Keep Out sign. I happen to know it's a public right of way, and in the ordinary course of events I should make a point of climbing over the wire and continuing, but in the circumstances it seems more politic to divert to the road, and walk up the drive. Which means that by the time I reach the front door I might just as well have arrived by car.

The house is even less welcoming in the daylight than it is by night. The cataract of rainwater from the gutters has ceased, but the pool it created is still half-blocking the approach to the door, and there are streaks of green slime down the walls in several places marking the site of other leaks and blockages. In the yard at the side I glimpse traces of enterprises in various states of incompletion or disintegration – a collapsed woodpile, a half-dismantled tractor, a pigeon loft with no pigeons, tangles of mud-splashed black plastic sheeting. A huge barking begins even before I've negotiated the protective moat in front of the door, and a great weight of thrashing dogflesh has come thundering out of the yard and hurled itself upon me once again, so that by the time Laura's opened the front door, in scarlet rubber gloves this time instead of a scarlet sweater, and pushed the draggled hair back out of her eyes, the painstaking patina of mud on my boots has vanished into a more general coating of filth. 'Is Tony in, by any chance?' I shout over the noise. 'I just happened to be passing, and . . .'

She holds the door open for me – rather reluctantly, I can't help feeling – and flails ineffectually at the dogs. I'm not absolutely sure she recognizes me, even after all the rich amusement I provided her with the other night. But when Tony emerges from some back corridor in the depths of the house and re-establishes control over the dogs, he's disconcertingly clear about who I am and why I've come.

'I just happened to be passing . . .' I explain hopelessly once again.

'Found me a customer?' he asks at once.

I commend my soul to heaven. 'Well . . .' I begin cautiously, to ease myself into my new career of fiction as gently as I can.

'Come into the office,' he says. He's as brownly dressed and greyly faced as before, and he's plainly had more trouble with his razor, but he has a pair of reading glasses perched on the end of his nose, which suggests some unsuspected scholarly depths. Perhaps he, too, is hurriedly reading up on art history. Laura's vanished without a word. I kick my boots off to follow Tony as he pads in his carpet slippers back down the corridor to a little room as brown as all the others, filled with a confusion of open box-files spilling papers, and bundles of brown envelopes and folders, some of them done up with pink baler twine. The dogs walk footprints over the papers covering the floor, and settle themselves in a nest of draft accounts. Tony moves a sheaf of what look like bills to reveal a scuffed leather armchair, and dusts it for me to sit down.

'Nerve centre of the whole estate,' he says. 'Where all the business gets done. Got to be businesslike about this thing, too. If you're going to be my art agent then we need to put our heads together and work out a proper deal that's fair to both of us.'

He perches on the edge of the desk, and a small glissade of dislodged documents slides smoothly away into the waste-paper basket. He puts his reading glasses in his pocket; he's moving into negotiating mode.

'So you've had a nibble?'

'Well,' I say once again, and once again I hesitate. I've spent my entire life up to this point hugging the shores of fact, paddling in the safe shallows of honesty. Now the moment has come when I have to launch out into the open sea of fiction. I have to cut free from the literal and start painting the picture, just as Bruegel did.

And I can't do it. The words won't come to my mouth. Creating a fiction isn't lying, I understand that. But suddenly it seems remarkably like lying, and remarkably unlike anything I've ever attempted in my life before.

I look out of the window. My imagination seems to be frozen. The only words that come to mind to end my now bizarrely long silence are a frank confession that I haven't found him a customer and never will, because I haven't the faintest idea where to look for one.

And then I remember that he's gone before me. He's written his own fiction – he's done a little painting of his own.

My work on Bruegel wasn't the only research I did in London yesterday. I also took the trouble to find out a few things about Giordano, since he stands guarding the route to my prize.

He came from Naples, apparently, like multi-coloured ice-cream. His first name was Luca, and he was known in the business as Luca *Fa Presto*, because that's what his father told him ('Get a move on, Luca!') and that's what he did. He could paint a large altarpiece in a day, and in his seventy-three years upon this earth he covered large tracts of southern Italy and Spain with Judgements of Paris and Solomon, Adorations of Shepherds and Magi, and Apotheoses of Jove. His favourite subject, though, was sexual intercourse, or rather the final approaches to it, particularly as occurring between females betraying various degrees of reluctance or resistance and males using various amounts of persuasion or coercion.

To find any trace of the great Upwood Giordano I had to move on from the V & A to the Witt Library, in the vaults of Somerset House, where all the visual art of the Western world over the last eight centuries is being assembled in the form of reproductions from sources such as museum and sale catalogues. File upon file, I discovered, is devoted to the industrious Neapolitan. They look like something out of Forensic. Here, from different angles and viewpoints, is Lucretia being raped by Tarquin, and Europa by the bull;

Proserpine being carried off by Pluto, and the Sabine women by the Romans; various gang rapes of nymphs by assorted gods and centaurs; and a number of last-minute rescues.

But what there's more of than anything is Helen being carried off by Paris. The Witt categorizes pictures as upright or horizontal and by the number of figures involved, but if you add up the totals in all the different categories Speedy Luca seems to have painted the scene no fewer than nine times. There are Helens being abducted left to right, Helens departing right to left, Helens being carried towards us, Helens being carried away from us, Helens with dresses riding up above their knees, and Helens with dresses slipping off their breasts. The model for the Helen being abducted in the Musée des Beaux-Arts in Caen, I couldn't help noticing, survives her trials in Greek mythology only to be raped by Tarquin at Christie's.

Among them all, in pre-war brown monochrome, I found Helen as I've come to know her and believe she really was, leaving Sparta left to right, landward knee and seaward breast out in the wind, and a definite touch of anxiety on her face about the possibility of a chill. The reproduction, however, came not from some work about the ancestral treasures of the Churts of Upwood, but from the catalogue of a sale to be held by Koch und Söhne, Kunsthändler, Berlin Charlottenburg, in 1937.

So the famous Churt Giordano, which has been in their family for so many generations, was only acquired in 1937. In Berlin, at a gallery almost certainly expropriated from its original Jewish proprietors, in a sale of paintings very probably acquired in much the same way.

It's no business of mine what the Churts were doing in Berlin in 1937 – it's evidently nothing that they wish to boast about. Or perhaps they acquired it later still. Maybe it was some local citizen who bought it at the sale in 1937. I can imagine it appealing to one of the new Gauleiters with a palatial home to furnish. In which case Tony's father presumably arrived with the invading Allies in 1945 and simply looted it, or purchased it from a starving war widow for cigarettes and instant coffee.

In other words I don't need to have any qualms. If the Churts can liberate *Helen* from the Germans I can liberate the *Merrymakers* from the Churts. Biff baff. Moral equilibrium.

And if Tony Churt can fictionalize a history for a picture I can surely fictionalize a future for it. This is what gives me strength and gets me going at last. I'm damned if I'm going to be outdone by Tony Churt!

And I launch boldly out into the deep waters.

'I was up in town yesterday', I tell Tony easily, turning back from my long study of the sky outside the window as if I'd simply been wondering whether the matter was worth mentioning, 'and someone I was talking to thinks he knows someone who might just possibly be interested.'

Tony frowns. 'Not a dealer?' he queries suspiciously.

'No, no – a collector. Said to be keen on Giordano. *Very* keen.'

'Money all right?'

'Money, as I understand it, is far from being a problem. Money coming out of his ears.'

So, it's all happening. The words are coming. And it's not at all a bad start, it seems to me. I'm impressed with myself. I've given him a good spoonful of jam to sweeten the tiny pill that's arriving next.

'Something of a mystery man, though, I gather,' I say solemnly. 'Keeps a very low profile. Won't show his face in public.'

Is this the kind of thing that people say? The subjects seem to be dropping off the front of my sentences, I notice, in deference to Tony's style. He looks at me thoughtfully.

And sees right through me. All my boldness vanishes at once. I feel the panic rise behind my eyes. I've been caught cheating my neighbours! How am I going to show my face round here after this? How am I even going to get myself out of the room?

'You mean he wouldn't want to come down here to look at it?'

'I don't know,' I flounder hopelessly. 'Perhaps . . . Possibly . . .'

'Take it up to town,' he says decisively. 'Get your chum to show it to him.'

I'm too occupied in breathing again to be able to reply. He misconstrues my silence.

'Bit of a bore for you,' he says. 'But it might be worth your while, you see. You'll make a bob or two if we keep this between ourselves. No auction houses, no dealers. Man to man. Arrangement among friends. Look, here's what you do. You take the old lady to Sotheby's and get her valued – and then you take her smartly away again. Right? They'll have knocked ten per cent off what they expect because they're being cautious, so you bump it up a bit. Yes? Then you add another ten per cent, because your mysterious chum won't have to pay the buyer's commission. Add on the VAT you're both saving, tell me what it comes to, and if it sounds half-way reasonable I'll tell you to go ahead. Then we'll split the commission.'

I gaze at him. I find all this remarkably difficult to follow, not being a simple countryman like him. Particularly the bit about splitting the commission. Splitting what commission?

'The nine or ten per cent I'd have paid if we'd gone ahead at Sotheby's, or if I'd taken it to a dealer,' he explains. 'So you get five per cent, I get five per cent, and we're both happy.'

I see. What I *think* he's saying is that since I'm a personal friend, and have somehow managed to find him a particularly satisfactory purchaser who may for obscure reasons be prepared to offer a top price even in the most dubious circumstances, and since I'm also prepared to risk prosecution for avoiding VAT, he'll pay me *half* of what he would pay a dealer.

'Fair enough?' he says, watching me. Plainly not; though fair enough is what it seems to me, I have to confess, because after all I'm *not* a personal friend, and I *haven't* found him his purchaser; and being cheated on the percentage would also relieve my conscience somewhat regarding the little corollary to the deal that he doesn't know about yet. For the sake of verisimilitude, though, I supposed I'd better bargain about it.

'Five per cent?' I query. 'I think seven would be more like it.'

'Seven?' he cries, pretending to be shocked, delighted to have drawn me to battle. 'Come off it, matey! You haven't got a gallery to maintain. You haven't got some smart little piece on the front desk to buy lunch for.'

True. 'Six,' I say.

'Five and a half,' he says.

I bow to the force of his personality. 'Five and a half,' I agree.

He's so pleased with this victory that he can scarcely contain himself. He jumps up from the desk. More papers fall into the waste-paper basket.

'Want to take her away with you now?'

It's like one of those dreams where you suddenly find you can fly. I struggle cautiously to get back to earth, and pat my pockets humorously.

'Money?' he says. 'Settle up when you've sold it. Good God – friends, neighbours. We can trust each other for a few thousand.'

Actually I hadn't even got as far as thinking about the money, let alone credit arrangements.

'I mean,' I explain, 'I don't think I've got a pocket large enough to put her in. I'm on foot.'

'Take the Land-Rover.'

I hesitate. I'm tempted, if only to get back into the breakfast-room, where I might find a moment to sneak another look at their excellent arrangements for stopping soot falling out of the fireplace. Then I see myself arriving back at the cottage, with Kate watching as I untie the baler twine on Tony Churt's tailgate . . . and unload *The Rape of Helen*. Not the kind of surprise that would go down well with Kate. I've a certain amount of preparation and negotiation to do there, I think, before I'm ready to roll. I also need to have a few words with the bank manager. Then again, a little seemly reluctance now may pay dividends later.

'I'd better find out first how interested this chap really is.'

'Suit yourself. Pick it up any time.'

The dogs get up to help see me out. But at the door of the office their master pauses, struck by a moment of doubt.

'I mean, I trust *you*,' he says. 'But I assume you won't go handing the goods over to whoever it is until you've got the money off him?'

'Of course not.'

'Something dodgy about him by the sound of it. Shady customer?'

'I've never met him,' I say carefully. 'I know absolutely nothing about him.'

No, that's too bland. I need to know one thing about him, one small but colourful detail for Tony's imagination to work on. I have one of my lightning flashes of illumination.

'All I know', I say, 'is that he's a Belgian.'

I've hit exactly the right button. Tony's immensely amused.

'Say no more!' he says. 'Cash down, tell him! Belgian banknotes on the table!'

He leads the way back to the hall, still laughing.

'I don't know why you think it's so funny,' says Laura, on her hands and knees, trying to fasten a loose rug in place with what looks like Superglue. 'Second time in a week this fucking thing has shot away under my feet. I nearly killed myself.'

'We're talking business, my sweetheart,' says Tony.

I look to see what's hanging at the head of the stairs, in the place where Helen of Troy should rightly be. I'm none the wiser, though, because it's a picture so small that from the bottom of the stairs you'd need a pair of binoculars. I feel confident enough of our newly established intimacy to inquire about my business partner's eccentric exhibition policy.

'Why don't you hang the good lady where we can all see her?' I ask.

'I *beg* your pardon?' snaps Laura, straightening up in amazement.

'Helen, Helen. Why isn't she gazing down at us from the top of the stairs?'

'Good eye you've got,' says Tony. 'Because you're right – she used to be over the stairs. I remember her up there when I was a boy. Been off on her travels since then, though.'

'His mother grabbed her,' says Laura.

'I wouldn't say "grabbed", exactly.'

'When your mother ran off with Dicky. They grabbed *Helen* and half the family silver as they went!'

'Spot of ill feeling about the marriage settlement,' Tony explains to me.

'Not to mention about Dicky being left to carry the can when the racecourse thing went phut!'

'Look, he was my father's man of business . . .'

'He was your father's life-support system!'

'It's a long story, and frankly, my sweet beloved, you know fuck all about it.'

'Anyway,' I say, to help their marriage back on to the rails, '*Helen* was a rather appropriate item to take.'

They're too irritated with each other to enquire why, but at least I've silenced them.

'She and Paris took all Menelaus's treasure when they ran off together,' I explain.

Whether they knew this piquant detail before, or whether they've taken it in now – whether they even know who Menelaus is – it's impossible to tell. One of the dogs, though, is polite enough to scratch itself in a way that suggests some mild passing interest.

'The point is, though,' says Tony to me, 'that she's back.'

'Not his mother,' explains Laura.

'Not my mother, no,' says Tony heavily. 'My mother's dead, God rest her.'

'So of course we've got the damned thing parked on us again.'

Is it Laura who dictates hanging policy in this house? Is this the answer to my question? I wonder what would have happened if they'd had mother-in-law herself parked on them. Would she also have been locked up in the breakfast-room? Dangled off a hook so low that she sagged at the knees?

'Well, my dear,' Tony tells her, as he opens the front door for me, 'you won't have to put up with it for much longer.'

'The only reason he hasn't sold it before is because it wasn't here to sell,' says Laura. 'He's sold everything else. And he always manages to get himself ripped off.'

– 108 –

'That's why I'm putting myself in Mr Clay's hands. You're not telling me *he's* going to rip me off?'

'I *should*, if I were you!' calls Laura to me, as Tony pulls the front door to behind his back, and she vanishes from my sight. 'Teach him a lesson!'

I don't like to catch Tony's eye. I edge away round the lake and the dogs who are helpfully trying to drink it up. But when I look up I see that it's the dogs he's gazing at.

'Not a clue about business, poor love,' he says mournfully. 'Can't understand that everything in the world's done by personal connections.'

It occurs to me that Laura's remark might be discreetly construed as a challenge to his authority, and that spurning this challenge will bind him yet more firmly to our new alliance.

'I don't want to cause any difficulties,' I say. 'I mean, if your wife feels I ought not to be involved . . .'

'Good God, don't take any notice of *her*!' he says. 'I never do. Fine mess we'd be in.'

I smile a dreadful little smile of male solidarity. I'm going to die of shame for this. But later.

The smile's such a success that it tempts him into new depths of confidentiality. He becomes solemn.

'Actually,' he says, 'a lot of people round here resent you chaps. Coming down at the weekends, taking up all the parking in Lavenage, turning the grocer's into a health food shop. But I say, look, if they're the sort of people who are prepared to pitch in and lend a helping hand, then they're neighbours, they're members of the community like the rest of us.'

'Thank you,' I say. 'That's generous of you. I'm very touched.' Do I detect a slight catch in my throat? Am I going to ask if I can sign a petition in favour of his scramble track? No, I limit myself to another little smile, a touched and grateful one. 'And I'll let you know if I get anywhere with our Belgian friend.'

On which note I withdraw down the drive. But I feel such a dizzy sense of achievement at the progress I've made that I have another of my sudden inspirations. On the spur of the moment I decide to attempt one stage further still. I stop and turn back to Tony.

'Oh, yes,' I call, with amazingly plausible belatedness. 'What about your Double Dutchmen? Do you want me to ask if he'd like to have a look at those?'

'Why not?' calls Tony. 'What have we got to lose?'

What has he got to lose? Nothing that he knows about. Really, it's like taking candy off a child. I should have become a confidence trickster ages ago.

I feel the physical force of the expression 'walking on air'; I float over the lakes and potholes of the drive as easily as a hovercraft. Then, as I turn into the lane at the end, this soft and balmy cushion of air under my feet solidifies with terrifying suddenness into a shrieking, flapping, rising *something*, and for some minutes after the pheasant has cleared the barbed wire and vanished I'm too shocked to breathe.

All right, all right, I think to myself, once I can think again. Point taken. There may be surprises yet to come.

I must stop talking about this strange and terrifying venture I'm now launched upon, even humorously to myself, as a confidence trick, because it's not – it's a public service, a contribution to the common weal at least as notable as anything that Rockefeller or Getty ever did. Tony Churt's unhesitating readiness to sell *Helen* to someone he assumes to be a criminal suggests very plainly the kind of fate that I'm almost certainly saving *my* picture from. If there were any justice in the world I should get my name incised in large Roman capitals across the top of the gallery that it's finally housed in.

Actually I do feel easier in my mind, ridiculously, now I know that the buyer I've found is a Belgian, however shadowy. He's taken on a little reality for me – he's shed a little of his stark non-existence. He *must* exist, if only because there's something so gratifying about the prospect of Tony Churt's being humbled by the race he feels so free to despise.

In any case, when I say, or allow him to believe, that I've found a shadowy Belgian, this is surely in terms of strict logic *true*, because I *have* found a shadowy Belgian. A Belgian rather more shadowy than my collector. About the latter we know at least that he's wealthy, whereas we know nothing about Bruegel's finances at all. It's also of course a classic *suggestio falsi*, which I must remember for my first-year Introduction to Formal Reasoning course, though one of the things contributing to my insane excitement as I come tumbling and stumbling downhill through the woods is the dawning realization that I'm never going to have to teach it again.

If I *am* in the woods, because by this time I'm too busy with my own thoughts to notice the reality of the very real piece of country around me. I've started to worry about exactly how I'm going to carry out my great public service. The rough outline which seems to be emerging inside my head is this. I'm going to take *Helen* and the two Dutch pictures to Sotheby's for a valuation, and I'm going to report the valuation absolutely truthfully to Tony Churt. Up to this point, everything's entirely straightforward and entirely clear to me. But here we leave the highway. If he accepts the valuation, I go ahead and sell the pictures for him. Since my admirable Belgian, wealthy and complaisant though he is, is still not quite real enough to produce real money, I shall have to sell them the way anyone else would, by finding a dealer who's prepared to buy them for something like the valuation, less his usual ten per cent. Then I go back to Tony, tell him I've persuaded my Belgian to pay the full valuation, and hand it over less my own five and a half per cent.

So I'm going to have to find four and a half per cent of the value of the three pictures. Which will be how much? Well, what's the valuation likely to be? Very roughly? Ball-park figures, as Tony Churt would say, though what ball-park figures are I have only a ball-park idea. Well, let's say the Giordano is £10,000, since this is the figure that Tony plucked hopefully out of the air, and surely out of the very thinnest air in the uppermost reaches of the stratosphere. A plausible figure for the skaters might be a couple of thousand, and for the cavalrymen a couple of thousand more. That's, what, £14,000. Add a thousand to be on the safe side. Five and a half per cent of £15,000 is . . . I can't do the calculation in my head, what with that maddening extra half per cent I've negotiated for myself, and the branches catching at my face, and my feet sliding away downhill in the mud a lot faster than the rest of me. But it must plainly be under a thousand pounds. A figure with only two noughts! This is ridiculously encouraging!

But then we come to the fourth picture, the Belgian picture, *my* picture. This one, of course, I'm *not* going to get valued at Sotheby's, or anywhere else, nor am I going to sell it to the dealer. I'm going to keep it. Eventually it's going to cover any possible outlay a hundred times over. In the meantime, though, I have to carry not just four and a half per cent of its price but a hundred per cent of it. So what's the price going to be? How am I going to concoct a plausible figure?

Simple. The label on the back implies that it's after Vrancz. I merely look in the records of sale-room prices in the V & A and see what kind of price paintings by his Circle or Followers fetch. What will it be? Another couple of thousand?

Simple as this procedure is, though, I'm not going to follow it. Since the rest of the deal's so reasonable, and since I stand to gain in the end, I'm going to make a quixotic gesture. I'm going to look up the price of a genuine Vrancz. Which will be, what, £10,000? Say £20,000. Then I'm going to go back to Tony and say, 'I hope you don't think I'm cutting too many corners, but I took a deep breath and decided not to get that unframed painting valued, because I knew what they'd tell me: if it was labelled "Vrancz" it wasn't by Vrancz. I thought I should try offering it in all innocence to my Belgian as genuine – and I'm afraid he fell for it. I feel a bit ashamed of myself, to tell you the truth, because I told him I wanted £20,000. So here you are –

£20,000. Less five and a half per cent. I hope you're not too shocked.'

So Tony will be pocketing £18,000 more than he can possibly have expected – and all his prejudices about the stupidity of Belgians will have been gratifyingly confirmed. Also, I shall have proved myself as unscrupulous as he is when I've a percentage at stake, which will probably be an even more gratifying confirmation of his general prejudices about human nature. Meanwhile, the picture will be on our kitchen wall, maturing with a graceful lack of haste into a Bruegel. As Tony says, there's something in this deal for everyone. A little more for me than for him, perhaps. But that's business.

Hold on, though. Isn't it going to come as a nasty surprise when Tony Churt opens his *Daily Telegraph* one morning, some months or years from now, and sees the photograph of me unveiling my newly discovered masterpiece to the world's media? Isn't it going to come as an even nastier surprise to me the following morning when I open my *Guardian* and see a photograph of Tony Churt telling another press conference how he'd entrusted the picture to me to sell for him, and how I'd carried out what he'll make sound rather less like an act of public service, and rather more like . . . well, yes, a confidence trick?

No, because it's not going to be like that. The deal's going to unroll slowly over the course of many months, like the slowly changing seasons, each with its characteristic labour. In the first panel I break the ground. In the next I plant my twenty thousand. Then, before the summer's too far advanced, comes a third labour. Somewhere in the rough ground I'm traversing now, where our two estates meet, I bump into Tony. We talk about this and that, as neighbours do, and in an afterthought as I turn to go, as artlessly performed as my afterthought this morning, I say: 'Oh, something I've always meant to tell you. This'll make you laugh. You remember that unframed picture of yours, the one you stopped up the fireplace with? You'll think this is very ridiculous, but I somehow fell in love with it while I was waiting to deliver it to my man, I don't know why. So it wasn't the Belgian who bought it – it was me! It's on my kitchen wall.'

'Good God!' says Tony in amazement. 'So where did the money come from?

'I scraped it together somehow,' I say modestly. 'Don't ask me how!'

'£20,000?' says Tony, astonished.

'Don't remind me! I just had to have that picture, though!'

'But it wasn't worth anything like that! It wasn't genuine! You told me!'

'I know,' I say, with heart-breaking simplicity. 'But I'd also told you I was going to get you £20,000 for it. I felt in honour bound to pay what I'd said.'

He gazes at me in incomprehension. In all his manifold wheelings and dealings he's never come across such a yearning for the higher things of life, or such punctiliousness in a matter of business. 'But this puts me in a terrible position!' he cries. 'It's one thing ripping off some unknown Belgian. But a neighbour . . . a penniless academic . . . a personal friend who went out of his way to make himself helpful . . . Why didn't you *tell* me?'

Why didn't I tell him? For a very good and honourable reason.

'Because I know *you*,' I say. 'You'd have refused to accept the money. You'd have insisted on selling it to me for £2,000.'

This confidence in the goodness of his nature, so naïve as

to border on idiocy, might arouse suspicion in anyone a little more acute. But on Tony Churt it has a completely unforeseen effect, or what would be a completely unforeseen effect if I weren't foreseeing it now. He has trouble with his voice. 'No one's ever said anything like that to me before,' he manages. 'Look, I'm going to repay you that £18,000 . . . Yes, I insist! I don't know how . . . I may have to sell the estate . . .'

Now it's my turn to be moved. I break down and confess everything . . .

Hold on. The painting of this particular labour has departed from any conceivable reality. There are many embarrassments which this scheme of mine may land me in. Tony Churt's offering to repay me money, I think I can say with reasonable safety, isn't going to be one of them.

Let's repaint the panel from where I told him I'd scraped the money together, I don't know how, and bought the picture myself. This is where I went wrong. He may well be surprised, but he doesn't show any signs of being softened by the news – of course he doesn't. What *does* he do? Laughs in my face, I should think, at the insane extravagance of my aesthetic and moral sensibilities alike.

But that's fine. In fact it's good, it's very good, for all the labours yet to come. Because I don't take his mockery amiss. I laugh with him. I make myself even more ridiculous. 'I know it's silly,' I tell him. 'But to me it's worth every penny. Because even though it's not a real Vrancz . . . I don't know, there's something about that picture . . .'

And the ground's prepared for the later panels in the series: my growing obsession with the *Merrymakers*, which eventually leads to my beginning to study late sixteenth-century Netherlandish art, and then, in growing excitement, as the grapes ripen on the vine, showing the picture to a specialist in the period, who takes one look and cries out with unprofessional astonishment, 'Holy shit – you know what this is . . .?'

Let's leave the last few panels unpainted for the moment, though. We'll come to them all in good time. Let's go back to the one where I tell Tony Churt that I scraped the money together I don't know how. Because I *don't*. Know how I scraped the money together. A few hundred for the other pictures is one thing. £20,000 is quite another. There are one or two more labours to be inserted here.

And suppose the cavalrymen or the skating scene are worth a lot more than I think. Suppose Sotheby's tell me that they're worth . . . I don't know, it could be anything . . . £50,000 apiece, even!

No, that's all right. Because then I shall find it perfectly possible, both psychologically and morally, to find that the so-called Vrancz is worth only a couple of thousand. If I get him a good price for the Giordano and the other two I can adjust the value of my picture to fit.

One way or another I can do it.

I realize with a shock that I'm approaching the cottage. I've no recollection of emerging from the woods, or of seeing the valley opening out in front of me as I picked my way through the cowpats, let alone the snow-capped crags and blue distances and beckoning sea that I saw on my outward journey. What I was seeing as I came back was the almost equally complex and wonderful landscape of the deal I'm setting up. The great diagonals of my scenario had taken my eye from the small, plausible details in the foreground – the comical dance of buyer and seller to the dealer's tune – and led it up to the snowbound whitelead peaks of the soaring prices, out through those endlessly alluring veils of mountain blue to the sea where my ship lies freighted with her cargo of noughts.

But now I have to convey this vision to Kate, if only because all our finances, such as they are, are held in common, so there's no possible way in which I could raise the six or ten or twenty thousand pounds I shall need without her knowing.

The high peaks vanish behind the winter grime on the windows of the cottage, still waiting for me to clean them. The swelling press of canvas on the high-pooped caravel becomes three of Tilda's sleeping-suits, washed by Kate and hanging accusingly out to dry.

Yes. Now comes the hardest labour of all.

Kate's sitting in front of the fan heater, holding two small feet in the air, and smiling down at the owner balanced on her knees. Her left breast is hanging free from her open shirt, like Helen's in the picture, but larger, whiter, softer and infinitely more beautiful. A drop of milk hangs on her nipple. She looks up, still smiling. 'Good walk?' she asks, with every appearance of polite interest.

'Fine,' I say. I'm not fooled by her smile. I know that tone of voice. There's something particularly irritating about her efforts to make me feel guilty for not getting on with a book in which she has neither interest nor belief – and something more irritating still about her refusal to do it openly. I know that things are going to get worse when I explain the reason, and worse still if I don't find exactly the right way to begin. Nevertheless, I bravely take in a good supply of air and open my mouth, eager to find out what's going to emerge. But she's absorbed in Tilda again already, and there's something so simple and concrete and complete about the two of them together, and something so confused and abstract and unfinished about what I have to say, that I let the air out again.

I take my coat off and sit down at the table to work instead. The ability to defer giving battle is the essence of strategy. I put out my hand to move the folder I left discreetly covering my stack of books – and find there's no need. The folder's lying beside them. *Pieter Bruegel the Elder*, the cover of the topmost book is screaming at the world, with a picture of a dancing peasant just to drive the point home in the most blatantly obvious way.

I look at Kate. She has her head down over Tilda, and she's shaking her loose hair back and forth over the baby's face.

I look back at the books. The stack's slightly out of true. She's read the words, in one spelling or the other, on all seven bindings. Never before, so far as I know, has she ever checked up on me behind my back. But then never before, so far as I can recall, have I ever kept anything from her. We've crossed some kind of watershed, and a new landscape's opened in front of us. It's not spring in this new valley. I realize that her absorption in Tilda is accusing me not just of neglecting my work, but of something worse. It implies a contrast with my failure to be absorbed in the wonderful little creature we've brought into the world together, and my cold-hearted absorption in something else. I don't believe her failure to replace the folder on top of the books was accidental. I suddenly feel the sense of injustice that must be afflicting the Hunters in the Snow, as they come back from their great expedition to secure food for the village and find that no one will give them so much as a glance, because they shouldn't have been out hunting at all – they should have been at home looking after the children and writing about nominalism. The injustice is even more marked in my case, since I've returned from *my* expedition not with one miserable, uneatable fox, but with enough meat to keep us, all three of us, for the rest of our lives. Or the prospect of it.

She looks up and sees me looking at her. We both look away.

'You didn't see the picture,' I say quietly. 'I did.'

I meant to begin quietly, it's true; but not like this, on a note of accusation. She carefully puts her breast away and buttons up her shirt.

'Bruegel,' she says neutrally, carefully draining any suggestion of doubt or query from her voice.

'I think it's just possible,' I reply, carefully draining any suggestion from mine of the conviction I feel, which has in any case begun to fade as soon as she uttered the name.

'Unsigned?' she inquires politely.

'Yes, but so are quite a number of them.'

Now I've moved from accusation to defensiveness. The conversation's come off the rails before it's even left the station. My idea, so far as I'd had one and can remember it, was to begin by simply describing to her what I'd seen, and letting her find her own way to the same conclusion to which it had led me. Too late for this now, and in any case Max Friedländer's wise words have come back into my head, warning against the vanity of attempting to describe pictures in detail. The 'strictest economy of words' is what he enjoins, and recommends limiting oneself to 'aphoristic remarks, put together unsystematically'. The shimmer on the leaves, the snow-capped peaks, the great diagonals, the feet stamping in the mud – they all flash through my mind and immediately fall victim to my drive for verbal economy. How can I condense it all into one unsystematic aphorism?

'It's the spring,' I say, and yes, not bad – in fact, perfect – I've got it in one. How aphoristic can you get? In a single word, the spring is what it is.

Whether it has the same full richness of meaning to her, I don't know. She doesn't give any evidence of the shock of delight that I felt when I saw the picture. Or any echo of my surprise. But then I suppose she remembers my questions about the iconography.

She fetches a clean jump-suit for Tilda. 'You don't mean something from the *Months*?' she asks, and of course at once I'm away. I've got my opening, like a salesman when the reluctant customer's foolish enough to display some passing polite interest.

'They're not months!' I say, just as the salesman might say, These are not brushes, madam, they're eco-friendly, fuel-efficient cleansing tools. 'That's the point! They're seasons!'

'I thought there were five of them extant . . .' she begins, as she eases Tilda's arms out of the old suit.

And now my spirits have really revived, my conviction's returned in full. It's plain that she doesn't know anything about the series. And I do. She's off her home ground. And on mine. Very calmly and coherently, I run through the history of the debate: the unpaid tax, the missing 'and', the misplaced *mit*, the old division of the year, the early spring and the late spring. I lay particular stress, of course, on her own decisive contribution in recognizing the iconography. Her hands stop working as I speak. Tilda lies half into her clean suit and half out of it. Kate's looking straight at me.

'And you seriously think . . .?' she begins carefully.

'No,' I say, 'I don't. I don't seriously think at all. I seriously know.'

She resumes work on Tilda.

'I thought you said before . . .' she begins again.

'That it was possible,' I agree at once, recalling with some surprise this now long-past stage in the conversation. 'I did. I was lying. I was trying to break it gently. I was saying, "I'm afraid your great-aunt's been taken ill," when what I mean is that she's dead.'

Another pause. More work on Tilda.

'There's nothing impossible about a missing Bruegel turning up,' I explain. 'Nothing even particularly unlikely. *The Flight into Egypt* didn't resurface until 1948. *Christ and the Woman Taken in Adultery*, which is a particularly important picture, only turned up in the fifties. *The Three Soldiers* in the sixties.'

She's no more interested in my newly acquired scholarship about Bruegel, though, than she was in my findings about the Master of the Embroidered Foliage.

'What did Tony Churt say when you told him?' she asks.

I've a long way still to go in explaining this thing to her, I realize.

'I didn't say anything to Tony Churt', I explain, very gently, 'because it would be a criminal offence. Yes! In effect! Aiding and abetting! It would be like giving a bank robber the key to the bank! Because that would be the last anyone would ever see of it! It would be out of the country and gone! Held as an investment in some millionaire's vault.'

Tilda's head is turned to one side, and she's watching me with unblinking seriousness and open mouth. *She* understands. *She* sees the dangers.

'So what are you going to do?' asks Kate.

'Buy it.'

Kate has been standing up to work on Tilda. She stops work and sits down. 'Martin!' she says.

'Don't start worrying about Tony Churt,' I reassure her. 'I'm not doing this to make money. I'm doing it to ensure that the picture goes to some place where everyone can see it. I'm doing it because it's a kind of miracle that's brought this picture and me face to face – because it's an opportunity that's not offered to many, and that will almost certainly never recur for me, to perform one truly worthy action before I die. There's something in that picture that cries out to me. Though if by any chance I do happen to make a little money in the process, I shall of course accept it gratefully. On behalf of both of us. And I shall give everyone, including Tony Churt, their rightful share.'

Tilda gives a sudden smile. She may not understand every nuance of this surprisingly eloquent speech, but she certainly senses and approves the passion that drives it. Kate, however, remains more resistant, and I was wrong – what's at the forefront of her mind is not the possibility of injustice to Tony Churt.

'How much will it cost?' she asks.

I make a rapid calculation. What I'm calculating is not exactly the answer to her question, but how much of my rather complex plans I should attempt to explain at this particular juncture. I can see that it's not the moment to get involved in a long, tangled exposition, or to mention the quixotic generosity I have in mind to show Tony Churt. I need to get the basic principle accepted first.

'I think something by a follower of Vrancz would probably be worth a couple of thousand,' I say. Another good *suggestio falsi* for my Introduction course, if things don't work out as well as I hope.

But the *suggestio* is evidently not false enough. She's appalled. 'Two thousand pounds?' she says in amazement. I was right to keep the ramifications of the scheme until later.

'Or so,' I say lightly, smiling back at Tilda, who's delighted to discover how modest the outlay will be.

'Where are you going to get two thousand pounds from?' demands Kate, as sharply as she's ever demanded anything. 'We haven't *got* two thousand pounds!'

'Overdraft,' I say. 'I'll tell the bank manager we're doing some improvements to the cottage. New septic tank, perhaps.'

I reach out to take Tilda. But Kate gets up without a word and carries her up to the bedroom for her nap.

And now, without Tilda there to encourage me, I feel some slight misgivings creep into the pit of my stomach. While it was actually happening, the conversation seemed to me to be bouncing along on a reasonably cheerful note, but I realize in retrospect that this was purely unilateral. Really it was just about as disastrous as I could have feared. She doesn't accept my attribution, this is the underlying trouble. She obviously wouldn't begrudge my investing a few pounds if she did, against such a huge return. Does this shake my conviction a little? Not for a moment. I saw it. She didn't.

But I can't help feeling the sadness of it all. Kate used to like what she thought of as my boldness and impulsiveness. She was dismayed by my swerve into the nominalist project, it's true, and a lot more dismayed still by my little fling with the Master of the Embroidered Foliage. But she liked it well enough on Lufthansa. Not just in my speed to proffer help with the ink, but in my almost equal speed to adapt all my plans in life to fit hers. She was on her way to monasteries to look at manuscripts, but I was on my way to somewhere no less important. I was going to visit Neuschwanstein, to research a book I was thinking of writing on Nietzsche and late romanticism – my first attempt to escape from the shackles of academic philosophy. She could have given up the monasteries and come to Neuschwanstein with me. But she didn't – the possibility was never even discussed. I gave up Neuschwanstein and went to the monasteries with her. She smiled and frowned when I announced my change of plan to her, as we came into land, and said I was being ridiculous. She frowned and smiled, and by the time the plane had reached the gate, had more or less agreed. This, incidentally, is how I first saw the South German and Danubian paintings that led me back from the nineteenth century to the fifteenth, and northwards from Bavaria to the Netherlands, then on again to my apotheosis in the late spring of 1565, in a rich valley beneath the snow-capped peaks of the Flemish Alps. This is how it all fitted together.

Our marriage – this was another sudden and amazing project of mine that turned out well.

The bedroom door softly closes, and Kate comes softly down the stairs again.

'Just promise me one thing,' she says concessively, and of course at once I'm ready to concede anything she likes in return. Or almost anything. 'You will let someone else see it first?'

This is so idiotic, so plainly impossible, so obviously at odds with the whole tenor of the delicate negotiations I'm involved in, that all thought of concession vanishes at once.

'Let who see it?' I ask, reasonably enough.

'Someone who knows something about Bruegel.'

She wants me to get it authenticated as the missing Bruegel – and then buy it for two thousand pounds? What do they do all day up there at the Hamlish? What do they dream about in the Ecclesiology Department? I love her strange, dreamy detachment from all worldly knowledge and values – I always have. It's written deep into the beauty of her face. But this is even more preposterous than my imaginary faith in Tony Churt's honesty. Then again, what's happened all of a sudden to her saintly disregard for money? Also, what does she mean – someone who knows something about Bruegel? *I'm* someone who knows something about Bruegel! Already I know almost as much as there is to know. By the time I hand over any money I shall know things that other Bruegel scholars never even knew there *were* to know.

But all I say is: 'I assure you I shan't go ahead if there's the slightest doubt.'

'In whose mind?'

In mine, obviously. But I don't reply. I'm going to let her do the talking for a change, while I borrow her technique of silence.

– 126 –

She tries another tack. 'Why do you object to its going out of the country? I've never heard you complain about the others being in Vienna and wherever it is. If this really is one of the series, it probably ought to be with them.'

I can't let this go by in silence. 'It won't be in Vienna! It certainly won't be in the Kunsthistorisches. Not if it's bought by some shady Belgian businessman.'

'Why should it be bought by a shady Belgian business-man?'

I revert to my previous policy. A slight confusion here, I realize; the mysterious Belgian comes into another chapter of the story altogether. A chapter which it's certainly not the moment to open now. In any case, she's already off on a fresh scent.

'Suppose Tony Churt simply asks you?'

'Asks me what?'

'If it's a Bruegel.'

'He won't. Why should he? I don't suppose he's ever heard of Bruegel.'

'But if he does? If he says, "Is this a Bruegel?"'

'I'll tell him the truth.'

'That it's a Bruegel?'

I say nothing again. I *could* say that it's disingenuous of her to suggest this is the truth, when she herself thinks it's not. But then she'd reply that what's at issue is not what *she* thinks ... etcetera etcetera. To which I should be forced to reply that the *truth* of a proposition is logically independent of what either of us believes . . . etcetera etcetera. Then it occurs to me, with a terrible sinking of the heart, that we're having the kind of conversation that other couples have, the kind that we've never had before, the kind that goes dully round and round in circles, with each of us scoring points that remain entirely obscure to the other.

We're on the road to becoming Tony and Laura.

'What will you tell him?' she persists.

'That I don't know.'

'I thought you said you *did* know?'

I shouldn't have offered her even that small response to work on, because now I shall have to give a little lecture about the criteria for knowledge, in any strict epistemological sense, that I should certainly be obliged to adhere to if my professional opinion were being sought; to which she will respond with . . . oh, who knows, who cares? How have we managed to avoid all this before for six long years? Because we've always conducted our disputes in silence. Or at any rate Kate has. I've always known what she was thinking, but since she's never uttered the objection aloud I've had no occasion or excuse for a counter-objection. It's her sudden abandonment of this policy, her complete reversal of it, that's landed us in this swamp.

'Martin,' she says quietly, 'listen to me. That picture isn't a Bruegel. I'm sorry – I know how much you want it to be. But it's not. It's truly not.'

'You didn't see it.'

'Martin, please! I *know* it's not! Please listen to what I'm saying! It's not a Bruegel, Martin! It's not, it's not! Of course it's not! How can you be so stupid?'

It's unsettling, I have to confess, to see someone as calm and rational as Kate give way to blind panic. I feel her terror creeping into my veins like an infection. But I resist it. I quietly repeat my unanswerable argument. 'You didn't see it. I did.'

I'm as isolated as Saul, in the great *Conversion* on the left-hand wall of the Kunsthistorisches. I'm lying at the side of the Damascus road, felled and blinded by the narrow laser beam from heaven that has sought out me and no one else. All around me the great army flows on, upwards and onwards into the mountains. That river of men is Kate and the rest of mankind, going about the settled business of their lives. I'm the small, unnoticed anomaly, the prostrate drunk, the collapsed down and out, the minor embarrassment at the periphery of their vision. What none of them knows is that I shall arise as Paul, and my awkward little fit will have changed the world.

Tilda cries. I'm on my way upstairs before Kate can move. Tilda's my one supporter, and I need a little support at the moment. I pick her up and walk her back and forth, and jiggle her gently up and down, until she settles again. It would be better to jiggle her box, because she'll probably wake again when I put her down. But I love holding her, and looking at her sleeping face. Particularly now. But the look and feel of her there in my arms, so real and solid, so present, undermines my faith instead of reinforcing it. My picture isn't in my arms, warm and breathing. My picture's absent. One glimpse is all I had of it, and even the memory of that glimpse has become indistinct. Once again my courage fails me, because now I suddenly see what the real worst-case scenario would be.

It's this: I've borrowed my £26,000, in the teeth of Kate's terrified unbelief, or perhaps without her knowledge at all, I've waited my decent interval, and I've shown the picture to the specialist I've found. He takes one look at it . . . and he doesn't shout out. He examines it for a long time, and then he says, 'I suppose you were hoping that this was an original Vrancz, but I'm afraid it's just something in his general style . . .' I sell it to a dealer, and I get £2,000 for it. So now I have to go back to Kate and tell her, 'I've borrowed £26,000, and I've lost over £20,000 of it, with no hope of ever recovering it . . .'

Nor any hope of repaying it. And whoever it was I borrowed it from, whether it was the bank, waiting to foreclose on the second mortgage I've taken out, or some firm I've found in the Yellow Pages, readier still to come round with dogs and iron bars, the real loser in the deal is right here, lying in my arms. I shall have borrowed the money against our daughter's future.

I'm not Saul but Icarus, in the Musée des Beaux-Arts in Brussels, who has flown too near the sun, and who has fallen, as unnoticed by the world as Saul, and as irrelevant; but fallen not to rise again in glory – to disappear ignominiously beneath the waves for ever.

With infinite care I settle my mortgaged child back into her box, and creep out of the bedroom. I'm going to sit down beside Kate at the kitchen table and take her hand, and kiss it. I'm going to confess that I've behaved wrongly, and ask her forgiveness. Then I shall tell her everything – the whole plan, with nothing kept back. Perhaps, when she sees how contrite I am, and realizes how much it must have meant to me ever to think of going behind her back as I did, she'll make a huge leap of faith and trust me to do as I think best. Then we'll be in it together, as we've been with every other venture since we first met. Perhaps she'll still say, lovingly, that she thinks it's wrong. And if she does I'll bow to her judgement. Without demur. I'll write to Caryl Hind, my friend at the National Gallery, to whom I should in happier circumstances have taken my picture for authentication, and suggest his spending the weekend with us. We'll take him to visit some of our neighbours. Then at least the NG will be on the case before anyone else is.

But Kate's sitting at the table working, and before I can sit down beside her, much less take her hand, she's looked up and said with a quite uncharacteristic sour irony, 'So how much are you going to give Tony Churt?'

I'm so taken aback by her tone, when I had such unsuspecting tenderness in my heart, that I can't understand what she's talking about. I frown in incomprehension. Her lips tighten. I see at once that she's misunderstood the signification of the frown. And up it all starts again.

'You said you were going to give him a fair share of anything you made,' she explains. Is this really what's worrying her? If so, there's a very simple answer that comes into my head even as I open my mouth to speak.

'I'll give him five and a half per cent.' As I hoped, the bizarre idiosyncrasy of this formula stops her in her tracks. Now it's her turn to frown in incomprehension.

'Because that's what *he's* giving *me*.' She can't understand this, either. Nor can I, now I've said it. Five and a half per cent for *buying* something? 'On the sale. On the sale of the Giordano.'

Too late I remember that this is something I haven't yet explained to her. She tries to look at me, but can't. She tries to look at her work, but can't. Faintly from upstairs comes the sound of Tilda beginning to stir and complain. I get up to investigate. 'Wait,' says Kate quietly. I sit down again, with terrible patience. What's happening to us? This is worse than ever. 'Martin, what's going on? You're selling the Giordano? How? What do you mean? Why didn't you tell me? What else have you arranged with him?'

I keep very calm. Suddenly the whole scenario, that appeared to me so complex and hazardous when I was worrying about it to myself, seems very simple and logical and easy to grasp.

'I take both pictures off his hands. I sell the Giordano, I keep the other one. He only has to pay five and a half per cent, instead of ten, so we're both happy. I was going to tell you, but I thought you'd just think I was getting distracted from the book again.'

This explanation is so satisfactory that for a moment I can't think why I need to find any money at all. The deal is practically self financing – my margin on the Giordano will almost pay for the other picture! I get up again to go, because at any moment Tilda's grizzling is going to change into a full-scale howl.

'Wait, wait. What about the other two pictures we saw? Does he want you to sell those as well?'

'We talked about it.'

'So you *are*?'

'Am what?'

'Selling them?'

It's absurd to be talking about these unimportant details when Tilda's crying. I look at the stairs, longing to be up them and comforting her.

'Are you or aren't you?' she demands.

'We can't talk about things in that tone of voice.'

'Are you selling the other two pictures?'

'I might. I'll see.'

Tilda's distress is gathering force. Kate's as aware of it as I am.

'*How* are you going to sell these pictures?' says Kate. 'Who are you going to sell them to? You don't know any-one!'

I'm tempted to say that I do, that I know a wealthy and reclusive Belgian who'll pay almost anything I like to ask. But somehow the fact of his being Belgian, that seemed so telling when I was explaining it to Tony Churt, now makes the words die away in embarrassment before I can utter them. Even the Belgian himself has become a little pale and ghostly. I say nothing, merely turn my head towards the stairs again, and the source of the increasingly urgent demands for our attention.

'You mean you'll take them to a dealer?' demands Kate. 'But then you'll have to pay the dealer ten per cent! It's stupid to tell me you're going to be making money! You won't be – you know you won't! He's tricking you! It's just a way for him to get rid of those pictures without paying the full dealer's commission! Martin, how much is all this going to cost? It won't be two thousand pounds, will it – it will be more! How much, Martin? How much will it cost?'

I should have told her the worst straight out. I see that now. I've completely mishandled this. I carefully recalculate the figure; this time it has to be the best and most honest estimate I can make. So, £10,000 for the Giordano – £2,000 each for the skaters and the cavalrymen – £14,000. Of which I have to find four and a half per cent. It's less than £700, for heaven's sake! Plus the £20,000 for my own picture, but I'll put that down for the moment at £2,000, because if it would make it easier for Kate to accept I can always drop the quixotic trimmings.

'Kate,' I say, 'we're talking about a total outlay of less than £3,000! A new sofa would cost us more than that! I told you, I'm not doing this for money – and I think you know me well enough to accept that – but have you any idea what kind of price a copy of a major Bruegel goes for these days? A *copy*?'

She's not listening, though. She's already on the stairs. All she can hear is Tilda, and the coming collapse of the world we've brought her into. 'You don't seem to realize!' she says, and all her unshakeable calm has changed into agitation. 'Things are different now we've got Tilda! We can't go on just doing as we like! We've got to think about *her*! We've got to think about the future!'

She disappears into the bedroom. When she says 'we' she of course means me. *I* can't go on doing just as I like. She makes it sound as if I've spent my days gambling and drinking, but what she means is that she's lost patience with my laborious struggles to find my way in life. Once again I'm choked by the sheer injustice of it. Just when by some miracle I've at last found the path that leads out of the maze, she wants to close it off! And all for the price of a sofa! I'm too angry to sit down. I walk up and down the room, unable to believe that she could behave so unfairly, with such small-mindedness.

This is the worst thing that's ever happened to us. The first real crisis, and we've failed.

Tilda gradually quietens, until all that can be heard from overhead is the creak of floorboards, and I realize that Kate's walking up and down the room, as if she were parodying me below. She's carrying Tilda in her arms, as intent upon her as I am upon the grievance I'm nursing down here. The fact that she now has our living, breathing child to hold, while I have nothing but my barren ache of injustice, seems an injustice in itself, as if I rather than she were the mere parodist. I stop and stand still, gazing sightlessly out of the grimy window at the three sleeping-suits hanging on the line. A moment or two later Kate stops as well. One way or another, even in separate rooms, we're locked into the absurd rituals of a row.

The house becomes absolutely silent. My anger slowly settles into sadness, much as Tilda has settled into sleep. I think of Lufthansa, and those first few days in Munich. I can see, not Tilda's washing, but the little café terrace where Kate and I drank *Gespritzten* one sweltering evening in the blessed shade of the Frauenkirche, and she smiled at me. Smiled and smiled, and everything in the world seemed easy. And when I think of that smile and remember that deep sense of ease, I know that something infinitely precious and good has slipped away from us for ever.

The silence goes on. But still Kate doesn't come down. I should go up, of course, but I'm too sad to. I sit down at the table, and go on gazing out of the window. She sits on the bed upstairs; by now, no doubt, as sad as I am – too sad to come down. Everything, it seems to me, is over. I have given up all thought of the picture. What worries me now is how we're going to manage. What are we going to do about Tilda? About lunch, even?

I look at my watch. Yes, somehow, unbelievably, it's long after lunchtime. I heat some soup, without the appetite even to cut bread to go with it. As I watch the sluggish brown liquid stir slowly into life I hear steps on the stairs behind me. It's Kate who's had to make the first move to rescue us from our impasse. Of course. Why couldn't I have done that, at least? I can't even turn round to look at her, though.

'I'm sorry,' she says, very quietly. I can hear from her voice that she's been crying.

'*I'm* sorry,' I echo her gracelessly. 'Do you want some soup?'

At least I've managed that much of a gesture. But there's no reply. Is she crying again? I turn round at last to look at her. She's sitting at the table, crumpling a handkerchief in her hands, but she's not crying.

'I've got some money my father gave me once,' she says. 'I'm not sure how much there is left. But it's probably enough. I'll pay it into our joint account.'

It takes me a moment to absorb the force of what she's saying, and another moment for the shock of reciprocal surrender to pass through me. Then I go over to her and kneel in front of her. I put my arms round her and sink my head deep into her softness. She's an inexhaustible and endlessly surprising treasure of goodness and love. She's never mentioned the existence of any money from her father before – probably, I realize, because she intended to use it for some private benevolence, perhaps even one directed towards me. Even more probably because in her sweet unworldliness she'd forgotten that she had it.

I lift my head and look up at her. She smiles down at me.

'My love,' I say, almost too choked to speak, 'I'm not worthy of you . . . I'm so touched . . . You'll never know . . . And of course I couldn't accept . . .'

'Why didn't you tell me before, though? That's what I don't understand.'

Nor do I, now the question's been raised. I think my way back through all the receding planes of silence and mistrust to the time when all this began. Why didn't I tell her? Well . . . because I knew she wouldn't believe me. And I was right – she didn't. Still doesn't, either. Not that it seems of much importance now. No picture in the world is worth losing this for.

'Because I'm a fool,' I tell her.

'I was keeping it for emergencies,' she says.

'Good. Go on keeping it. I couldn't take it, my love. Not in any circumstances whatsoever. Not if it was my last hope in the world.'

She strokes my hair. Everything's as it was. We've faced our first great crisis together and, thanks entirely to the goodness of her heart, in spite of the deviousness of mine, we've come out of it closer than ever.

'The soup's boiling over,' she says softly.

I go on holding her. Let it. So am I.

A Hint of Thunder

So here's the fundamental principle that I've settled in my own mind:

I shan't risk any money on my great scheme unless I can find evidence, objective evidence, for my conviction that the *Merrymakers* is what I think it is. Kate says that she doesn't have to be consulted – doesn't *want* to be consulted. She entirely accepts my judgement. But I realize I can't expect her to share my *prima vista* intuition sight unseen, or my feeling that the anomalies in the iconography count in favour of my attribution rather than against it. What I think I've tacitly agreed with her, and what I've certainly agreed quite explicitly with myself, is that I must be in a position to make out some kind of reasoned case to her.

We've spent a happy weekend together, all three of us. We haven't talked about my scheme. Or scarcely. I haven't even thought about it. Not all the time, anyway. And first thing Monday morning I'm back on the London train again. I've rung our bank in Kentish Town and arranged to see our 'personal banker' – with the full agreement of Kate, I should explain, because she understands why I can't accept her money if I do go ahead with the scheme, even though she's still offering it. On the way to Kentish Town, though, at Kate's excellent suggestion as she drove me to the station – where we kissed with a newly regained tenderness that takes us right back to those first few glowing months of our marriage – I'm going to the V & A to do what I should have done when I was looking up the sale-room records for Bruegel: to check the kind of prices that Giordano fetches, just in case my uninformed guesses are too wildly out. Such good, practical advice. And such a delight to be working on this together. Even though she's doing it for love of me, not out of any real confidence in my attribution. Yet.

The question is how to find objective evidence. What kind of thing am I looking for?

Details of style and technique? Not a very plausible line of inquiry. I can't ask to examine the picture again at the length that would be necessary without revealing too much interest, and I haven't the specialist knowledge to know what I was looking for even if I did.

The iconography? This is more hopeful, particularly with Kate's help. But will the iconography differentiate Bruegel from his followers and imitators? More likely, it seems to me, is my own pet discipline – iconology. I might be able to show that Bruegel's using the iconography of the picture in a way that relates it to his particular outlook and philosophy.

At once a difficulty arises. What *are* Bruegel's outlook and philosophy?

I sat on the train with my pile of books, now mercifully lodged not in plastic bags but in Kate's holdall for Tilda's things, and went through them all once more. I was even more struck this time by Bruegel's extraordinary elusive-ness and ambiguity. It's not just the biographical detail. It's *everything* about him – the whole sense and intention of his pictures. Every scholar reads them differently.

Here's Grossmann's catalogue of the possibilities: 'The man has been thought to have been a peasant and a towns-man, an orthodox catholic and a Libertine, a humanist, a laughing and a pessimist philosopher; the artist appeared as a follower of Bosch and a continuator of the Flemish tradition, the last of the Primitives, a Mannerist in contact with Italian art, an illustrator, a genre painter, a landscape artist, a realist, a painter consciously transforming reality and adapting it to his formal ideal – to sum up just a few opinions expressed by various observers in the course of four hundred years.'

Or Gibson on 'the amazing number of different interpretations by scholars of Bruegel's attitude to the peasants: descriptive, moralising, mocking, good-humoured, sympathetic.'

Friedländer stresses the humour. Stechow dismisses all such readings as out of date, and presents what he calls a 'darker' Bruegel, for whom nature is the 'one realm in which Bruegel sought and expressed relief from human folly, selfishness, and hypocrisy.' Tolnay, however, insists that his works are philosophical comments upon 'the essence and necessary evolution of human life,' though he agrees that Bruegel sees this life as 'the kingdom of the mad'. Bruegel's later years, says Tolnay at one point, are 'an attempt to synthesise the rational reign of nature and the insensate reign of man;' at another, 'the stoical contemplation of a human life fatally subject to the eternal laws of the universe.'

Friedländer thinks that paintings of this later period are attempting to be 'ethically neutral'. Cuttler, too, dismisses the moralistic view of 'some modern scholars' that Bruegel was concerned with man's duty to overcome his foolishness and sinfulness. He doesn't see man represented in Bruegel as insane or as helplessly subject to forces beyond his control. Human actions are not 'manifesting a rootless existence' on the surface of the world, but participating in its underlying order. Harbison takes a similar view. The cycle of the year in particular, he says, demonstrates the human 'response' to the passage of time and the rhythms of nature.

Bruegel, in other words, is an absence, a ghost, which scholars characterize more or less however they choose. So instead of trying to relate his iconography to Bruegel himself, perhaps I could relate it to what was going on around him at the time. If I can't see Bruegel, perhaps I could try to put myself into the space he occupied at the centre of his world, and see what he saw.

So I'm not yet in the V & A – I'm back in the Reading Room of the London Library, doing a little historical research. I know something about the Netherlands in the fifteenth and early sixteenth centuries from my nominalist studies. But the late sixteenth is *terra incognita*. My plan is to start with the more familiar territory, and then explore gently forwards.

Before I can make out a case to Kate, it seems to me, I have to be able to make out a case to myself. Now let me be absolutely honest with myself. If I *can't* make out a case to myself, will it change *my* feelings? Not in the slightest. Supposing, though, that the objective evidence I turn up destroys my case instead of proving it; supposing that it proves the picture *isn't* what I think it is . . . This is one of those ridiculous hypothetical tests like, 'If the house was on fire, would I save Kate or Tilda first?' Supposing, though? Would I still want the picture? Of course! It wouldn't change the picture itself one iota, even if it turned out to have been painted by Tony Churt.

Would I want it *as much*? – Yes!

Really? Enough to go through with all the financial and moral complications of the deal? – Certainly! All it would mean is that the picture was valuable for itself alone, and not for what it told us about Bruegel and his works. And that it was worth a few thousand pounds instead of a few million.

Not that this is what I'm thinking about. Though of course I'd have to reconsider the finances rather radically . . .

Odd, though, all these dealings of mine with myself. First I've agreed a principle with myself, now I'm making out a case to myself, and debating my own feelings and intentions with myself. Who is this *self*, this phantom internal partner, with whom I'm entering into all these arrangements? (I ask myself.)

Well, who am I talking to now? Who is the ghostly audience for the long tale I tell through every minute of the day? This silent judge sitting, face shrouded, in perpetual closed session? Sometimes I think there's something recognizable about the way he listens. It's Kate! It's God! It's my old history teacher! No, there's something even more familiar about him than that. It's some allotrope of myself, a twin lost in the womb, an alternative version of myself who might have been me – and who might yet be, after he's heard what I have to say.

You, yes. In the Reading Room with me, occupying my chair. Who are you? You're almost as elusive as Bruegel. How much do you know already? How much do I have to explain? How formal do I have to be?

Quite formal, I think. Experience suggests that you tend to leap to conclusions. You're not good at grasping a long train of evidence and arguments unless they're laid out quite pedantically.

So here's what I'm going to do. I'm going to treat you as if you were one of my students. A reasonably able one, but a bit short on concentration and tenacity. I'm going to spell things out to you rather laboriously, and spring sudden questions on you to make sure you're following me.

Agreed?

I think it must be, because here I am, doing it.

The history of the Netherlands in the sixteenth century has a remarkably familiar ring to anyone reading about it today. However much allowance you make for the unbridgeable dissimilarities between one age and another, it reads like a first draft for the history of Occupied Europe under the Nazis, or Eastern Europe under the Soviets. The imperial power was Spain, and the two great pillars of their Netherlandish policy – as with Germany and Russia in their dependencies – were economic exploitation and ideological repression.

There's a painful irony about the way in which the Netherlands became enslaved by Spain. It wasn't the result of weakness and failure but of strength and success. Their rulers did too well for themselves.

The Netherlands . . . (And how many Netherlands were there? I told you I was going to spring the occasional question on you . . .! Seventeen – yes, good.) . . . the seventeen Netherlands were assembled into a nation around the end of the fourteenth century by the Dukes of Burgundy. The great skill of the Burgundians was not war but marriage. They married first north into Flanders, then out into the surrounding provinces. The huge revenues from the wool and linen trades, the brass industry and the great entrepôt of Bruges made them immensely wealthy. Philip the Good, who kept thirty-three mistresses and invented the rules of courtly etiquette, was the richest ruler in Europe, and in the fifteenth century the Netherlands became the new heartland of European art, the northern centre of the Renaissance.

The family had a setback when they lost Burgundy itself, their original power base, to France. They protected their interests by once again exercising their great skill at marrying. This time they married southwards into the power of Spain. They did it with such success that their man, the son of Philip the Handsome, moved on to the Spanish throne as the Emperor Charles V. It was the master-stroke that crowned their achievements – and it was the fatal move that brought the Netherlands down. Charles gradually became accommodated to his new world, and lost to his old one. He was like a provincial English scholarship boy who's absorbed into the London establishment. The Flemish King of Spain, ruling there through his hated Flemish advisers, slowly became the Spanish King of the Netherlands, ruling *there* through his hated Spanish councillors. By their success in colonizing the throne of Spain the Netherlands themselves became colonized.

So that's how the economic exploitation and ideological repression began. The two were connected. Charles V, in the first half of the sixteenth century, bankrupted Spain by borrowing at high rates of interest from German bankers to pay for his defence of the Catholic faith, which was threatened by the Turks from without and by the Reformation from within. In 1555 he abdicated in exhaustion, and split his huge dominions into two: in the east, the Holy Roman Empire; in the west, the Kingdom of Spain. When his son, Philip II, succeeded to the Spanish half, the bankers would lend him no more, even at forty per cent. Everyone knows that he depended on the income from the precious metals mined in Spain's South American colonies. What people forget is that he derived four times as much from the huge commercial prosperity of the Netherlandish provinces.

I'm way past my period by this time, and I'm following the story in John Lothrop Motley's great nineteenth-century classic, *The Rise of the Dutch Republic*. Motley was an American Protestant, and openly committed to the Dutch in their struggle against Catholicism and colonialism, so I'm balancing it with Edward Grierson's *The Fatal Inheritance* and various other, more temperate works from the middle of this century – Rowen, Geyl, van Gelderen and Arnould and Massing. Whatever source you go to, though, the savagery with which Charles struggled to suppress Protestantism in his Netherlandish colonies remains impressive. He introduced the papal inquisition into the provinces in 1521, and in 1535 reinforced it with an imperial edict specifying that, although unrepenting heretics were to be burnt, repentant males were to be executed with the sword, and repentant females were to be buried alive, though whether this bizarre form of sexual discrimination was intended as oppressive or chivalrous remains obscure. Motley doesn't believe that Charles was a religious bigot. 'It was the political heresy which lurked in the restiveness of the religious reformers . . . which he was disposed to combat to the death. He was too shrewd a politician not to recognise the connection between aspirations for religious and for political freedom.' Whether for spiritual or political purposes, further edicts were promulgated as the reign progressed, until by the time Charles abdicated, according to Motley, between 50,000 and 100,000 Netherlanders had been burned, strangled, beheaded, or buried alive.

This was the happy land in which Bruegel passed the first twenty-five or thirty years of his life.

Then things got worse. Charles was succeeded by Philip. Philip II was obsessed with extirpating religious dissent for its own sake. Motley calls him an 'insane tyrant'. And by this time the threat to Catholic orthodoxy in the Netherlands was not so much Protestantism as Luther had first conceived it in Germany, but the more extreme version preached and practised by Calvin, that came in from Geneva through the French-speaking provinces.

Motley asserts that Philip was 'filled with undisguised hatred' for the Netherlands. In 1559, four years after his accession, when Bruegel was painting *Netherlandish Proverbs* and *The Fight Between Carnival and Lent*, and changing his name from Brueghel to Bruegel, the King announced to a convocation of distinguished local citizens in Ghent that he was leaving the country, and he never set foot there again throughout his long reign. On the same occasion he took the opportunity to proclaim the enduring twin goals of Spanish policy in a crude juxtaposition that made clear both their brutality and their ultimate incompatibility. He announced the renewal and enforcement of the various edicts and decrees for the extirpation of all sects and heresies; and he entered a 'request' for three million gold sovereigns.

The King said none of this in person, though. He couldn't speak Flemish or French, so thoroughly Spanish had the family become, and the words were uttered for him, like his part in the ceremony where his father had formally transferred his powers, by a spokesman. His voice on both occasions was supplied by the same man – Antony Perrenot, the Bishop of Arras.

Perrenot was plainly the coming man. So was Bruegel. Their paths were converging.

No one could have known at this stage, of course, quite how great Bruegel was going to become. But then no one can have realized to quite what heights Perrenot would ascend.

No one, that is, except Philip. The King had secret plans to bring the Netherlandish church under his personal control. He intended to replace the four bishops who'd run it up to then with fifteen new ones, all his own nominees, and each with his own staff of inquisitors. Ruling the new bishops were to be three new archbishops. The senior of the three archbishoprics was to be Malines, and the Archbishop of Malines was to be Perrenot. So Perrenot would be primate of the Netherlands, and the managing director of this great conglomerate of religious enforcement.

To execute his policies in his absence, Philip installed a Regent – Margaret, Duchess of Parma, his father's illegitimate daughter. According to Grierson, she was an excellent and popular choice. She was Netherlands-born, though Motley says the only language she knew was Italian. He agrees, however, that she was 'most strenuous in her observances of Roman rites, and was accustomed to wash the feet of twelve virgins every holy week.'

She was not, however, to be the real conduit of royal power in the provinces. A Council of State was set up to advise her – and the President of the Council was none other than Antony Perrenot, the ubiquitous Bishop of

Arras. In fact he was more than President, because Margaret had secret instructions from the King not to be guided by the Council as a whole, but only by a cabal of them, the Consulta – and the Consulta, it need hardly be said, included the good bishop, who governed the Regent with what Grierson calls 'adroitness and the natural delight in ruling that mark the born man of affairs.' He also maintained a direct correspondence with the King, behind Margaret's back, so that he was in effect, as Motley says, the real ruler of the Netherlands.

Perrenot wasn't a Netherlander but a Burgundian from the Franche Comté. Motley credits him with outstanding force and intellect, and describes him as serene and smiling, smooth in manner, and plausible of speech – but also as overbearing and blandly insolent. In the Anthonis Mor portrait of him in the Kunsthistorisches he looks elegantly and sceptically askance at us, in the manner made fashionable by Titian (who, as it happens, had painted his father). You can hear the bland insolence, though, in his contempt for 'that wicked animal the people,' and in his opinion that the rebelliousness of the Netherlands arose from the country's excessive prosperity, 'so that the people were not able to resist luxury and gave in to every vice, exceeding the proper limits of their stations . . .' He also thought, like Stalin and his henchmen, that great harm, especially in the matter of religion, resulted from the unfortunate commercial necessity of contact with foreigners.

In the Gaetano portrait, in the London Library's edition of his collected correspondence, Perrenot seems slightly surprised, perhaps at his own ever-growing eminence. Motley says that he frequently instructed not only Margaret but the King himself what to say. He also told the King to conceal the source of his instructions, and the King habitually obeyed. One of the earliest measures of Philip's reign was undertaken on Perrenot's express advice – the re-enactment of Charles V's notorious 'Edict of Blood' of 1550. It seems at first sight surprising that he opposed the King's restructuring of the church, the device by which Perrenot rose to his position; but he confessed, with engagingly open cynicism, that it was because 'it was more honourable and lucrative to be one of four than one of eighteen.' He claimed that he lost money by becoming Archbishop, and perhaps he was forced to undergo further financial sacrifices for his faith when the Duchess of Parma, as a charming secret surprise for him in 1561, persuaded the Pope to give him a red hat, and make him cardinal. Over the gate of La Fontaine, his delightful country house outside the walls of Brussels, which he preferred to his palace within them, he carved a stoical motto: *Durate* – 'patiently endure' – though Motley says that 'by trading on the imperial favour and sparing his Majesty much trouble' he grew enormously rich. It says a lot for his character that he himself felt able to resist the evil effects that excessive prosperity had produced upon the people he ruled.

All in all, he was the Seyss-Inquart of his day – a Burgundian brought in by the Spanish to repress the Netherlands just as the Austrian later was by the Germans. And how did the Nazi Reichskommissar's predecessor use his new-found wealth? What did the newly created Cardinal Granvelle spend his rapidly accumulating guilders on?

On paintings by Bruegel. He had become Bruegel's most important patron.

Not, so far as anyone knows, his *biggest* patron, who was Nicolaes Jongelinck, the Antwerp merchant. Jongelinck, according to the famous schedule of security for the debt to the Wine Excise, owned sixteen Bruegels. The inventory of the archbishop's palace at Malines lists seven. Jongelinck, though, was just another member of the subject people, on the same level as Bruegel himself; his brother Jacques was an artist, a sculptor, and also under the Cardinal's patronage. The Reichskommissar himself was something else again, the incarnation of absolute power.

He may actually have owned more than seven Bruegels. Which the seven at Malines were, and what happened to them, no one knows, but they were still there long after Granvelle left. The only Bruegel ever traced to Granvelle's possession is *The Flight into Egypt*, which Bruegel didn't paint until 1563, the year he left Antwerp and followed the new cardinal to Brussels, so it probably wasn't one of the Malines seven. Granvelle may well have bought it to decorate one of his two new establishments, and if he bought one picture for Brussels he may have bought others.

Am I beginning to think of Bruegel the way we think of the artists and entertainers in Occupied Europe who worked for the Nazis – as some kind of collaborator? I don't know. You can't project modern sensibilities back on to the Renaissance; no one holds it against Michelangelo or Raphael that they worked for Alexander VI, the bad Borgia Pope.

All the same, the regime over which Granvelle presided was quite strikingly loathsome. Under Charles V, between fifty and a hundred thousand people had been executed for religious reasons over the course of fifty years. Under Philip II, according to the calculations of the Prince of Orange, who eventually emerged as the leader of resistance to Spanish rule, some fifty thousand people were slaughtered in the first seven years alone.

You have to keep a sense of proportion, of course. There was nothing particularly remarkable about people being slaughtered by the devout for practising slightly variant forms of devotion, even by the tens of thousands. In any case, if those fifty thousand victims of the re-enacted Edict hadn't been burnt at the stake or hanged or beheaded or buried alive they'd have died one way or another – probably painfully and before their time, of any one of a hundred different natural plagues and pestilences. No one would have counted them; no one would have remarked upon it. It would be unreasonable to expect some wretched painter to turn down professional success, even if he had much choice about it, just because some of his fellow citizens had died of burns and asphyxiation rather than smallpox or typhus.

All the same, fifty thousand is quite an impressive total to run up, given the limited technology of the time. It's in the range produced by dropping an atomic bomb, or by the collision of a hundred or so Boeing 747s. You can't help wondering what Bruegel thought about his patron, and the reign of terror that he was presiding over.

Nothing at all, if we're to believe van Mander, the only writer who might have known him personally. Van Mander could have told us without any danger to Bruegel if he'd ever heard of him expressing the odd reservation, because by 1604, when his book appeared, the painter was long dead.

He could have told us without any danger to himself, for that matter, because he published it in Haarlem, and by then the Dutch north had fought its way free of the Spanish and their thought police. For van Mander, though, he was simply 'the very lively and whimsical Pieter Brueghel,' always ready with the jokes, but not, apparently, with any opinions.

None of the scholars seems to show any interest in Bruegel's relationship with Granvelle. There's something a bit odd about it, all the same, however indifferent he was to what was going on around him. The re-enacted Edict made it a capital offence for any lay person 'to converse or dispute concerning the Holy Scriptures, openly or secretly, especially on any doubtful or difficult matters.' It also promised death to anyone not having 'duly studied theology and been approved by some renowned university' who taught or expounded the Scriptures – or even *read* them. Well, Bruegel was a lay person, so far as anyone knows. He can scarcely have had time, before he took up his pupillage as a painter in Antwerp, to study theology or graduate from any university, renowned or otherwise. So he was forbidden on pain of death to read the Bible. And yet he somehow managed to paint *The Conversion of Saul, The Procession to Calvary, The Tower of Babel, The Adoration of the Kings,* not to mention Granvelle's own *Flight into Egypt.* On the face of it, the Cardinal was buying self-evidently illicit merchandise from a flagrant criminal.

All the artists in the Netherlands who worked on religious subjects were in the same position, of course; maybe they were allowed a little latitude. Their status had improved somewhat since 1425, when Philip the Good hired Jan van Eyck to be his *peintre et valet de chambre.* All the same, they were still members of craft guilds, very like the other craft workers and small tradesmen who were the readiest converts to Protestantism, and the most frequent victims of its suppression. Let painters indulge their vices, and how do you draw the line at weavers and candlestick makers? Difficult even to turn a blind eye, because there must have been plenty of people ready to out a closet Bible reader. The Edict required everyone to inform upon suspected heretics. If you failed to, you were liable to the same punishments as the heretics themselves; if you succeeded in getting a heretic executed, you were entitled to up to a half of his property.

What did Granvelle think about the traffic he was abetting? It's not as if he were above taking a personal interest in the prosecution of religious offenders. The records are full of his letters urging on inquisitors throughout the provinces, and pursuing individual cases wherever the zeal of others flagged. When the local authorities in Valenciennes proved reluctant to prosecute two dissenting ministers, Faveau and Mallart, the good Cardinal pressed forcibly for their condemnation, and then, when the local powers dragged their feet again over carrying the sentence out, specifically ordered their execution by burning. The crowd rescued them from the flames, whereupon troops were despatched by Brussels to arrest everyone who might have been among the rescuers, and burn or behead them in place of the original victims.

Perhaps Bruegel was able to give the Cardinal a solemn assurance that he hadn't read the stories himself – that he'd simply heard them in church, or had them read over to him by a properly qualified specialist. Then again, Granvelle was a worldly and cynical man – think of his regret at having to share the spoils of office with all the new bishops. If Bruegel was a favourite, the Cardinal might well have been prepared to overlook small personal weaknesses. He was well placed to protect him, after all. But Bruegel must have been acutely aware how precarious his position was.

And if Tolnay's right, he was also vulnerable in another way. He had a bit of a past. Tolnay believes that while Bruegel was living in Antwerp he was in contact with a group of geographers, writers and artists called 'the Libertines' – not rakes, but 'liberal spirits, tolerant on questions of faith, enemies of confessional fanaticism, with a Stoic ideal of life, founded on the great belief in the moral dignity of the free man.' Tolnay curiously insists that this didn't mean Bruegel was ever a heretic. But they were strange ideas, to say the least, for the Netherlands in the sixteenth century – and a number of the Libertines, according to Tolnay, had stranger ones still. They were members of a sect that he calls the *schola caritatis*, founded by Hendrik Niclaes, the author of *The Mirror of Justice*, a work in which salvation is envisaged as being brought about by the power of universal love alone. All external cults are secondary, Niclaes believed; all religions are symbols of a single truth and Holy Scripture has merely an allegorical sense.

I imagine the Cardinal dropping in at the studio one day to check progress on his latest commission. The two men chat about this and that, and the conversation turns to philosophical matters. Bruegel tells him about the views of his friends in Antwerp. Human freedom and the moral dignity it confers. No need for the intercession of the Church. Catholicism and Calvinism much of a muchness. The Cardinal's very interested. 'You must let me meet these friends of yours,' he says. 'Invite them round one evening, why not, and we can . . . stoke up the fire and have an enjoyable evening together sorting out our little differences.'

I suspect that Bruegel didn't mention his old Antwerp

friends. They all seem to have survived. A dozen years later, one of them, Abraham Ortelius, even went on to become geographer royal. Failure to inform upon suspected heretics: another charge hanging over Bruegel's head. Another little capital offence.

No wonder he had to be somewhat elusive. Either he had to conceal his past, or if the Cardinal knew about it already, he had to be discreet enough to allow him to overlook it. Or perhaps Bruegel distanced himself from his youthful vagaries even more firmly, by persuading Granvelle that he'd become a sincere and useful supporter of the regime. Art was one of the most powerful instruments of the Counter-Reformation. Another Netherlandish artist, Frans Floris, also collected by Jongelinck, travelled to Rome to study the heroic style favoured by the Catholic Church at this period, and then did a *Fall of the Rebel Angels* in which St Michael, with obvious topical symbolism, is striking down the heavenly dissidents with great violence and effect. Eight years later, in 1562, with the Cardinal installed in Brussels and the new terror well under way, Bruegel weighed in with a *Fall of the Rebel Angels* of his own.

So what am I saying now – that Bruegel was simply a hired hack of the Counter-Reformation? It might explain why he went back to the old Books of Hours as the source for his great cycle of the year. He was merely serving up the same old reassuring myth, so carefully sustained from generation to generation, of a happy bucolic world untouched by the conflicts and savageries of real life, one more episode in the long-running story of Arcadian shepherds and Bourbon milkmaids, of Soviet tractor drivers and Merrie England.

I offer this interpretation with judicious scholarly detachment. But I don't feel detached about it at all. I don't believe it. Not for a moment. I refuse to believe it. If Bruegel is all things to all men, then he certainly isn't that to *me*.

Do I have any evidence for this? Yes – the evidence of my eyes! Of plain common sense! Those six magnificent panels can't have sprung from such base origins! The suggestion's ludicrous!

But I need something a little more objective than this. What other evidence can I find?

There's one other fragment of contemporary testimony apart from van Mander, though it looks at first sight too insignificant to consider. Abraham Ortelius, the Antwerp geographer with whom Bruegel shared his dangerous past, must have remained a friend, even after Bruegel moved to Brussels, because it was probably in the following year that he commissioned a picture from him, *The Death of the Virgin*; and in the 1570s, after Bruegel's death, he began assembling an *Album Amicorum*, a collection of tributes to his friends, in which he included an epitaph for the painter – the only contemporary account of him still extant apart from van Mander's. An epitaph isn't the kind of source that usually provides much illumination, and when I glanced at it before, in Tolnay's end-notes, unable to understand more than a few words of the Latin, I assumed it was the usual bland tribute, and passed on. Now that I look at it again, though, in the light of all those fires, with the smell of all that burning flesh in my nostrils, and His Eminence the Reichskommissar looking over my shoulder, I start to wonder if it's quite as innocuous as it seems.

Multa pinxit, hic Brugelius, quae pingi non possunt . . .' begins Ortelius. 'He painted many things, this Bruegel, that cannot be painted . . .'

Why can't they be painted, these things that he did in fact paint? Because they're in some way elusive, hard to observe, difficult to render pictorially? The rawness of early

– 157 –

spring, the heat of summer? Or does the difficulty go deeper? Is he referring to things that can't be seen? To the feelings that landscape and the changing seasons induce? To the lift of the heart as the spring draws on and the mind goes out to the far blue horizon?

Or does he mean things more abstract still? Beliefs? Ideas? Strange ideas, perhaps, like religious tolerance and the moral dignity of the free man? Ideas which are unpaintable for more reasons than one?

My spirits have suddenly begun to lift. All my senses are alert. How does the epitaph go on? *Multa pinxit, hic Brugelius, quae pingi non possunt, quod Plinius de Apelle* . . .

But here both my Latin and my grasp of classical allusion give out. Also, I suddenly realize that I have to get to Kentish Town before the bank shuts.

Multa pinxit, hic Brugelius, quae pingi non possunt . . .

The nice thing is that Kate can translate it for me. She can read the Latin in a breviary or a Book of Hours as easily as the English in a newspaper. As with the iconography, we can work on this together.

I walk round our cold flat in Oswald Road, still wearing my overcoat, turning on the central heating. I'm going to stay in town overnight and go off to the V & A first thing in the morning to do what I should have done today – investigate Giordano prices – since I'm determined to leave nothing to chance, and to have a clear-cut plan of action for Kate's approval.

I look in at each of the cold rooms, checking that nothing's changed behind our backs. Nothing has. Everywhere there are the traces of Kate and Tilda, and our life together. Tangles of tights and underwear on the stairs, waiting either to be washed or put away; plastic ducks and buckets scattered across the bathroom floor; the newspaper I was reading at breakfast the morning we left propped up against a lurking bag of muesli. One of the things we like about each other is that we're neither of us obsessively tidy, and Tilda seems set to take after us. *Multa pinxit* . . . In the rush of our departure we've forgotten to make the bed; the pillows still have the shape of our heads in them, the piled duvet the mass of our warmly twined bodies . . . *Quae pingi non possunt . . .*

I sit down amid the sweet wreckage of the bed and phone her. As I listen to the phone ringing in our distant cottage, and imagine her coming indoors, or laying Tildy down, or drying her hands, I put my head down into the bedclothes to inhale the deliciously lingering smell of us, and I feel the life stir inside my trousers.

The dear familiar caution of her 'Hello?' thrills me, as it always has.

'I'm faxing you some Latin to translate.'

'Where are you?'

'At Oswald Road. I'm going to have to stay overnight.'

'Oh,' she says, and I realize how much she was looking forward to the moment when my smiling face separated itself from all the meaningless faces emerging around it into the station yard.

'I know,' I say. 'But I still haven't got round to Giordano. I've been working on our man.'

Our man. Yes. Now.

'Not because of what *I* said?'

'Not at all. Because of what *I* said. I just want to be absolutely sure in my own mind before I go ahead. As sure as it's humanly possible to be.'

'Don't give Tony Churt a chance to get rid of it some other way first,' she says. She's being so sweet about it!

'No, but I'm not going to rush, I'm not going to panic. How's Tildy? What's she been doing? What's the weather like down there? No sign of Mr Skelton yet? The sink hasn't blocked up again? Oh, Kate, I miss you so much!'

And love her so much. Perhaps even more at this distance than I do when we're together. She's like my picture. No painting in the world has ever meant as much to me as that briefly glimpsed panel, so difficult of access. I think of it all the time, almost as much as I think of Kate – I'm thinking of it now, even while I'm talking to her. By the time I've had it on the kitchen wall for three months I'll probably have ceased to look at it.

'Everything's fine,' she says. 'I took Tildy to see the cows. The sun came out just after lunch. Did you get to the bank?'

She's even taken the initiative in talking about the bank! It transforms life, now I can say everything to her quite openly again, now we're in this together.

'Just!' I confess. 'No problems, though. We can simply increase our mortgage. It should only take a week to go through.'

We – yes. Joint account. I've applied for the maximum they'll offer, which against the equity we've got is £15,000, just in case I decide to go ahead with my original plan of getting Tony the full price of a genuine Vrancz. On my vague estimate this might leave a few more thousand to find – not from Kate! – but there must be other sources. It's a useful possibility to keep at the back of my mind, that's all. No point in going into hypotheticals with her at the moment, though. Time enough if the occasion should actually arise. I'm not going to do anything until I've really identified that picture. I can't, in any case, until the bank's come through with the money.

'So what's this Latin?' demands Kate. She's beginning to be caught by the mystery. I can hear it in her voice.

'You tell me. I'll put it on in a moment.'

'Don't forget to look up the Giordano tomorrow. You don't want any surprises.' She's becoming as obsessed as I am.

'First thing on my list for the morning,' I assure her. 'Kiss Tildy for me. I miss you both so much!'

As soon as I put the phone down, of course, I remember that I've no fax, because Kate's got it – we took it down to the cottage. I'll have to ask Midge, our usual standby in emergencies. I write the epitaph out in carefully legible capitals, since the laptop's relaxing in the country as well, and run downstairs with it. So much more plausible and congenial, one's neighbours in town – and so much closer.

'Emergency,' I say, when she opens the door. 'Yet again. Could you send a fax for me?'

'I thought you were in the country,' she says, as she ushers me in and takes the page, trying not to look at it.

'Kate is. It's to her. She's got the machine.'

'Nothing wrong?' she asks, glancing at the desperate capitals in spite of herself.

'No, no,' I assure her, but she's not listening – she's reading. *MULTA PINXIT, HIC BRUGELIUS, QUAE PINGI NON POSSUNT* . . . And she's storing it away for future use, because she writes a column for one of the papers, I can never remember which, about the more comical aspects of life in Kentish Town. We feature in it from time to time, our names changed but otherwise our lovably eccentric and absent-minded selves, locking ourselves out and locking each other in and overflowing the washing machine into her flat. Now we're going to be in it again, coyly corresponding about our domestic arrangements in Latin. Well, she helps us out – we help her out. Exactly like me and my good friend Tony Churt.

I'm back upstairs by this time, anyway, looking through the various commentators again to find any possible candidates for the things Bruegel painted that can't be painted. Almost at once I find the converse – things that *can* be painted and that he *didn't* paint. 'Bruegel,' says Friedländer, 'was the first artist successfully to eliminate the lingering echo of religious devotion.'

I make another trip through the pictures, and yes, the absence is striking. Even when he *did* do religious subjects the sacred events tend to be diminished in size, off-centre, offstage even, left at the edge of the onward rush of the everyday world, like Icarus in his fall. Saul's converted, to become the great founding father of the Christian church, and no one notices. The citizens of snowbound Judaea pour into Bethlehem for the census, and you have to search among them to find the pregnant woman arriving on the donkey. The Kings arrive to pay homage to the holy child, and what occupies almost the whole of the picture is their train of retainers and pack animals waiting in the softly falling snow. Three-quarters of an inch further to the left and Jesus himself would have been out of frame.

I turn back to *The Fall of the Rebel Angels*. And no – it's not a contribution to the Counter-Reformation. It's totally unlike Floris's picture. The fallen angels aren't devilish muscular warriors, but fantastic creatures with the bodies of fish, the heads of birds and the wings of butterflies – figures straight out of Hieronymus Bosch. They don't look like anything that might be described as angels, and they don't appear to be engaged in anything that might be described as rebellion.

And then, in the great cycle of the year, not so much as a nod to religion, even in the remote background, even at the outermost edges. Not a ghost of a saint – not a prayer – not an uplifted gaze – not a sigh – nothing.

Perhaps this creeping secularity is what the Cardinal appreciated in Bruegel. At last, a painter who was trying to sober up and cut down on his biblical intake! For a senior churchman, a little breather from all that Christianity must have been as good as a holiday.

Multa pinxit . . . Even as he ushered the religion out of the back door, he was smuggling something else in, and under the Cardinal's very eye. What was it?

A sudden loud hammering on the door makes me jump out of my chair in the empty flat, full of a confused terror that the inquisitors have read my thoughts. But it's Midge, holding out a curling sheet of fax paper.

'Sorry,' she says, as I gaze mutely at her, still too shocked to speak. 'I've been tapping and tapping. I thought you must be asleep.'

'No, sorry,' I explain, 'I was . . .' Was what? I gesture helplessly. In the Netherlands, I want to say. In the sixteenth century. I can see from the little amused tightening of her lips, though, that she's got enough for another paragraph or two already.

Well, pleased to be of some use. I'm already sitting down at the kitchen table again and reading Kate's translation. What was it he painted that can't be painted?

Thunder.

This seems to be what Ortelius is suggesting. That Bruegel painted thunder.

I was through the door of the London Library next morning as soon as it opened, and now I'm sitting with Kate's translation on the desk in front of me, together with a pile of classical dictionaries and Vol IX Book XXXV of Pliny's *Historia Naturalis*. What Ortelius was trying to say in his epitaph takes a lot of puzzling out even translated into English, because it's wrapped up in a series of obscure classical allusions.

This Bruegel [begins Kate's neat handwriting] *painted many things which cannot be painted, as Pliny said of Apelles.*

I dimly recall that Apelles of Kos was a painter, and I discover from my books that Pliny thought he was the greatest in classical Greece, though nothing of his work has survived. And, yes, according to Pliny he 'painted the unpaintable, thunder, for example, lightning and thunderbolts.'

I can't see what's so unpaintable about the last two, but thunder would certainly present problems. When I run through the works of Bruegel in my mind, however, no suggestion, however oblique, of thunder in any literal sense, or even of lightning or thunderbolts, can I recall. If Bruegel contrived to paint an electrical storm it must have been a metaphorical one.

Then comes a reference to another Greek painter:

The same author said of Timanthes that in all his works more is always understood than is painted.

Also a suggestion of something hidden. Not thunder in the case of Timanthes. What his reputation rested on was a picture called *The Sacrifice of Iphigenia*, in which Agamemnon conceals his uncontrollable grief by covering his head with his mantle. Is this the 'thunder' that Bruegel was hiding – feelings too terrible to reveal?

Actually, Apelles, like Timanthes, was famous for concealing something, though in his case it was himself. 'It was also his habit', says Pliny, 'to exhibit his finished works to the passer-by on a balcony, and he would lie concealed behind the picture and listen to the faults that were found with it, regarding the public as more accurate critics than himself.'

So perhaps Bruegel was also concealing himself in some way – not just his feelings but his whole character and identity.

There are two more allusions to come, though, that seem at first sight to sit oddly with the idea of concealment:

Eunapius, in his Iamblichus, said that painters who paint people made beautiful by the bloom of youth, and who want to add some allurement and charm of their own to the painting, debase the whole portrait they produce, and depart equally from the model placed before them and from true beauty. Our Bruegel is free from this weakness.

Eunapius, I discover, was a historian, and he was chiefly famous for being an obstinate opponent of Christianity, and for trying to establish the great Neoplatonist philosophers as alternatives to the Christian saints. One of these philosophers was Iamblichus, and Eunapius wasn't praising him for his powers of concealment, but quite the contrary, rebuking him for failing to tell the unadorned truth.

Whereas our Bruegel did. So he was a good portrait painter? Not literally, because he never painted portraits at all, any more than he did thunderstorms. What Ortelius is saying in his epitaph, then, as I understand it, is that a truth of some sort lies concealed but unadorned in Bruegel's work – much as it does in this epitaph – a truth about the painter himself, perhaps; and that this truth is as startling and ominous as thunder.

He's saying, I guess, that Bruegel didn't merely know about the heterodox ideas shared by Ortelius and his circle in Antwerp, didn't merely sympathize with them – but that he found some way of expressing them in his pictures.

How, though? Where? In which pictures?

In *my* picture, perhaps?

I should move on to the V & A and look up Giordano – I don't think there's any more meaning to be squeezed out of the Ortelius. But instead I sit gazing out of the windows of the Reading Room at the tops of the trees in St James's Square, where the spring's advancing by the minute in the April sunshine, just as it is in the *Merrymakers*, and I think.

What I'm thinking is this: *why* should one of those six pictures in Jongelinck's house have gone missing?

It's not very surprising at first sight, perhaps. A lot of Bruegel's pictures have gone missing. But this particular one should have been well cared for.

Let's follow its trail as far as we can. In 1592 the Duke of Parma, the current Governor of the Netherlands, dies (just before the King can stab him in the back, as he did most of his other loyal henchmen), and in the following year his successor arrives. The Archduke Ernst, the new incumbent, is from the Austrian branch of the Habsburgs. According to

Motley he is 'very indolent, enormously fat, very chaste, very expensive, fond of fine liveries and fine clothes, so solemn and stately as never to be known to laugh, but utterly without capacity either as a statesman or a soldier.' Nevertheless, the city of Antwerp welcomes him with the traditional ceremony of the Joyous Entry, one of the grandest ever accorded, in the course of which they present him with a number of paintings. They include Jongelinck's cycle of the year, which they've acquired either by foreclosing on the pictures when de Bruyne failed to repay his debt, or by buying them, as the account book kept by the Archduke's secretary suggests, from an art dealer, Hane van Wijk. They seem to be intended as a kind of thank-offering to Ernst from Antwerp to show its gratitude to Spain for having sacked the city twice through the good offices of Ernst's predecessors, the Duke of Parma and the Duke of Alva. According to the account book, there are six of them. They're shifted by barge to Brussels, to the Governor's official residence. The following year the Archduke dies, having accomplished nothing, says Motley, and passing out of history like a shadow. But leaving behind him the pictures. Six of them still, listed once again in the post-mortem inventory of the Archduke's collection made on 17 July 1595.

Then, for half a century, like the Archduke himself, they pass out of history.

From 1646 to 1656 the Governor of the Netherlands is the Archduke Leopold Wilhelm, and the curator of his collection in the Royal Palace is the artist David Teniers. Teniers does a number of paintings of the collection, but in none of them is there any sign of the Bruegels, which suggests that they'd been shipped off to Vienna after Ernst's death together with the rest of his collection. From Vienna they seem to have been passed on to the Emperor himself, Rudolf

– 168 –

II, in Prague. But by 1659 they're back in Vienna, listed in the inventory of Leopold Wilhelm's collection after his return from the Netherlands, and in 1660 Teniers publishes a letter from an unnamed friend in Vienna which describes seeing the series in the archducal gallery in the Stallburg. Teniers' correspondent says there were six pictures on display, but the sixth must have been an odd one, put in to make up the total (as happened again in the nineteenth century, when the series included two substitutes) because in the Archduke's inventory there are by this time only five.

So the first picture in the series – my picture – has disappeared somewhere between Brussels, Prague and Vienna, at some time between 1595 and 1659. 'The loss can well be put down to the account of transportation,' says the Kunsthistorisches catalogue nonchalantly.

I wonder. Does a picture on its way between branches of the most powerful dynasty in Europe simply fall off the back of a lorry in transit? Unremarked? One of a set? The first of a set?

Or was it removed from the collection by its curators, for some good reason?

I have a feeling that one day some official looked a little more closely at this innocent series of pastorals hanging on the walls of the Royal Palace in Brussels, or awaiting shipment to Vienna. Someone with a fresh eye, perhaps. A prelate, one of Granvelle's successors, being shown over the collection for the first time, or for the last before it was crated up. And suddenly he sees in one of the pictures something that no one had seen before.

A number of Bruegel's pictures have been censored at various times. The prominent erections of some of the peasants in *The Wedding Dance* were painted over, and only recently revealed. In the seventeenth century the children's bodies in *The Massacre of the Innocents* were repainted to turn them into sacks of grain, and conceal the real horror of what's happening. Now the curious prelate bends to look at some detail in one of the pictures of this charming series of the year – in the first picture, to be precise, the one that establishes the mode of the whole set . . . and is transfixed. Within hours it's being lifted down from the wall, or removed from the shipment, and carried down to the palace cellars before further scandal can be caused.

What was it that my keen-eyed and public-spirited cleric might have seen? What might *I* see, if I looked at it now with an informed eye?

Had Bruegel in this one picture lifted Agamemnon's mantle from his face, and for a moment shown some terrible truth beneath? Had he emerged in person from behind the canvas? Painted the thunder? Expressed what can only be implied?

Well, I must look! I must go back to Upwood. Ask to see the Giordano, perhaps, to check one or two points that my Belgian has raised, and then, as soon as I'm alone . . .

The Giordano, yes. Before I do anything else I have to get back to the V & A for the prices.

Bruegel shows his face quite literally in three of his pictures. Or so some scholars believe. I'm sitting in the library at the V & A, distracted from my quest for the Giordano prices by these three rare materializations. In his drawing of *The Painter and the Connoisseur* he works away, grim-faced and wild-haired, while a bespectacled patron watches over his shoulder with a vacant grin and a hand already in his purse, too stupid to be able to see or understand what he's about to pay for. In *The Peasant Wedding* he sits at the edge of the picture, listening expressionlessly to the expostulations of a Franciscan friar. In *The Sermon of St John the Baptist* he lurks very small and inscrutable among the preacher's congregation.

I can't help noticing that in the first picture his beard seems to be grey, in the second brown, in the third black. The only evidence adduced for believing that any of them is a self-portrait is the similarity that various scholars have been able to discern to his appearance in the two copper engravings of him done by Dominicus Lampsonius and Aegidius Sadeler, in both of which he's clearly identified by name.

It's easy to find the Lampsonius – it's reproduced over and over again in the biographies. It shows Bruegel in a crude and simple profile, his face half-hidden by his long beard, his expression and character unreadable. The Sadeler I eventually track down in Hollstein's *Dutch & Flemish Etchings*, and in this one he looks out at us from above the beard, now elegantly trimmed, with sad and serious eyes, and for a moment . . . yes, he seems real and human.

But then Sadeler didn't do the portrait until 1606, thirty-seven years after Bruegel died – which was a year before Sadeler was even born. The portrait's framed in an allegorical surround by Bartholomeus Spranger, who worked with Sadeler in Prague at the court of Rudolf II; and the most scrupulous scholarship, by Bedaux and van Gool, on the unbelievably arcane images and even more arcane Latin text that Spranger has written – both in the most esoteric Rudolfine tradition – suggests that it was a mystical attempt to portray both the Elder and the Younger Bruegel as a single entity, since they were reputed to look alike, and using the son, whom Sadeler may have met, as the model. In plain language, then, it's not a portrait of Pieter Bruegel the Elder at all.

I turn back to the Lampsonius. Lampsonius *was* a contemporary of Bruegel's, but there's no evidence that they ever met. For most of Bruegel's working life Lampsonius was in England as secretary to Cardinal Pole, Bloody Mary's Granvelle, who had formally received Engalnd back into the bosom of Rome, and when he returned to the Netherlands in the year before Bruegel's death he went not to Brussels but to Liège, where he was kept fully occupied as secretary to the Bishop. The portrait comes from a series he did of famous Netherlandish painters, and it's in much the same style as the ones of van Eyck and Hieronymus Bosch, who died long before Lampsonius was born. The chances that Lampsonius's picture is in any real sense a portrait are vanishingly small.

And if neither the Sadeler nor the Lampsonius is a likeness of him, then there's no reason for thinking that any of his three supposed self-portraits are, either.

Every time you think you catch a glimpse of Bruegel, he slips away like this as soon as you look closer. The mantle comes down; there's no one looking out from behind the canvas. So, the Giordano prices, then back to Upwood. But as I pull out the first volume of sale-room records, I have a stroke of luck. I make one of those almost random discoveries that sometimes happen after hours of patient, systematic effort. I realize that I'm standing next to one of the computer terminals which list current research, and that for once no one's using it. I push the sale-room volume back.

It takes only a moment to tap in 'Bruegel' . . . and then the system takes over. It's so swift and seductive – so unlike hunting back and forth through the broad fields of the microfiche reader, or stooping like a potato harvester over the dog-eared cards in the filing cabinets. No sooner has that merest hint of a wish been formulated than up come 114 different ways of satisfying it.

They're mostly contributions to scholarly journals, none of them, so far as I can see, of any imaginable relevance to me – until I get to the eighty-seventh item on the list: the *Gazette des Beaux-Arts*, February 1986, with a contribution on *Pieter Bruegel, peintre hérétique*.

A heretic? This is way beyond what even Tolnay claims. The author is Pastor H. Stein-Schneider, I discover when the item arrives on my desk. He's evidently a French Protestant clergyman, and he describes himself as a heresiologist and a historian of the sixteenth century. He makes no bones about his claim. Bruegel, he says, was 'a manifest heretic, and his paintings Manichaean and neo-Cathar charades.'

Wow, as Laura Churt might say. Manichaeanism, a strand of thought that keeps recurring in Christianity, however often it's suppressed, insists on the reality of darkness and evil as fundamental constituents of the world. Once upon a time good and evil, light and darkness, were clearly separated, and in the last days they will be again. Our present state, though, it sees as a mixture or balance of the two, half day and half night. The Cathars, or Albigensians, were brutally suppressed by the Inquisition in the thirteenth century. If this is what Bruegel was painting, then he was certainly playing with thunder and lightning.

Stein-Schneider, like me, has been struck by the cryptic hints in the Ortelius epitaph. The key to the epitaph, he says, is a letter written by Ortelius that came to light in 1888. It was found in a drawer in an old printing house in Antwerp owned in the sixteenth century by the publisher Christophe Plantin, and it establishes that both Ortelius and Plantin were members of a sect founded by Hendrik Niclaes called the Family of Love, which is presumably the *schola caritatis* referred to by Tolnay. Between 1550 and 1562, while Bruegel was living in Antwerp, Plantin had printed many works relating to the sect. He'd done it clandestinely – and for good reason. Stein-Schneider takes a very different view of the Family of Love from Tolnay. To a heresiologist, a reading of Familist documents entirely confounds Tolnay's view that the sect was faithful to the Roman church. The Familists' doctrines of irenicism and ethic soteriology . . . I run to the shelf where the dictionaries are kept – their doctrines of pacifism and salvation through goodness . . . together with their sexual asceticism, identify them as a Manichaean movement in the Cathar tradition.

A heretic, yes. I think of that little figure in the background of so many of Bruegel's pictures, the ordinary-looking man no one's paying any attention to, the Icarus, the Saul, the condemned Christ, the one whose view of the world is different, whose fate is against the grain of the everyday world around him, and whose unremarked presence changes everything. The unobserved observer with dissent hidden in his heart.

'One volume in particular of this Familist collection,' says Stein-Schneider, 'entitled *Terra pacis* ('Land of Peace'), printed by Plantin at Antwerp between 1555 and 1562, is not only completely clear, but seems to contain the description of a certain number of Bruegel's paintings. It even contains the enumeration and explication of forty heretical symbols that Bruegel seems to have used in his Familist charades . . .'

If I can lay my hands on a copy of *Terra pacis*, all my problems may just possibly be over. Where would I find one? The British Library, of course. I'm on the Piccadilly Line before I remember why I was in the V & A in the first place.

I gently open the ancient cover of the little volume. *Terra pacis. A true testification of the spirituall Land of Peace; which is the spirituall Land of Promyse, and the holy Citee of Peace or the heauenly Ierusalem; and of the Holy and spirituall People that dwell therin: as also of the Walking in the Spirit, which leadeth therunto. Set-foorth by HN: and by Him newly perused and more-playnly declared. Translated out of Base-almayne.*

The British Library's English edition is undated, but from the style it must have been published not too long after Plantin's 'Low German' original. I slowly turn over the packed, irregular pages. It's a kind of novel – the story of the pilgrim's painful journey out of this sinful world, which it identifies as 'the North Country', or 'the Country of Ignorance', to the New Jerusalem, the promised land of the soul's peace. The journey is entirely on foot, and the laboriousness of the travel is brought out by the archaic spelling of the word.

For as long as one is in the Journey, he must account of him self, as a Pilgrim or Walker in strainge Landes . . . This great unpathed Lande that he travaileth thorow is named Many-maner-of-walkings because the Travaillers do travaille and passe from all Quarters thorow the same Lande to that one good Lande of Rest . . .

The Travailler crosses a landscape of topographical allegory assembled from biblical sources, all scrupulously cited in the margins. There are fayre Hills, that seeme to be somwhat delytfull, but the Travailler must beware of them, because they are nothing but Deceit, Vanitee and Seduceing. He must pass a daungerous Ryver wherin many Travaillers be drowned and choaked, named A-delyte-in-the-pleasurs-of-the-flesh. His life is threatened by divers Natures of Beastes that are mynded to Devouring, the which also do pursue the Travaillers very stoutly, and a crafty Murderer lurking in the thickets, whose name is Unbeleefe.

I look at my photocopy of Stein-Schneider. A number of his forty heretical symbols enumerated and explained by *Terra pacis* occur in the cycle of the year. The North Country, he says, is shown in *The Gloomy Day*, and its cold and hunger in *The Hunters in the Snow*. The deceptive hills are represented in the Hay Harvest, while the treasure that is to be found in the field (see Matthew 13, v 44) is described in *The Corn Harvest*.

The cycle can't exactly be a record of the great hike, I realize, because if *The Gloomy Day* is the last of the series, the wretched travailler would be ending up back in the North Country where he started. It might, though, be intended to show not the consecutive stages of the journey, but various views in Many-maner-of-walkings at different times of the year. So what we're looking at is a kind of illustrated almanac of the North Country and the 'wildernessed Landes,' where the snowy crags remind us that 'God wil now bring-downe all high Hills, and make the high Stony-rocks and the Vallyes playne that Israel may walke and dwell free without Fear; to the Honour of his God.' In each of the pictures is one of the Castels thorow the middest of the which the Travailler must passe, and half-seen, or just out of sight, at the end of all these valleys is a town – the Citee of Peace that he finally hopes to reach.

'But in all the same Lande named Many-maner-of-walkings there is not one playne pathed Waye.' And in the whole of Bruegel's cycle, apart from the village streets in *The Hunters in the Snow*, there's not a single path or road. 'The most-part of the Lands are besett with greevous Laboure, and with much Trouble . . .' And so they are – the traditional labours of each season.

Long before I've travailed the length of the book I feel I could name all the topographical features in the series, as if I were standing in front of the pictures with a gazetteer in my hands. *The one of these Castels is named The-power-of-the-devils-assaulting, the second The-forsaking-of-hope, the third is named Feare-of-death . . . These Hils are named, Taken-on-witt-or-prudence, Riches-of-the spirit, Learned-knowledge, Taken-on-freedom, Goodthinking-prophecie, Zeale-after-chosen-holynes, Counterfeit-righteousness, New Invented-humilitee, Pryde-in-ones-owne-spiritualnes, Unmyndful-of-any-better . . .* And those unseasonably early swimmers in the *Merrymakers* must be plunging into A-delyte-in-the-pleasurs-of-the-flesh – the daungerous Ryver wherin so many Travaillers be drowned and choaked.

Or am I wandering off into great unpathed Landes myself? Am I getting close to the edge of the dizzy precipice named You-can-fit-almost-anything-into-any-pattern-you-like-to-name? I remember all the hikes and other travails I've been on myself where I've stood looking from land-scape to map and back, seeing the shape of the hills in front of me in six entirely different parts of the contour lines. If only I could see one single detail in the landscape that related unambiguously to one single sign on the map. One church spire. One lighthouse, one narrow-gauge railway.

And here I have another of the unpaintable flashes of lightning that are guiding my steps forward on this vertig-inous day.

Maps! Yes! The maps in *Theatrum orbis terrarum*, the great atlas of 1570 by Abraham Ortelius! Perhaps they also contain some reference to the heretical symbols of the Family of Love! Something that's reflected in some detail of the *Merrymakers*!

I rush back to the catalogue. It lists various editions of the *Theatrum*. The first four were published by someone called Aegidius Commenius Diesth. But from 1579 onwards publication was taken over by . . . by Christophe Plantin of Antwerp, Ortelius's brother Familist, the underground distributor of Terra pacis.

I'm on my way to the Map Room.

I work my way slowly through the first Plantin edition of the *Theatrum*. I don't know exactly what I'm looking for. Some reference to the great unpathed Lande, to the Walking in the Spirit. I can't imagine what it would be.

What emerges page by page under the protective sheet of talc is a historical document: a view of the world seen from a particular place at a particular moment just as surely as the landscapes of the cycle are. What I'm looking at is the world of the late Renaissance as viewed from the Netherlands. In the foreground, like the dancing peasants on the hillside from which the *Merrymakers* was painted five years earlier, is the close-up detail of the Netherlands themselves; in the middle ground is the rest of Europe, stretching away like the valley in the picture to the new horizons opened up by the great navigators.

'The wholl Earth', says Niclaes in *Terra pacis*, 'is unmeasurable great and large: and the Lands and People are many and divers.' So are the scales and colours and cartographic styles of the various mapmakers whose work Ortelius has assembled in the *Theatrum*. And yet the world it shows is strangely static. It's a place of rivers, mountains and forests, of kingdoms and duchies, of towns and cities. But there's no sign of any communications connecting the isolated human settlements, any more than there is in Bruegel's landscapes. No railways, obviously – but still no roads worth marking, either. It's as trackless as the great unpathed Lande. Only on the seas, exactly as in Bruegel, do a few symbolic ships set sail for emblematic destinations.

The map of Salzburg appears to curl back from the page to reveal the city itself behind it, seen as Bruegel might have seen it from the same high foreground. On the other side of the Alps, Lake Como curls back in the same way to reveal a scene even more like one in the cycle of the year, with a distant city and green mountains beyond . . .

And there in the foreground is what I'm looking for. A little Travailler. A walker, striding along past what might be a wayside cross or a signpost, or both.

He's coming down out of the north, on his way from the Country of Darkness. He's descending from the Alps, from the high passes through the deceptive hills, into the balmy air of Italy, the New Jerusalem, the promised land of the soul's peace.

No, of course he's not. It's just a casual thumb-nail sketch, a decorative flourish by the Italian cartographer.

Or is it? I order up the earlier editions of the *Theatrum*, published by Diesth. And in the first edition of 1570 . . . no little walker. He doesn't appear until the second edition, in the following year. So he's presumably been added, not in Italy by the cartographer, but in Antwerp by Ortelius himself. Why? I can think of only one good reason for such a small but strange editorial intrusion: it's a secret sign to the initiated, like a masonic handshake. By setting that little walker on his travels and travails through the unpathed Lande of his roadless world, Ortelius was quietly signalling to his fellow adepts that the entire terrestrial theatre was the setting of life's great journey. He was declaring it all to be the land named Many-maner-of-walkings.

And this is the thought that comes to me as I sit there in the Map Room, at the end of this extraordinary day: if there were also a little walker in the *Merrymakers* it would identify the whole cycle of the year as a Familist document. It would explain why this particular picture was removed and hidden. If I could find a little walker coming down from the cold north lands of March I should have identified it beyond a doubt.

I should be the man who'd finally solved the mystery of Bruegel. I should have lifted the veil, revealed the hidden figure behind the canvas. I should have found the thunder.

Another thought strikes: there *is* a little walker in my picture. I can see him as clearly as if I were standing in front of it in the breakfast-room at Upwood now.

Check, though! Yes? Somehow!

And already I'm out on the street and heading for home. The season that my picture shows, it seems to me now, is the moral equinox, the uncertain days we live in, when light and dark in the world are equally balanced. Or perhaps, more accurately, the weeks just after it, at the start of the old New Year, when the long winter nights behind us are beginning to give place at last to the long summer days ahead. Outside the windows of the train the north-western suburbs, too, are full of sunshine, and everywhere there's the same shimmer of green that's spreading across the woods in the picture. There's also a travailler here – me, coming down from the winter air in the high passes, heading for the soft lands of summer, where the ship's waiting to weigh anchor and set sail for Jerusalem. And what a delight it is to have some great journey to undertake, some great enterprise under way, so that all one's thoughts and efforts are guided by the onward momentum of it.

Everything we do has bad as well as good in it, dark as well as light, and that includes the enterprise I'm embarked upon now. But the days are drawing out and the nights are drawing in, and I know now that the good is going to pre-dominate.

I open the *Country Life* I bought at St Pancras; not a journal I've ever bought before. As the train rolls north, and the land named Many-maner-of-commutings rolls south, I flick through the property ads looking at the price of country estates. For a million pounds, say, we could get something really rather impressive. Somewhere not entirely unlike Upwood, perhaps. Upwood itself, it occurs to me, may come on the market sooner or later, in spite of all my efforts to help Tony out.

I remember I still haven't looked up the Giordano. But by this time the exact figures involved in the stupendous deal I'm about to do seem to me of remarkably little importance.

The Little Walker

'He's just gone out,' says Laura. She's only half-opened the great front door to announce this, but even so it's a warmer welcome than I'm used to at Upwood. At least she seems to have some idea of who I am. Also, there are no dogs barking and thrusting themselves at me.

I look at my watch, and make what I hope is a wry face. Kate's waiting for the results of this little expedition almost as eagerly as I am. I told her all about the Lande named Many-maner-of-walkings, and the great question of whether there was a little walker in my picture, as soon as she collected me at the station last night. 'You'd better take my magnifier with you,' she said.

'I've got to fax off some details about *Helen* to this friend of mine,' I explain to Laura. 'You know he's found someone who's interested in it? I just need to have another quiet look at it, and write a few notes.'

Actually, I knew Tony was out. I knew there'd be no dogs. I saw them all in the Land-Rover as I drove up Taken-on-witt-or-prudence Hill, on my way here to The-power-of-the-devils-assaulting Castle. I could have stopped him and made an appointment to come back later, but even as I put my hand on the hooter it occurred to me that it might be easier with him out of the way. I don't think Laura will have the patience to wait in the breakfast-room with me as I peer wearisomely at the detail of Helen's *déshabillé* through Kate's magnifier. I've also got her tape measure in my pocket, because the very first thing I'm going to do as soon as Laura's out of the room, even before I turn the magnifier on to the middle distance of the *Merrymakers*, is the simplest test of all – checking that the panel measures three foot nine by five foot three, like all the others in the cycle.

She hesitates, then reluctantly opens the door a little wider. I hesitate in my turn, uncertain whether I'm supposed to give her a kiss or not. Almost certainly yes, since I'm now assumed to be on social terms with her. There's something about the remoteness of her cheek, though, and the emptiness of the house, that makes the kiss die on my lips.

'I'll have to leave you to get on it with on your own,' she says. 'I've got things to do.'

'Of course. Just head me in the right direction.'

'I'll get my keys. He keeps the breakfast-room locked.'

While she fetches her handbag I look round the hall with a different eye. Yes – a little fresh paint and a lot of fresh money and this house could make a very suitable country retreat for a couple of serious-minded art historians and their growing family . . . But already she's back and leading the way through the maze of discreetly shabby, unimproved glooms. She's wearing not apron and rubber gloves this time, but another of her oversize sweaters, an abundance of emerald that contrasts strikingly with the worn browns all around, and shifts disconcertingly all over, I can't help noticing, with the lateral movement of her hips as she walks.

'Some mysterious Belgian, I gather,' she says over her shoulder, as she turns the key in the lock. 'Which of course Tony thinks is hysterical. I just wonder if he's for real.'

She's holding the door open for me, and for the first time, I realize, she's looking straight at me. There's something speculative about her gaze, and it occurs to me that she's a good deal shrewder than her husband. I have a nasty feeling that she's on to me. I keep entirely calm, though. Amazingly calm. My tongue simply takes over, as it did when I first discovered my Belgian for Tony.

'What, Mr Jongelinck?' I say. 'I *think* he's real. Rather splendid house just outside Antwerp, by all accounts.'

I almost laugh at my own ingenuity. I've just discovered something else, too – why Mr Jongelinck keeps such a low profile. It's nothing as banal as drugs or arms dealing. It's because his family made their money during the Occupation, just as the original Mr Jongelinck must have done. There were unpleasant hints of slave labour this time round, I think, of Resistance workers betrayed to the Gestapo. I keep this shameful little secret to myself, though. As I should, of course, have done with Mr Jongelinck's identity.

'Actually,' I say, even more plausibly, 'you'd better forget his name. I don't think I'm supposed to know it.'

I go over to the fireplace. I can't help noticing that it's open; the soot guard has gone. But of course I'm looking at *Helen,* and she's still where she was, sagging hugely down at me from above the mantel. It's still cold in the room, too; I'm rather pleased I wasn't invited to take my coat off. I get out my pen, and an old V & A requisition form to write on, and peer learnedly through the magnifier at Helen's left foot. 'Paint apparently applied with lavatory brush,' I note down judiciously.

I glance over my shoulder to see where *my* picture's got to, and find that Laura's still standing there, in spite of her natural impatience and all the things she has to do.

'Thanks,' I say. 'I won't be long. I'll come and find you as soon as I've finished.'

I turn back to my scholarly labours. Behind my back I hear the sounds of a cigarette being lit.

'I mean,' she says, 'is he for real about wanting to buy it?'

I see. My little flourish of plausible detail was unnecessary.

'Oh, I think so,' I say. 'Why shouldn't he be?'

'I just can't see why anyone would want to buy that thing. What's so marvellous about it?'

What? I've not only got to look at it – not only find some fool to buy it – I've got to give a tutorial on it? 'I'm afraid I'm not an expert on Giordano,' I say. 'I'm just an intermediary. It's not my period at all.'

'Please. I'm asking a serious question. I'd really like to know.'

I step away from it and look at it. We both look at it. Come on, tongue!

'Well,' says tongue, 'the composition's well organized. No? The figures have a certain . . . plasticity and strength. Rather bold chiaroscuro.'

Not a bad effort by tongue, in the circumstances. Also, this new interest in art appreciation offers me an opportunity. 'Where are the other three?' I ask. I can see the skaters and the cavalrymen where they were before, one propped up against the serving hatch, the other lying beside it. 'They're a bit closer to my period. Would you like a brief introductory lecture?'

But she's still gazing at *Helen*. She slowly lets out a mouthful of smoke, absorbed and reflective. Her attitude's changed. Good God, what did I say? Was it the plasticity or was it the chiaroscuro?

'At least I'm not as fat as her,' she says.

Oh, I see. 'I don't think she can offer you much competition in any way,' I reassure her politely. She gives no sign of taking in this little gallantry. Though as it happens it's perfectly true. She goes on gazing, lost in thought. 'Which one's Paris?' she asks.

I indicate a muscular figure in a helmet. She gives a little dry laugh.

'*He* never looked much like that, even when I first met him,' she says. Tony, presumably. This time I remain diplomatically silent. 'He'd already got a paunch. He already looked like someone's uncle. Pretty much what happened, all the same. Suddenly, out of nowhere – wham! Phone calls at all hours. Flowers. Weekends on someone's yacht. Christopher went mad, of course, but Tony just ignored him, just shoved him out of the way. We'd only been married for a couple of years, too. I felt absolutely sick about it, but I was hypnotized, I was helpless, I didn't know what had hit me. And all these stories about Upwood! He made it sound like Chatsworth or somewhere. Showed it me through the trees one moonlit summer's night. Couldn't actually bring me here, of course, till he'd got shot of Margaret. But then – I couldn't believe it! – she made some kind of muddle with her pills, and there we were.'

I gaze at Laura, trying to take in the implications of this, which seem to be that Tony either drove his previous wife to suicide or else murdered her. Laura, meanwhile, gazes at the great abduction – wistfully, it seems to me now, seeing her own life in that preposterous scene. The power of art! 'I suppose what a woman always finds irresistible is feeling that a man's really determined to have her,' she says.

Silence. I should say something, obviously, but I'm so taken aback by this sudden shift into confessional mode that I can't think what. I'm not sure she notices the lacuna, though. She seems completely absorbed in her own thoughts, and after a while she simply continues where she left off.

'My God, though, what a shock when I did get inside the house! Rain coming through the roof, mouse droppings everywhere. And of course by this time he'd realized – I didn't have any money! He'd looked at Christopher and me – house in Chelsea, place in Barbados – and Christopher earning practically nothing, of course, poor sweet – and he'd thought all that was *me*, but it wasn't, it was a trust. I took Tony down to Somerset to meet Daddy and it was a total disaster. As soon as he heard we'd got married he simply switched off the money.

'I'm not saying the money was the *only* thing Tony liked about me. He gets a kick out of knocking women off their feet quite regardless, but it's always over pretty fast, and I just think that if I *had* got a bit of money, if I *had* been able to get the estate straightened out for him, then I might have lasted a tiny bit longer. God knows, I've *tried* to adapt, I've *tried* let him go his own way. Where he is at this very moment, for instance, I have not the faintest idea, though I can guess . . . He's got this workshop place in the yard, and he says he's going to be working on things all day, and then when I go to look he's vanished. He's working on things all right. But not broken pheasant feeders. He's always telling me to get a life of my own, and I've done my best, believe me, though when I do of course he doesn't like it.'

She pulls up her emerald sweater. We're looking at her rib cage, and the soft, silken underswell of her left breast. Across the bottom of her heart stretches a large, irregular indigo storm cloud surrounded by a greenish nimbus.

'It's where the handle is,' she explains. 'On the fridge.'

I try to go on looking at it. I try to stop looking at it. I try to do both at once. She goes on gazing at it herself for a long time, either too absorbed in the sight to remember my presence, or else waiting for me to respond to this new advance in our sudden intimacy. I'm still not sure whether I'm merely the inert catalyst for this explosion, or whether I'm by any chance part of the life of her own that she's attempting to make. If I'm honest with myself, I do feel a slightly sick excitement, a kind of sympathetic creeping in my own flesh. Her left breast, even inside its silk covering, certainly has more effect on me than the naked right breast waving in the wind above our heads. I have another of my sudden convictions – that I should kneel down in front of her and gently kiss the bruise. I don't act on all my impulses, though, whatever Kate thinks, and I allow this one to die away. 'I'm sorry,' I say instead, and the moment passes. She lets the sweater tumble back into place.

'Poor Tony,' she says. 'He's such a fool. He gets everything wrong. His sons won't speak to him. And he always ends up cheating himself. All this ridiculous business with you just to avoid inheritance tax.'

Inheritance tax? I gaze at her, even more obviously disconcerted than I was by the bruise.

'Well, of course,' she says. 'She only gave it to him when she was on her deathbed. It's got to be at least three years before you die. Otherwise you pay forty per cent. He says it *was* three years before – she just didn't write anything down. Of course she didn't – no one in that family ever did anything as simple and obvious as writing things down. She *told* him she wanted him to have it. He says. But she *didn't*, she can't have done, because they didn't speak to each other for thirty years, they didn't see each other. No one speaks to anyone in that family! He only went when she was dying. First time in thirty years. His own mother!'

Of course. Obviously. It's not just four and half per cent commission he's trying to save; it's forty per cent tax. I should have thought of it. It seems ridiculous in these surroundings, where everything's been inherited in one way or another, but I didn't think of it because inheritance isn't part of my world. Never in my life have I either bequeathed or inherited anything except my genes. Never in my life, for that matter, have I attempted to avoid paying tax.

I plainly look as stupid as I feel. 'He didn't tell you?' she says. 'No, of course he didn't. Which is wonderfully clever, because if you don't know what's going on and you make a mess of it, he'll end up with some whacking great fine and be worse off than ever.'

So will I, of course. So will I.

I snatch at a faint shred of hope. 'The other three pictures, though . . .?' I suggest.

'Forty per cent. They all came back in the Land-Rover. Though what he means about her *giving* them to him I don't know. She couldn't speak to anyone by that time – she couldn't move! Anyway, he hitched up the trailer when he went to see her, so he must have been clairvoyant.'

I feel panic closing over me. I just want to get out of the house, away from these terrible people and a way of life in which I'm completely out of my depth. I move blindly towards the door.

'Oh,' says Laura in surprise. 'Have you finished? You've found out everything you wanted to know?'

'I think so, thank you.'

She stubs out her cigarette. Rather reluctantly, it seems to me. But half in and half out of the door I take a hold of myself and make one last attempt at the real business of the day.

'I'm supposed to be selling the other three for him as well,' I say, with an attempt at ruefulness which is now beginning to demand heroic efforts. 'But I can only see two of them.'

'Yes, what happened to that one in the fireplace . . .?' she says. She looks vaguely around the room. 'Oh, I think he took it out to his workshop. Something about cleaning it up a bit.'

I get into my car and start the engine, still in shock, unable to think because my mind's totally occupied by a huge and shapeless mass of panic, through which all I can see is the agonizing image of the picture, left propped up on some workbench while the paint stripper takes effect.

I look back at the house. The front door has closed. I turn off the engine again and get out of the car. What am I going to do? I've no idea. I find that my feet are taking me round the side of the house, past the rusting remains of the cannibalized tractor, into the yard. I suppose I'm going to look for the workshop. And do what? I can't imagine. Wash the paint stripper off. Put my arms around the picture. Protect it. It's the irony that cuts at me. All he has to do, for heaven's sake, is nothing! If he just keeps his hands off it, I'll get him £20,000 for it!

I stand still for a moment and control my panic.

He won't have put paint stripper on it. Or oven cleaner or sheep dip or anything else. I understand that perfectly well. Whatever he means by cleaning it up, he's not a fool, he's perfectly used to handling pictures, and his weakness is for entrusting them to others, not for meddling with them himself. What I'm going to do is simply to seize the chance to look at it again *before* he puts the rust remover on . . .

Never mind the rust remover. But I *am* going to measure it and look at it. This is what I came for, after all. Check the size and find the little walker, before a flying splash of

Nitromors expunges him and the answer to the problem for ever . . . No, no. No panic.

There are a number of stables and outhouses in the yard, but I find the workshop quite easily; it's the only door that hasn't collapsed on its hinges, or started disappearing behind the first growth of spring grass. There's a security fastening – a length of pink baler twine, of course – but it's dangling idly. The door gives slightly under my knuckles when I tap on it, and judders open as soon as I push. Inside is a bench with a muddle of tools on it and the guts of various pieces of household equipment – a tangle of pipes and wires, of heavy electric armatures, and miniature cityscapes of electronic components out of television sets or computers, all of them looking unlikely to have water or electricity flowing through them ever again. A breath of warm paraffin fumes hangs in the air; he was obviously working in here before he went out this morning.

In the gap beside the bench are jammed various offcuts of wood and synthetic boarding, collapsed cardboard boxes and empty picture-frames. Picture frames? Curious . . . And mixed in with the paraffin fumes, it occurs to me, is another familiar smell. I can't quite place it. It has agreeable associations, but in here, for some reason, it makes me feel uneasy . . .

And then, with a sudden sense of foreboding, of the ground disappearing under my feet, I realize what it is. Linseed oil.

Beyond the workbench is another door. I push it open. The smell of linseed oil becomes stronger. I'm in another little room with another workbench. But on this one is a different sort of confusion. I'm looking at a chaotic battlefield of muddy colours – splashes and solidified lumps of paint, with scrubby thickets of brushes in pots, filthy rags and the broken corpses of old tubes of paint . . .

He painted it. The picture – the *Merrymakers*. He forged it. The Giordano isn't the bait that I'm using to make a fool of him; it's the bait that *he's* using to make a fool of *me*.

Who whom? The fundamental question, as Lenin said. I thought it was I him. It wasn't. It was he me.

The whole thing was a charade from first to last. The implausible appeal for my help, the pantomime of artistic innocence and financial dishonesty, the trail of pictures leading me into the trap. It's a classic sting! It was using my own dishonesty to lure me on, my own vanity to blind me.

The whole world has become the negative of itself. All the shining whites have become black, all the blacks transparent white. The picture itself has turned inside out. Everything that I thought was good about it now seems a manifest weakness, all the signs of its authenticity proof of its falsity. All my secret cleverness has turned into public foolishness, my absolute conviction into universal distrust. Yes, when I think of that flash of certainty in the moment that I first saw it, when I think how I've run from library to library, from step to step in the identification, following the false clues that my supposed victim has left for me, winding myself deeper and deeper into self-deception at every turn, I feel the hot burn of shame in my flesh.

Against the back of the bench several pieces of board are propped, with still-lifes and landscapes on them in various stages of completion. My eye darts from one to another, searching for the *Merrymakers*. None of them is it. None of them is even remotely similar. They're all far too small, for a start. And far, far too . . . what? What's the word I want?

Far too clumsy. Far too amateurish. Far too *inept*. The man can't paint at all!

Slowly I take a hold on reality and come to my senses. I was having an attack of moral panic. Tony Churt couldn't forge his own signature, let alone a sixteenth-century panel painting. He can't maintain the landscape God gave him, let alone create a completely new one. He could no more execute a confidence trick upon someone else than he can shave without cutting himself.

The colours of the world gradually return to something more like normal, the whites to dark greys, the blacks to lighter ones.

There's something familiar about the paintings, I realize. I remember the pictures I saw in the living-room that first evening. Yes; their provenance wasn't the local Women's Institute, as I'd supposed. They were painted by the master of the house himself. This is what he's up to – not forging Bruegels but replacing the family's Guardis and Tiepolos with authentic new Churts.

I almost laugh aloud. But then I feel a little embarrassed to have discovered this secret weakness of his. In all our discussions of paintings and painters he never mentioned being a painter himself. Not the slightest interest in looking at the efforts of others in the field, and yet he has some ridiculous yearning to produce the stuff himself. How soft people are inside their hard shells! I think about him sitting out here with the oil heater going and his reading glasses on the end of his nose, cack-handedly daubing his heart out, trying to paint his way out of all his personal and financial problems, and I feel . . . yes, embarrassed, as if I'd seen him on the lavatory.

Slightly ashamed of myself now, I quietly close the inner and outer doors and go back to the car. I start the engine once again. Then once again I turn it off. So where *is* the picture? What *is* he doing with it? I can't get the smell of the linseed oil out of my nostrils. He's not . . . I don't know . . . *retouching* it somehow?

I get out of the car again, go back to the great front door, and crash the heavy knocker up and down, though what I'm going to say I'm still not sure. It occurs to me as I wait that if Laura's been looking out of the window during the past twenty minutes and following my various changes of direction, she'll have a strange impression of my state of mind.

I don't think she can have been watching, though; she seems surprised to see me.

'Sorry,' I say. 'I've just been reflecting on your parting remark.'

She waits. Or perhaps it's not exactly surprise that her manner suggests. Thoughtfulness might be closer to it.

'About cleaning the picture. I suddenly started to get a bit worried.'

'How far did you get?' she says.

'How far did I . . .? Oh – not far. Nowhere, in fact. I've been sitting in the car thinking about it.'

She gives a very slight smile. Her eyes flick briefly past me to see if there's anyone coming up the drive. Then she holds the door open for me. I walk in, a little baffled.

'I just wanted to ask you to give him a message . . .'

'We'll find something to write on,' she says. She closes the door behind me and leads the way into the kitchen.

'Just tell him I don't think it would be a good idea . . .'

'Sit down. I'll make us some coffee.'

I sit down at the bare wooden table, not knowing quite what else to do. It seems a bit late in the day to be offering me coffee. In any case, she's apparently already forgotten about it again. As also about the writing materials. She's lighting another cigarette and leaning back against the rail in front of the Aga, watching me through the smoke.

'Pictures are very easily damaged,' I say. 'It doesn't matter about dirty varnish. A buyer might even find it gave the picture an added authenticity.'

Her eyebrows have risen by a millimetre or two. I remember when I've seen that look on her face before – when I told her about nominalism, about iconography and iconology. What she's doing is struggling not to laugh.

'And that's what you've been thinking about out there in the car for the past twenty minutes?' she says. 'Wow.'

At this, of course, I see what's got into her head. And yes, now I think about it, I realize that my reappearance must seem a little suggestive. The message I've come back to deliver, so desperately cogent to me, must sound to her like the lamest excuse ever invented by a timid seducer. I realize yet again how easy it is to misread everything in front of one's eyes. At once I'm paralysed. I can't think how to correct her misapprehension without discourtesy. I suppose I should simply get to my feet and go. But this will look even more absurd. I stay sitting, unable to formulate any words. This, evidently, is the absurdest option of all, because suddenly she loses her battle to control the head of laughter building up inside her. It comes fountaining out like oil from a blown well.

I've piled Erwin on Panofsky again.

'Sorry,' she manages. 'It's just . . . everything . . .'

She turns her head aside so as not to go on seeing me and reinfecting herself. It doesn't seem to help, though. She puts a hand in front of her face to conceal her agony.

And somehow I start laughing, too. She stands leaning against the Aga and laughing. I sit at the table laughing. God knows what *I'm* laughing at. Everything, too, I suppose. Myself. Her. Life. Nothing at all.

Where we go from here I can't begin to imagine. Joint suffocation, possibly. Two corpses without a mark on them. Forensic experts baffled. But help's at hand. Her laughter dies away, and she turns her head towards the door, listening. There's the sound of heavy bodies thumping against woodwork, and paws scrabbling on stone. The door crashes open, and in bursts the familiar boiling, smelly mudslide of dog. My own laughter, too, departs.

'Dead cow in Long Meadow . . .' Tony's saying as he follows them, and then stops in the doorway at the sight of me. His glance flicks to Laura for an instant, and then back to me. Laura continues to lean against the Aga and smoke. I struggle to my feet, encumbered by the dogs – which have now, I notice, accepted me as so much a part of the household as not to need even a preliminary barking at before licking and trouser-exploration can begin.

Tony comes on into the room and throws his cap down on the table. 'I don't know what that portends,' he concludes.

'Vet's bills, I imagine,' says Laura. 'Martin says you're not to try cleaning that picture.'

'What picture?'

'The one in the fireplace. The one you took away.'

He turns to me in surprise.

'Cleaning it?' he says. 'What's all this?'

'I just looked in to get my Belgian some details of *Helen*,' I explain, 'and Laura said . . .'

'Oh, for God's sake! Don't take any notice of her. She doesn't know what she's talking about.'

'But you told me . . .' begins Laura.

'I said I was going to get some advice about it. I did. I got some advice. That's what I've been doing this morning.'

He looks at me and makes a face that seems intended to express amusement at knowing something that I don't, perhaps also at the alarm I'm failing to conceal. He's been out getting advice about the *Merrymakers*? From whom?

'You look worried,' he says.

'Not at all.'

'I don't know why *you* should be losing sleep over the bloody thing. You said it was another dud.'

That is of course not what I said, but I let it pass, because any attempt at an explanation might suggest more interest still.

'All I was going to do was to get a bit of gunge off the corner. Thought there might be a signature hiding away there.'

Gunge? Signature? What's all this?

'Anyway, set your mind at rest,' he says. 'I took it to an expert. Expert says leave the gunge on. So on the gunge stays. The caustic soda goes back in the cupboard. Joking, joking.'

But I'm no longer worrying about the cleaning arrangements. I haven't time to – my mind's moved on to the expert who gave him the good advice. He *took* it to him? *Showed* it to him? Is that's where it's been this morning – out in the Land-Rover with Tony and the dogs? Being examined by an expert? Being examined by *what* expert?

I manage to raise an eyebrow, so far as I can tell, in passing surprise. 'I didn't know there were any art experts round here,' I say, with passing interest.

He laughs. 'Certainly there are.'

'Anyone I'd know?'

He laughs again. Art's providing us all with a great deal of life-enhancing mirth this morning. 'You'll find out,' he says.

I get to my feet, and start making my second stunned exit of the day from Upwood.

'Poor Martin didn't realize you were trying to avoid paying tax on *Helen*,' says Laura, as she follows Tony and me to the front door.

'Avoid paying tax?' says Tony. 'What do you mean? What nonsense have you been feeding him now? There's no question of tax! Because (a) my mother told me donkey's years ago that she wanted me to have it, and (b) it didn't matter whether she told me or not, because it wasn't hers, it was mine anyway. Not to mention (c), that you're getting cash for it, so no one's ever going to hear about it. At least I *assume* you're getting cash for it. Good God – you weren't thinking of putting this through your books, were you? You'd have to pay gains tax on it yourself!'

I don't think I can manage any reply to this. I just smile and wave my hand in a way that means – I don't know what. I'm past knowing what I mean by anything.

'Just don't stir the buggers up!' he says. 'I certainly don't want to start paying the government for the privilege of keeping my own possessions! Look – serious word. I know all you lot are socialists, and that's fine by me. No business of mine. Keep it for London, though. All right? We're in the country here, and what we are in the country is country-men. Simple countrymen. Neighbours. We all try to give each other a helping hand.'

'Watch out!' cries Laura, as I back away through the remains of the puddle outside the front door. 'Mind the . . .'

Land-Rover. Parked right in front of the door. The pain in my elbow is blinding, and made no less easy to bear by the sound of Laura's laughter starting up again behind the closing door, but I wait to massage it until I'm safely concealed inside my own car.

The only thing that makes the burden of anxieties and indignities swirling round inside my head bearable is the anticipation of sharing them with Kate. I'm in such a hurry to get back to her that I'm out of the drive of The-power-of-the-devils-assaulting Castle and halfway down Taken-on-witt-or-prudence Hill before it occurs to me that the picture was probably still there inside the Land-Rover when I walked into it. One glance through the window and I might have seen the little walker.

The spring sunshine comes and goes as I drive down the hill, lighting our quiet valley with hope and plunging it into despair as bewilderingly often as my own moods change in the shifting circumstances of my quest. It fades as I make the turn into our track, and I bump along in gloom and anguish. But then, as I make the second turn beyond the elders, a flood of sunshine blesses our cottage with the glowing colours of a Book of Hours. The front door's as green as the new season, the daffodils we planted around it last autumn as yellow as the sun, the blossom fallen from the crab-apple trees as white as the sun's innocent light, Tilda's carry-cot on the stump of the old maple tree as blue as a distant sea. And in the foreground – my own fat peasant, legs planted wide in the freshly turned brown soil, bending to her emblematic planting and sowing, the traditional April labours. She straightens up at the sight of the car, arching her back against the ache of standing upright, and brushing a loose strand of hair out of her eyes with the back of her muddy hand, as all the generations of toiling women have done since first they bent to labour, then smiles as only Kate can.

'Well,' I begin as I jump out of the car, 'an eventful morning!' There's so much to tell her that I don't know what to say first. All I know, at the sight of her smiling there, is that the anxiety and uncertainty will fade from the story as I tell it, and that all will once again be well. We lean towards each other, touching our extended lips together like the couple in my picture, in our own simple, earthy echo of the gentry's pleasures.

The first thing that comes into my head to tell her is the last one that happened – my belated discovery that Tony Churt's using me to cheat Inland Revenue. But even as I open my mouth, it occurs to me that this may merely evoke Kate's alarm, and introduce yet another element of uncertainty into the situation, since I haven't yet worked out quite what I'm going to do about it. I go back to the event that immediately preceded this one – my managing to reduce Laura once again to helpless laughter. Then I remember the ridiculous misunderstanding of my intentions that evoked it . . . and my own laughter . . . and I realize I can't now recall exactly how the misunderstanding arose, or easily explain why I was laughing as well.

Kate goes straight to the point, though, as usual. 'So do you think you saw anything?' she asks.

'I didn't see anything at all!' I cry, finding immediate relief, once again, in being able to share everything with her. 'I couldn't! It wasn't there! He'd taken it away to show it to someone! Some art expert! But who? And what did they tell him? What did they think? Who could it have been? He wouldn't say! Perhaps he was lying . . . I don't know what he's up to . . . What art experts are there living round here?'

She laughs. Which is of course what *he* did, and at once my heart contracts, because what she means is what he meant – that there *is* someone. Someone obvious. Someone so eminent that I should know about him.

'What?' I say. 'Who? You mean someone like us? Someone with a cottage? Someone *you* know?'

And now it comes back to me. There's some colleague of

hers at the Hamlish who has a place somewhere near here. She's always threatening to invite him over.

'Your friend!' I say. 'Over at wherever it is! What's his speciality? What's his period?'

Kate frowns. 'You mean John Quiss? Oh, I see. Well, French eighteenth century . . .'

But he writes about European art in general – I remember now – he's one of those tiresome people who are famous for knowing everything, and who even more tiresomely probably do. My heart contracts still further. There's no possibility that John Quiss can have seen that picture and failed to recognize it.

'It's the middle of the week,' says Kate. 'He'll be in town. Anyway, I didn't mean him.'

'Someone *else*? Round here?'

'Of course. You.'

Me? What's she talking about?

'He brought it here,' she says.

'Brought it *here*?' I repeat stupidly, gazing round even more stupidly, as if some last confirming trace of it might be lingering in the air.

'He wanted you to look at it.'

'But . . .' I can't find words to express my multiple bafflement, and my outrage at the exquisite unfairness of events. All the adventures I've undertaken to get a sight of it were in vain – because the idiot had taken it away to show to me!

'But I wasn't here!' I manage finally. 'I was there!'

'I told him. Didn't he catch you? There's what looks like a patch of something on the surface. He'd got it into his head that there might be a signature underneath it. You mean – you haven't seen it?'

I sit down on the broken kitchen chair that's waiting in the garden until we have a bonfire. I put my head in my hands and groan. And I *still* can't make sense of what's happened!

'But he said he *had* showed it to someone!' I cry. 'He said he'd got advice from an expert!'

'I suppose he meant me.'

I take my head out of my hands.

'You?'

'Well, you weren't here. Don't worry. I told him not to touch it.'

'He showed it to *you*? You've *seen* it?'

'It was a rather cursory glance. I didn't like to demonstrate too much interest.'

The first thing I feel, I have to confess, is a stab of jealousy. Up to now I was the sole interpreter of the picture, the only priest admitted to its mysteries. Now a second priest has arrived in the sanctuary. Not an acolyte, introduced and initiated by myself, but one of equal or superior standing, who's found her own way in independently of me.

Now she *has* seen it, though, I want to ask her a thousand questions. The only one that emerges is: 'He brought it into the house?' Ridiculous, I know – but *I* was the one who was going to carry it in triumph into our cottage!

'No, I was working out here. He just untied the back of his Land-Rover and slid it out a bit.'

Jealousy gives way to curiosity. What did she see? What did she think? And instantly curiosity gives way in its turn to uneasiness. The great advantage that I had over her in the debate, the circumstance that disqualified all her doubts about the picture's authenticity, was that I'd seen it and she hadn't. This advantage has abruptly vanished. Her opinion's now at least as good a mine. And no, I don't want to know what she saw, I don't what to know what she thought! I already know what it was: nothing that I'd have liked her to see, not what I need her to have thought.

I have to know, though, whether I want to or not. I wait. I can see she's going to take her time.

'I had a look at the patch in the corner,' she says. 'I don't know what it is – it could be anything. Dirt. Ink, even. I think he's right, though – it's on top of the varnish. He could probably take a damp rag to it without doing any harm. I thought you might not want the signature on display, though.'

Good God! I hadn't even thought that he might have been just about to reveal the word 'Bruegel' to the world!

She goes over and takes a look at Tilda. I wait.

'I couldn't really see any little walker,' she says when she comes back. 'Though the varnish is considerably darkened and there's quite a lot of cracking and paint loss, so some of the detail is rather difficult to make out.'

And of course at once I'm irritated. She *should* have seen a little walker. She didn't see a little walker because she was looking in the wrong places, in the wrong spirit. And she thought I might be frightened to have a signature revealed, I realize, not because it would be Bruegel's but because it wouldn't be. I now absolutely do not wish to hear anything else she has to say about the picture.

'I can't really read the iconography as religious at all,' she says nonetheless. 'It's pretty much in the standard pastoral convention, isn't it?' The very slightly patronizing, reductive tone of this judgement puts my back up even further. I know what prompts it. Her territory's threatened. *She's* the expert on religious iconography; she's not going to have a bold new extension of the vocabulary foisted upon her by some amateur like myself.

'There's something a bit worrying about that swimming party, too,' she says. 'I've checked – there really are no examples in the calendars of swimming as an activity for any of the spring months.'

I listen politely. What I'm thinking, though, is that there *is* now an example of swimming in spring, and that I'm just about to announce it to the world. It's a further hint, like the courting peasants, that the picture's the work of a painter who was great enough to bend the conventions rather than bend beneath them.

She stoops and resumes her planting. I watch her in amazement. Is that the end of her assessment? This is breathtaking. I thought we were in this together now! She knows, she *must* know, that what I really want to hear – yes, still, in spite of all my reservations about her judgementis what she *thought* of the picture. Does she accept that I'm right, does she support me? I suppose her silence makes her assessment clear enough. I respect her unbudgeable honesty. Of course I do. But her way of expressing it I find intolerable. This performance of delicacy, of tiptoeing around my idiotic, amateurish enthusiasms, is even more hurtful than open dismissal. It suggests that she's dealing with a child.

It also makes it very difficult to know where we go from here. Do I humbly have to *ask* her to be explicit? Or do we simply drop the subject and never refer to it again?

We're back to where we were before the great row. The compromise we patched up then, that she'd pretend to trust my judgement because she'd had no opportunity to exercise her own, has come unravelled.

What suddenly blinds me with irritation now, for some reason, is how much longer she had than I did to study the picture, and what poor use she made of the time.

'So you've been gazing at the thing all morning?' I say. She glances up at me, hearing the displeasure in my tone.

'No, for a few minutes.'

For a few minutes? But I passed Tony Churt heading in this direction while I was on my way to Upwood . . .

'What?' says Kate, straightening up completely again, knowing there's trouble in the air. She arches her back again, and brushes the hair away from her brow. This time, though, I feel I've seen the performance once too often.

'You really don't have to worry,' she says. 'I was very offhand about it. Most of the time we were simply chatting.'

Chatting? Kate doesn't chat. She *can't* chat. And with Tony Churt? For two hours?

'He says that as far as he's concerned we're all countrymen together.' She laughs. 'He really is the most awful person!'

In that case, why's she laughing? Perhaps this is his approach to all the women Laura says he knocks off their feet. He's so awful he makes them laugh. The famous aphrodisiac.

'Long chat,' I say ridiculously, looking at my watch.

'No, he wouldn't stay. He said he was going back to catch you.'

'Fitting in another little rendezvous on the way, evidently,' I suggest, even more ridiculously. 'Laura says he's a great womanizer.'

Kate frowns, puzzled, still pretending to be uncertain what her offence is. 'Are you warning me?' she says. 'Or trying to make me jealous?'

I let this pass. She knows perfectly well what I'm upset about.

'Quite a character, your new pal,' I say sourly. 'He beats his wife. With the refrigerator.'

The expression on Kate's face suggests that she find this no more convincing than my attribution of the picture.

'Or else he beats the refrigerator with his wife,' I concede. 'If so, she's not really quite up to the work. She showed me the bruises.'

'Where?'

'Where?' It occurs to me that Kate is jumping to conclusions – that she thinks we retired to Laura's bedroom to view the evidence. 'In the breakfast-room,' I explain patiently. 'While I was looking at the Giordano.'

'I mean, where were the bruises?'

Oh, where were the *bruises*. With lightning discretion, I shift them to Laura's neck . . . to her upper arm . . . and back to their rightful place, since there's no earthly reason for them not to be there.

'On her ribs,' I say flatly.

But perhaps I hesitated a few microseconds too many, because for another microsecond or two Kate looks at me. If I thought her chat with Tony went on for a disturbingly long time, I realize, then she must presumably think the same about my examination of Laura's ribs. All she says, though, is, 'Poor woman,' and goes back to work.

It's Kate, as always, who makes the first move towards reconciliation. 'John Quiss,' she says, as we get the lunch together. 'That's rather a good idea. If you could tell Tony Churt that you wanted to examine the mark in the corner, and get the picture down here for the day, I could invite John over, and he could have a look at it without knowing where it came from.'

She's demonstrating that she's still on my side, still trying to help me. She's showing that she's prepared to descend to a certain amount of deception for my sake. She's even giving me all the credit for the idea. Unfortunately, what she's also making absolutely clear once again is that she doesn't believe me. The possibility that her colleague might agree with me has not for one second crossed her mind. If it had, her imagination would presumably have moved on to the later stages of the conversation, after he's said: 'Yes, I'm pretty sure that this is one of the most famous missing masterpieces in the world that you've got propped up on the draining board in your kitchen' – and then wanders off without any inquiry about how it happened to get there, and without mentioning this odd little detail of our domestic arrangements to anyone else.

'I'll think about it,' I say. I smile. She smiles.

I'm not sure I didn't prefer open warfare.

As the day wears on, and Kate and I sit working in silence at opposite ends of the kitchen table, I feel the balance of power in this uneasy alliance of ours begin to shift. I've lost the one advantage I had, my exclusive acquaintance with the picture. It's as if the table were a seesaw, and Kate were rising above me, right and victorious, and I were sinking, defeated and wrong.

My first thought is to go straight back up the hill and look at the picture again for myself. I'm sure *I'll* find my little walker in it somewhere. I can perfectly well go back yet again without seeming to be too interested. All I have to say to Tony is: 'Kate said you wanted me to look at this patch you've found . . .' But then supposing it's not Tony I'm saying this to? Supposing he's out, and it's Laura? I can see the little mocking smile starting on her face again . . .

I feel the terrible exhaustion that comes with having some great enterprise under way, of being on some great journey through unpathed lands, across unbridged rivers. I'm overwhelmed by the perpetual preoccupation, the perpetual anxiety, the perpetual load of decisions and judgements to be made, swaying and teetering like the piled chairs and china on the tightrope walker's head.

And when I look at Kate, bent over her books at the other end of the table, absorbed and professional, my defiant conviction fades. Her observation's scrupulous, her objectivity unshakeable. I don't need to see the picture again. If Kate says there's no little walker, then there's no little walker.

I bend over my own books. And now I reread my photo-copy of Stein-Schneider's article, and my transcriptions from *Terra pacis*, all the supposed links between Bruegel's pictures and the Familist ideas begin to fall to pieces in front of my eyes. The narrow mountain defile in *The Conversion of Saul*, says Stein-Schneider, is the Strait Gate of Righteousness through which the soul must pass. Yet out of all the great army of people in the picture, almost the only one who's *not* going through the Strait Gate of Righteousness is Saul himself, since he's been struck down by divine illumination just short of it. Everyone in the Tower of Babel, according to the pastor, is 'the prisoner of a strange light.' But there's nothing strange, so far as I can see, about the light in either of Bruegel's pictures of it.

The 'deceptive hills' in *Haymaking* aren't deceptive in any way that I can detect. The 'treasure hid in a field' of Matthew 13:44, which represents the Kingdom of Heaven, and which is supposed to be illustrated in *The Corn Harvest*, remains as hidden from me as Matthew said it was. The 'lack of food' shown in *The Hunters in the Snow* is evidently not preventing the villagers enjoying winter sports, or roasting a pig or whatever it is in front of the inn.

All the drunken and lubricious peasants in Bruegel's pictures, says Stein-Schneider, are caricatures of the sexual life so frowned upon by Niclaes. But Bruegel and his wife managed to produce children by one means or another – and in Antwerp earlier, if we're to believe van Mander, during the years when Bruegel was in contact with the Familists, he was living in sin with a servant girl. Presumably his peasants are the people the Travailler through the wildernessed lands sees besett with greevous laboure, and are named Striken-in-Heart, Cumbered-in-Mynde, Wofulnes, Sorow-

fulnes, Anguish, Fear, Dismayednes, Perplexetee, Uncomfortablnes, Undelytfulnes, Heavymyndednes, Many-
maner-of-thoughts, Discourage . . . I turn back to the cycle of
the year. If those three girls striding along with the hay-
rakes in June are poor Striken-in-Heart and Cumbered-in-
Mynde and Wofulnes, then I can only say that they're
putting a pretty good face on it; and if that's Mrs Sorow-
fulnes and her friends picnicking in the July shade of the
cornfield, then the sunshine and the prospect of lunch must
have distracted them for a moment from their troubles. And
what about my *Merrymakers*? In the spring sunshine, as I
recall it, Dismayednes and Perplexetee are dancing to the
music of Uncomfortablnes with surprising abandon. And if
the young woman kissing Undelytfulnes in the bushes is by
any chance Many-maner-of-thoughts, then I suspect that
she has – well, yes – many manner of thoughts in her head,
not all of them totally despairing, and that for a moment, at
any rate, she finds poor old Undelytfulness somwhat delytfull, like the wicked hills around them.

I've failed. I promised Kate – promised myself – that I
shouldn't risk any of our money unless I could demonstrate
to her beyond all reasonable doubt that the picture was what
I think it is. And I can't. All my researches have led nowhere;
all my great conjectural Tower of Babel has collapsed. The
little walker in the atlas is merely a decorative doodle. The
only other little walker to be found is me, plodding slowly to
a Land of Peace that seems to lie as far off as ever.

I haven't even been able to convince myself. Perhaps I'm
wrong about the picture . . . I *am* wrong. I know it. Once
again. That half-witted customer looking over the artist's
shoulder in *The Artist and the Connoisseur*, too stupid to be
able to see or understand what he's about to pay for, is me.

Kate looks up. I realize I've been absently gazing at her.

She smiles, and blows a little kiss. I suppose she can see the dismay written all over me. I smile, and blow a little kiss back. She returns to her books. I return to mine.

And now I remember what Laura said about how Tony acquired these four pictures. From his mother, when she was dying. He went to see her when she couldn't even speak, and came back with them. How did he know that she wanted him to have them? He didn't know. He simply took them. Stole them, in plain English. So if I buy them, I shall be receiving stolen property. Property stolen by my accomplice from his own mother, in front of her eyes as she lay dying.

I admit total defeat. I'll ring in the morning and say that I'm withdrawing.

Kate looks up once more, and frowns. 'What?' she says. I suppose I was gazing at her again.

Multa pinxit, I find myself thinking, *quae pingi non possunt* . . . He painted many things which cannot be painted. In all his works, more is always understood than is painted . . .

So what *was* it he was painting that couldn't be painted, if it wasn't the theology of the Family of Love? And, yes, more *is* always understood than is painted. In all his pictures; in *my* picture. There is, there is! I can feel it, as palpable as the uneasiness in the air between Kate and me. I just can't put my finger on it.

I suppose now I never will. Kate's still looking at me. I put my copies of Stein-Schneider and *Terra pacis* and all my notes away in my folder. I'll tell her I'm giving up. Stop her worrying. Get it over with.

But I don't. I say nothing. I open the folder again and take out the small handful of original evidence that's survived: Van Mander's biographical sketch; the Ortelius epitaph; and the pictures themselves.

And I start all over again.

Whatever he was painting that couldn't be painted, whatever's understood rather than shown, whatever indiscretions he'd committed in his past, one thing's certain. It leaps out at me as I go through the evidence once again. I can't think how I missed it before, except that none of the commentators I've read remarks upon it.

In the last years of his life Bruegel was a frightened man.

What he seems to fear is that he might be accused of something. The something's never identified. Sometimes he seems to be suggesting indignantly that the charge is false. At other times he seems to be admitting that there might be something in it – even that there's material evidence to be disposed of.

The entire population of the Netherlands must have been in a permanent state of fear at the time, of course. By the 1560s the province had become a police state where denunciation was not merely encouraged but required, and where, true or false, it led almost certainly to torture and death. Bruegel's anxiety, though, seems to be not a general one but to relate to something more specific.

It's there, for instance, in *The Calumny of Apelles*, the drawing he did in 1565 – the same year in which he painted the six great panels of the calmly changing seasons. Yes, Apelles again. Concealment and the art of painting thunder aren't the only things that Bruegel learnt from him – he took over wholesale the allegorical scene depicted in Apelles' most famous picture. It's a curious piece. The characters in it are all labelled, as in an old-fashioned political cartoon, and their names are the Latin terms for the abstractions they embody. The central figure's a woman identified as *Calumnia*. Boiling with righteous indignation, she's approaching a king on his throne, ushered forward by *Lyvor* . . .

'More Latin,' I say to Kate. '*Lyvor*.'

'Envy?' she suggests. 'Malice?' She's too tactful to give any indication of curiosity about what tangent I am off upon now.

So Calumny's being guided by Envy or Malice, and urged on by . . .

'*Insidiae*?' I ask Kate. '*Fallaciae*?'

'Plots,' she says. 'Tricks and stratagems.'

And she's dragging by the hair an unidentified boy whose hands are raised above his head in supplication. What's the boy accused of? There's no way of telling, but since his accuser's Calumny the charge is presumably false. This is the work that van Mander seems to be referring to under the title *Truth Breaking Through*, which he says Bruegel himself described as the best thing he'd ever done.

It's not, by any stretch of the imagination, but if van Mander's right then it clearly meant a lot to Bruegel. So presumably did another picture that he produced in the same year, a grisaille entitled *Christ and the Woman Taken in Adultery*, since he retained it in his own possession for the rest of his life. Once again the accused stands surrounded by her accusers. But this isn't a text against false accusation – the woman, according to St John's Gospel, was taken 'in the very act'. Accusers and accused alike have turned to look at Christ as he stoops and writes in the dust '*Die sonder sonde is . . .*' – 'He that is without sin . . .' Christ is deprecating our pretensions to accuse and condemn our fellows in any circumstances, however true the accusation, however justified the condemnation.

Two protests against accusers and accusation in one year. Bruegel returns to a similar theme with one of the last pictures he painted, in 1568, the year before he died – *Landscape with the Magpie on the Gallows*. This strange work was obviously important to him, too, because on his deathbed, according to van Mander, he bequeathed it to his wife. It could almost be a scene in the cycle of the year; yet another view from a high foreground looking out over yet another river winding past yet another castle; yet more crags; yet another sea. The pleasant landscape is dominated, though, by a feature very out of keeping with the mood of the cycle – a gallows. Tolnay identifies the tiny outline of a far-off gibbet in *The Return of the Herd*, but this one is quite different. It stands in the foreground, dominating the picture, in a nightmarishly impossible perspective that prefigures Escher, with two uprights, one foreshortened by being further away from us – and a cross-bar leading away from us that connects the uprights back to front. The gibbet is untenanted, but there is a small crowd of peasants gathering at its foot. One of them's having a quiet crap in the bushes. Three of them, two men and a woman, are dancing together in an odd, unaccompanied, self-absorbed round dance. Are they all too wrapped up in their own concerns to bother about the ghastly structure that towers over them, or too inured to the sight of such things in the Spanish Netherlands even to notice it? Neither, I think, because one of them seems to be pointing it out to the rest of them. Is he indicating that for once no one's being hanged? Is this what they're celebrating? Or are they, like the cheerful crowds pouring out of town in *The Procession to Calvary*, assembling in holiday mood to watch an execution which is just about to occur?

The iconography suggests that happy anticipation is the mood. On the crossbar at the top of the gallows, in the dead centre of the picture, perches a magpie. The magpie's a symbol for gossip, and by it, says van Mander, Bruegel 'meant the gossips whom he would deliver to the gallows.'

So Calumny's still at work, though here it's her instead of her victim who's to be dragged off for punishment. If van Mander is right.

But is he? Hasn't he got the iconology back to front? The magpie's on top of the gallows, not under it; it's not the magpie who's going to be hanged. Gossip is triumphant, not punished. According to Stechow, there's a Netherlandish expression that means gossiping someone on to the gallows. Is this what Bruegel is threatening to do? To calumniate the calumniators? To gossip the gossips to death?

Or is he saying, once again, that the gossips, the slanderers, the true or false accusers, will calumniate *him* into the noose, to the satisfaction of a world waiting to be entertained?

Now I've noticed the theme, I realize that the power of malicious rumour was already preoccupying Bruegel in 1564, the year before the great cycle. *The Adoration of the Kings* in the National Gallery offers what Stechow calls 'an iconographic rarity.' While Mary and the Kings gaze with traditional reverence at the child in Mary's lap, Joseph's attention is distracted. A young man standing behind him has put his hand on his shoulder and is slyly whispering in his ear, his gaze averted in the classic evasiveness of the insinuator. Joseph's turning aside from the holy scene to listen with interest. What poison is the young man dropping in his ear? Stechow suggests that it's doubts about the paternity of the child. But it's no news to Joseph that he's not the father himself, because according to the Gospels God had already told him. So if Stechow's right, then the young man must be telling him that God's not the father, either – it was the milkman or the lodger. In which case God was lying. God doesn't lie, though, so the young man's story must be false.

And here it is again, in the same year, if that's when Bruegel painted *The Slaughter of the Innocents*. Why has Herod sent his cavalry to massacre all the boy children in this little Flemish village? Because he's heard a story about a child being born who will one day usurp his throne.

And again, in the year before this, 1563, when Bruegel painted the biblical subject which is complementary to the slaughter – *The Flight into Egypt*, the story of Christ's escape from death at the hands of the political power. This is even more striking, because Christ escaped by his abrupt removal from Bethlehem to Egypt – and 1563 was the year in which one of the few known events in Bruegel's own life occurred: his abrupt removal from Antwerp to Brussels.

Bruegel had just got married, to the daughter of Pieter Koeck van Aelst, the Antwerp painter from whom he'd learnt his trade. Van Mander says he'd carried the girl in his arms when she was a baby and he was her father's apprentice. By the time he married her, Koeck was dead, and she seems to have been living with her widowed mother in Brussels. According to van Mander, it was her mother who insisted that the couple should set up home in Brussels as well, because she wanted to make sure that Bruegel got right away from the servant girl he'd been living with in Antwerp. Bruegel, says van Mander, had been so attached to his mistress that he would have married her. The only reason he didn't was that she was a terrible liar, and van Mander, who writes more like a raconteur than a historian, gives a characteristically breezy and anecdotal account of what must have been an awkward episode. Bruegel, he says, 'made an agreement or contract with her to the effect that he would procure a stick and cut a notch in it for every lie she told, for which purpose he deliberately chose a fairly long one. Should the stick become covered in notches in the course of time, the marriage would be off. And indeed this came to pass in a short time.'

I wonder. A woman who tells such lies to her lover that he leaves her is presumably not fibbing about whether the cat was fed or how the milk jug got broken. Were they lies of the sort that traditionally poison relationships – attempts to cover up infidelity? If so, would Bruegel have been patient enough to tolerate a record of infidelities long enough to cover his stick? And wouldn't van Mander have cited the infidelities, rather than the lies about them, as the real cause of Bruegel's departure?

Van Mander's story is the kind of thing that might have raised a laugh from his friends in the pub, but like a lot of pub stories, it doesn't quite make sense. He doesn't say who told him, which makes it sound more like gossip than a firsthand account, and I can't help wondering if it hasn't got slightly mangled in transmission. Bruegel discards his mistress – and what happens, surely, is what's happened a million times since the world began when a couple splits up. He puts out his side of the story, she puts out hers. Each indignantly denies the other's account of events, each blackens the other's character. He tells everyone that she's a liar, because she's started claiming that . . .

That what? That he used to beat her? Or dress up in women's clothes? Or something worse? Something that makes it seem prudent for him now to hastily abandon the field and get out of Antwerp?

Is she telling people that he used to have some connection with certain mysterious figures who advocated religious freedom and circulated clandestine pamphlets offering salvation by the power of love alone?

In *The Calumny of Apelles*, I notice, Calumny herself is a handsome woman in spite of her moral shortcomings, and she's full of the righteous indignation of a woman wronged. She's also carrying a blazing torch, which is odd if you take it literally, because it appears to be broad daylight, and odder still if it's part of the iconography, since her role is to obfuscate the truth rather than illuminate it. It would make sense, though, if she were hoping to light a fire with it.

So was it heresy once again that was hidden in Bruegel's heart, even if not in his pictures? Or at any rate the fear of its being found there?

But then at once another mystery opens up: if Antwerp was becoming too hot for Bruegel, why on earth did he think of taking refuge in Brussels, of all cities? It was the centre of the Spanish administration. He was jumping out of the frying pan and into the fire – only too literally, in all probability.

I turn back to the *Calumny*. I examine it again, like an investigator in a crime story who comes to think that a witness he interrogated before might have kept something back.

The story it tells is oddly detailed and circumstantial. At the front of the court, standing beside the throne for the best possible view of the case, are twin sisters with their arms fondly twined around each other, labelled *Suspicio* and *Ignorancia*. At the back of the court *Penitencia* waits for sentence to be passed. But there's a hint of a surprising last-minute twist coming in the story. Penitence is turning to look at a naked man who's sinking pleadingly to his knees beside her, unnoticed by anyone else in court. His name is

Veritas. We begin to suspect that it won't be the accused whom Penitence finally hauls out of court for punishment at the end of the case – it will be the accuser herself.

There's something familiar, too, about the appearance of *Lyvor*, the figure of Malice or Envy, who's egging Calumny on. His shock of long grey hair projects from beneath a large skullcap, so that he looks like a tonsured monk – or the painter in *The Painter and the Connoisseur*, the drawing that Bruegel did probably somewhere around the same time as the *Calumny*. He has the same skullcap perched on the same shock of long grey hair – but no beard. So, even if the painter with the connoisseur really were Bruegel himself, as some scholars believe, this one's someone else. Another painter, by the look of it. Calumny's being urged on by the malice and envy of one of Bruegel's fellow artists.

It all seems too particularized to be simply an allegory of false accusation in general. Some actual story's being told, some definite charge is being laid. What is it?

Bruegel took the subject from a picture he'd never set eyes upon – Apelles' original vanished some time in the Dark Ages. His source was a description of it written in the second century AD by a Syrian essayist called Lucian. Which I will no doubt find in the London Library.

Kate yawns and starts to close up her books. I wonder whether to share my new line of inquiry with her; this is certainly something we could work on together. But all I say is: 'Would you mind driving me to the station again?' I've just remembered how she sank my last theory by failing to see the little walker. I think I'll keep my new thoughts to myself. Like the little walker, I'll plod on alone.

'Whenever you like,' she says, still yawning. 'Shall we have the sausages for supper?'

'I mean now.'

She stops for a moment in mid-yawn. This is going to test our new arrangements.

'I know,' I say, 'but I want to be in the library tomorrow first thing. If he's started carting that picture round and showing it to people, then I've got to be ready to move just as soon as the bank's got the money through.'

She unhurriedly finishes her yawn. Of course; she's entirely confident now that I'm not going to meet the conditions I've set myself.

'Don't forget to look up the Giordano prices this time,' she says mildly.

Bruegel, I discover next day, sitting with my back turned obstinately once again upon the real spring in St James's Square, wasn't the only artist to attempt a reconstruction of Apelles' vanished masterpiece. The detailed description that Lucian gave was evidently so vivid that a dozen centuries later, in the Renaissance, it caught the imagination of a considerable number of artists, and the scene was illustrated by, among many others, Botticelli, Mantegna and Dürer. A French art historian, Jean-Michel Massing, has devoted a whole book to the subject. There's something profoundly odd about Bruegel's version, though, that Massing sets out but doesn't comment on, and that no one else seems to have noticed at all.

I think about it to myself. (Yes, we're still working on this together, myself and I, even if Kate's out of it.) Lucian wrote in Greek, and the knowledge of Greek wasn't widespread at the time of the Renaissance. The great rediscovery of classical civilization was made through Latin, either from original Latin texts or from Greek ones translated into Latin. Bruegel had plainly read Lucian's account of the *Calumny* in translation – the figures are all identified by their Latin names. The labels in the other famous versions of the picture, by Botticelli, Mantegna and Dürer, don't correspond to any of the various known translations. But Massing's able to identify the one that Bruegel had read, because his labelling follows, exactly and to the letter, the version done in 1518 by the German humanist Philipp Melanchthon.

The more I ponder this to myself, the more astonishing both I and myself think it is. I happen to know something about Melanchthon because he began life as a nominalist, but in the sixteenth century he was notorious throughout Catholic Europe as one of the founding fathers of Protestantism. He was a personal friend of Luther – out of transubstantiation even before Luther himself – and the principal author of the great statement of Lutheran beliefs, the Augsburg Confession. In the Spanish Netherlands, in other words, he was Satan's archangel. Bruegel had already taken amazing risks by reading God's word in the Bible, but to start on the Devil's works as well was insanely reckless.

And at once a practical question arises: where in Brussels at that time could Bruegel have possibly laid his hands on a text by Melanchthon?

Well, where would you look for a copy of Trotsky's writings in Stalinist Russia? Where would be the likeliest place to find *The Satanic Verses* in Iran? I know where I'd look first: Beria's bedside, some ayatollah's coffee-table.

My guess is that Bruegel found Melanchthon in Cardinal Granvelle's library.

Bruegel's all-powerful patron was possibly the only man in Brussels who could possess heretical texts with impunity. He had a professional obligation to read them, to know what it was that he was protecting everyone else from. In any case, it might have amused him to own forbidden books, even to display them. It's a demonstration of the great man's power, to permit himself liberties denied to lesser men. They're in chains; he holds the chains.

So maybe this is why Bruegel fled from Antwerp to Brussels – to secure a foothold inside the lion's den, because he knew that no one would dare to touch anyone living so close to the lion. The Cardinal perhaps found Bruegel as chic as the writings of Melanchthon. He might have found it even more piquant to tolerate a live pet radical about the house, a painter with heretical leanings, like a jester licensed to mock the king, or a wild tiger cub permitted to foul the carpets and bite the courtiers – a living demonstration that not only did he hold the chains, but that he kept the key to them, and locked them and unlocked them at his own good pleasure.

The pilot fish survives all the lesser predators of the ocean by having a shark right behind it, and survives the shark by swimming just in front of its nose. Perhaps *The Flight into Egypt*, which Bruegel painted in the same year as his move to Brussels, and which is known to have been owned by Granvelle, was a graceful allusion to the sanctuary that the Cardinal was offering him.

I see Bruegel settling into the same easy terms with the Reichskommissar as Apelles was with Alexander the Great, according to Pliny. When Alexander visited Apelles in his studio and ventured a few opinions about art, Apelles felt free to tell him how ridiculous they were. I hear Bruegel uttering a short insulting laugh when the Cardinal tells him, over a bottle of white wine amidst the genial chaos of the artist's studio, how much he admires Frans Floris and *The Fall of the Rebel Angels*. I see the Cardinal smiling good-naturedly at this touching little sign of professional jealousy. Alexander gave Apelles a most handsome present – his favourite mistress. I imagine the Cardinal making a few knowing remarks about the little servant girl Bruegel had abandoned in Antwerp, who keeps sending his officials long letters in green ink full of wild allegations. The Cardinal has her ravings filed away for possible future use, but in the meantime orders a huge birthday cake to be delivered to Bruegel, and when Bruegel cuts it – out jumps a very pretty little nun as a substitute . . .

Or perhaps not. The following year, 1564, when he paints the *Adoration*, Bruegel's still evidently worrying about gossip. The pilot fish must always remain a little anxious, in spite of the mighty bodyguard at his back. One moment's inattention, one brief failure to anticipate which way your great friend's turning next, and – snap! – no pilot fish. And by the spring of that year this particular pilot fish suddenly had an urgent reason for paranoia. A sudden commotion in the water behind him, and when he looked round – no shark!

What had happened? The Cardinal had gone home to Burgundy to see his mother.

It was a neat reversal. Granvelle had often prompted the King what to say and do, and modestly told him not to mention the source of the suggestion. By 1564 the ubiquitous prelate had made himself so loathed by all parties in the Netherlands, from the Prince of Orange to the Duchess of Parma herself, that the King was obliged, after endless hesitation, to make a decision of his own at last without the Cardinal's assistance. He instructed Granvelle to go and visit his mother in France. And he modestly told him not to mention who'd prompted this little filial piety.

So Granvelle left, and never returned. There was wild rejoicing in the capital, though possibly one abruptly abandoned pilot fish didn't join in. Once again Bruegel was as alone and unprotected in the great ocean as he'd been in Antwerp.

Put not your trust in princes . . . The Spaniards and their local hirelings, like all failing imperial regimes, were particularly dangerous friends to have. If Bruegel could have foreseen what would happen after his death he might have been even more anxious. In 1572 Granvelle's palace at Malines was wrecked and looted, not by the Protestant rebels, but by the Spaniards themselves, under the command of the Duke of Alva, who'd come to put an end to the Netherlanders' disobedience once and for all, and who sacked not just Malines but a number of cities, all with spectacular and ghoulish brutality.

What happened to the Cardinal's collection of Bruegels inside the palace? Some of them, at any rate, had remained there up to then. Granvelle, still in exile, sent an envoy, Provost Morillon, a devoted and conscientious-looking priest in his portrait in the *Correspondance*, to inspect the damage. Morillon reported that Don Frederic, the Duke of Alva's son, who was acting as the local Spanish commander, had sold a collection of loot to a certain captain Erasso, and that 'this fine brigand' would make a handsome profit if he got the chance, 'because he was still taking the pictures while I was there, and has declared that he will carry off all the casketing and wainscotting, beds and chamber doors, if they are not redeemed to his satisfaction.' Nine days later he reports again. 'I have sent Christian the painter to buy the XXV canvas perspectives and Antwerp landscapes . . . but you must not expect to recover the Bruegel pieces, or only at a price: because they are more sought after since his death than before, and are estimated at 50, 100 and 200 escudos, which is unconscionable.'

Whether Granvelle ever did recover them, the correspondence doesn't record. Perhaps he did, and they disappeared again later, in the seventeenth century, when one of his descendants, the comte de St Amour, began to sell or give away *mille belles choses* from among the late Cardinal's effects. What the Count valued least, papers and books, was abandoned to the mercy of his servants. The Cardinal's dispatches, says his editor, were treated as waste paper, and could be seen used as wrapping and 'undergoing the uttermost indignities.' Maybe the last record of the fate of the Cardinal's Bruegels disappeared into the staff latrine.

On the other hand, it may well have been the approach of war in the provinces that preserved some record of Jongelinck's Bruegels in Antwerp, by ruining his friend de Bruyne and forcing Jongelinck to list them for his pledge to cover de Bruyne's debt. The pictures themselves, for that matter, were probably saved only by the City's seizure or purchase of them, because Jongelinck's villa, for which he'd commissioned the great cycle, was in the suburbs – a luxury spec development put up by a builder who'd acquired a plot outside the city walls. When Alessandro Farnese besieged the city in 1584 this early experiment in suburban living turned out to be premature, and the defenceless villa was destroyed by the Spaniards like so much else.

Back to 1564, though, with Bruegel in Brussels – and his great patron gone.

There he is, unprotected again, and in the following year he's defending himself against actual or potential accusers with the *Calumny* and *The Woman Taken in Adultery*. His fears remain with him to the end of his life and *The Magpie on the Gallows*. But by then the story's taken a slightly different turn.

The bequest of *The Magpie* to his wife wasn't the only disposition he made on his deathbed, according to van Mander. He also ordered her to burn a number of pictures. Exactly what they were van Mander doesn't say, but he describes them as 'strange and full of meaning . . . careful and beautifully finished drawings to which he had added inscriptions,' and says that Bruegel wanted them destroyed 'from remorse or for fear that she might get into trouble and might have to answer for them.' It seems unlikely, though, that they showed the great unpathed Lande named Many-maner-of-walkings, because van Mander says that they were 'compositions of comical subjects' and that 'some of them were too biting and sharp.'

Comic drawings that might get their possessor into trouble because they're too biting and sharp sound like caricatures of some sort. If so, they must have been most carefully retained in Bruegel's own possession up till then, and most comprehensively suppressed by his widow, because there are no known caricatures of identifiable individuals among his extant works. There are plenty of sardonic representations of peasants and beggars, of course, and some of these were apparently taken from life, but I can't believe Bruegel was worrying about peasants and beggars recognizing themselves and bringing lawsuits. Van Mander suggests that the drawings which Bruegel ordered to be burnt were like others of which engraved copies have survived. But the extant engravings of comical subjects are all fantastical scenes scarifying human vice and folly in the most general way, and I don't find it any easier to believe that Bruegel thought his widow might be troubled by group actions brought by misers and lechers who thought their interests had been damaged. So perhaps these dangerous drawings, with the inscriptions he'd added, were something more like . . . yes, *The Calumny of Apelles* once again.

And so I turn to Lucian. He was a rhetorician, I discover – a performer, a kind of early Eddie Izzard, who toured the Greek world in the second century after Christ reciting witty essays he'd written. One of them was about slander, a subject which he says was long before pre-empted by Apelles for his famous picture. Lucian calls him Apelles of Ephesus, Pliny Apelles of Kos, but he seems to be the same man, and from the way he talks about the picture it's plain that Lucian actually saw it and had some kind of guided tour of it.

He says that Apelles had a good personal reason for wanting to do a picture about slander, because he'd once been falsely accused himself, and almost executed. A rival artist called Antiphilus was jealous of him, and denounced him to the king. He told the king that Apelles had been seen whispering in the ear of one of the provincial governors and inciting him to revolt. The king's judgement, according to Lucian, had been corrupted by flattery, and without further inquiry he began raving and shouting that

Apelles was an ingrate, a plotter and a conspirator, and was going to have him beheaded until one of Apelles' fellow prisoners spoke up and absolved him of any part in the plot, whereupon the king was so ashamed that he gave Apelles his rival as a slave.

The circumstances of the revolt identify the credulous monarch as the debauched and drunken Ptolemy IV, otherwise Ptolemy Philoprator, one of the Macedonian kings of Egypt in the third century BC – which means that the story, like so many others, has got corrupted in transmission at some point, because Apelles had been dead for nearly a hundred years when the incident occurred. The details are so circumstantial and vivid, however, that Lucian's account must be based on some sort of actual events, even if he or his informants have elided them with something that happened later. What's most striking about the allegation – so striking that it's survived the change in the story's setting – is its nature; it's a political one.

But then so was the allegation against Christ, as Herod understood it, that led to the great massacre and to the hurried removal of the infant Christ from Bethlehem. The charge in both cases was sedition, committed or threatened.

Was the allegation haunting Bruegel in those last six years of his life also a political one? Was he in fear of being denounced as a danger to the state? Of being revealed not so much as a heretic but as a dissident?

This is the new tower of Babel I'm building: politics. Can I find room here for the cycle of the year?

I look through the five known panels once again. I can see not a ghost of a political idea in them anywhere, except the general air of disconcerting quietism, the suggestion that life in the Netherlands was one long rural idyll.

Could there be some detail in the first picture in the

series, in my picture, that suggests otherwise? That puts a different spin on the whole series? I can't imagine what it could be. I could easily imagine the little walker. But what sort of detail might carry a political meaning? Barricades? Rick-burning?

Or could swimming earlier in the year than the Books of Hours allow for be a form of political protest?

There's nothing more to be discovered in London. What I have to do is head north once again and make another attempt to see the picture. I'll go to Upwood and offer my services with the mysterious patch in the corner of the picture – but before I knock on the door I'll reconnoitre carefully to make sure that Tony's Land-Rover's in the yard, and the dogs are at home. If not, I'll lurk patiently in the undergrowth until he returns and extinguishes any possibility of embarrassing misunderstandings.

Because there's *something* in that picture of mine! I know that. Something that explains why it disappeared. Something that unlocks all the mysteries. Something that identifies it beyond any reasonable doubt.

Actually, there *was* one thing more to be discovered in London, I realize, as I roll north through a sudden sobering downpour of spring rain – the Giordano prices. Damn.

The First Shipment

I don't walk up the drive – I don't go anywhere near the roads. I climb quietly over the rusty barbed wire in the woods and slither through the mud beneath the dripping trees, fearful of scaring up another pheasant and getting shot by one of the pheasant security staff, or putting my foot into a mantrap. Never has the country seemed so much less appealing than the London Library.

It's the back of the house that appears first, across a muddled no man's land that seems to be some kind of abandoned kitchen garden. I struggle sideways through the woods, with not even the ghost of a suppressed right of way under my feet, more and more like a poacher, or a burglar reconnoitring his target. No dogs come crashing out to challenge me, and when at last I get a view over the front of the house and the yard there's no sign of the Land-Rover.

So I stick to my plan. I find a reasonably dry, firm spot behind a tree, and I wait.

I wait for an hour and a quarter.

I begin to get surprisingly cold, and also to feel surprisingly ridiculous. I modify the plan slightly. I go for a little walk in the woods. Horrible as it is, it's not quite as cold or ridiculous as standing still. When I come back . . . still no dogs, still no Land-Rover.

I wait.

I take another little walk.

Then I undertake a major review of the situation. I'd

somehow assumed that Tony's travels wouldn't take him too far afield. Some outlying part of the estate, perhaps. The shops in Lavenage. A neighbour's house. But he might equally well be out for the entire day, I realize. Or destroying some variety of animal life in Scotland. Checking his bank account in the Cayman Islands.

Or at a neighbour's house, yes, where he knew the husband would also be out for the day. And where he might stay until the husband returned.

The thought that he might be at the cottage again, back with some other artistic matter he wants Kate's advice on, is so ridiculous that it makes me laugh aloud. But it's also ridiculous my lurking about in the cold and damp, like some boy hero in a children's detective story, just because Laura might misunderstand my turning up for a third time when she's on her own. I'm not a boy in a children's story – I'm a man in a story for adults – man enough, certainly, to ride out minor social embarrassments. And I'm damned if I'm going to be intimidated by the half-educated wife of some layabout landowner.

I scramble out of the woods and march straight up to the front door, raise my hand to the knocker, see in my mind the front door dissolving in front of me, and Laura standing there with that mocking, knowing smile pushing at the corners of her lips, and march straight back into the woods again.

I have a feeling that I've spent half my life walking backwards and forwards across the hard standing in front of the Churts' house.

Another rethink. I'll go home and tell Kate about all the idiocies of the morning, and I'll come back later. Then at least I'll be certain that Tony's not at the cottage.

I haven't struggled very far back among the trees when I

hear a vehicle thumping through the potholes on the drive. I stop and turn back, all my stratagems justified. By the time I reach the house there's the Land-Rover in front of the door, and there are the dogs, one lapping at the lake, the other preserving the natural balance of nature by urinating into it. They look up as I approach, and come bounding over, barking joyously to greet their new-found friend. I fence humorously with them, in the way that I've seen people do with dogs, for once as pleased to see them as they are to see me. I must find out what they're called – bring them titbits – inquire solicitously after their health and education.

The front door stands welcomingly open. I step into the hall. 'Hello,' I shout humorously. 'Anyone at home?'

'Only me,' says Laura, emerging from the kitchen. 'How did you guess? Watching the house?'

No words frame themselves.

'Don't take your boots off, though,' she says. 'You can help me carry all the stuff in first – I've just done my weekly stint at Kwik Save. Don't I get a kiss?'

A kiss, certainly, yes, of course. I make some kind of disjointed gesture in the direction of her cheek.

She laughs. 'Don't worry,' she says. 'I dropped him off at the station. He's going to be in London all day. Here – three dozen eggs. Watch what you're doing.'

'Chuck your boots in the hall,' says Laura, when we've carried in substantial sections of several frozen animals.

I come back into the kitchen in my socks and make the speech I prepared for Tony. 'I gather he wants me to look at this patch of his.'

She doesn't reply. She hands me a huge ancestral carving knife and indicates one of the cardboard cases we've carried in. 'Get that open. I'll find a lemon.'

Inside the case are a dozen bottles of gin. She takes one out and cracks the lid open. 'Tony's going to go ballistic when he sees what I've bought,' she says, pouring two half-tumblers. 'But I'm sick of pheasant and I'm sicker still of that brown muck he puts in the decanter.' She hands me the tumbler. Gin is the drink I hate most in the world, and there's more gin in this one glass than I've drunk in my entire life so far. 'Don't want tonic, do you? Don't say yes, because I forgot to get any.'

She lights a cigarette and leans back against the rail of the range, as she did before. She's not wearing one of her amazing sweaters today but a man's shirt, several sizes too big, with rather formal blue stripes and a tail that hangs outside her trousers. One of Tony's, perhaps, and on him, I imagine, not very remarkable. On her, though . . . I look away into the depths of my gin.

She raises her glass. 'Well, here we go again,' she says. 'Perhaps we'll get a bit further this time.'

Oh, my God. This is even worse than I'd feared.

'I gather', I repeat pathetically, 'that he wants me to look at the patch. Tony does. Kate said. This patch that he's found. He wants me to look at it.'

It sounds incoherent. It sounds desperate. Worse, it sounds suspiciously insistent. What's happened to all my new-found skills as a hustler?

'Patch?' repeats Laura, baffled. 'Which patch? This patch?'

She's gazing at a livid bulge on the ceiling where water seems to be coming through. 'Look at any patches you like,' she says. 'The whole bloody house is patches. Brown patches, green patches. Dry rot, wet rot. Black fungus, blue fungus. Mushrooms, toadstools. Help yourself.'

'No, no,' I say stiffly, making myself more ridiculous by the second. 'On the picture. In the corner of the picture.'

She looks at me, and tilts her head disbelievingly.

'You're not trying to get us back in that breakfast-room?' she says. 'How about the game larder? Might be a bit warmer. Or the local morgue?'

I realize that we're at cross purposes.

'Not *Helen*,' I say. 'The other one. Or is that back in the breakfast-room, too?'

She frowns. I've been so successful in concealing my interest in it that she's forgotten about it once again. The trouble is, I can't think how to refer to it. I can't call it 'the *Merrymakers*'. Not in public. I want to say 'the Bruegel'. No other way of describing it presents itself – it's Bruegelness is the only quality I can bring to mind. What's wrong with my tongue today? All its glib and flashing silver has turned to base metal. 'The one he was going to clean,' I manage finally.

'Oh, right,' she says. She laughs. 'The one that was in the fireplace. That's the one you want to see?'

'*I* don't want to see it,' I say, 'but there's apparently a patch in the corner . . .'

'Oh, the thing in the corner.' She laughs again. 'Well, that's different. I'll be delighted to show you *that* one. Bring your glass. And the bottle. You're not going to believe this.'

She leads the way out into the hall, glass and cigarette in hand. I follow, with glass and bottle, already apprehensively beginning to believe what she tells me I'm not going to. And, yes, up the great staircase we go, the stripes on the striped shirt-tail swaying vertiginously left and right in front of my eyes at each step. I tear my eyes away as we reach the landing, and stop to inspect the picture I'd noticed before from below, too small to be made out, hanging in the place of honour occupied when Tony was a boy by the great *Helen*. It's not that I find it more interesting than the shirt-tail. I'm simply trying to demonstrate my lack of any overmastering sense of urgency in regard to the picture we're going to see. Or its whereabouts.

My interest contracts even further as I look. English, eighteenth century, a dog of some sort. Of some brown sort, about the same colour as the two now lying in the hall below and most of their master's clothes and furnishings. It's standing in a brown landscape, with various dead brown birds on the brown ground in front of it. I get the impression that everything was even browner in the eighteenth century than it is now.

'That's the one picture he'll never sell,' says Laura, coming back to see what's holding me up. 'I think it actually does belong to him. Apparently it reminds him of the first dog he ever owned. If the house burned down this is what he'd grab. This and his Purdey.'

I offer up a brief prayer that the wiring in the house is in better condition than the crumbling fabric that encloses it, then turn and follow the shifting stripes of the shirt-tail up the last few stairs.

And there it is.

Propped up, in a good natural light from the window, amid a confusion of socks, bills and sporting cartridges on top of the dressing table, facing the unmade bed.

Shimmering spring leaves – dancing peasants – broken-toothed crags – distant sea . . . My first glimpse of them since the evening when the whole spiralling madness began. At last!

What am I thinking? I don't know. Nothing much, this time. Disappointment, then? Not really. I stand in front of it, glass of gin in hand, running my eye over it this way, that way, unable to take in more than I did before, and feeling . . .

Feeling Laura's arm, linked through mine as she stands gazing at the picture herself.

'God knows why he's brought it up here,' she says. 'I think he's rather taken with it. Like the dog. Reminds him of looking out over his precious estate.'

She puts the cigarette back to her lips with her free hand, then stops.

'You don't like me smoking, do you?' she says.

I make the resigned gesture that non-smokers usually make when smokers ask if they mind, that's always taken to mean they don't but privately means they do.

'I know you hate it. So does Tony. That's probably why I do it. I'll put it out.' She looks round the room. 'Only no ashtray, of course. He won't have ashtrays in the bedroom.'

She suddenly darts towards the dressing table. The insane idea flashes into my head that she's going to stub the cigarette out on the picture. I hurl myself convulsively after her, with a kind of little groan, and fling out my arm to prevent her. My hand still has the glass of gin in it. It catches her on the elbow. She looks down at the silver splash of gin leaping out of the glass at her like a flying fish, then looks straight up into my eyes, startled.

'Wow!' she says, and laughs, amused and gratified by my cack-handed eagerness. She puts down her glass, and stubs out her cigarette in a saucer full of cufflinks and collar studs.

'I'm sorry,' I say, 'I thought . . .'

But she's put her finger to my lips.

'No more thinking for today,' she says.

She becomes serious. She takes her finger away from my lips, inspects them intently, then stands on tiptoe and gently presses her own lips against them.

She tastes of gin and cigarette smoke and . . . I don't know . . . something intolerably soft and sweet. What do I taste of to her? Gin and fear, I imagine, and . . . perhaps just a little of that same sweetness.

I look into her eyes an inch away from mine, as they look into mine an inch away from hers. It's her being on tiptoe that melts me more than anything else.

She sinks back on to her heels, and puts her arms around me. I put my arms around her. I can't think quite what else to do. She looks up at me seriously, then tucks her face into the hollow of my neck. Which brings the picture into my eyeline. I have my tape measure in my pocket, but I don't think I can produce it just at the moment and attempt to use it behind her back. I try to make some kind of systematic examination, though – try to focus on each detail in turn, and think whether it could have any religious or

– 246 –

political significance. I can't make out any little walker, I have to admit, but yes, I was right, there *is* a tiny splash of reflected azurite sky which I think must be a millpool in the midst of the spring verdigris, with a little party of people beside it, one of them defiantly taking an unseasonable plunge . . . She's so distractingly soft against me, I find it extremely difficult to take in what I'm looking at . . . Or the raised foot of the dancing peasant – could that suggest some kind of rebelliousness? The yearning lips of the kissing couple . . .? I can feel my heart beating; I can feel hers . . . Oh yes, and there's the dark patch in the corner . . .

'I had a feeling you'd come today,' she says. I can feel her voice buzzing against my throat.

Foot. Patch. Swimmer . . .

I realize that she's taken her face out of my neck, and is smiling up at me.

'Or do you want to look at the thing on the picture first?' she asks, as mockingly as ever, though now I know she doesn't mean it.

'Of course not.' What else can I say?

She tightens her arms around me. I tighten mine around her. She winces, and gives a little cry.

'What?'

'Bruise.'

And at the thought of that dark cloud of pain beneath her left breast I feel an aching tenderness for her. She suddenly seems like a lost child in a fairy story, shut away here with that terrible man in this terrible house, but also brave in her refusal to give up and go under, in her desperate clinging to whoever she can find to cling to.

I gently detach myself from her, and smile at her. Sadly, I think. Mostly sadly. She kicks off her shoes, and takes me by the hand. We pad across to the bed in our stockinged feet.

'Listen,' I say. 'Wait. Sit down.'

She waits, puzzled but obedient. I take her hands in mine, and we sit down side by side on the edge of the crumpled bed. Now I can see the picture only out of the corner of my eye, and too far away to make out anything but the most general outlines.

She waits for me to say whatever it is I'm going to say. I wish I knew what it was. In the end she has to say it herself.

'You mean you don't want to?'

'I'm sorry,' I say. 'I can't. I wish I could, but I can't.'

She looks away, at the sky outside the window. Silence. We sit, her hands still in mine. I suppose what she's thinking is, 'He's thinking about *her*.' Is that what I'm thinking about? Yes, I suppose it is, now I've thought about her thinking about me thinking about it. Yes, certainly. Kate. And Tildy. And everything.

She looks at our four hands for a bit. I look at them as well. Then she looks out of the window again. I look at her face, in profile to me, and the distant mountain landscape beyond her. I can't think quite where we go from here, or how we're going to get out of this.

She gives a little chastened laugh. 'Well, it must be different among your sort of people in London,' she says absurdly. 'It's not like that round here.'

'Look,' I say, 'it's not just . . . you know, things. It's you.'

Another laugh.

'No, seriously.' And now I've said it I *do* mean it seriously. 'I don't want to start something we can't finish. I don't want you hurt. I don't want it all to end in tears and desperate phone calls.'

She takes her hands away. 'Why did you keep coming here, then?' she says sharply. 'You just wanted to talk about . . .' She moves her head from side to side, casting around for some suitably ludicrous subject of conversation to impute to me. I can't think what she's going to hit on. The plasticity of Giordano's forms? The chiaroscuro? '. . . about *normalism* or something?'

Oh, normalism. I don't even think of correcting her and Erwinning the Panofsky. I've got beyond that stage, at any rate. And yes, I think wistfully, I *shouldn't* mind a bit of a chat about normalism, or even nominalism, for that matter. I suddenly feel a great nostalgia for it.

I can't help noticing, though, that she's remembered the term, or half-remembered it, from that very first conversation of ours. I made an impression on her from the first moment. I knew I had. Her mockery was a sign of interest. I knew it was.

And now she looks so mortified! I lean forwards and gently kiss her mouth. She doesn't look at me, just gives a little rueful laugh. I give her another gentle kiss, then sit back and inspect the result. She manages only a bit of a smile this time, and goes on looking down. I kiss her again, then sit back and look at her again. Give her another kiss, take another look.

I do it about nine times, I think.

Gradually she lifts her eyes to mine, and a smile spreads all the way across her face.

'You are a frightful little wet fish, you know,' she says tenderly.

'Am I?' I say, and kiss her again.

I kiss her at some length, and it comes to me that if I simply let events take their course, in half an hour or so from now I could be examining the picture on the dressing table at my leisure, with a cup of coffee in my hand and a serene mind, and that if I still hadn't looked my fill I could come back and examine it again more or less as often as I wanted.

And, really, now that the first shock has passed, now that we've both had time to recover from our mutual surprise and confusion, and to make clear to each other, even if only by silent implication, exactly where we stand and how we view the matter, wouldn't it simply be the easiest and most natural and least hurtful way out of the situation? The quickest way back to normalism and nominalism alike?

It plainly would, because already she's sinking back beneath me into the tangled duvet, and pulling a cold hot water bottle out from behind her. And I'm somehow following her down, and starting to unbutton Tony Churt's spare shirt . . . then becoming aware that some other foreign body – like a cold hot water bottle, only disconcertingly moister – is becoming improbably wedged in my crotch. I reach behind me to get rid of it, and it sneezes and licks my fingers.

'Wait,' I say.

'*Now* what?'

I get up and escort the dogs out of the room. I take them all the way to the head of the stairs, and put a friendly boot up their backsides by way of returning the compliment. They go thundering and tumbling away down the stairs at gratifying speed, barking with insane indignation.

'Yes, well, that'll teach you to go shoving your snout into places uninvited,' I shout after them.

'I'm so sorry,' one of them shouts back over the noise.

My heart stops. The world stops. *What?*

'The door was open . . .' it shouts. 'Down, boy, down . . .! I'm sorry, I thought . . . Get down, get away from me . . .! Mr Churt? Is that you . . .? Would you, could you . . .? Mr Churt!'

The voice is becoming as desperate as the barking. I take a hold of myself and go back to the bedroom. Laura's standing looking out of the window. She's put her shoes on again.

'We left the front door open,' I explain.

'Not the little rector man?' she asks. 'There's a bicycle outside.'

'Oh dear. I'm afraid I told him to shove his snout elsewhere. I'm sorry.'

She glances at herself in the mirror, then goes quickly out of the room without looking at me.

I listen through the crack of the door as Laura shouts at the dogs, and the barking gradually subsides. Then I close the door and go and look at the picture. At last I'm completely on my own with it. But I can take in even less of it than I could before. All I can think is the *rector*? My embarrassing amours have been nipped in the bud by the local clergyman? This is the most shameful touch yet.

I go back to the door. There's a murmur of voices from below. I go back to the picture. All I can see is the absurdity of the couple who have been caught for all eternity on the point of that glutinous kiss. I yearn to be more like the man diving so cleanly into the chill waters of the millpool . . .

I listen at the door. Silence. I go back to the picture, and look at the bottom right-hand corner, where it ought to say, in neat Roman capitals, *BRVEGEL MDLXV* . . . Yes, there's an ill-defined, somehow anomalous black patch, that perhaps doesn't look quite part of the landscape, and perhaps doesn't have quite the same surface texture as the varnish. I rub my thumb over it. It doesn't affect the patch, but it leaves a slight grubbiness on my thumb. Dirt, then? Possibly. Ink, as Kate suggested?

Door. Voices again.

Picture. The swimming party, I see, isn't a swimming party. The man who's diving into the millpool is fully dressed. In fact I don't think he's diving at all – he's simply tumbling in head first, presumably drunk, while the people around him reach out to save him. My healthy sporting citizen has been caught in as embarrassing a posture as all the rest of us. Well, at least it solves the iconographic problem of swimming in spring.

Door. Silence from below.

And I do a bunk. I could get out my magnifier and study the details while Laura gets rid of the clergy, then put it away and try to resume where we left off. I could at least get out my tape measure and measure the thing. But I don't even do that. I just want to get out of the house.

Look, the picture's a Bruegel, there's not a shadow of a doubt in my mind now I've seen it again, if ever there was. Kate's wrong; I'm right. I haven't forgotten that I'm going to make out some kind of objective case for its identification before I go ahead – but I have to balance that against the chance to extract myself while I still can from the nightmare of dishonour and misery that I was just about to plunge into with Laura.

I'm not going to emerge from this story with any great credit, I can see that. But I *am* going to emerge a great deal richer and more famous. Even if I do have to pay gains tax, which I must admit I hadn't known about until Tony mentioned it. Gains tax? I'll be glad to pay it! The more gains tax I pay the less bad I shall feel. As soon as I've some gains to pay it on.

So, I take one last look at my prize, then pad softly down the stairs. Laura's presumably taken the rector into the kitchen for a glass of gin. What I'm going to say if he suddenly emerges I haven't really worked out. Nothing, probably. Firm handshake, a clear, straight look into his eyes – no explanation called for or offered. In any case he doesn't emerge. I slip my feet quietly back into my muddy boots, and disappear quietly through the still open front door.

Normalism, at last. It seems a little excessively normalistic, though, to walk straight down the drive; I'm not quite sure what you can see from the kitchen window. More agreeable, anyway, to go home through the woods, the way I came. I set out, keeping close to the unused wing of the house. As I pass the last mullioned window a little spurt of flame on the other side of the glass makes me jump out of my wits. There's some mysterious presence haunting the house!

Laura, I realize as I turn to look, lighting a cigarette. And beyond her, on the other side of the breakfast-room, the gleaming backs of two projecting ears. It's the little rector man, sunk in a reverent genuflection in front of *The Rape of Helen*.

Tilda's lying on the picnic rug in front of the cottage, waving her little woollen arms and legs about in the soft spring air with uncoordinated delight, bubbling merrily at the mouth like a newly poured glass of champagne. I snatch her up and keep the effervescence going by running her three times round the outside of the cottage. Kate, sitting with her book on the broken kitchen chair by the maple stump, looks up thoughtfully each time I pass but makes no comment.

I'm propelled and energized by the sheer joy of being with my little bubbling daughter. I've often felt a spontaneous surge of delight at coming home and seeing her, but I've never thought of running wildly around with her in my arms before, and it occurs to me that I'm perhaps behaving just a touch *normalistically*. Normalism, I realize, now that the term's been introduced into the discourse, is an important concept. It's the art and science of behaving normally. A difficult thing to do, perhaps, at any time, and particularly difficult – and particularly important – if your life's become in some way abnormal, as for instance in the midst of a complex commercial transaction where different forms of confidence have to be maintained simultaneously with parties whose interests are mutually antagonistic. It involves skill not only in performance, but in observing and remembering what normal behaviour's actually like.

My glimpses of the expression on Kate's face as I pass suggest that I may have misremembered slightly. I may be over-normalizing. Though why I should be normalizing at all just at the moment I've no idea, since I've actually resisted all the temptations to abnormality that were put in my way by other parties to this particular deal. I stop running round, and plump down breathlessly on the rug. Tilda gazes at the sky over my shoulder. To her the sky is evidently at least as surprising as her father's behaviour.

'So did you see it?' asks Kate.

'Yes! I did!' A triumphant tone. Reasonable enough; I set out to see the picture – I saw it. If she asks me *where* I saw it I'll of course tell her. And since Tony's in London he wasn't here, so there's no reason for Kate to jump to the conclusion that he wasn't at Upwood. All the same, if she asks me who was there . . . I'll tell her that as well. Probably.

But she doesn't. She doesn't ask any more questions at all. There's something a little unnatural about this restraint. Should I disingenuously burst out with my renewed certainty about the attribution? Would that be normal? Or would it be over-normal? It might be safer to stick to aspects where I've come to agree with her assessment.

'You're right about the patch in the corner,' I say. 'Some of it came off on my thumb. It might just possibly be covering up a signature.'

No comment. Some kind of trouble's brewing, certainly. But what? I wonder whether to try to amuse her with my bizarre last glimpse of the rector bowing the knee to *Helen*, but I realize that it would involve explaining a lot of circumstantial detail. As would any attempt to communicate the even more comic image that keeps coming into my mind of the rector being taken upstairs to admire the rest of the art collection . . .

I decide to persist with stressing the convergence of our observations.

'I also agree about the absence of any religious symbolism. Not a trace, so far as I could see. Though of course I only had time for a fairly cursory examination.'

No comment on this, either. Though I suppose the lack of comment is comment enough. What I believe she may be ironically remarking upon, when I think about it, is the exacting scholarly standards I must have set myself if I regard an examination lasting the entire morning as only fairly cursory. I should perhaps explain that I spent a large part of the time concealed behind a tree, waiting for Tony to return, and then another longish period carrying bulk supplies of groceries into the house. And that most of what little time still remained went on tactfully coping with the Churts' personal problems, not to mention dealing with their dogs. So that out of the entire time I was away I doubt if I managed to spend more than two or three minutes in front of the picture.

But on second thoughts I say nothing. I feel a growing indignation, though, at the unfairness of Kate's unspoken suspicions, and of the tangled circumstantiality of the truth that makes them so impossible to answer. For several long minutes we sit in silence, apart from various little gurglings and burblings from Tilda as I jig her up and down on my shoulder.

'What I suspect', says Kate suddenly, and at once I freeze, 'is that you think Bruegel was some kind of Netherlandish freedom fighter.'

I still can't speak. But now it's because I'm too astonished. Is this what all that silence was about?

'No?' she says. 'You were asking me about the Latin in the *Calumny*. You think that's supposed to be Bruegel himself being hauled in front of the Inquisition? A lot of people have tried to read some kind of political content into the pictures. *The Massacre of the Innocents* is about Spanish atrocities, etcetera. Actually there weren't any Spanish troops in the Netherlands at the time. They were all withdrawn in 1561 – they didn't come back until 1567.'

I'm still too taken aback by this outburst to offer any reply. Also, I'm beginning to realize that this is how she's spent the morning – looking through my books and files.

'I've been rereading your Motley,' she says. 'I haven't looked at it since I was about nineteen. I'd forgotten what a blatantly one-sided account it was. There were plenty of horrors committed by the Protestants, you know. Particularly the Calvinists. Not even Motley can gloss over the image breaking in 1566. In the cathedral in Antwerp the mob destroyed everything. All the pictures, all the statues.'

I know, I know. But on she sweeps, becoming more and more agitated. It's worse than her great spasm of anxiety about the money. Now all her banked-down resentment has been transferred to a cause in which she can feel the most selfless indignation. Her voice hurries and shakes.

'Every beautiful thing that had been so lovingly and painstakingly made over the centuries. And not just in Antwerp – in hundreds of churches across the Netherlands. No one knows how much was lost. Whole lifetimes of devotion thrown away in two days and nights of barbarism.'

Yes – all that raw material for iconographic studies! Also, she was brought up as a Catholic. In her anger and distress she's reverting to a long-forgotten tribal loyalty.

'I know,' I say, 'it was loathsome. Though of course the Catholics did a lot of image breaking of their own. When Alva's troops sacked Malines, for example. They systematically desecrated all the churches. And that wasn't the mob – it was sanctioned by Alva. He didn't even have any ideological pretext. It was the Catholic commander unleashing

Catholic troops on what Catholics held sacred, simply to make up their arrears of pay.'

Perfectly true – but what am I saying it for? Am *I* reverting to old tribal loyalties? Our attempts to dress our obscure personal squabble up as a great historical debate are very silly. And there's more to come.

'In any case,' I say, rocking Tilda tenderly back and forth, 'however terrible it is to destroy works of art, it isn't as terrible as torturing people to death.'

'Isn't it?' she says coolly. 'Though the Calvinists did plenty of that, too, in the areas they controlled.'

I ignore the irrelevant provocation, and swoop like a hawk on those first two shocking words. 'Are you suggesting that destroying pictures and statues might be worse than destroying people?'

'Of course not,' she should reply, if she had any sense. But she doesn't. She allows herself to be manoeuvred into a position far more extreme than she intended, as people do when they're angry. 'Isn't it?' she repeats. 'Isn't what people do more important in the end than what they feel? Isn't what they leave behind more important than what they were?'

This is art history grown monstrous in its self-importance. I drive home the implications of what she's said with complete ruthlessness. 'You're implying that a painting might be worth more than *us*? Than you and me?'

She thinks. She's become very quiet and still. It occurs to me that she's perhaps not just allowing herself to be manoeuvred – that she really does think that she means what she's saying. I have a glimpse into the depths of her, into the quiet darknesses that usually remain hidden. And yes, she has some kind of hard obstinacy lurking down there. Some element of fanaticism, even, that I lack completely. And without which, I realize with dismay, even in the midst of my merciless pursuit of her, human beings never leave anything much behind them anyway.

'More than me, yes,' she says finally. She *does* mean it, too. I should take her hands in mine, of course, and smile at her tenderly, and tell how much more she is to *me*, at any rate, than any painting in the world could ever be. But I don't. I've not finished with her yet.

'More than *me*?' I ask her quietly.

She thinks once more. 'Possibly,' she says slowly at last. OK. Fine. This is damage I can take, because she still hasn't seen the ambush I'm leading her into. I don't even say the words. I simply kiss the top of Tilda's head, very gently, as she lies against my shoulder, and then look up at Kate with the question in my eyes.

And again she thinks. She seems to change in front of my eyes. She looks away, and all that hardness in her is transmuted into a kind of terrible sadness.

I break. I shouldn't have done this to her. I repent unreservedly. I love her. I feel the most wrenching tenderness towards her.

She gets up and gently takes Tilda from me. I as gently let her go. Kate carries her towards the front door, then comes back.

'There seems to be at any rate one picture in the world', she says quietly, 'that *you* think is worth more than either me or Tilda.'

She turns and disappears into the house. I remain sitting on the picnic rug, unable to move, like someone who's been knocked down in the street. That happened to me once. The first difficulty afterwards is to discover whether you're alive or dead. The second is to make some estimate of who you are, and how it feels to be that person. The third is to work out how it's come about that you're in this unusual situation, lying down in the middle of the road.

The first coherent feeling that I manage to identify now is mortification, and the first coherent thought is this: Not I her – she me. It was *she* who was manoeuvring *me* into position for the kill. No, worse still: she who was letting me manoeuvre myself.

I can remember having some very similar feeling, and thinking some very similar thought, in another context recently, though I can't remember what the context was. I'm losing my sovereignty all round. I'm becoming a mere object.

And then I'm overcome once again by the sheer unfairness of it. To pretend that she was holding some kind of serious discussion about religious rights and wrongs in the sixteenth-century Netherlands, when all the time she was simply waiting to air a supposed grievance, of crude vulgarity, about my faithfulness! And for me to find myself lying here in the road like this when I was obeying every law that a pedestrian should! To be half dead when what felled me wasn't even some serious vehicle like a bus or a truck – when it was a bicycle, a skateboard, a child on a scooter – when it was a mere notion so completely false and frivolous!

And finally: how in heaven's name did this accident ever happen? *Why* has she jumped, as I must assume she has, to the grotesque conclusion that I was alone with Laura all morning, when I *wasn't*? So far as *she* knows! When I was with Laura and Tony together? Not even that – with Tony on his own? When I didn't so much as set eyes on Laura? For all that I or anyone else has said! Why should Laura come into the story at all? Why should Kate think she did? It's a pure, blind leap in the dark, made on no rational basis whatsoever, that betrays a lack of confidence in me which nothing I've ever done can justify.

Eventually I pick myself up, as I did after I was knocked

down by that car in Kentish Town High Street, and go on my way as best I can. I walk into the kitchen, where Kate's washing a bowlful of Tilda's clothes. I'm going to normalize once again, since I can't think of anything better. My plan, in so far as I have one, is to make no reference to the conversation we've just had, or to the reckless insinuation it culminated in, but to let fall in passing one or two remarks which suggest, without any actual misstatement, how ridiculous is her idea that I wasn't talking to Tony this morning.

'I'd better saw some more firewood,' I say, as if nothing had happened.

'Don't you want any lunch?' she says, likewise. She's normalizing, too. I think. 'We've had ours.'

Overtones there still, of course, but I ignore them. 'I'll make myself a sandwich later.' I look in the cupboard under the sink at her feet for the saw. 'Tony's still on about that scramble track, by the way.'

Not bad. Pretty casual, pretty off the back of the hand. And probably true. Also, the indignation that Kate and I share on the subject makes it a powerful bond between us to appeal to.

But it's not the scramble track that catches Kate's attention. 'Oh, yes, I meant to tell you,' she says. 'He phoned this morning. He's up in London.'

She does it perfectly, I have to say. Much better than me. With exactly the right suggestion of apology for not remembering earlier. I've underestimated her.

I pick myself up from the roadway once again as best I can. I don't attempt to explain anything. I simply ask, with passing curiosity in my voice – even if I have to keep my head in the cupboard under the sink to hide my face – 'What did he want?'

'He couldn't remember the name on the label,' she says.

– 261 –

For a moment I go on trying to pull the saw out from the muddle of old string and wire it's become entangled in. Then I slowly take my head out of the cupboard and gaze at her.

'Vrancz,' she says. 'He was on his way to a library to look something up.'

On his way to a library? To look something up? About Vrancz? About my picture? In London?

I think my mouth's open, but no more words emerge from it. She glances up at me.

'He's obviously starting to take a personal interest,' she says. 'I'm sorry.'

I take the saw and escape into the garden. To be run over once may be regarded as a misfortune; to be run over twice in the same day looks like carelessness. To be run over *three* times, as I've been, suggests an attempt at murder.

I gaze unseeingly at the scavenged fragments of tree waiting to be sawn. I haven't the faintest idea what to do next. Not that it matters. The next thing happens of its own accord, like everything else today, without any assistance from me.

A man on a bicycle teeters round the bend in the track. He has a red face and ears like jug handles. The face is new to me; the ears are familiar. He's not wearing his dog collar, but the ears are the ones I saw from behind, lowered reverentially before *Helen*.

He sets one foot to the ground and stops. 'You're Martin,' he says.

The rector's never appeared in our lives before. I can only assume that Laura's confessed everything to him, and that he's come round to remind me of my duties as a husband and father. I could deny my identity, I suppose, but I merely nod, and wait helplessly for the pastoral care to commence.

Confidential counselling, however, is evidently not what he has in mind; it's family therapy – shock treatment – the full and frank confrontation. 'Is your wife in?' he says.

Again I could say no. But I've given up the fight. I simply indicate the cottage. Let him tell her the whole story in every unfortunate detail, exactly as Laura's confessed it to him.

He gets off his bicycle and shakes my hand. 'I'm John Quiss,' he says. 'One of Kate's colleagues at the Hamlish.'

'Delectable,' says John Quiss, as he examines Tilda. 'Such delicate flesh tones. The moulding of the cheeks is particularly fine.'

He sits himself down at the kitchen table. So Laura was wrong, and it's not some harmless local clergyman that I saw worshipping her pictures. It's the deadly John Quiss, the art hisorian who knows everything.

I make some coffee. I think it's coffee I'm making – it may be an infusion of rat poison – I can't really see what I'm doing. The calm resignation I achieved when the horror in prospect seemed to be marriage counselling has been replaced by the most intolerable anxiety yet. Did he see the *Merrymakers*?

I try to keep a grasp on plausibility. It's really not possible. She can't have taken him upstairs! Or can she?

'We've been meaning to ask you over ever since we came down,' says Kate.

'I know – I couldn't wait any longer! I adore seeing the insides of other people's houses.'

He glances round the homely confusion of the kitchen with carefully imprecise benevolence. 'Lovely things,' he says. 'But I think the most important piece is your beautiful little daughter. I have to confess I really came over to look at your neighbour's house. I gather I have *you* to thank for that. Mr Churt rang and said you'd been kind enough to mention my name.'

Of course. It was Kate who put Tony on to him. It's the most monstrous betrayal she could have committed. It makes her imaginary grievance against me even more outrageous. But did he see the *Merrymakers*?

'I'm so sorry,' says Kate, without so much as a glance at me. 'I don't know how he got hold of you – I simply mentioned your name. I didn't mean him to go badgering you.'

'No need to apologize!' he cries. 'I know most of us hate being asked to tell people how much their ghastly heirlooms are worth. But I adore it! I always spring into the saddle and pedal off with the utmost alacrity – it's such a chance to peek and pry! Anyway, there's always the hope you might find something lovely.'

And has he? He might simply have asked to use the bathroom, it occurs to me, then taken off on his own tour of inspection . . .

'I assume you've been in and done your stuff already,' he says to Kate.

'*We* had to go to dinner,' she says ruefully.

'Oh, you poor loves!' he cries. 'Peeking's one thing – eating's another. I always decline the honour. Simply hop on my bike and drop in. So you sat there all night with those dreadful people – and all an utter waste of time, because of course he didn't trust you. They never know *who* to trust, people like that! So they end up advertising their wares to every shark in the business.'

Whether he humorously means to include himself among the predators I'm not sure. But has he seen it?

'Anyway,' he says to Kate, 'what did you make of it all?'

He speaks as lightly as before, but now I detect a shadow of seriousness, even anxiety, in his voice. He wants to know Kate's assessment almost as much as I want to know his. This is why he's come here. It's not a

social visit. He thinks he's on to something. He's desperate to make sure that no one else is.

'I didn't really look at anything,' says Kate. 'I'm no good
at these games. Martin was quite interested, though.'

Quiss turns to me, surprised. I think he'd forgotten that
this silent figure fussing with the coffee pot was a part of
the household.

'I didn't know you were one of us,' he says. 'I thought
you were something respectable. A philosopher or a book-
maker or whatever.'

I shrug. 'Slight amateur interest.'

'Oh, my God,' he says, 'that's what really puts the wind
up the pros – the thought of some amateur pipping them to
the post.'

I smile politely. He's seen *something*, I'm sure of that now.

'So what do you make of the mighty Giordano?' he asks.
'Why is it bulging about in the breakfast-room like that?
The poor love looks as if she's being crucified. Is it on the
HP? Are they hiding it from the repo man?'

From creditors of some sort – yes, very possibly, now I
come to think about it.

'I'm not a great fan myself,' says Quiss. '*Fa Presto*, by all
means – *fa* as *presto* as possible. But he always seems more
like *Fra Pesto* to me. Forty different kinds of pasta, but the
same jar of Marks and Spencer's sauce poured over all of it.
What about the other bits and pieces, though? Anything of
interest there, do you think?'

The other bits and pieces – this is what he wants to know
about. 'No idea,' I say.

'Not making any offers yourself, then?' he persists.

I smile, and shake my head.

'Well . . .' says Kate, frowning.

It's not my dishonesty that's going to finish us – it's her

honesty. Quiss looks at her, then at me, waiting for us to agree on our story.

'I said I'd look around,' I say finally. 'See if I could find anyone interested.'

'And have you?' His curiosity is getting slightly beyond polite limits.

I hand him his coffee, and smile.

'I see,' he says. He glances at Kate, then back at me. 'What, someone in the Bahamas? Some little tax dodge?'

Kate looks at me as well. The idea hadn't occurred to her before, any more than it had to me before Laura mentioned it.

'Not anyone in the Bahamas,' I smile. But what I'm thinking is: did it occur to *him* so readily because this is what *he's* proposing?

'So which one are you trying to shift?' he asks. 'The Pesto?'

'Milk?' I ask.

'Thank you. Or one of the others?'

All pretence of polite conversation has broken down. I feel licensed to respond in kind. 'Which one are *you* proposing to shift?' I ask rudely.

For a moment he gazes straight at me, trying to decide how seriously to take me. Then he smiles. 'How flattering,' he says. 'I'm afraid I'm merely a humble woodsman in the groves of academe.'

He sips his coffee for a moment, then abandons me and turns back to Kate.

'Not some great bosom pal of yours, is he, Mr Churt?' he asks Kate. 'No, of course not. Heartbreaking, that house, you know. I believe they had several really rather good pieces at one time. All gone to feed the pheasants. Fool of a man, by all accounts. Not that I've actually met him. Only the chatelaine in residence when I called.'

He laughs. 'I don't know what to make of her,' he says. 'Rather a . . . what shall I say . . .? Rather a juicy little number, isn't she?'

Kate smiles tautly, and doesn't look at me. 'Is she?' she says.

He laughs again. 'Actually she wasn't entirely on her own. Some gentleman upstairs when I arrived. Certain amount of excitement and shouting going on up there.'

Kate gives another of her dreadful little smiles.

'It was probably just the plumber,' says Quiss. 'Working himself up over the plumbing. I must keep my somewhat rococo imagination under control. Though when the good lady eventually came downstairs I couldn't help feeling she seemed a trifle *distraite*.'

He looks at me. I smile in my turn. I assume he's not suggesting that there was anything familiar about the voice. In my anxiety about Quiss's artistic discoveries I'd forgotten about my ill-timed suggestion to the dogs. Something to do with shoving their snouts elsewhere, I recall. It was a more apposite suggestion than I realized at the time. I feel like offering it again. In the end, though, Tilda wordlessly makes much the same proposal herself. Quiss sniffs and then delicately coughs. 'I think I'd better change her,' says Kate.

After he's gone a silence settles over the cottage. Kate and I both have a lot to think about.

Halfway through the afternoon she speaks. 'So it's in the bedroom now?' she asks politely.

No reply seems to be necessary. Around teatime, though, I initiate a short conversation.

'It's the picture I'm after,' I explain. 'Not her.'

'So I assume,' she replies, as politely as before. 'But maybe they come as a pair.'

As we sit at dinner she tries again. 'You'd better go back

tomorrow', she says helpfully, 'and find out how far John got with them both.'

I think about this for some time. 'Thank you,' I say finally.

'No – I just want to get the whole thing over as soon as possible.'

Actually, it's not the thought of his having seen it and recognized it that's preoccupying me by this time. It's an even more disturbing possibility: that he's seen it and *not* recognized it.

The Land-Rover's in the yard at Upwood next morning, but once again it's Laura who opens the door to me.

She smiles helplessly; she's undisguisably happy to see me – and I, of course, am helplessly pleased by her helpless pleasure. 'He's in the breakfast-room,' she says quietly. All the way up through the woods I've been planning the kiss to greet her with, trying to design something that will strike the exact balance of closer acquaintance and continuing emotional distance, but before I can execute the graceful compromise I've settled for she's glanced over her shoulder, then pulled the door to behind her, stretched up and kissed *me*. It's very swift and light, but it's on my lips instead of on her left cheek, and it's not at all what I had in mind.

Disconcerting as this is, it's a relatively minor setback. What I've also been planning, more importantly, is how to find out if Quiss saw the *Merrymakers*, but without suggesting any misleading curiosity about the degree of intimacy he achieved with her, or any pressing interest in the picture itself. What I'm going to do is this: I'm going to ask what he thought about the dog picture on the stairs. If he didn't get as far as that, he plainly never reached the bedroom.

'Listen,' I begin at once, before any interruption or distraction can occur. But she puts her finger to my lips, as she did before. 'Don't say anything,' she says, keeping her voice down. 'It was all my fault. I'm feeling horribly ashamed of myself.'

I'm lost. I don't know what's happening. My carefully planned speech has become undeliverable after the first word.

'Yesterday,' she explains softly. 'Springing on you like that. As soon as I saw the look on your face, I realized – I'd fucked it up once again. So stupid! It's just that . . . I didn't know what else to do! People round here – well, they *expect* it. That's how they pass the time when there's no shooting . . . Oh, my God, now you're looking all shocked and disapproving again. *You're* not like that – I know, I know. Obviously. One look at you and I should have realized. I suppose I thought, well, *intellectuals* – everyone knows what they get up to. Just shows how ignorant I am. Playing way out of my league, that's the trouble.'

She smiles ruefully.

'Please!' I babble, and I think what a fool I made of myself yesterday, what a chance I threw away. 'For heaven's sake! Entirely my fault! I'm sorry! Let's just forget about it! Listen . . .'

She closes my lips again. Not with her finger this time, but with another quick kiss.

'And you were so sweet about it!' she says. 'Only now you're going to think that's what I'm like, and I'm *not*, as a matter of fact, I'm absolutely *not*. I really would like to . . . well, just be *ordinary* together. Just talk about things. Anything. Pictures. I really would like to know about pictures! And your work, your normalism thing. Everything. I mean, I understand about Kate, and so on. I don't want to cause any trouble. I'd just like to be friends.'

Friends, yes. Why not? A few simple but enjoyable tutorials on art and philosophy, pretty much as I'd imagined to myself that first evening. What do I feel about this sudden access of moderation? Relief, I suppose. Also a simultaneous stab of disappointment. Plus a suspicion that I'm being some-how made use of in her ongoing private war against Tony. That once again it's not *I her*, as I'd supposed, but *she me* – that it's yet another of the nightmare shifts from nominative to accusative that are undermining my position in the world.

One other thing I certainly feel: an almost overwhelming sense of her physical proximity. She's wearing one of her oversized sweaters again. Dark blue, this time, and made of some very soft wool. She's so close to me that I have the warmth of it on me. We're standing there in the porch, with the wind rippling the water in the puddle behind me, and the front door pulled to behind her, and her grey-faced, razor-nicked husband presumably somewhere not far behind the door, and all I can think of is the softness and warmth and abundance of her.

Well, this is *almost* all I can think of. I make a great effort to concentrate on the other topic of the day.

'Listen,' I say, but under the pressure of events the care-fully planned casual legato I had in mind has somehow become abrupt and staccato. 'The dog. On the stairs. The picture. That man. Did he see it?'

'What, yesterday?' she says, puzzled. 'That little art per-son?'

'What did he say? Did he say anything? About the dog? On the stairs?'

She frowns. 'It's the *dog* you're interested in, is it? I *thought* you seemed rather taken with it.'

'No, no. I just wondered. Did he see it? The dog?'

She suddenly laughs. 'Or do you mean did I take him upstairs as a substitute for you?'

'No, no . . .'

'You're worried about that little man with the ears?' she asks incredulously.

'Of course not. I just wondered . . . if he said anything. About the dog.'

She gazes at me, smiling rapturously. I'm evidently jealous. I'm even jealous of a little man with ears the size of rhubarb leaves who's patently never so much as cast an unchaste look at a woman in his life. April for her has suddenly turned to May. 'What about the one in the bedroom?' she says. 'Don't you want to know what he said about *that*?'

I laugh. I can't think of any other answer. No, as a matter of fact I can. I stop laughing.

'Yes,' I say. 'What *did* he say about it?'

Now it's her turn to laugh. She presses her index finger against the tip of my nose. 'I'm not going to tell you,' she says.

There's a huge snuffling and snorting around my knees, a massive wetness of muzzle and thrashing of tail. The front door's open behind her, and Tony Churt's standing on the threshold.

I start back. *He* starts back. What *I'm* trying to do is to get my nose away from Laura's finger. What *he's* trying to do is to conceal something behind his back. It leaps out of his hands, though, describes a yellow curve through the air, then comes slithering across the porch to my feet.

'Martin knows all about your other art person coming here,' says Laura calmly, as Tony joins the dogmass scrabbling around my feet. She's addressing him, but keeping her eyes on me, and still helplessly smiling. 'He's terribly jealous.'

'Second opinion,' says Tony, as the yellow object escapes him again. 'I always get a second opinion.'

He stands up. He's balancing a wet bar of yellow soap on the bristles of an upturned nail brush.

'Don't worry,' he says, 'it's her Crabtree & Evelyn. I

thought I might just have a little go with it. If it's safe enough for her to soap her tits with, then it's not going to eat through paintwork.'

'I thought some great expert told you not to touch the thing?' says Laura. 'Why do you waste people's time asking for their advice if you're not going to take it?' She turns to me. 'He's getting obsessed with that picture. He still thinks it's a Rembrandt or a van Dyck or something.'

'Well, it's certainly not what it says on the label,' says Tony. 'I've ploughed through the complete works of your friend Mr Vrancz, and even I can see it's nothing like him. A little splash of soap and water, and I think it may turn out to be a . . . you know . . .'

I wait with sinking heart.

'Who do I mean?' he demands.

Nothing in the code of practice I've agreed with myself says that I have to read his unarticulated thoughts for him. I wonder whether to suggest one of the Valckenborch brothers, or Mompers, attributions which are just about imaginable. But Tony's never heard of Mompers or the Valckenborches. There's only one remotely plausible author of this work whose name he *has* heard of, and even if I don't say it he's just about to.

He gazes frowning into the distance, and at last the word forms itself on his lips. 'Fuck,' he says.

I'm so relieved that it's not the name I was expecting that for a moment I'm ready to endorse the attribution. Then the dogs rush barking off into the distance and I realize that he's gazing at something behind my back. I turn to look. Another four-wheel-drive is bumping over the potholes towards us. A much larger, cleaner, more modern and streamlined one than Tony's.

'Fuck,' says Tony to himself again. 'Oh, *fuck*!'

Out of the car, bizarrely, climbs Tony Churt. A much larger, cleaner, more modern and streamlined Tony Churt than Tony Churt himself. Not painted in yellowy-brown ochres, like the old Tony Churt, but in a discreet dark blue that matches the new four-wheel-drive. Dark blue blazer, well filled with flesh. Dark blue vertical stripes on the shirt clashing impressively with the light blue diagonal stripes on the dark blue regimental tie. A study in exotic indigo and expensive ultramarine. And above the shirt, where the old Tony Churt has tried to set off the overall brown of his colour scheme with a face of azurite blue-grey, this new Tony Churt achieves the contrast no less inappropriately with a face pigmented in red lead, or the dark exudations of Oriental lac insects. It's curious; if they'd swapped heads they'd each have achieved a considerably more harmonious effect.

The dogs have gone mad with simultaneous recognition and non-recognition. 'Shut up, you fools,' says their alternative master, lifting his arm at them, and they cower away from him, beating their tails on the ground and growling. He turns to the original Tony.

'I've just been going through the contents of Mummy's house,' he says.

'I thought you were in South Africa,' says the original.

'Well, you were wrong. Once again. I just want the answer to one simple question: where is it?'

'Where's what?'

'Come on, let's not fart around.'

Pause. The fresh Tony Churt takes a long look at the house and grounds. 'My God,' he says, 'you've let this place go in the last twenty years.'

The final item of the property that his inspection falls on is the old Tony Churt himself, parked in front of the porch as immovable as a piece of mouldering brown sculpture, and still holding the nail brush and soap.

'Are we going to stand out here and catch cold?' says new Tony.

'All *you've* done in the last twenty years, so far as I can see,' says old Tony, 'is get high blood-pressure.'

'Or do you want me to come back with a writ and a tipstaff?' says new.

Reluctantly, old Tony moves to one side. And into the house marches new Tony. He gives no sign of noticing my existence, but he nods at Laura as he passes. 'You're the new wife, are you?' he says. 'The one with the money?'

He laughs. Perhaps he's making an effort to break the ice.

New blue Tony goes straight to the foot of the stairs and gazes up at the landing, where *Helen* once hung. Old brown Tony watches him. So do Laura and I and the dogs.

'No, of course not,' he says. 'You wouldn't have the nerve. You knew I'd be coming sooner or later.'

'If I'd ever got my hands on the bloody thing,' says brown Tony, 'it wouldn't be here. I'd have sold it.'

'No, you wouldn't. You wouldn't have the nerve for that, either. I assume it's not in the sitting-room . . .'

He marches on into the depths of the house. 'I know you've got it here somewhere,' he calls back over his shoulder. 'Mummy got rid of it!' calls brown Tony, following him. 'Ages ago! I thought she'd told you . . .'

The soap escapes from him as he departs, and goes skating away across the flagstones.

'What happens when he tries the breakfast-room and finds it's locked?' says Laura quietly to me. 'I *told* Tony it was hopeless. He'll just break the door down . . . Oh, my God, you *do* look sick.'

I imagine I do. Because what about *my* picture? He's going to find *that*! And seize it as well! It's going to walk out of the house in front of my eyes!

'I'm so sorry,' says Laura. 'I've never been absolutely sure what you're up to, but I realize it all depends on getting rid of *Helen* for him.'

I open my mouth to deny it, too panic-stricken even to be

taken aback by her percipience. But all I manage to babble is: 'The other one, the other one!'

Laura frowns. 'What other one? Which other one?'

'The one upstairs!' And there we are – I've told her. She knows the whole story now. I've made her my accomplice. Or else delivered myself into her hands.

I see from the look on her face that she'd guessed it all, anyway. But the procession of brothers and dogs is coming back.

'I told you!' says brown brother. 'She sold it! Five, ten years ago!'

'Of course she didn't.'

'How do *you* know? You weren't there!'

'Nor were you.'

'Look, matey, I nursed her when she was dying!'

'No, you didn't. You looked in once for half an hour.'

'You don't know what I did!'

'I know more about you than you know about yourself.'

'*You* didn't even look in! You sat on your fat arse in Cape Province guzzling Piesporter, and you couldn't even be bothered to step on to a plane.'

They stand facing each other across the hall like two contrasting images lingering in a pair of funhouse mirrors after the customer's laughed and moved on. I look from one to the other with helpless anguish, unable to think of any way to save the situation. Neither image gives any sign of noticing my presence. I've become entirely irrelevant to the affairs of the Churt family. I turn to Laura, to see if by some miracle she might have come up with an idea, now that I've enrolled her in the enterprise, but she's vanished.

'I'm not leaving till I've got it,' says Blue.

'It's not here!' says Brown.

'I don't believe you.'

'Search the house if you want to.'

Another pause for thought. 'Listen . . .' I say, though I've not the slightest idea what I'm going to ask them to listen to.

'You're a fool to play poker with me, Tony,' says Blue. 'You're not good enough. See you.'

'You want to search the house?'

'From cellar to attics. From gun-room to pigsties. And I know more nooks and crannies here than you've got unpaid bills to put in them.'

'Help yourself. Go where you like.'

'Listen . . .' I begin once again.

This time, for some reason, old brown Tony does. He glances round at me. 'I'll just show poor Mr Clay out before we go any further,' he says. 'You're embarrassing him.' And before I can say anything else, he's ushered me through the front door and pulled it to behind us. 'Quick,' he says. 'This way.'

He sets off past the unused wing of the house, half walking and half running, following the same devious route I took myself when I left the day before. I struggle to keep up. It seems that poor, dim Tony, unlike me, has some kind of plan in mind.

We turn the corner, and hurry along the side of the house, snatched at by bare branches and sucked at by sodden earth. Tony's in worse case than me; he's still in his carpet slippers. We turn another corner to the muddled back parts of the house. He fumbles desperately for his keys, and unlocks a warped and blistering door. 'What's happening?' I ask, as we trail mud along a stone-flagged corridor, though I'm pretty sure I know the answer. Tony says nothing – simply waves at me to keep my voice down, unlocks another door, and pushes me inside.

We're in the breakfast-room, of course. And there's my picture, not upstairs in the bedroom at all, but balanced on two chairs, waiting for the Crabtree & Evelyn. Shimmering leaves – dancers – crags – sea . . . No time to look at it, though, because he's propelling me across to the fireplace, and dragging two more chairs over for us to climb on. Arms straining and chairs wobbling, we release *Helen* from her sagging torment and lower her to the ground. She's at least as heavy as she looks. I wonder once again about the physical plausibility of all those *Depositions*.

He heaves the seaward end towards the door. But what on earth is he intending to do with her? 'Come on!' he says. 'Your end! Up! Lift! What are you waiting for?'

'The other ones!' I cry. 'What about the other ones?'

'Never mind about them. Little tit's forgotten about them.'

'He'll remember them when he sees them!'

Tony hesitates.

'Several thousand pounds going begging there!' I urge.

He flings the window up, and hurls the two small Dutch paintings out of it. They break their way through the twigs of the shrubs outside and vanish. 'Get them later,' he says. He grabs a corner of the *Merrymakers*, and drags it towards the window in its turn. I grab another corner, and try to stop him.

'What?' he demands.

'Damage it,' I say, trying to keep the desperation out of my voice. 'Scratch it.'

'Got to prioritize,' he says.

We struggle awkwardly. It's twenty or thirty pounds of solid oak, with no handholds.

'Too big,' I gasp. And, yes, it must indeed be something like three foot nine high by five foot three long, though once again it's not quite the moment to get my tape measure out of my pocket and check.

'Try it,' he gasps back, heaving it out of my hands. And he's right – it just goes, on the diagonal, scraping paint off the window frame, and vanishing in a confusion of snapping twigs and tearing thorns.

He slams the window down; I try to close my mind.

There's no question of *Helen* leaving the same way – in her frame she stands nearly seven feet off the floor. Tony hoists her seaward end again, I take her landward end. It's an intolerable load – I sympathize even more warmly with Paris's men. The strange equanimity she's preserved for all these years in the face of her abductors' huge efforts to load her on to the boat remains equally undisturbed as she watches us struggle to ease her through the door.

'Don't crash it around like that,' whispers Tony. 'He can't be far away.'

He relocks the breakfast-room. 'Get the little shit's hopes up for a moment,' he says.

What's all this *little* shit and *little* tit? He's vast! I suppose he's the younger brother.

We stumble back along the corridor, and out to the rear of the house, arms racked and backs breaking in the service of art. One of Tony's slippers has vanished, I notice, and the sock's beginning to follow it. We manoeuvre round sheds and outhouses, then Tony dumps his end of *Helen* while he rips open the gate of a muddy trailer. He hurls sacks of pheasant feed out of it. 'In here!' he grunts.

'Won't go!' I grunt back.

'Will go. Done it before.'

'He'll see it.'

'This over it.'

He drags a tangle of black plastic sheeting out of a stinking puddle and pushes it nauseatingly into my hands. I shake off the unidentifiable liquids pocketed in it, cover

Helen's nakedness as best I can, and tie her up in various lengths of pink baler twine I find lying around. When I turn to Tony for help, I find only a single sock of him remaining. At once an engine roars, and the aged Land-Rover reverses in a series of wild zigzags back to the trailer.

'Too big!' I report. 'Gate won't shut!'

'Tie it!'

He finds yet another piece of baler twine in a heap of ordure and throws it to me. I tie the gate half-closed as best I can while he slams the towbar on to the coupling. God knows how far he's intending to drive with it like this.

'Brakes,' he says. 'Bit worn. Give them plenty of welly.'

And I realize he's holding the driver's door open for me. I look at it stupidly. I look at him. 'Buck up!' he says. 'You want him chasing you down the drive?'

'But . . .' I say. 'But . . . where am I going?'

'Where?' he repeats, baffled by my incomprehension. 'How should *I* know? Wherever he is!'

'Wherever *who* is?'

'Your bloody Belgian!'

I get into the car. My own intentions have overtaken me. They've assumed a life of their own – merged with a faster and faster flowing current of events in which I'm being swept along with less and less control over even the actions of my own limbs. My foot's already pushing the clutch down, I notice. My hand's grinding the gear in.

'But your brother,' I say, as Tony slams the door. 'If he goes to court . . .?'

'He won't,' says Tony. 'He can't. Nothing in writing. It was my father's. It's mine.'

'And what about the other ones?' I cry. 'Mr Jongelinck wants *all* of them! I've got to take *all* of them!'

'Later, later! Let's just get *this* bugger off the premises!

He'll be round that corner any second!'

I make one last stand against the floodwaters. My foot remains down on the clutch – the car stays where it is. 'The other ones!' I insist.

'Martin!' says Tony, his eyes suddenly filling with tears. 'I'm begging you! He's always had everything! I've always been cheated out of it all! That little toad has sat on my chest from the moment he was born! It's not just *Helen*! It's the estate! That's what he wants! I have three years tax to pay! I'm going to lose the *estate*! He wants the *estate*!'

I'm aware that this summing up of the case begs a few questions, but what can I do? The tears add the last few cubic centimetres to the torrent snatching at me. I sigh. My hands sketch a gesture of helplessness. My foot thumps up off the clutch. The car thumps forward.

Tony appears hobbling frantically beside the window, banging on the glass, as I struggle to change up into second. 'Tell me what he's offering before you do anything, though . . .! Ring me . . .! And Martin, Martin – cash, remember, cash!'

I thump off the clutch into second, and Tony disappears astern. The unfamiliar tank of a car, with me in nominal command, and *Helen* bouncing madly in the trailer, goes howling out of the yard, past its sleek blue waiting counterpart, and into the cratered moonscape of the drive, pursued so far only by an insanely barking escort desperate for martyrdom beneath its wheels.

What I'm going to do at the end of the drive, whether for instance I'm going to turn left or right, I've no idea. I put my foot on the brake to stop while I consider things, but the car's in no mood for reflection. It continues across the road at a steady twenty miles an hour, and up the muddy green bank opposite, into the great unpathed lands.

What happens in the next few seconds, while the steering wheel spins through my hands and the universe bounces wildly around me, I'm not absolutely sure. I see the advantages of four-wheel drive for off-road motoring, though, because eventually, to my surprise, the world settles down, and there's asphalt beneath us again. It seems that the car's chosen to turn right, possibly because it thinks downhill's the easier option. I try to take stock of the situation. Tony was evidently right about the brakes. Also, the steering wheel and the steering seem to share some of the same difficulties that their master has in forming close relationships. My head and the mirror have come into confusing conflict while we were off in the open countryside, so I can't see what's behind me, but judging by the crashing and clunking *Helen's* still in the trailer and the trailer's still attached to the car.

Where are we all going, though? The car has a plan, I believe, to shake off any possible pursuit by plunging down the hill at great speed. And after that? If there *is* an after that. I get the impression, from the way we're heading, that we're making for London. Sell *Helen*, the car's thinking, then come back with sackloads of cash, and Tony will be only too pleased to get the other three pictures off the premises as well. It may have forgotten that it's Saturday, and that the weekend's probably not a good time to start selling major works of art. Perhaps its plan is that we should lie up in Oswald Road, all four of us, car, trailer,

Helen and me, until the dealers and banks are open on Monday. It's suggesting that I could do with a short break while the great river of time emerges from its headlong plunge through the rapids, and settles back into its more usual placid meanders. It's telling me to normalize a little, to regain control over my destiny.

Fair enough. What it doesn't realize, though, (and how could it?) is that I've undertaken to Kate not to do what I'm now doing until I've made finally certain of the identity of the *Merrymakers*. I've forgotten this myself, I have to admit, until I see the turning into the track up to our cottage fast approaching. I struggle with brakes and steering to get it into the car's thick head that we have to make a brief detour, so that I can explain to her about the changed circumstances and assure her that I'll complete my studies over the weekend. The car concedes the point only at the last moment, and between us we just manage the turn, up the bank again beyond the track and through the dustbins that I filled that morning.

Kate comes out of the cottage at the sight of the Land-Rover. There's something slightly odd about her manner. She has a polite smile on her face. She's tucked her hands self-deprecatingly into the pockets of her cardigan, and her shoulders are defensively braced. It's her social manner; she's politely ready to be amused, because she thinks I'm Tony Churt. When she sees it's me getting out, her shoulders settle and her smile vanishes. She turns to look at the car instead. Then at the trailer, and the huge black parcel bursting out of it.

'It's *Helen*,' I explain frankly. Her manner's now far from social. 'I know, I know,' I say. 'I can't *tell* you what's been going on up there!'

And as soon as I've said it I realize I'm right – I *can't* tell her what's been going on up there. She's discovered from John Quiss's visit that the sale of *Helen* is a tax-avoidance scheme. What I haven't told her, though, because I didn't know myself, is that the whole enterprise is even more dubious still – that Tony wants me to get rid of her for him because her rightful ownership's in dispute. My new lady friend may very possibly be about to start a second Trojan War. This is why she's outside our cottage, modestly wrapped in black plastic – because she's hot. I don't believe the release of this information at the present moment would be helpful.

'Great ructions!' I sum it all up briefly. 'I can't explain, but I just sensed that it was now or never.'

She says nothing. She simply turns and walks back into the cottage. I follow her.

'I haven't forgotten what I said about being absolutely certain,' I assure the back of her neck. 'I'm almost there, as it happens. Just one or two more things I want to look up – and I can do that between now and Monday.'

Silence. I collect up all my books and files to take with me, so that she can see I'm serious. Then I realize that as I take things off one end of the table she's laying things out at the other. Lunch things. For two.

I obviously haven't made completely clear to her the plans that the Land-Rover developed on the way down here. Difficult to do, because I can't give a proper account of the reasoning behind them – that at any moment another four-wheel-drive is somehow going to sniff out our hiding place and come screaming up the track after us.

Not easy, either, to explain that if I'm going to eat the rest of the weekend meals in silence, I'd rather do it on my own. After Monday it'll be different. After I've got back and collected the other pictures. After I've taken the skaters and the cavalrymen to London. After I've got my share of the spoils propped up against the wall there. Then we can start to normalize again.

I carry my things to the front door. She stops half-way between dresser and table, a dinner plate in each hand. 'I'll ring you,' I say. 'Kiss Tildy for me.' She doesn't reply. She simply puts one of the plates on the table, and the other back on the dresser.

This time I persuade the Land-Rover to let me share the driving. It agrees to stop at the end of the track, in the midst of the cans and bottles from the overturned dustbins, and check that there's no avenging angel tearing down the hill before we turn out in an orderly manner in the direction of London. Soon we're swooshing through the last dregs of the lake in the dip by the wood where Kate and I found the dead tramp . . . turning out on to the Lavenage road . . . passing Busy Bee Honey . . . moving on into the country that always seemed so suspiciously unreal to Kate and me before everything else got even more unreal. What we were missing, perhaps, was simply the authentic smell I'm now enjoying inside the car, of dirt and dog and oily rags and leaking petrol. And in the mirror, now I've adjusted it, no sign of pursuit – only *Helen*, in her new black chador, trotting submissively at my heels.

The one thing I'm missing to complete my satisfaction is some reassurance that my picture hasn't been found and seized. I try to put it out of my mind, since there's no way of knowing. Just as I'm joining the motorway, though, a sudden loud electronic burbling, somewhere around my left knee, makes me jerk the wheel wildly to the right, though fortunately the car stolidly ignores this ill-considered suggestion. I fumble under the dashboard, and locate a grimy mobile phone.

It's Laura, of course.

'He's gone,' she says. 'And don't worry – he didn't find it. I kept moving it from room to room behind him.'

'Brilliant,' I say. 'Wonderful. Thank you.' Though what I'm trying to imagine now, of course, is how she managed to drag it around like that, and how much of the painted surface got knocked off in the process. Also, what the price of her co-operation is going to turn out to be.

'That was Georgie, by the way,' she says. 'His younger brother. They don't get on.'

'You don't say?'

'Things got much worse after you'd gone – he went off in a tremendous rage. He took a great piece out of his hand with the crowbar getting the breakfast-room open. He's coming back with writs and things . . . Listen, I've got to be quick – Tony keeps coming in and shouting about all the burdens he has to bear. I just wanted to let you know that the dog's safe and sound . . . Hold on . . . Sorry, I'll call you back.'

The *dog's* safe and sound? It's the *dog* picture she's hidden for me? My skill at deceit seems to be taking over – I've even deceived my own accomplice. Not to mention myself – because what's happened to *my* picture while Laura was busy hiding the wrong one? He's found it, obviously! He's taken it! An exit to somewhere's coming up. I turn off and pull up on the edge of the ramp, gazing at the phone, waiting for it to ring again, ready to . . . I don't know . . . turn round and go back, pursue brother Georgie across England . . .

I've snatched it up even before it's completed the first note of its burble.

'Sorry about that,' says Laura. 'This brother's going bananas, too. Martin, listen . . .'

– 288 –

'What about the other three?' I interrupt with insane casualness. 'Did his brother find them?'

'He'd given up looking by then. He was just trying to stop the bleeding.'

My anxiety subsides a little. But if he didn't find them . . .

'They're still out in the shrubbery?'

'I think Tony's hidden them away with the pheasant chicks.'

Oh, my God. How are pheasant chicks housed? In the warm and the dry, presumably. How warm? How dry? Is there any check on the humidity . . .?

'Now, Martin, listen to me,' says Laura. I listen. 'You're going to need money, aren't you?'

'Money?'

'For whatever you're doing with the pictures. I just wanted to say that I've got a bit, not much, but he doesn't know about it, and if you wanted it . . .'

First Kate, now her. My anxiety's overtaken by shame.

'That's very sweet of you,' I say, 'but it's all taken care of.'

'Well, don't forget, if you get any surprises. Where are you now?'

'On the motorway.'

'I wish it was me with you instead of *Helen*,' she says wistfully.

I try to work out a judicious reply, but the task seems to be beyond me.

'Shall I tell you when I first knew what my fate in life was going to be?' she says. She sounds serious. 'When you explained that it was *Erwin* someone.'

Not true, of course. She didn't foresee for a moment what was going to happen. I feel a pang, though. It all seems a very long time ago now, part of some lost prelapsarian world.

'Erwin Panofsky,' I remind her.

She laughs. 'You've done it again,' she says.

So I have. 'I'll be back at the beginning of next week,' I tell her.

'Martin!' she cries, as I try to switch off the phone. 'Martin!'

I wait. She's serious again. What now?

'I've given up smoking,' she says shyly.

I drive on towards London, full of uneasy foreboding. I thought *friends* is what we were going to be – innocent, uncomplicated *friends*. Or at any rate accomplices – innocent, uncomplicated accomplices. Now suddenly she's offering me her life savings and giving up smoking. The same question as before comes back to me: I her or she me? I her, by the look of it, after all. But now it's beginning to seem even more alarming than the converse.

And what about the competition? I've a head start on my rivals, but how long's it going to last? How long before brother Georgie comes back with his writs? How long before Quiss cycles over for another look around? I don't think he's seen the *Merrymakers* yet. But he's seen *something* that's caught his interest. I can't do anything until the bank gets clearance for the mortgage increase, which is supposed to be on Monday. But then there's nothing that brother Georgie can do until he can get his lawyers into action, and even the omniscient Quiss will want to check current prices while he's in London during the week before he makes any offers. If I can get *Helen* valued at Sotheby's on Monday . . . If I can find a dealer to pay spot cash . . . If I can get the rest of the cash from the bank . . . If I can arrive back at Upwood with my hands full of crackling banknotes on Monday night . . .

I come round the great bend above Edgware, and London opens out in front of me. Slowly my fears begin to recede, and my hopes once again get the upper hand. Everything's possible! Laura's miles away behind me. So's Kate, so are my enemies, so's normal responsible life. And here's me, hitting town with the most beautiful woman in the world.

Yes, after all the preparation and delay, after all the anguish and study, the great abduction's finally occurred. The lady's loaded into the boat. The die is cast, the mighty enterprise is under way. Sparta's falling astern. Ahead lie Troy and immortality.

Hard Cash

The Spanish troops left the Netherlands in 1561, amid general rejoicing, three years before Bruegel painted *The Massacre of the Innocents* – Kate's right about that. But she's wrong in telling me that this means the picture doesn't allude to them. Why should Bruegel have forgotten them? Why should *anyone* have forgotten them? Their behaviour had been infamous, and they went only after years of outrage and agitation, only after the most strenuous political efforts by William of Orange, only after it was made a condition for granting Philip's 'Request' for the three million gold sovereigns. Had the peoples of Holland and Belgium stopped thinking about the *German* Occupation by 1948? Kate's being absurd. She's simply repeating what most of the commentators on Bruegel have said. They're *all* absurd. I feel like throwing them across the room. They none of them seem to have used their common sense. They've all put their noses up against the surface of the panels and squinted at the details with myopic literal-mindedness. They don't stand back and look at the general sense of the pictures in the context of the times.

They're all iconographers. What this problem needs is an iconologist.

It's Sunday. I'm sitting in our flat in Oswald Road going through all the books once more at the kitchen table, trying to make good my pledge to Kate before tomorrow morning, when I go out and sell *Helen*, and take almost the very last step before I'm totally committed. Though why I should be so scrupulous about Kate's feelings I'm not sure, because the more I think about what she said, and about all the massed choir of art historians who sang the same tune before her, the angrier I become. How can they not see what's in front of their eyes? How can they be so *wrong*?

Meanwhile, Helen sits on the other side of the table, occupying considerably more of the room than me and myself and the table together, still with that unshakeably indifferent expression on her face, still with her right arm raised in mild concern. I've taken her out of the wet black plastic to let her dry out and breathe a little. She seems none the worse for her elopement apart from smelling rather strongly – she's acquired the rancid dirty-hair smell of sheep, that attaches itself to everything they come into contact with.

What she's mostly concerned about now, I think, is not her personal hygiene, or her exposure to the weather, but the suspicion that she's even less covered by our household insurance than she is by her dress. It's worrying me, too. This is a moderately high crime area, and our policy, I imagine, requires that any individual item of value has to be specified. By the time I rushed back from the shops on Saturday afternoon I was convinced that I'd find she'd taken off again with another suitor already, leaving me with £20,000 odd to find. My one reassurance is that it would take a whole team of burglars to get her out of here. It had plainly not struck the Victorian architect who designed this house that its occupants might one day want to hang a canvas covering 42 square feet, in an elaborate gilt frame, in one of the upstairs rooms. I had to ask Midge, of course, to help me get her in. But we also needed her boyfriend Alec, her son Jeremy and the Japanese couple in the basement. Midge crushed a finger against the newel post on the stairs, and won't be able to type for some time, though when she can she'll have her best column yet.

Now I've got to get the poor old soul out again tomorrow morning. I've also got to run to the window every few minutes to see if the Land-Rover's still outside, since I have a feeling that the baler twine holding the tailgate shut may not be proof against the more sophisticated sort of car thieves we have in London.

And when I think of what the rest of tomorrow's going to be like, manoeuvring all this lot around the West End . . . I'm pleased to have a quiet day at home with her first. I'm getting quite fond of her, as a matter of fact. She's a peaceful person to be with, after the last week or two. She hasn't made any alarming advances to me, or announced she's given up smoking. Her silence isn't pointed, in the way that Kate's was when I rang her last night and told her humorously that I was sitting at the table here gazing into Laura's eyes – a silence that continued even after I'd explained that 'Laura' was a slip of the tongue for 'Helen'.

Another of Helen's virtues: she hasn't got any art historian friends of hers to come and buy her behind my back. Also, she isn't a closet Catholic, and she hasn't tried to tell me that the troops in the *Massacre* aren't Spanish! Anyway, even if they *aren't* it doesn't make any difference to the sense of the picture, because after the Spanish had gone there was still the local mounted gendarmerie, the Bandes d'Ordonnance, ready to put down religious or political dissent. It was detachments of this security police, together with a company of the Duke of Aerschot's regiment, that rounded up the victims for mass execution in Valenciennes after the crowd rescued Faveau and Mallart from burning. That was in 1562, after the Spanish troops had gone, probably just two years before Bruegel painted his *Massacre*. Do you really think that he hadn't made the connection? That everyone who saw the picture didn't make it in his turn?

I look at Helen. She says nothing; there's nothing she can say.

There are more troops in *The Adoration of the Kings*. Why? There are none in the Bible story. More again in *The Procession to Calvary*, wearing the red coats of the gendarmerie. A complete army in *The Suicide of Saul*, painted in 1562, as the new campaign of religious persecution got under way. This is another iconographic rarity – the Saul of the Old Testament, falling on his sword because the crushing of his nation by its enemies the Philistines has reduced him to despair. Are you trying to tell me that the Netherlanders looked at that and didn't think of their own nation, also crushed by its enemies?

There's another army marching up into the mountains in *The Conversion of Saul*. This is the other Saul, the Saul of the New Testament, and his accompaniment by an army on his journey from Jerusalem to Damascus is exceedingly odd. In Acts 9, where the story's told, there's no mention of either mountains or army. Saul was trained as a rabbi, not a soldier, and he's on his way to Damascus ('yet breathing out threatenings and slaughter against the disciples of the Lord') accompanied only by unspecified 'men which journeyed with him,' and bearing letters from the High Priest to the local synagogues authorizing him to arrest Christians.

But in 1567, the year when the *Conversion* was painted, there *was* an army marching through the mountains. It was the Spanish army under the command of the Duke of Alva, on its way through the Alps from Italy to put an end once and for all to dissent and rebellion in the Netherlands. Alva was a reasonably good model for the unconverted Saul. According to Motley, 'the world has agreed that such an amount of stealth and ferocity, of patient vindictiveness and universal bloodthirstiness, were never found in savage beast of the forest, and but rarely in a human bosom.' Like Saul, he was coming with orders to extirpate heresy. Like Saul, he was bearing letters from higher authority – what Motley calls 'a whole trunkful' of blank execution warrants, already signed by the King. I can't see in Bruegel's picture any indication of the two thousand specially enrolled prostitutes who were travelling with the Spanish troops, but perhaps they're further back in the column, or perhaps Bruegel didn't know about them. But if God had taken the hint he'd surely have struck the Duke of Alva down at the roadside, just as he did Saul, and converted him into a Protestant.

Glück agrees that the theme of the picture may have been suggested by Alva's approach, but other commentators are scathing about any explanation so vulgarly obvious. I wonder what the Spanish security services in the Netherlands thought. I'm sure they were too sophisticated to fall into any simplistic interpretation themselves, but they must have been a little surprised at the coincidence – and a little anxious lest local malcontents and agitators made something of it.

Or go back to the *Calvary*. The crucifixes waiting for Christ and the two thieves aren't the only engines of execution set up on the muddy hillsides that bright spring morning – the landscape's studded with gibbets, and with those cartwheels on top of poles on which victims were exposed and left to die. Never mind what Bruegel's intentions were – what did his Spanish and Netherlandish contemporaries think the scene represented, at a time when five thousand or so people were being executed each year by a variety of means? What did they think when they turned to another landscape of gibbets and wheels in *The Triumph of Death*, with one victim actually being beheaded in front of them? What came into their minds, in a land where so many towns were to be sacked and subjected to mass reprisals, when they lifted their eyes to the horizon of the *Triumph* and saw it prophetically smudged with the smoke of one burning town after another?

Once you start seeing it, the apparatus of persecution, and the allusions to oppression, leap out at you from almost every picture. Another Flemish village in winter, like the one in the *Massacre* – and how often it's winter in these pictures painted during the long winter of Spanish rule! – is the setting for *The Census at Bethlehem*, at an earlier stage of the story of the Nativity. Why are Joseph and Mary, together with the rest of the population of Flanders, going to Bethlehem to be counted? Because 'it came to pass in those days, there went out a decree from Caesar Augustus, that all the world should be taxed.' It also came to pass, from the mid-1550s onwards, there went out successive decrees from Philip II to the same effect; inquisition, occupation and taxation – these were the three heads of oppression that the Netherlanders rebelled against.

Scholars furrow their brows over the mysteries of *Two Monkeys*. Heaven knows why. There sit the two dejected creatures, in chains, in what looks like part of a dungeon, with Antwerp in the background, and the shells of what scholars identify as hazel nuts scattered around them. To my eyes they're almonds, but even if they're not, hazel nuts are Barcelonas, and in either case they come from Spain. They're the trifling return for which the wretched pair have traded their liberty.

All right – look at the *people* in these pictures. *The Triumph of Death*, bottom left: a king being shown the fatal hour-glass by a skeleton, and gesturing helplessly in his death throes as another skeleton dressed as a soldier helps himself to a barrel of gold coins. Next to him: a cardinal, dying in the arms of a stick-like figure of death who's also wearing a cardinal's hat. All resemblance to any real person, living or dead, as it used to say in the front of novels, is purely coincidental. All the same, there weren't all that many cardinals around for this one to coincidentally resemble, and only one king. So Granvelle, who'd got *his* round hat only the year before this picture was painted, must have wondered if there wasn't just a bit of a secret tease in it. How he must have wished Philip could have been there to enjoy the joke with him.

I suspect that Granvelle smiled, too, in spite of himself, at *Dulle Griet*, or Mad Meg, a crazy old biddy staggering out of hell with her pinny full of the swag she's looted from its unfortunate inhabitants. I'm sure *he* didn't suppose for an instant that this had any reference to his nominal boss, Margaret, Duchess of Parma, Governor of the Netherlands, and the hell she ruled over, but he must have speculated what others might think – you know how people's minds work!

The Triumph and *Dulle Griet* were probably both painted in or around 1562, and their imagery's a throwback to the grotesque world that Hieronymus Bosch was creating some fifty years earlier, as if this was the only way to come at the unfolding horrors of the times. The same fantastic creatures recur in *The Fall of the Rebel Angels*, also painted in 1562. The title makes it sound as if it predicts the victory of the Counter-Reformation, like Floris's altarpiece of the same subject. But in the context of the other two pictures, a cautious church official might have wondered if he'd understood it aright. The suspicion might cross his mind that it displayed the horrors not of dissent but of its violent repression, and that what it prophesied was the downfall not of the Lutherans and Calvinists, but of the Cardinal and his inquisitors.

I put myself into the clogs of an ordinary Netherlander in 1568, gazing at *The Parable of the Blind* that Bruegel painted in that year. I look at the five blind beggars in the picture who follow their visionless leader into the ditch, unable to grasp the realities of the world around them. The Eighty Years' War, the long struggle for Netherlandish independence, is just beginning. Not being trained as an art historian, what I see in my simplicity is the King of Spain and his successive lieutenants and local collaborators, stumbling uncomprehendingly into disaster.

I look at *The Bad Shepherd*, who runs off and abandons his flock, and what I see is the Church that's left me to my fate.

I look at *The Death of the Virgin*, the mysterious grisaille that Bruegel probably painted for Ortelius, since Ortelius had an engraving made of it, and I see . . .

Yes, what do I see here? Nothing obvious, nothing that leaps to the eye. This is an altogether much more difficult picture to read. As I look at it I get more and more caught up in the multiple puzzles that it presents.

We're in a room in a house at Ephesus belonging to St John the Evangelist, where according to legend he took the aged Mary to end her days. It's night, and a positively Manichaean darkness surrounds the room. Almost the only sources of light are the radiance emanated by the dying Mother of Christ in the bed, and the glow of the hearth on the very left-hand edge of the picture, beside which sits St John himself. Mary Magdalene's smoothing the Virgin's pillow, St Peter's offering her a candle.

Now, here's the first puzzle: at this crucial moment, John himself is asleep. According to Glück, he's exhausted by his noble vigil. According to Grossmann, though, he's dreaming the whole scene. If he is, it may provide an answer to the next puzzle – who the figures are on the left-hand side of the bed.

Traditionally, the dying Virgin's surrounded by the Apostles, and here they are, all eleven remaining after the suicide of Judas: Peter on the right-hand side of the bed, with eight others in the shadows around him; John, sleeping by the fire; and one other, almost completely lost in the shadows at the foot of the bed. But on the left-hand side of the bed is a crowd of extra figures, *not* accounted for by the traditional iconography, pressing in out of the blackness of the night to kneel at the bedside around Mary Magdalene. Who are they?

Grossmann believes that what Bruegel's showing, through the device of John's dreaming vision, is not only the scene at the deathbed, but also a moment yet to come, after the Virgin's assumption into heaven. Here, according to *The Golden Legend*, the collection of lives of the saints made by Jacobus de Voragine, who's quoting an apocryphal work by this same sleeping John, she's reunited with her son in the presence of a multitude of patriarchs, martyrs, confessors and holy virgins. These, says Grossmann, are the figures on the left-hand side of the bed. And they may well be, from what little detail can be made out. But to me, a simple Netherlander, standing here in my wooden shoes, looking at the picture in a very dark hour, they're something else as well: they're me and my wretched fellows, pressing in from the darkness to ask succour from the Virgin, the traditional channel of intercession for the ordinary humble citizen.

There's a third puzzle in the picture, too – a small but curious anomaly that seems to go unremarked by the commentators. None of the Apostles on the right-hand side of the bed has any of the traditional attributes which are normally used to identify them. They all kneel in anonymous worship. Except for one. In the darkness at the back of the group one of the Apostles is silently holding a cross aloft. It's not the usual Latin cross but the *crux gemina*, the twin cross, the Cross of Lorraine, with the smaller bar above the main one that represents the inscription nailed over Christ's head.

I stand here in my Netherlandish clogs, searching this mysterious nocturnal scene for meaning. Almost every single iconographic clue that I expect to see in a religious painting has been withheld. This is almost the only recognizable symbol I'm offered. It has a meaning for me. It must do – that's why it's there. It has a meaning for me because it refers to something I already know. What is it?

The complete and authoritative answer, of course, is at hand, waiting at the other end of a telephone. I feel the same delight I felt before at finding a problem that Kate and I can work on together. I'm so excited that it's only after I've heard the instant of silence after my eager 'Help! Help!' and the cautious coolness of her 'What is it?' that I remember we're not supposed to be on that sort of terms at the moment. Never mind – collaboration may help to restore peace between us. I'll kill two birds with one stone.

'Kate, listen,' I say. 'The *crux gemina*. What's the significance?'

Silence. Good God – she doesn't think I'm sitting here studying religious iconography with *Laura*, does she?

She sighs. She's ceased to believe in any aspect of my enterprise.

'It's sometimes called the True Cross,' she says flatly at last.

The True Cross. Yes. Well. It might have some reference to

truth in general. The concealed truth, the unadorned truth referred to in the Ortelius epitaph. I know there's more to come, though, if I can just get it out of her. I wait. She sighs again.

'It's the cross carried by an archbishop,' she says.

An archbishop? I feel a terrible dismay. It's not simply a respectful reference to Bruegel's patron, the appalling Archbishop of Malines? The idea of the corrupt and cynical Granvelle gatecrashing this particular scene, that even I find holy, is peculiarly nauseating.

'Where is it?' she says, very slightly interested in spite of herself. 'What's the context?'

'*The Death of the Virgin*,' I explain. 'One of the Apostles is holding it.'

'Oh, I see,' she says. 'Well, that's obvious, then. The figure sleeping by the fire is St John. It's St John's house they're in.'

'I know.'

'The *crux gemina* is the symbol of St James the Great. He's John's older brother.'

Oh.

'Is that all you wanted to know?'

I suppose it is. No – I also want to know if she still loves me, if we're ever going to get back to normal, if I still love *her*.

'That's all,' I say, as coolly as her now. 'Thank you.'

I put the phone down. Oh, well. My suspicions about this particular picture were obviously misplaced. I push it aside, and now my mood begins to change. I'm probably wrong about all of them, I realize. I am, I know I am. I feel the great wave I've been riding ever since Tony rushed me round the side of the house slip quietly away from me into the shallows, leaving me floundering in the slack water behind it. I put my head down on my folded arms. I'm wrong about everything. I'm stuck here on my own, with nothing but the inept image of a long-dead trollop for company, and I've lost my way through life.

And there I stay for the rest of the afternoon. The sky outside the window begins to fade, the details of the room slip away into the dusk. Two tears run down my face. The first tears I've shed since . . . I can't remember when. Since maybe the very first row that Kate and I ever had, outside the Amalienburg Palace in Munich, four days after we met, when suddenly the whole amazing world we'd been living in seemed to have crumbled into dust. What the row was about I've not the faintest recollection.

Why, though? That's the word I find I'm left with in the end. Why am I here? Why are things like this? Why did I ever begin this terrible enterprise? Why am I going ahead with it tomorrow when I still haven't honoured my pledge to Kate to find some objective evidence – when I no longer believe in it myself?

Ahead with it tomorrow morning I'm going to go, nonetheless, as soon as the auction rooms and dealers and banks are open. No turning back now. I feel like Lensky, on the eve of his futile duel with Onegin. Still, it will at least put an end to all my doubt and anguish. I go to bed early to prepare mind and body for the critical action.

And just as I turn out the light I remember. Tomorrow's a Bank Holiday.

Why, though? The question's still in my mind when I wake up. What I'm wondering now, though, is why St James on one side of the room is signalling his identity to his brother on the other side, when his brother knows perfectly well who he is.

Yes! Kate's explanation doesn't explain anything. It's obvious, she said. It's not obvious! It's extremely weird! James may need to wear a name tag when he goes to international church conferences where no one knows him, but with his fellow Apostles? In his own brother's house? It doesn't make any sense at all! It's just as wilfully obtuse as all the other explanations offered by art historians!

I've woken up fighting, in other words. Well, the sun's shining. If it's Bank Holiday for me, then it's Bank Holiday for Quiss and brother Georgie, too, so I'm still one step ahead. And it gives me an extra day to find the objective correlative I'm looking for, and redeem a few shreds of my honour.

All right – the sorceress can't or won't reveal her mysteries. But I've got all her books of spells. There's something I know I've seen on the shelves in the bedroom, where Kate keeps most of her reference books. I'll look it up for myself. *We're* still on speaking terms, myself and I. We search as we help each other dress . . . Yes! Réau: *Iconographie de l'art chrétien*. Exactly.

St James the Great, I discover, has other claims on our

attention, apart from being John's brother. He's reputed to have been the first Archbishop of Spain, and on the pilgrimage to Compostela he's credited with saving the life of a man falsely accused of theft by a woman whose advances he'd spurned. The man was convicted and hanged. St James supported him as he dangled on the gibbet, and kept him alive for several weeks until his parents had him cut down.

Réau says there's no evidence for St James ever having been in Spain. But his supposed achievements there, however apocryphal, would have been familiar to anyone in the Spanish possessions. So even *The Death of the Virgin* contains yet another reference to false accusation and wrongful execution.

I haven't finished with Réau yet, though. The *crux gemina*, it turns out, is the symbol not only of St James the Great, but of St Bonaventure, St Claude, St Laurent Giustiniani and St Parascève. One after another I look up their lives and works. Bonaventure, Laurent and Parascève I quickly dismiss from the case. But St Claude of Besançon is another matter. Although he was a much more obscure figure than the illustrious James, he'd have been known to Granvelle, because Besançon was the Cardinal's home town. He'd almost certainly have been familiar to Bruegel, too, and anyone else in Brussels, because his story's featured in a sixteenth-century Brussels tapestry called *The Miracles of St Claude*. And one of those miracles was to cut the rope of a wrongfully hanged man.

I put my ancient Netherlandish clogs on again. I come in out of my wasted land, where the bodies of my fellow countrymen twist in the wind beneath so many roadside gibbets, and take refuge for a moment in that quiet and darkened room in Ephesus, alongside the dim multitudes praying before the radiance of Our Lady. What the artist intended I shouldn't presume to guess, but I know my saints, and this is what I see in my extremity: the great Apostle and his mediaeval shadow silently interceding once again for the wrongfully condemned.

Yes, even *The Death of the Virgin*! And twice over. My reading of the pictures was right all the time; my confidence has returned. But of all the wobbles so far, that was the worst. I pick up the phone to ring Kate and tell her the whole story. Then I remember: she doesn't believe a word I'm saying, so I put it back.

I pick it up again and start dialling the Churts' number, in the hope that it might be Laura who answers. Once again I put it back. What could I ever say to Laura? What could she ever say to me? I'll just have to sit here with Helen in silence.

What I actually do in the end is take another look at *The Death of the Virgin*. It's the figure at the foot of the bed I'm puzzling about now. Is it really the eleventh Apostle? The faces of all the others are towards us, catching the holy light from the dying woman. This one kneels apart from all the others, his back towards us, entirely in shadow, a dim, uncharacterized silhouette. But it's powerfully and mysteriously placed – in the foreground on the right-hand edge of the picture, exactly balancing the sleeping John on the left-hand edge. I can't help asking myself – yes, the elusive I consulting my elusive interlocutor once again – if this isn't the equally elusive *painter*, making what may be his only appearance in his works, busy dreaming John, and also the dream that John's dreaming.

Then I think of the great cycle of the year. Suddenly, in the midst of all this wilderness of gibbets and broken bodies, of sacked villages and desperate prayers, Bruegel begins to *normalize*. He produces six major works in which the rural year goes on its sweet, untroubled round as peacefully as it did in the days of Philip the Good, with only one tiny distant gibbet to link it to the desolation all around.

I don't believe it. If even *The Death of the Virgin* makes such a powerful allusion to persecution, then so does the cycle of the year.

If it does, though, there's only one place where that allusion can be.

In the Churts' hatchery.

The only way I can fulfil my pledge is to study my picture until I find what I'm looking for. The only way I can study it is to acquire it. The only way I can acquire it is to break my pledge.

An antinomy, as we call it back in the department.

I feel about twelve years old, standing in the elegant foyer of Christie's in my open neck and slightly mud-splashed brown cords, unwrapping *Helen* from her black plastic in front of the immensely charming young man with bow tie and crisply waved hair who's come down to look at her for me. No, I don't, I feel about sixty-five – a flyblown theatrical agent who's helping some ageing show dancer he represents to step out of her clothes and audition for Cleopatra at the RSC.

The charming young man's perfect manners reduce me even further. 'You must have got a horse-box out there for this one,' he says. 'Are you on a yellow line? Are our people keeping an eye on things for you . . .?' He glides away to talk to the doorman. I hadn't liked to ask the doorman for any more favours – I'd already had to get him to help me carry my huge client into the building. It was a mistake coming to Christie's, I see that now. I set out to go to Sotheby's, but I've never set foot in either before, and suddenly the idea of Christie's seemed a little less intimidating, because it's just round the corner from the London Library. Also, there was a long enough piece of unoccupied yellow line outside to accommodate car and trailer for a moment.

By the time my charming expert gets back, Helen's grimy underwear is scattered all over the floor around her. Our sordid traffickings are occupying a fair amount of the foyer. People waiting at the enquiry desk and along the catalogue racks are beginning to stare.

My man remains completely unfazed. The first thing he does is to sniff at her and identify the smell she's giving off. 'Sheep's urine,' he says. 'What a witty idea! Some pastoral scene?'

He steps back and examines her. 'No, of course – it's Helen,' he says at once, with the gracious ability of the really polite to place the names of people they hardly know, and to find the right things to say. 'Oh, yes! Yes, indeed! What a splendid piece! Such a bold, free treatment.'

I wonder if I should tell him the name of the painter, before he embarrasses us both with a wrong guess. But he already knows. 'Absolutely off the cuff,' he says thoughtfully, 'my feeling is that it may perhaps be the best of all his *Helens*. How good of you to bring her in. She's been hiding away at Upwood for so long. Very exciting! Let me fetch Mr Carlyle.'

And before I can compliment him on his amazing knowledge he's vanished back into the depths of the building. All his insincere flattery has made me begin to feel slightly defensive about my poor client; I think I'd prefer him to look down his nose quite openly. She's not *that* bad, for heaven's sake. She covers up a lot of wall. And then there's all that strength and plasticity . . . all that chiaroscuro . . . Though what I feel worst about is knowing that I'm not even going to let Christie's have her at the end of all this, however well-informed and gracious they are about it. I'm just going to get a valuation to satisfy Tony, and then I'm going to hawk her round the streets in an even sleazier manner.

I have a moment of panic as I stand there waiting for my man to come back. What's he doing? They haven't already had a call from brother Georgie, have they? He's not phoning the police?

He reappears, as charming as ever, looking through a file of papers. 'I'm afraid Mr Carlyle's doing a valuation in

Somerset today,' he explains. 'I'm so sorry. You've taken us a bit by surprise. It *was* Mr Carlyle you saw when you came in before, wasn't it?'

I can't understand what he's talking about. A crossed line here somewhere.

'When you came in last week,' he says. 'With the documentation.'

He takes a piece of paper out of the file and holds it up. It's what I have folded away in my pocket ready to show *him* – a photocopy of the catalogue entry on *Helen* from the Witt.

'Oh, right,' I say uncertainly. What I'm uncertain about is whether to confirm it or deny it, and why I'm uncertain is because it takes me at least two seconds more to work out what's happened. Of course! That's what Tony Churt was doing in London! Not just pursuing his scholarly researches into the works of Sebastian Vrancz. He was looking out the documentation on *Helen*, and checking up in advance on what I was going to tell him about the price. He thought I was going to Sotheby's, and he wanted a second opinion from Christie's, not to mention a third from John Quiss, and probably a fourth from some man he met in a pub. How absolutely characteristic of him! And how absolutely characteristic of me not to have seen it coming!

'I don't think we quite realized you were intending to bring it in,' says my man. 'I do apologize, Mr Churt.'

Mr Churt? He thinks *I'm* the double-dealing, incompetent, pathetic Mr bloody Churt? This is too much!

'It *is* Mr Churt, isn't it?' he says, shaken in his outrageous assumption by the expression on my face.

I open my mouth to scotch the libel at once, then close it again and nod, because if I'm *not* the razor-nicked, tax-evading, thick-witted Mr bloody Churt and I'm even so standing here with the brother-cheating, wife-beating, first-wife-murdering, mother-neglecting, neighbour-seducing Mr bloody Churt's picture, then I can't think for a moment quite who I *am*. I should have got this straight in my head on the way here, of course, but what with the traffic, and the brakes, and the steering . . . I've got so used to lying that it takes me a little time to realize that I could simply tell something more or less like the truth, and by then the conversation's moved on.

'It doesn't matter too much, though, Mr Churt,' my man's saying, 'because Mr Carlyle and I did have a chance to talk about it together on Friday, and we've done a little homework. The picture appears to be in very reasonable condition, now that I see it – though of course we'd want to take it in and get our people to go over it absolutely thoroughly – and it is an important piece. I can certainly confirm that we should be more than delighted to try and sell it for you. I think Mr Carlyle suggested that we should be looking for a hundred to a hundred and twenty, didn't he?'

I stop thinking about who I am. A hundred to a hundred and twenty? I'm stunned. A hundred pounds odd? For a painting this size? But that's frankly insulting! It's insulting to me – it's more insulting still to Helen! And once again I want to spring to her defence. To humiliate her like this to her face, when she's in no position to defend herself! Caught at a disadvantage, half-dressed, a complete mess in every way, certainly – but a hundred pounds? All right, my ten or twenty thousand was perhaps a little over-gallant, but . . . 'A *hundred*?' I say, in frank amazement.

'To a hundred and twenty,' he repeats, obviously a little taken aback once again by my outrage. 'Though that was very much a first rough guess. The figures are only intended as a guide, of course, but having actually seen the piece I feel that we were being perhaps a shade conservative. It does have something of the same quality as his *Rape of Proserpine* in that ceiling he did for the Medici Palace in Florence.'

Giordano did a ceiling for the Medici? A sudden chill of unease checks my outrage.

'I'm always reluctant to raise people's hopes too much,' continues my man, as courteously as ever. 'But I think we could probably quite safely make that a hundred and ten to a hundred and thirty.'

And I suddenly grasp what he means. He doesn't mean pounds. He means thousands of pounds. He's saying £110,000 to £130,000. He's telling me it's worth something like ten times as much as I'd supposed. He's informing me that my whole scheme is based on a complete misapprehension.

I don't think I've ever felt such a fool in my life. It's as if I'd gone round to the local recreation ground to knock a tennis ball about with Kate, and found by some dreamlike transformation that I was facing a major international star on the Centre Court at Wimbledon. I can't find any words to cover my retreat. I silently put on an expression that I hope suggests regretful refusal even to debate such a paltry figure, and start to wrap *Helen* up again. The young man hands me pieces of fetid black plastic, as courteous as ever.

'I'm sorry if that seems disappointing,' he says. 'Do by all means see if you can find a more ebullient view elsewhere.'

He hands me pieces of baler twine. I silently tie my parcel together. I'm still in shock.

'And do of course feel free to come back, if our friends round the corner don't feel they can say any better. I'll talk to Mr Carlyle again. He might feel on reflection that a hundred and twenty to a hundred and forty was more realistic.'

I heave one end of the parcel up off the floor. 'No, no – let me!' he cries, taking it from me and signalling to the doorman to take the other.

'It may well go above that, of course,' he says, as he watches me tie the tailgate of the trailer half-shut. 'A long way above, even. We sold a rather larger piece by Giordano a few years ago, *The Raising of Lazarus,* that achieved £298,000.'

'Thank you,' I manage at last, as he opens the driver's door for me, and closes it behind me.

'Thank *you*, Mr Churt,' he replies. 'It was a pleasure to see it.'

I drive up King Street and into St James's Square, my mind blank of anything except shock and humiliation. I drive slowly round the square. I've plainly got to reconsider my plans. By the time I've gone round twice, though, I've realized that thinking's not really possible to combine with driving round St James's Square. I need to find somewhere to park for a moment. But there isn't anywhere to park. I need two spaces together, one for the car and one for the trailer, which obviously increases the difficulty, and there isn't even a single space. I drive round the square a third time. Still nowhere. What I should do, obviously, is to think of somewhere else to look. But I can't even focus my mind on anything as simple and concrete as this. I drive round a fourth time.

I can't go round a fifth time! People will begin to talk. The police will take an interest. With a great effort I snap out of the loop, and drive on down into Pall Mall. And there's a parking space! No – two parking spaces together! But by the time I've made seven attempts to reverse into them, and each time succeeded only in pushing the trailer in the opposite direction, out across the traffic, my nerve breaks, and I drive on. Along Pall Mall, up St James's Street, along King Street again, and back into St James's Square.

Where's this car going? It found London all right. Now it seems to have lost its way in life completely.

By this time, however, a few thoughts are beginning to

come back into my head. Incoherent rage, for a start, at Tony. For what? For knowing what the picture was worth and not telling me! For going behind my back! For finding out what it was worth, if he didn't know before – and still not telling me! Then rage at the world in general. For much the same thing – for knowing about Giordano and keeping it from me!

At myself next, for never getting round to looking up the sale-room prices, as Kate kept urging. At Kate, for being right.

No, at myself, myself, for making such a mistake about Giordano – for ever getting involved in all this. As I pass the London Library in the corner of the square for the sixth time, I recall, with a bitter sense of irony, the long days of peaceful research in the Reading Room, when everything seemed clear and hopeful and accessible to reason, when I thought my life was moving towards some great goal, not towards driving round and round St James's Square, unable to set foot to ground, shackled to an ageing Land-Rover, like the Flying Dutchman to his ship, for all eternity, or at any rate until the petrol runs out, which I calculate will be after I've gone round the square something like a thousand times.

By now the circuit of the square is beginning to settle into such a routine that calculations like this are becoming possible. It occurs to me that some of my panic may be misplaced. £100,000 to £120,000 – this is what he told Tony – forget all the wilder guesses that Tony knows nothing about. Terrifying figures, certainly, for a man who's had difficulty in extending his mortgage by fifteen thousand pounds. But £100,000 to £120,000, it slowly comes to me, isn't what I should have to find, because if that's what the picture's worth, then it's also what I should presumably be getting from the dealer I sell it to. All I have to find is the difference between his commission and mine – between his ten per cent and my five and a half per cent, which is . . .

well, I can't do the sum precisely while I'm driving round St James's Square, but it's something like – I don't know, five thousand pounds.

Five thousand pounds! But that's nothing! I'll still have ten thousand in hand to buy the other three pictures! All it means is that I'll have to scale back my absurdly over-generous plans to pay Tony twenty thousand pounds for the *Merrymakers*. Since he's behaved so badly he doesn't deserve it, though. And since he's also going to be getting five times as much as I thought for *Helen*, I don't see that he'll have much to complain about.

Five thousand pounds! Good God! All my despair was completely misplaced, as it has so often been before! Just double-check that I don't mean five *hundred* thousand pounds . . . Or five *million* pounds . . . No! I'm in business!

Another thought comes to me. I may possibly find a dealer who's prepared to pay *more* than a hundred to a hundred and twenty. I may find one who's prepared to follow Christie's thinking upwards to a hundred and thirty . . . a hundred and forty . . . If by any chance I do, I can't see that I need feel obliged to be any franker with Tony than he was with me.

I could be *making* money on the deal.

All I've got to do is to find a phone to ring Tony on, to give him my edited report on the Christie's estimate. I break boldly out of the St James's Square loop, and drive down into Pall Mall again. I simply need a double parking space with a phone near enough to it for me to keep an eye on the trailer, and large enough for me to drive into forwards. In my new positive mood this seems not too much to hope for.

There's no such parking space in Pall Mall, however. Nor in St James's Street nor King Street. I go round again. As I wait in traffic outside Christie's their charming young man in the bow tie emerges from the door. At the sight of the

Land-Rover, and the great black plastic parcel in the trailer, he stops and smiles more welcomingly than ever. So, I've been to Sotheby's and I haven't liked what they had to say. I've come crawling back, just as he foresaw. He beckons me into my old place on the yellow line. But the traffic loosens, and I drive straight past him, with a gesture that may mean I've a wealthy Belgian impatient to pay everything that Christie's are estimating and more, or may mean simply that I'm on my way back to St James's Square.

Which I am. On the corner of York Street a young woman stands laughing, I assume at me until I observe, the next time I pass her, that she's sharing the joke with a mobile phone. I feel a bitter pang of jealousy. I might have some faint chance in life if I had the basic equipment like a mobile phone that everyone else takes for granted . . .

I *do* have a mobile phone, though! This is the one thing I *have* got! One more trip round the square and I've found it. One more again and I've found Tony Churt's number. Another two and I've discovered how to get the latter into the former.

'Hello?' says Laura tensely, and I realize at once that she's hoping it's me. 'I *knew* it was!' she cries, as soon as I confirm it. 'Where are you? Are you still in London? How's it all going? I tried to ring you! When are you coming back? What's the weather like? Everything here's ghastly beyond belief! Have you got shot of that great fat tart yet? I'll scratch her eyes out!'

'I'm in St James's Square,' I tell her. 'The weather's OK. Is Tony there?'

'Does it sound like it?' she laughs. 'No, it's all right – he's out in his beastly little workshop place. I'm all on my own. Now – sound of trumpets! – I'm still not smoking! Not a single one since you left! Are you proud of me?'

'Very good,' I say. 'Listen.' Because I might as well tell her the whole story before she fetches Tony. I'd be interested to know if he's told *her* what kind of money was involved. At that moment, though, I catch sight of a blue four-wheel-drive in the mirror. It's following me slowly round the square.

'Go on,' she says impatiently.

It's still right behind me. It's been there for some time, it occurs to me. I think this is our second go round together.

'What's happening?' says Laura. 'You've gone all quiet. Are you still there?'

The four-wheel-drive turns off into a parking space in the centre of the square, nose first, that I might perhaps have got into if I hadn't been watching it instead of parking spaces. Damn. Not Georgie, though, presumably. Might be sensible not to hang around waiting for him, though.

'Did you say Tony's in his workshop?' I ask.

'Yes! Don't worry!'

'No, I mean, could you fetch him for me?'

A brief but wounded silence. 'I see,' she says in a rather different tone of voice. 'It's *Tony* you want to talk to?'

I realize I haven't handled this as well as I might.

'I'll tell him to call you,' she says coolly, before I can explain, and hangs up. Well, all right – but I can't do *everything*! I can't drive round and round St James's Square, *and* look for parking places, *and* watch in my mirror, *and* calculate five and a half per cent of some vast sum of money, *and* tiptoe around people's feelings . . .

Now there's a police car behind me. I drive down into Pall Mall, up St James's Street, along King Street again, and I'm just getting back into St James's Square when Tony calls.

'So what do Sotheby's say?' he demands. 'How much?'

I resist the short-term satisfaction of telling him that I

went to Christie's, not Sotheby's, so I know that he knows already, and stand out for the longer-term benefits of getting credit for my honesty. 'You're going to be amazed,' I tell him. 'A hundred to a hundred and twenty.'

He's not amazed, though. 'So tell your Belgian a hundred and forty,' he says.

Of course. I should have seen it coming. I've been pushed far enough, though. I'm not going to let myself be pushed any further.

'I'll tell him a hundred and twenty,' I inform him flatly, 'since that's what they said.'

'Don't be a fool! You're saving him the buyer's commission! That's ten per cent, for a start! Plus half the seller's commission!'

Oh yes. I'd forgotten the commissions.

'All right,' I concede. 'A hundred and thirty.'

'No, but you've got to bargain, you've got to fight! For God's sake! How is it that I always find myself in the hands of some amateur without a grain of business sense? Start high! Try him on a hundred and forty! Tell him you'll take it elsewhere! And all right – be prepared to settle at a hundred and thirty-five.'

'I'll start him on a hundred and thirty-five,' I say. I've got the picture, after all. And I'm very sick of St James's Square, and the stink of petrol in the car. Also, I need a pee.

'A hundred and thirty-five?' he shouts. 'A hundred and thirty-five is your absolute rock bottom after you've tried every trick in the book!'

'My bottom is a hundred,' I say calmly. 'Since that's what they said.'

'A hundred? What *is* this? Whose side are you on?'

'No one's,' I say simply. 'But I'm not going to be a party to cheating Mr Jongelinck just because he's a Belgian.'

'In that case bring the thing back and I'll find my own bloody Belgian!'

'Bring it back?' I say calmly. 'Sure. Delighted to. Save me a great deal of trouble. With any luck I'll roll up the drive just about the same moment as your brother and his lawyers.'

I switch the phone off. I feel I've regained control of my destiny at last. What I'm going to do if he doesn't back down, I haven't the slightest idea. But something. With my newly recovered autonomy I break effortlessly out of the loop in which I've spent so long. I turn out of St James Square into Charles II Street, as if it was the easiest thing in the world. I don't know where I'm going, but at least it's somewhere else.

The phone rings again as I'm driving across Piccadilly Circus.

'A hundred and twenty,' he says. 'And not a penny less.'

At once I feel I can be generous. 'A hundred and five,' I counter.

Silence. But now I know where I'm going. There's a car park in Old Burlington Street with a number of galleries close by. I shan't be able to stir far, of course, in case the tempting whiff of sheep's urine on the breeze lures some tearaway into investigating the contents of the trailer.

'A hundred and ten,' says Tony at last, pathetically. 'There's no point in selling her at all if you go under that.'

'I'll do my best,' I tell him noncommittally, and switch the phone off.

I've become battle hardened. I can shove the bayonet in now without a second thought.

Koenig Fine Art is the place I decide to try, because it's the first one I come to, as I run from the underground car park in Old Burlington Street, that seems to deal in Old Masters. There's a fair-sized *Death of Actaeon* in the window that suggests they may have a taste for the grandiose. I'm attracted by the subject, too. I can't help feeling a touch of sympathy for someone who's been changed into a beast and torn to pieces because he happened to catch a glimpse of transcendent beauty. Though in my case I now have renewed hopes of avoiding at any rate the second half of this fate.

The gallery inside is panelled, with period furnishings and a woman sitting at the scrolled table in the corner who appears to be carved out of various highly burnished hardwoods herself, hair included. A concealed mechanism snaps her lips into a brief smile as I approach, but it also flicks her eyes briefly down at what I'm wearing, and almost audibly registers a disposable income too low to allow my adventures in the art market to get much beyond postcard reproductions. This time, however, I'm not the slightest bit disconcerted, because *I* know I have high chips to play with. I fling them down on to the table with complete openness.

'A Giordano,' I announce. 'Valued by Christie's at £140,000. Is that something you might be interested in making an offer on?'

She doesn't blink. 'I'm afraid Mr Koenig's in a meeting,' she says. 'If you'd like to bring it in some time . . .'

'I've brought it. It's in the car park round the corner. In its frame it's about seven feet high by nine feet long. I don't imagine you want to help me carry it, and I don't want to leave it for more than a few minutes. When will Mr Koenig be free?'

'I've no idea.'

'I'll wait ten minutes, then I'll try elsewhere. May I use your lavatory?'

Is there any tonic in the world that bucks you up the way money does?

She hesitates for a fraction of a second. She doesn't like me. But the days when I cared about being liked are over. I'm as much a beast as poor Actaeon now. She leads the way to an ornate door that opens out of the eighteenth century on to a muddled twentieth-century backstage corridor, separated from an adjoining office by a battered hardboard partition, and lined with files and copiers and stacks of catalogues. She indicates another door at the end. As I pee (and I even pee arrogantly in my current mood), I become aware of a man's voice on the other side of the partition. 'Charles,' it says pleadingly, 'will you please hold your horses a moment, will you please listen?' But Charles, who's presumably at the other end of a telephone, is plainly not inclined to restrain his horses at all. 'I know that, Charles,' says the man at my end. 'I know, you're right – I should have done, and I didn't – but, Charles . . . Charles . . .!' There's a defeated note in the voice. Behind the panelling at Koenig Fine Art, perhaps, all is not as well as it should be.

I wonder, with my brutal new-found realism, if it's really worth waiting even ten minutes for this broken reed. But then the same realism even more brutally prompts me to wonder whether a little desperation on Mr Koenig's part might not prove helpful in the negotiations.

Let's see how desperate he really is. Now I've got the pressure in my bladder back to normal I'm even more insolent in my power.

'On second thoughts,' I tell the woman when I re-emerge, 'I think I'll wait in the car park.'

'I don't think Mr Koenig would want to . . .'

'Luca Giordano. *The Rape of Helen*. From the Churt collection at Upwood. I'm on Level Three.'

I stroll up the street until I'm out of the woman's sight, then I run all the rest of the way, suddenly overcome with the certainty that the importance of my cargo, projecting ostentatiously out of its parking bay, will already have attracted a gang of international art thieves – or Georgie – or the police. As soon as *she's* out of *my* sight, no doubt, she goes running to Mr Koenig.

He keeps me waiting twenty minutes, none the less. Quite nicely judged, I have to say. It's very quiet and peaceful down in the clean white underworld of Level Three, and by far the most congenial place I've been in all morning. I'm within a couple of minutes of giving up on him, all the same, by the time he comes sauntering across from the lift, his off-hand buyer's manner and ironic condescension visible at a range of a hundred feet, and I'm not feeling quite as cocky as I did. If I hadn't heard him pleading on the phone I should start cutting my price.

'Maybe I should move the business down here,' he says, shaking my hand. 'Rather nice ambience.'

He looks like Gustav Mahler: high bony forehead, a bush of dark hair on either side, small gold-rimmed spectacles. Crumpled shirt, tie half an inch off centre. Not a dealer at all – an academic; a version of myself. Perhaps this is his problem.

I say nothing. I'm not going to make a social occasion of this, however much like me he is. I've got the goods; he needs them. He can take it or leave it. I undo the twine, and we slide the huge package out. He sniffs.

'Sheep's urine,' I explain briefly.

Once again Helen steps out of her drapes and shows her charms. But now I know that I'm pimping for a very high-class girl indeed, an international *poule de luxe*. He pushes his spectacles up on to his forehead and gazes at her for some time.

'What's the documentation?' he says.

I unfold my crumpled photocopy from the Witt. He examines it in the way that an immigration officer might examine an out-of-date Nigerian driving licence offered in place of a passport. It doesn't worry me in the least. I know what I know.

'And Christie's told you . . .?'

'A hundred and forty.'

He laughs. Let him. I've heard him in another mode.

'What about Sotheby's?'

'I haven't tried Sotheby's.'

'Why not? They might say a hundred and fifty.'

He's as rude as I am. Would he be less cocky if he realized I'd overheard him?

'Why have you brought it to *me*?' he asks.

'I don't want to pay the premiums, and you were the nearest gallery to the car park.'

He pulls the spectacles back on to his nose and transfers his scrutiny to me. Pictures he can see unaided. It's the rest of the world he has difficulty in focusing.

'Also, you want cash,' he says.

I say nothing, because of course I do. I'd intended to demand it boldly, though, not to confess it meekly. He goes on looking at me for a moment. He can see tax avoidance written in my soul just as I can see bankruptcy written in his. Or perhaps what he sees is more than mere tax avoidance. I realize he hasn't asked me my name, and it occurs to me that this isn't because he thinks I'm Mr Churt – it's because he knows I'm not. He suspects that my title to the picture won't bear too much examination.

He goes on gazing at me. My confidence ebbs a little. I'm beginning to feel a little like the wretched Nigerian with the driving licence.

'Family situation,' I say. 'I won't bore you with the details.'

'You *are* the owner?'

I nod, after the briefest pause for thought. What the pause means to me is that I shall have become the owner retrospectively, in a sense, after I hand the money over to Tony. What the pause means to Mr Koenig, I imagine, is confirmation of his hypothesis.

'You'll put something in writing?' he demands. I nod again.

'Very well, then,' he says decisively, handing me back my piece of paper. 'I'll give you £70,000 for it. In cash. Tomorrow.'

I suppose I should laugh in my turn. £120,000 . . . £150,000 . . . £70,000 . . . The figures balloon and shrivel as arbitrarily as one's fingers in a fever. I don't laugh, though; I think. Because of course it probably *is* stolen, though not by me, and the longer I negotiate and wait for my money the more likely it is that the efforts of brother Georgie and his lawyers will make it unsaleable. This is the weakness of my position. I pluck another figure out of the great emptiness of the car park.

'A hundred and ten.' What I'm holding on to is the fact

that he's prepared to deal at all, even though he thinks there's something dodgy about it. This is the measure of his desperation. This is the weakness of *his* position.

He smiles, and starts to wrap the picture up again for me. What he's indicating is that we're not within signalling range of each other. If this is really what he means he ought simply to walk out of the car park. He's found an excuse to linger in case I soften. What *I* ought to do, obviously, is to walk out of the car park myself, and find a few more deal-ers. It's manifestly worth a great deal more than he's offer-ing, or he wouldn't be offering it. But of course the advantage of overhearing any more moments of defeat and weakness is unlikely to recur. And in any case, at the thought of running back and forth to the car park, of dress-ing and undressing *Helen*, of laying out further stocks of aggression and cunning, all the energy drains out of me.

'A hundred,' I say, ignominiously.

He's got me on the run, and he knows it. 'Seventy-five,' he says at once.

Now *he's* made a mistake. If he could only have brought himself to say ninety, I'd have said ninety-five and been on my way home. But for him to go up five when I've come down ten is insulting. I find the twine, and he puts his finger on the first half-hitch for me as I tie the second. We glance up at each other at the same moment, and catch each other's eye. This is ludicrous! Two nicely brought up, well-educated mother's sons, and here we are, me trying to sell a picture that's not mine, him trying to buy it with money that's almost certainly not his. How have we got into this situation?

And we're both at the end of our tether. He's got to go back and wearily cajole a lot more money out of someone who doesn't want to let it go. I've got to go back and find some way to make that money up to . . . I don't know. The figures balloon and shrivel again . . . I can't even remember what I told Tony. Was it a hundred or a hundred and five?

We're both the creatures of unseen proprietors. Two old boxers at the point of collapse, holding each other up.

Yes, if he said £95,000 I could persuade myself. Obviously I'm not going to get anything like the full auction price from a dealer. I have to accept that. In any case, it's a question of perspective: £95,000 standing as close as the merrymakers in the foreground looks bigger than £110,00 standing way off among the mountain blue.

'Ninety-five,' I say. Yes, ninety-five plus the fifteen from the bank might just about do it. If I told Tony a hundred and five, then I'd still have a few thousands left over towards the other three pictures.

'Eighty,' he says. 'And that's absolutely final.'

'All right,' I say. 'Ninety.'

Ninety? What am I saying ninety for? I can't settle for ninety! It would leave me at least five thousand still to find!

'Eighty,' he says again.

'Eighty-five,' I hear myself saying, to my despair. Because this is madness! I must go elsewhere! I must try at least half a dozen places before I even think of going below ninety-five!

'Eighty,' he repeats blankly.

'Eighty-five,' I repeat, no less blankly. Madness, madness! But I can't go through this again!

'Eighty.'

'Eighty-five!' And here I have to stand, whatever the outcome.

Silence. He gazes into the distance, waiting for me to weaken. I don't weaken. At eighty-five I finally stick. I say nothing. I wait for him.

And in the end he breaks.

'Eighty-one,' he says flatly.

'Eighty-one,' I agree.

Because I can't go through it again, I really can't.

Together we tie the tailgate half-closed. We avoid each other's eye. We both know we've made a terrible mistake.

'And you'll have the money tomorrow?' I say with insulting sternness, to compensate for my humiliation. 'In cash? By what time?'

'By midday,' he says.

'Midday. Right. And you'll be there to help me unload it if I stop outside the gallery?'

'No need to bring it to the gallery,' he says. He takes a little notebook out of his pocket, writes something, and tears the page out for me. It's the address of a forwarding company, in a unit on an industrial estate in Rotherhithe.

The deal's not going through his books, any more than it is through mine. He has a Belgian of his own.

'Fifties all right?' he says. 'You don't want it in fives and tens?'

I drive back to Kentish Town in a state of mild post-traumatic shock. So now I'm a thief, on top of everything else. Fives and tens? But I'm *not* a thief! I'm *not*!

A receiver, possibly. A fence . . .

Oh, nonsense. I'm merely trying to help out in someone else's family dispute.

I find somewhere to stop outside the flat, but neither Midge nor any of the others is at home to help me carry *Helen* in, so I simply designate the Land-Rover as my command post. I sit back as comfortably as I can in a headquarters smelling so strongly of leaking petrol, and I review the situation.

I've got the major part of the job done. Not done as well as I was hoping. But done. All I have to do now is to raise the balance of the money.

I run all the way to the High Street for a sandwich and a bottle of mineral water, and then I set to work with Tony's mobile. First a rather enjoyable call to the bank. Yes, the mortgage extension has gone through – £15,000 has been credited to our joint account. Fifteen thousand! It seems small change now, to a man who's spent the morning bandying figures up to ten times as large. I treat it as such. 'I'll come in tomorrow morning and draw it out,' I tell the voice at the other end. 'In cash. All right? In fifties . . . Yes, three hundred fifty-pound notes . . . Thank you.'

The voice gives no sign of surprise, but it must be speculating. Does it think I'm buying a consignment of heroin? Paying blackmail? Hiring a hit man? Let it think what it likes. I no longer care what anyone thinks about anything.

Now, the eighty-one from Koenig plus the fifteen from the bank makes ninety-six, so I need another nine to pay Tony for *Helen.* Dare I deduct from that the five and a half per cent commission I negotiated for myself? I don't know. I've no idea whether Tony understood the figures I mentioned on the phone to be net or gross. I've no idea, for that matter, whether *I* did. My fingers bulge and waste away . . . In either case I'm going to need several more thousand on top of that to buy the other three pictures.

He hasn't been hawking photographs of *them* around, too, has he? I'm not going to get three more horrible surprises?

I assume not. I *have* to assume not, because if he's shown a picture of the *Merrymakers* to anyone then the game's up.

So how much more money am I going to need?

It's like trying to measure fog. Nothing's fixed, nothing's solid! My head swims. Another two or three thousand should do it, shouldn't it, on top of what I'll actually be getting for the skaters and the cavalrymen? No idea. Sounds plausible. So altogether I need about another twelve thousand. If my original calculations are right. But supposing they're not? Supposing I'm as far out with the skaters and the cavalrymen as I was with *Helen*? In that case I should need . . . I can't begin to guess.

The question really is how much I can get.

Yes. The next phone call's going to be the difficult one. I sit gazing at the great eventlessness of Oswald Road for half an hour or more while I nerve myself. And then the phone's in my hand and the number's been dialled.

'Hello?' says Kate, as cautious as always. I used to love that guardedness of hers. Now my spirits sink at once.

'Hi. It's me.'

I wait for a response. None comes. I hurry on.

'How's Tildy?'

'All right.' Her tone is as neutral as if I'd inquired about the weather.

'Still no sign of Mr Skelton?'

'No.'

'Anyway, I've managed to sell *Helen*. I've got to wait until tomorrow to collect the money, though. I should be back around the middle of the afternoon.'

'I see.'

I close my eyes for the next part. Why do we close our eyes when we're talking on the phone and we're ashamed of what we're saying? Is it because we're trying to become invisible to ourselves? Or because we're hoping to abolish the accepted everyday realities of the world?

'Kate,' I say through my closed eyelids, 'you once with great sweetness, with great generosity, with a sweetness and generosity that made my heart almost burst, offered to lend me some money your father had given you, and I said that I could never accept it, not in any circumstances what-soever, not even if it was my last hope . . .'

'It's in the joint account,' she interrupts. 'I transferred it last week.'

Silence. What can I say? The tears run down my cheeks.

'Kate . . .' I begin.

'I'm not lending it to you. I didn't really think of it as mine. It's ours. It's just part of our money.'

'Kate . . .' But I can't get any more words out. 'Kate . . .'

'I'd better go. I left Tilda on the rug.'

'Wait!' I beg her. 'Wait!'

Because there's something more I *have* to say, and it's the most shameful thing yet.

'Kate . . . how much?'

Another moment of silence, that lasts until the end of time.

'Six thousand and something.'

What words could I ever find to thank her? I can't even begin to try because she's already put the phone down.

The important thing is not to think. Just to act. These things have to be. There might once have been a time for turning back, but that time's now behind us. All this will be over soon, that's the important thing, and we can get back to where we were. Until then I must close my heart and act, act, act.

A somewhat ridiculous call next – the bank again. 'Was it you I was talking to before? About collecting £15,000 tomorrow in fifties . . .? Right, slight change of plan. Could you make that £21,000?'

A few kilograms of crack cocaine on the side, obviously. Now another embarrassing call. I dial the Churts' number. If it's Tony who answers, I'll tell him he's getting a hundred and five less five and a half per cent, which he's going to shout about. That'll be bad enough. If it's Laura, though . . . It *is* Laura.

'Hi,' I say for the second time today. 'It's me.'

'You want to talk to Tony?' she says coolly. My spirits sink once again. Another icy blast. Why is she being like this? I thought this one at any rate would be pleased to hear from me. Then I remember the slight misunderstanding that arose at the end of our last conversation.

'Yes! Sorry about that! I didn't mean I didn't want to talk to *you*! I did! I do! You're *just* the person I want to talk to, because, Laura, listen, listen . . .' I close my eyes again. 'Something very embarrassing I need to ask you . . .'

'Hold on,' she says coolly. She turns away from the

phone to speak to someone else. 'It's Skelton about that bloody stove,' she says. She turns back to the phone. 'I'll check the number on it and call you back.'

Oh, I see – Tony's in the room. So now I've become the man who cleans the septic tank. Fair enough; I feel as if I've cleaned a few septic tanks in the last few days and hours. I wonder how much practice at lying I shall need, though, before I'm as quick at it as Laura?

'Sorry,' she says in a completely different voice when she calls back a few minutes later. 'I can't go near the phone at the moment without his popping out from somewhere. I don't know why he's quite so suspicious all of a sudden – I think maybe he's only just noticed I've stopped smoking. So what's this frightfully embarrassing question? Shall I be shocked? Will it make me blush and giggle?'

'No, Laura, listen, it's serious.' I close my eyes again. 'You very sweetly and generously offered to lend me some money . . .'

'Oh, *money*,' she says, disappointed. 'I thought you meant something quite different.'

I struggle on, eyes still closed. 'And I said . . .'

'And you said, "No, no, no! Never, never, never!" So how much do you need?'

'Laura, I'm sorry about this . . .'

'Martin, my sweet, just tell me how much! He'll be coming into the kitchen any moment to see if it's Skelton I'm carrying on with.'

How much? The question is how much can I reasonably ask for. How much was she thinking of? How much has she got?

'Well . . .' I say.

'My honey, I'm not clairvoyant! Five pounds?'

She's joking, of course. I think. 'Actually . . .' I say.

'Five *hundred* pounds? Five *thousand*?'

'*Could* you?' I say quickly. 'Could you really?'

'Which – five thousand?'

'Only if you could spare it.'

'*Exactly* five thousand? I've guessed exactly right?'

A bit implausible, I agree. Particularly since I need about six. I pluck another figure out of the petrol-laden air. 'Five thousand eight hundred' has a solid ring to it. I close my eyes again. 'You couldn't manage *seven*, could you?' I hear myself ask.

She laughs. 'Cash? Used fivers?'

'I'd prefer fifties,' I say frankly.

'Fifties. All right. Fine. This means you've got rid of *Helen*?'

'Yes.'

'But not for as much as you thought.'

'No, well, let me explain . . .'

'Never mind explaining. As long as we're giving Tony a poke in the eye. Just let me know when you want it.'

'Well . . . tomorrow.'

'Tomorrow?' She laughs again. 'If only you were as quick off the mark in other ways, my sweet!'

'Yes, I'm sorry. It's just that something's come up rather suddenly.'

More ribald laughter. 'Martin, you're such a sweet, funny boy! Don't worry, I'll call the bank at once. Only you've got our car, so here's what you'll have to do . . . When are you getting back?'

'Tomorrow afternoon.'

'You'll have to pick me up and drive me into town before the bank shuts.'

'Laura, this is so kind of you! I don't know how to begin to thank you. I'll explain it all tomorrow.'

'Explain about normalism instead. There's only one condition – that you don't let *him* know I've got any money left.'

'Of course not. Where shall we meet?'

'Somewhere secret,' she says. She starts to laugh again. The only salve to my conscience is that she's possibly getting seven thousand pounds worth of entertainment out of it all. 'The end of the drive. Four o'clock. I'll be hiding behind the sign.'

'What sign?'

'*His* sign,' she says, still laughing. 'Private Property. Hands Off.'

Once again I fumble helplessly for words of gratitude, and once again I'm spared the effort, as she hurriedly breaks off the call and puts the phone down. I assume Tony's appeared in the kitchen. I'll give them a bit of time to sort themselves out, then I'll try ringing *him*. I now have £109,000 to juggle with, so perhaps it would be money well spent if I surprised him by giving him a bit more than I said. After I've deducted my commission I'm going to need how much to cover the balance on the other three pictures? Can I get away with, say, five thousand pounds?

As I sit in the Land-Rover gazing at Oswald Road, juggling all the imponderables once again, I can't help brooding once again about how relative poverty is. Six thousand pounds is Kate's complete life savings. Seven thousand pounds isn't a sum that seems to trouble Laura at all. I could probably have borrowed the entire amount off her. I assume, from what she said, that she realizes I'm going to be paying it all straight over to her husband.

I dial their number once again. This time it's Tony who answers. 'I just thought you might like to know', I say, 'that I got him up to a hundred and seven in the end.' I decide not to mention my commission for the moment. Let him enjoy the thought of a hundred and seven for another day. I hope I might hear some signs of satisfaction, perhaps even a word of commendation for my efforts. But all that comes is a pause, then a sigh.

'Well,' he says gracelessly, 'if that's the best you could do. You're not much of a businessman, Martin, I'll tell you that. You *have* got cash?'

I swallow down my irritation.

'Fifties. In your hands tomorrow afternoon.'

'And the other three pictures?' he demands querulously. 'I know that little tosser's coming back. I can't have them trailing about the place indefinitely.'

'Tomorrow afternoon,' I assure him. 'I'll put the money in your hands. You put the pictures in mine.'

I switch off the phone. Tomorrow afternoon, yes. And the whole nightmare of shame and duplicity will be as good as over.

'The uneasiness, the terror, the wrath of the people seemed rapidly culminating to a crisis,' says Motley.

We're moving into the spring and summer at the beginning of 1565 – the old 1565, equinox to equinox – the year that Bruegel fixed for the centuries to come in his great cycle, and I'm sitting at the kitchen table in Oswald Road making one last great effort to redeem my pledges to myself and Kate before the die's finally cast in the morning, when I bundle *Helen* off to Unit 47 on the Tidewater Industrial Estate in Rotherhithe, and who knows what shameful destination thereafter. Every now and then I look up from my books and catch her eye as she watches me with her usual faint disquiet. Our last night together. I feel a slight pang of guilt, I have to admit, even about Helen. And I'll miss her company. My evenings aren't going to be as peaceful again for a long time.

I turn back to my books. The 1560s were a harsh decade for the Netherlanders in every way, with bad harvests raising the price of bread and the depression of trade bringing unemployment and low wages. But by 1565 the economic misery had been overtaken by the political crisis. 'Nothing was talked of but the edicts and the inquisition,' says Motley. 'Nothing else entered into the minds of men. In the streets, in the shops, in the taverns, in the fields; at market, at church, at funerals, at weddings; in the noble's castle, at the farmer's fireside, in the mechanic's garret, upon the merchants' exchange, there was but one perpetual subject of shuddering conversation.'

Nothing else entered into the minds of men. Except, apparently, into Bruegel's. Bruegel, who'd painted so many things that couldn't be painted, who'd shown his fellow citizens what they, in their unscholarly way, must have thought were the security troops and the engines of execution that surrounded them, the despair to which they were reduced, the depredations of the Regent, and the downfall of King and Cardinal – this Bruegel, who'd painted so much and so much, suddenly closed his mind to the events that obsessed everyone else, and began to create a happier Netherlands of his own invention.

Well, why not? We all need a break from reality at times, and the reality of 1565 grew steadily more savage and departed further and further from Bruegel's alternative version as the months went by.

You can't precisely compare the chronological progress of the year as Bruegel experienced it and as he painted it, because no one knows in which order he did the panels. All we know is that he can't have completed any of them (with the possible exception of the trimmed and undated *Haymaking*) before 25 March, when the year began, and that he'd finished them all, and delivered them, at the very latest by the following 21 February, the date on which Jongelinck listed all *De Twelff maenden* among his securities for the Wine Excise.

Nothing else entered into the minds of men. Whatever order he painted the scenes in, though, the year they represent has its own chronology. What's happening month by month in the Netherlands outside the studio door while the fictitious months unroll in the Never-Neverlands within? In *my* months, for a start, 25 March to 25 May?

This is when the Count of Egmont (to be beheaded by Alva along with the Count of Horn on the Grand Place in Brussels three years later) is returning from Spain confident that he's persuaded Philip to moderate the repression. In reality, though, he's being shadowed (characteristically) by simultaneous dispatches from the King with a completely contrary message: Philip is writing to say that he's determined to suppress heresy at whatever cost, and would prefer to die a thousand times rather than to allow a single change in matters of religion. As a result, the terrible edicts are republished in Brussels. In spite of his ringing declaration, though, the King *is* instituting a change. One single change. To avoid giving heretics the opportunity of public martyrdom they're henceforth to be executed at midnight in their dungeons, by binding their heads between their knees, and then slowly suffocating them in tubs of water. Who says Philip's inflexible?

Summer comes. The Regent reports to the King that the popular frenzy is becoming more and more intense. The people are crying aloud, she says, that the Spanish Inquisition, or something even worse, has been established there.

In Bruegel's studio the girls go singing to the hayfields, the harvesters doze in the midday shade.

Autumn, and in the streets of Brussels the violent debate among the Netherlandish leaders bursts out into the open. The excitement, says Motley, spreads at once to the people. Inflammatory handbills are circulated. Placards are posted up every night outside the palaces of Orange, Egmont and Horn, calling upon them to champion the people and their liberty.

Far, far away, in another Netherlands altogether, the herds amble placidly down from their summer pasture, past the golden vineyards, to the rich meadows of the valley.

Now it's winter, and the whole nation's in shock as the government in Brussels releases the King's letter 'from the wood of Segovia,' in which he declares that all hopes of compromise are at an end, and that the Inquisition will continue as ordained by the laws of God and man. There's a mass exodus of refugees. Inflammatory broadsheets appear in the towns. Prisoners of the Inquisition are freed by the mob. Petitions to the Regent are nailed on the doors of Egmont's and Orange's palaces. There are rumours that a general massacre of Protestants is planned.

And away in that other, better land, the hunters are returning to the still valley we know so well, where every sound is muffled by the snow.

The year winds on to its close. In February and March, as the carnival revellers eat their waffles in that muddy little village above the stormy estuary, and the peasants prepare for the coming of another spring, the conditions of life in the rest of the country grow worse and worse. This is the beginning of the Year of Hunger, when shortages deepen into famine, and the economic desuetude is exacerbated by the flight of skilled craftsmen from the terror. By summer, clandestine 'hedge preaching' will be spreading through the land, from the Walloon provinces northwards, with twenty thousand assembling at Tournai to sing the Psalms in French, and tens of thousands more outside Harlem to sing them in Dutch. By August, the image breaking will sweep across the country from south to north, devastating the ecclesiastical treasures of Poperinghe, Oudenaarde and St Omer. It reaches Antwerp, where the whores hold up wax tapers from the cathedral altars to light the work of the men as they put on the priests' vestments, burn the missals and manuscripts, smear their shoes with sacred oil and drink the sacramental wine. Then on the fury goes, to

Ghent, Valenciennes, Tournai, Amsterdam, Utrecht, Leyden, Delft, Friesland, Groningen.

And to replace the old images burnt, our amazingly detached artist in Brussels has produced those six new images of his own. Six pictures of a historyless land in a historyless year. The hunters haven't caught much on the winter hills, it's true, but the village they're returning to seems prosperous enough. In the whole cycle there's not the slightest shadow of hunger or economic misery, of repression or political ferment.

It's breathtaking. Particularly since, as soon as he'd finished the cycle, he emerged from that other happy Netherlands and returned to the wretched one around him. In 1566, as the wave of hedge preaching passed across the land, he painted a *Sermon of St John the Baptist*. Who knows, any more than with the earlier pictures, what his intentions were? Who, though, in that particular year, looking at a picture of John preaching the bright beginnings of Christianity to a crowd of Netherlanders under the trees in the open air, can have failed for one instant to see a parallel with the potential martyrs who'd turned their backs on the churches to preach the new reformed religion in the fields outside the towns?

Tolnay and others believe that one of the faces in the crowd is Bruegel himself, and there's been speculation about a much more prominent figure, a swarthy, black-bearded gentleman who sits with his back turned dismissively towards John, and who seems to be having his hand read by gypsies. I can tell you what Helen and I think he is: a Spaniard who's turning his back on John's revolutionary message, and instead consulting the divinations of priests. His back's also turned upon another member of the congregation, and an iconographically much more surprising one: Christ himself, who stands listening to the great hedge preacher with every sign of attention and respect.

Then in the following year Bruegel painted *The Conversion of Saul*, with its amazingly coincidental likeness to the Duke of Alva on his march through the Alps from Italy. By now the terror was beginning to spiral out of all control. Within a few months of Alva's arrival, says Motley, 'the scaffolds, the gallows, the funeral piles, which had been sufficient in ordinary times, furnished now an entirely inadequate machinery for the incessant executions. Columns and stakes in every street, the door posts of private houses, the fences in the fields, were laden with human carcasses, strangled, burned, beheaded. The orchards in the country bore on many a tree the hideous fruit of human bodies.' In the following year, 1568, the Holy Office condemned the entire population of the Netherlands to death as heretics, and the King ordered the sentence to be carried out at once, without regard to age, sex or condition.

This, however, seems to have been beyond even Alva, and that same year the Prince of Orange was provoked into armed revolt. The consequences of 1565, the year when Bruegel was apparently otherwise engaged, spread outwards across Europe and onwards through the centuries. The war of Dutch independence that grew out of Orange's revolt continued on and off for another eighty years. Malines was sacked, and Granvelle's palace with it; Antwerp, and Jongelinck's hopeful suburban villa. In 1598 the Duke of Parma reconquered the south from the rebels, but only at the cost of destroying its economy and reducing its farms to ruin. By then, in any case, the rebels were firmly established in the north. Antwerp itself, enriched by the civil war of the 1480s that had driven the entrepôt trade away from Bruges, was ruined in its turn, cut off from the sea by the rebel forts downstream. Its trade passed to Amsterdam. The wealthy provinces of Flanders and Brabant remained Catholic and were reduced to wasteland; the wasteland of Holland became Protestant and grew rich.

Outwards and onwards the ripples spread. To destroy support for the rebellious provinces in the north, Philip had to invade England. To cover Parma's crossing of the Channel in defenceless flat-bottomed barges, he had to send a naval task force. To restore Spain's failing position after the destruction of this Armada, he had to intervene against the Protestants in France. To stem the haemorrhage of wealth after his failure in France, he had to declare bankruptcy . . . Down went the old empire of Spain. Up came the new empires of the north.

And what happened to the pictures themselves, those six historyless panels painted as the torrents of history swept round the studio door in 1565? They were swept along in the current like everything else, and tumbled in the world's changing politics. First they were taken back to Vienna, and so passed away from the failing Spanish empire into the second Habsburg empire that Charles V had separated from Spain when he abdicated. But one of them vanished in transit, so then there were five.

Five little pictures, hanging in a row. Five largish pictures, and not hanging in a row at all, because *Haymaking* went off on its travels again, no one knows when or how, but probably one of the Habsburgs gave it away to someone as a present; Grossmann thinks Maria Theresa to her favourite, Count Grassalkovich. So then there were four.

Four oil-paintings, hanging on the wall. On the wall of the Belvedere, to be precise, one of the imperial palaces in Vienna, where in 1781 they were arranged under the title of *The Four Seasons*. A simple solution to all the problems that have beset later scholars, but one even less related to reality than it appears, because spring and winter in this group were represented by two pictures that weren't part of the cycle at all, *Children's Games* and *The Massacre of the Innocents*. The genuine pair, *The Gloomy Day* and *The Hunters in the Snow*, had gone into store, unrecognized and unregarded. So then there were two.

Two lonely pictures, remaining from the six: *The Corn Harvest* and *The Return of the Herd*. Then in 1805 Napoleon entered Vienna, and secured his position by defeating the Austrians and their allies at Austerlitz. Four years later the French took away a number of the Habsburg Bruegels amongst their booty, and though they later returned the others, *The Corn Harvest* remained behind in the possession of Count Andreossy, who'd been the French commander in the city. So then there was one.

One single picture, quaking in its boots: *The Return of the Herd*. Until . . . until, just before this one in its turn got struck by lightning, or chopped up to make a campfire at the Battle of Königgrätz, and the whole cycle vanished, they began to reappear.

First came *Haymaking*. In 1864 it was inherited from Princess Grassalkovich by Prince Lobkowitz, and was discovered in his collection in Prague by the art historian Max Dvořák. In 1884 Engerth recognized the two pictures languishing in the store room in Vienna, *The Gloomy Day* and *The Hunters in the Snow*, and returned them to their rightful place on the walls. In 1919 the new empire that had arisen across the Atlantic entered the story, when *The Corn Harvest* came up for sale in Paris, and was bought by the Metropolitan Museum in New York. Then for a few years the three pictures remaining in Vienna vanished once more when Austria was annexed by Nazi Germany and Europe was closed by the Second World War; and for a few more years after that, with the extension of the Russian empire to central Europe, the Iron Curtain was drawn down upon *Haymaking* in Prague.

Since when, as relative stability has returned to the Western world, they've settled in their places, three in Vienna, one in Prague and one in New York, not to be disturbed again. Five happy pictures, hanging on the wall.

Until *I* came on the scene, and then there were six. Or very soon will be. As I believe. As I *know*. And am on the verge of proving, if only I could see what's eluding me.

One way of proving my picture's identity would be to trace it back to its hiding place since it disappeared from the late Archduke's baggage.

Does it bear any evidence of its passage through the last 350 years of European history? Well, at some point it seems to have passed through the hands of someone who covered up the signature. It's not the only time that something like this happened. Think of that neat three centimetre-wide strip missing from *Haymaking*. That didn't come about by accident – you can't knock a complete horizontal section off a solid oak panel half an inch thick by banging it against a doorpost. Someone deliberately and laboriously sawed it off. Why? Why should anyone want to conceal the signature that establishes the identity of a major work of art? Only one reason comes to my mind: because its owner didn't want it to be recognized. Why might its owner not want it to be recognized? Again, only one reason comes to mind: because he was frightened that it would be stolen.

My picture has another clue, perhaps left by the same person who concealed the signature, perhaps not – the label on the back:

Vrancz: Pretmakers in een Berglandschap (um 1600 gemalt).

Who wrote that? Someone who knew Dutch or Flemish, plainly. And although the paper was yellowing, it was typed, so it was someone in this century. As I think about it now, though, I seem to recall that for some reason the date at the end *isn't* typed. *(Um 1600 gemalt)* is handwritten, as if it were an afterthought, added after the label had already been stuck on. A little odd. And suddenly I'm struck by something much odder still about this postscript. Why hadn't I noticed it before? *(Um 1600 gemalt)* isn't Dutch or Flemish. It's German.

A Dutchman, or a Fleming, frightened that the picture will be stolen if anyone realizes what it is, types a false label in his own language, then adds the date in someone else's . . . No. It's the someone else who adds the date, in his *own* language. A German, then. Why is the German writing on the Dutchman's picture? Because what the Dutchman feared has come to pass. It's been stolen. It's been stolen by the German.

A scenario:

1940, and the Wehrmacht is requisitioning houses in Brussels. Or Antwerp, or Amsterdam. In some of them they find pictures on the walls. A lieutenant who knows approximately as much about art as Tony Churt looks at the labels on the back of them all, hoping to find a Rembrandt or a Vermeer. He's never heard of Vrancz, but this one looks quite nice, so he takes it anyway, breaks it out of its frame to make it easier to carry, and looks up the name in the local library before he takes it home as a present for his girlfriend the next time he goes on leave. 'Painted about 1600,' he writes on the label, to impress her.

Possibly. But then how did it get into the Churts' possession?

Another scenario:

1945, and the British army is requisitioning houses in

Hanover. Or Gütersloh, or Osnabrück. In some of them they find pictures on the walls. Major Churt, who knows approximately as much about art as the son he will beget when he returns home from the war, has no scruples about relieving the local Gauleiter's family of *The Rape of Helen*, which will look impressive at the head of the stairs back home, but is most careful to press packs of Naafi cigarettes on various other, more modest citizens as recompense for two or three vaguely Dutch-looking paintings that have also taken his fancy.

Well, possibly. We can guess this much about my picture, though – that it's been tumbled along in the great stream of history like the others. Tumbled and tumbled, all six of them, until they've reached the placid waters of our own times, and come to rest. Three in Vienna; one in Prague; one in New York; one in the Churts' hatchery.

And, yes, there's something about them that I haven't put my finger on yet. Something that I'm just about to locate. Because even in that idyllic year of 1565 *something* was worrying Bruegel; it was at some time in those same twelve busy months that he was also doing *The Calumny of Apelles* and *Christ and the Woman Taken in Adultery*, his two great appeals against denunciation, false and true.

The answer hovers at the edge of my mind, like an elusive word or a half-remembered face. I've a feeling that I've got what I'm looking for in front of my eyes already, if only I could see it.

And when I wake in the morning, alone in the double bed at Oswald Road, I have it: baler twine. Everything fits together! The pink baler twine that you can see in my picture when you look closely is binding it to a whole series of other pictures scattered around the world. These pictures make a terrifying historical pattern that ties them in with the Churts' estate, and clearly connects them to the peasants who go squawking up into the air from under your feet at every step, only to be shot dead and roasted alive by faceless figures cowled in black plastic sheeting – the brutal henchmen of the German Inquisition.

Even after I'm on my feet and cleaning my teeth, my mind keeps slipping back to this vision. And later still, long after I've thought my way out of everything else in the tangle, long after I've got *Helen* loaded up for the last time, and set out with her for south London, one element of it somehow ridiculously persists at the back of my consciousness:

Baler twine.

But what this unlikely detail might conceivably signify I can't imagine.

Almost over now. By the end of the day I'll have my picture in my hands.

I've got the baler twine out of my mind by this time. It's 'almost over' and its variants that are filling my head now. I'm standing outside the NatWest in Lavenage holding a Sainsbury's plastic carrier bag. In the bag are not groceries but neat bundles of banknotes: 1,920 fifties in seventy-eight fat packets of twenty-five, and an assortment of loose notes. Sixty-two of the packets are from Mr Koenig's unsavoury-looking associate on the Tidewater Industrial Estate in Rotherhithe, sixteen from the bank, filled with the mortgage extension and the money from Kate. Now I'm waiting while Laura collects the final seven thousand pounds. I'm waiting on the pavement outside because I feel that curious glances might be directed at me by employees and customers who know her if I stand next to her while the clerk counts out the fifties, and she drops them into my carrier bag.

I'm not only waiting for Laura – I'm also waiting to be mugged. It seems unlikely that people are attacked for a bag of groceries in the middle of the afternoon in Lavenage, but rural crime's on the increase, and then again I may have been followed from Rotherhithe by some of Mr Koenig's associate's even less savoury friends. In any case I'm also waiting for the police, for court officials, for private security staff hired by brother Georgie. I'm waiting for Tony to spring out of nowhere, just as Laura comes out of the bank waving her money at me, though how he can get into Lavenage when we've got his Land-Rover I'm not sure. I'm waiting for Kate to appear, in town for a little implausible last-minute shopping.

But mostly I'm waiting for it all to be over. Which it will be very soon. Half an hour or so. Say an hour or two, to be on the safe side. By the time the sun goes down this evening, everything will be beginning to get back to normal.

Out of all the eventualities I'm braced for, some likely, some unlikely, the one that actually materializes is Kate. Of course. I knew it would happen. I knew it as surely as I know who painted the *Merrymakers*. Tilda's dangling in the sling in front of her, and she's carrying a plastic carrier bag like mine. I realise without surprise that she's crossing the road towards me, and the very first thing that goes through my head, in spite of all my fears, is a flash of tenderness and delight. It takes her a moment or two longer to realize that it's me, since she's not expecting me as I am her – and then the first thing that crosses her face is that same brief flash of happiness. In the next instant, though, she's remembered how things stand, and the light's gone again, almost as soon it appeared.

'Hello,' she says, as cautiously as if she were answering the phone.

'Shopping?' I ask fatuously.

'One or two things.' She doesn't enquire what I'm doing there, in the middle of the afternoon, on my way from London to the cottage. I lift my carrier bag an inch or two, as a self-evident explanation, though whether I'm suggesting I've money or groceries in it I'm not sure. I don't need to ask her what she's got in hers. It's some small treat to offer me for dinner later, as a wordless gesture to mark my homecoming.

'I take it you don't want a lift home?' she says.

'No, thanks,' I say, and start to explain that I've got to drop the Land-Rover off at Upwood. But a more graphic explanation has already materialized beside me.

'Seven thou,' says Laura, dropping five more fat packets and another handful of loose fifties into my bag. 'Though frankly I think we should blow it all on a weekend in the Bahamas . . . Oh, hello!'

'Hello,' says Kate.

A pause. Almost over, though. Almost there. Soon, soon, soon be there.

'Why's there always someone just in front of you in the queue who seems to be paying in their life savings in five pees?' Laura asks Kate in a tone of humorous complaint.

Kate says nothing. For a moment she simply stands there, not knowing what to do. Then she walks away. I run after her. 'Listen,' I say, 'I'll be back very shortly . . . I've just got to . . .' I gesture with the bag, but she can't see it, because she's walking away from me and she doesn't turn round.

1565. The uneasiness, the terror, the wrath . . . Yes, rapidly culminating to a crisis.

'Sorry,' says Laura humbly when I get back to her. 'I should have looked first.'

'No, no,' I say gallantly. 'My responsibility. Don't worry.'

'You hadn't told her about the money?'

'No.'

'Oh dear.'

Oh dear indeed. But then I haven't told Laura about Kate's money. Oh dear, oh dear, oh dear.

'And that was a joke,' says Laura.

'What was a joke?'

'About the Bahamas.'

– 353 –

'I realize.'

'She wouldn't have thought . . .?'

'Probably. We've been going through a bit of a rough patch.'

We walk towards the car park.

'*My* fault?' she asks quietly.

'You come into it.'

'But that's crazy!'

'Yes.'

'Nothing happened!'

'No.'

We get awkwardly into the Land-Rover.

'Just take me back and drop me off where you found me,' she says. 'Then you won't ever have to see me again.'

'Thank you,' I say. She laughs, wounded.

'I mean for the money,' I explain.

'Unless you *want* to see me.'

'Yes, yes. And I'll pay you back as soon as I can.'

'Of course,' she says, but she doesn't ask when that will be.

We sit in silence as I drive her towards Upwood. When *will* I be able to pay her back, in fact? As soon as I've completed my gradual discovery of the real identity of my picture. I adjust the time scale for this as we drive; I can't keep Kate and Laura waiting for their money just so that I can observe the kind of niceties I originally had in mind. 'I should think I'll be able to let you have the money in a month or two,' I tell her. 'Will that be all right?'

'Don't worry. I'm not going to start ringing you up. I'm not going to go bombarding you with letters.'

'Thank you,' I say again. I can't think of anything else. She glances at me.

'I do realize how bloody it was for you,' she says gently,

'running into Kate like that. I'm sorry. I can see how sick you are about it.'

'Yes. *You* don't have to think about it, though. I'll be all right. Thank you.'

'I wish you wouldn't keep saying thank you.'

I stop just short of the drive. 'You'd better leave it twenty minutes or so before you put in an appearance,' I tell her. 'Just in case he starts putting two and two together. I'll probably be more or less through with him by then, anyway.'

'I'll give you ten minutes,' she says, as she gets out. 'I can't hang around for ever. Even for you.'

'Fifteen,' I counter-offer. All my old aspirations to the transcendental truth of the universe have crumbled into a life of endless chaffering.

'I'll smoke a cigarette, then,' she says defiantly, closing the door. Then she pulls it open again, fumbles in her bag, and throws a crumpled pack of cigarettes into the car. 'No, I won't,' she says. But she looks as bleak as I imagine I do.

I drive on, past the Keep Out sign, prudently remembering to conceal the cigarettes in my pocket. Almost over. By the time the sun goes down I shall be there.

Yes, the sun's still shining. We're coming to the end of a warm spring day, well down the green hillsides towards that happy blue town beside the sea, where the ship's just spreading its sails.

By sunset I shall be there.

The Deal Done

As I knock on the great front door, and start the dogs barking, my spirits revive. What I feel now is that I've been
through some kind of initiation rite to test my fitness to
handle high art. I've passed through stage after stage of
humiliation and hardening. I've rolled my trouser leg up,
I've drunk my yard of ale down. I've had my head shaved
and my skin slashed and I've watched all night in the
Chapel Perilous. Now I'm hammering on the temple doors
to claim my reward.

'Got the money?' says Tony anxiously, even before the
door's open enough for the dogs to squeeze through. I hold
up my carrier bag. He smiles. 'Sainsbury's! Excellent! Must
be good stuff!' The dogs slaver and prostrate themselves.
We're welcome guests, my carrier bag and I.

He leads the way into the dark room with the threadbare
carpet and the deconstructed sofa where we went that first
evening. I count out eighty-four packets of notes and seventeen loose fifties from the stock in the bag, and lay them on
the long table behind the sofa, while he pours two glasses of
his cut-price aperitif. We seem to have come full circle.

'£112,000,' I say crisply. 'Minus five and a half per cent. I
make that £105,840. Call it £105,850, because I haven't got
change.'

I'm braced for an outburst of fury at the mention of the
commission, which I suspect he's completely forgotten.
Not a word, though. Now the deal's done he behaves in the

most gentlemanly manner. He re-counts the packets, but trusts me for the number of notes in each of them and scarcely glances at the loose fifties, then normalizes most gracefully.

'Sorry if I got a bit raw-arsed at times.'

'Not at all,' I say magnanimously. 'Life's a battle. We've all got to fight our corner.'

'Also, things here were somewhat on my tits.'

'I can imagine. Happier days ahead, though.' I raise my glass. 'Is Laura going to join us?' I ask, with effortless disingenuousness. All my newly learned skills in *suggestio falsi* have returned in the hour of victory.

'She's out somewhere,' he say. 'God knows where.'

He sits down in his old armchair, in front of the great empty fireplace, and gazes gloomily into his drink, suddenly overtaken by melancholy.

'Meant quite a lot to me, you know,' he says. 'Your help in all this. Not just the money. I sometimes feel I'm fighting a pretty single-handed battle here. Government's doing its level best to destroy me for a start. Neighbours aren't much better. Two sons – total washout. One's mucking out in a dogs' home. Which I thought was a job for girls. The other's a *social worker*. Another girl's job, isn't it? What do you make of that? According to Laura they're trying to tell me something. God knows what. And now that charming brother of mine's crawled out of the woodwork. I sometimes wonder what the point of it all is. Get you to tell me some time, perhaps.'

As a philosopher, presumably. 'Well, one of these days,' I say with a sympathetic sigh, though I'm absolutely determined that I'll never set foot in this house again. 'Except that I'm not sure I've much idea myself.' The only idea I have in my head is impatience to take the pictures and get out of here. I hadn't foreseen grateful speeches and sudden confidences. I'm becoming consumed by an irrational fear that Georgie will return in the next few minutes with enforcers and sniffer dogs trained to nose out arsenic sulphide and copper carbonate, and just pip me to the post.

'Well,' I say regretfully, looking at my watch.

'You've brought the Land-Rover back? I'll drive you home.'

'Thanks,' I say, getting to my feet, and picking up my Sainsbury's bag, with the three thousand pounds or so left of my hard-won money in it. 'I don't think I can really walk it carrying those three pictures.'

He remains sitting, though, gazing into the black depths of the cold fireplace. 'I just struggle to keep the old place going,' he says mournfully. 'All I can think of. Waste of time, even if I manage to hang on to it. Sons don't give a monkey's about it. Anyway it's breaking up around my ears already, however hard I try.'

I attempt to murmur something appropriate, but all I can think of is getting the next three bits of it away from him. 'Perhaps we'd better hustle those Dutchmen out of here', I say, 'before anything else happens.'

The dogs lift their heads and look at the door. One of them utters a brief bark. There's the sound of the front door opening. It's Georgie – he's here.

Footsteps come down the corridor outside, and Laura puts her head round the door. Oh, yes. I'd forgotten about her.

'What are you two up to?' she says. 'Not boozing already?'

'We're celebrating,' I tell her. 'I've sold *Helen*.'

'Oh, great,' she says vaguely. 'I was out for a walk. How much did you get for her?'

I open my mouth to tell her, then glance at Tony. He's still gazing into the fireplace, apparently unaware of Laura's question or even her presence. I turn back to Laura, uncertain how much he tells her about his business arrangements. She glances at him in her turn, then makes me a little private funny face.

'Hundreds or thousands, though?' she enquires. My caution was right. 'Thousands,' I confess boldly. 'Unbelievable,' she murmurs, and disappears.

'Yes,' says Tony, 'and then there's her.'

Long pause. I sit down on the arm of the sofa. I force myself. I can't do otherwise.

'Out for a walk!' he says. He gives a short laugh. 'She's never walked as far as the end of the drive!'

I could reassure him that he's wrong about this, at any rate, but I don't.

'She's stopped smoking,' he says.

'Has she?' Again, I could offer informed comment – I could tell him that I share his forebodings about the significance of this. Again, I don't. 'Good,' I say.

Another long pause. I get the impression that the room's growing darker. We're getting visibly a little nearer to sunset.

'I admit that I haven't kept absolutely to the straight and narrow myself,' he says. 'Neither of us has. But I am actually rather fond of her. Rather devoted to her. Rather dependent on her, though you might not think it. I don't know what she's up to, but I do know it's something serious this time. I may be a fool, but I'm not *that* big a fool. And, Martin, if she left me . . .'

He looks up at me. There are tears in his eyes once more. I suppose these ones I've helped to put there. I'm past caring about his tears, though. Or about any responsibility I may have. Past caring about anything except pictures and go.

'Don't worry,' I say fatuously, then advance from fatuity to simple lying. 'She loves you. I've seen the way she looks at you.' I get to my feet again, repeat the performance with my watch, and shift from simple lying to brutal practicality. 'Now, if you're going to give me a lift . . .'

Laura comes back, carrying a bottle of the gin she bought. 'I'm going to have a glass of this,' she says. 'Anyone want to switch?'

Tony at last gets to his feet, and walks out of the room. 'Come on,' he snaps at me. 'Let's go if we're going.'

'No?' says Laura to me, holding up the bottle.

'Tony's giving me a lift home,' I explain.

She mimes a silent kiss to me. 'Love to Kate,' she calls aloud, as I vanish through the door and follow Tony and the dogs up the corridor.

'If I ever get my hands on the gentleman concerned,' he says, as soon as the front door's shut behind us, 'I'll run a harrow over him.'

'Don't forget the pictures,' I say.

He uncouples the trailer from the Land-Rover, then opens the door for me. The dogs jump in ahead of me as he walks round to the driver's side.

'I'll put him through the combine,' he says.

'Pictures.'

'Get in. What pictures?'

'The Dutchmen. The other three pictures I'm selling for you.' I fight to keep the panic out of my voice.

'Oh, *them*,' he says. He gets in and starts the engine. 'You don't have to bother. Got someone else to take them off my hands.'

I get in beside him and close the door, too stunned to think. We bump down the drive. Something about the huge silence that's fallen over the world, perhaps, makes him glance at me, and what he sees on my face suggests that something more needs to be said.

'Thanks for offering, though. Sorry. Should have said that before.'

Half-way down the hill we have to pull into a passing place to make room for a car on its way up. The driver winds down his window to speak to us, and a smiling pair of ears emerge. It takes me a moment to recognize them – the last time I saw them they were departing on a bicycle.

Tony winds down his window as well. 'I'll be back up there in a moment,' he calls. 'Tell Laura to give you a drink.'

'I feel so guilty!' cries John Quiss. 'Roaring around like Mr Toad in a hired car, poisoning a fine spring evening. But I don't think I can ride all the way back to London with them tied on my *handlebars*.'

We continue on our way.

'He thinks one of those buggers could be worth quite a bit,' explains Tony.

Faster and faster flows the river. The uneasiness, the terror, the wrath culminate to a crisis. Then all at once the current dies away in the flat calm of the millpool. We enter a land where history has ceased.

So it's over before sunset, just as I said, with an hour or so still to go.

I move about the cottage kitchen like a ghost, putting books down and picking them up, saying nothing to Kate, unable to speak. Our paths cross and recross, as she moves silently about preparing a bottle for Tilda. We step aside to let each other pass, shifting in and out of the low golden rays of the declining sun from the window, now gilded and blinking, now dark and blinded. It's like a very complex formal dance, but one conducted in total silence.

I suppose this is the worst thing that's ever happened to me. It's certainly the worst that's ever happened to *us*. I don't know how to begin to explain to her. I still can't take in the scale and suddenness of the catastrophe, the total alteration of the world around me.

Perhaps I could start like this: I could tell her that in the end I kept my word. That I didn't find the objective evidence I was looking for, and that I consequently didn't go through with my scheme. Or I could try leaving out 'consequently'. But I *didn't* go through with it! That's the important part. Not all the way.

I could tell her quite straightforwardly that all I have left, out of the £15,000 I borrowed from the bank, and the £6,000 I borrowed from her, is the £3,150 in the carrier bag. That I will repay her, and the bank, I don't know how, but *somehow*, even if I have to do nights at the local petrol station to raise the money. That I pledge myself to this utterly. As utterly I as I pledged myself to my earlier undertaking.

I could tell her that at any rate I will never again have to take part in shabby schemes to evade tax, never again have to handle stolen goods or be caught out in apparently clandestine meetings.

I could tell her how ludicrous her misreading of the situation with Laura is, and how hurtful to me.

I could tell her that really I *succeeded* as a confidence trickster – succeeded only too well, because Tony had no idea at all that I was after those other three pictures. I'm like the Netherlandish rulers getting their man on to the throne of Spain. I outsmarted everyone, even myself.

I could tell her that it was she who finished it all, for better or worse, with just two words to Tony. That it was she who brought down the whole cloud-capped Tower of Babel I'd constructed for him with her passing mention of John Quiss.

I could point out that as a result of our joint efforts it is at least a respectable academic who's getting his hands on the picture, so it will presumably find a proper home.

I could tell her how bitter I feel that she betrayed me in this way.

I could tell her that I've gone down into the pit, and will not return.

I could tell her that in some secret part of me I'm relieved to be spared the terrible burdens that victory would undoubtedly have brought.

But I tell her nothing. I sit down at one end of the table,

gazing sightlessly at the Sainsbury's carrier bag. She sits down at the other end of the table, holding the bottle she's made for Tilda. And in the end it's she's who speaks. Of course. Once again.

'Martin,' she says quietly, 'I love you, and I think in your own way you love me. So can I ask you to do something for me? For both of us, in fact. For all three of us, because I know you love Tilda as well.'

I wait, my hands still, my head bowed.

'Can I ask you to go away until all this is over?' she says.

So now at last I know what to say. It's very simple.

'It *is* over,' I tell her.

She watches me. I go on looking at the carrier bag. I can hear Tilda beginning to stir upstairs.

'You mean you've got the picture?' she asks.

'I mean I *haven't* got it. I'm not going to get it. I've lost. You've won.'

I get up and put the carrier bag on the table in front of her. 'There's a bit of the money left. I'll get the rest of it somehow.'

She looks at the bag sadly. She doesn't even react to the news that I've managed to lose most of the money in the process of achieving nothing.

'I'm sorry,' she says.

I'm not quite sure what's supposed to happen now. I have a feeling I should kiss her. Awkwardly I take hold of her arms, to indicate that she should stand up. Awkwardly she does so. Awkwardly we stand facing each other. She's still holding Tilda's bottle.

The phone rings.

I make a wry face, and go on standing there, waiting to kiss her. She goes on standing there, waiting to be kissed. We seem to have become frozen in time, like my lost couple in the bushes. But that flatly insistent demand for our attention, like the grizzling of a baby, makes it somehow even more awkward to proceed to the next stage of our reconciliation. She turns to look at the phone. 'Leave it,' I say. She goes across and picks up the receiver. For a moment she listens in silence, and then silently passes it to me.

'Sorry,' says Laura, as soon as she hears my voice. 'I know I said I wouldn't. But I've *got* them! You'll have to jump in the car and get up here *immediately*!'

She puts the phone down. I put the phone down. I look at the table. The inside of my head's completely anaesthetized.

'Listen . . .' I say to Kate.

I see her hand, still holding Tilda's bottle, as it pushes the carrier bag back towards me.

'You'd better keep the rest of the money,' she says. 'Because it's not over, is it? It's never going to be over. So, Martin, will you just go now? And please don't ever come back.'

The river lies motionless in the millpool. Then on it plunges again, into the race. History ceases for a year. Then on it surges again, into the Eighty Years War.

As soon as I turn into the drive at Upwood, Laura comes running over from where she was waiting before, behind Private Property, Keep Out, tremendously excited and pleased with herself.

'They put them in the boot of his car and then they went back into the house for a drink!' she cries. 'So I simply took them out again!'

I jump out of the car. She's already running back to the sign to fetch them.

'You *took* them?' I query despairingly. 'You just . . . *took* them?'

'I couldn't believe it when I realized he'd cheated you out of them!' She opens my boot and flings the pictures in.

'But if you *took* them,' I say, 'then that's . . .' Something. Some sort of crime. Isn't it? What sort of crime, though? I don't know.

'Not *stealing*!' cries Laura. 'Certainly not *stealing*! Not if you send him the money!'

No, all right, not *stealing*, exactly. But . . .

'He made some kind of arrangement with you, didn't he?' she says, slamming the boot down. 'We're just sticking to the arrangement!'

Yes. Possibly. I'm not sure quite how definite the arrangement was, but morally, I suppose . . . perhaps . . .

'You *have* still got some of the money left?' she asks. She picks up the Sainsbury's carrier bag on the front seat and looks inside. 'Swads and swads! Just send him a few thousand – he's not going to complain! He can't! One word and his brother'll have writs out for these as well!'

I get uneasily into the car. But she's running back to the sign and dragging something else out . . . It's a suitcase. What's this?

'I'll ring him tomorrow,' she says, as she heaves it on to the back seat. 'It's usually safer to be at the other end of a phone before you tell him things he doesn't want to hear.'

She's leaving him? A sound move, certainly, and high time. But where do *I* come into all this exactly?

She gets in beside me. 'Come on!' she says. 'That horrible little art person's going to stop somewhere and look in his boot, and then he's going to come screaming back up the hill again!'

Yes. We'll have to discuss all this as we go along. I turn the car, and we start back down the hill. She starts to laugh. 'It's like Tony's mother, taking off with Dicky and *Helen*.'

'Now, Laura,' I say firmly. 'It's very kind of you to get the pictures for me, and I'm very amazed and very touched and very grateful. But perhaps we should just get one or two things absolutely straight . . .'

She stops laughing. 'We've got everything absolutely straight. Don't worry. You couldn't afford me, anyway. You're just giving me a lift. Drop me off in London somewhere – I'll stay with my sister. I *assume* you're taking the pictures to London?'

Am I? I suppose I am. The whole thing's got way beyond me once again. I plainly can't go back to the cottage. Not for some time yet. Though Kate doesn't mean *ever*, of course. No one means absolutely literally what they say. Not even Kate.

I can feel Laura looking at me. 'Or are you worrying about Kate again?' she says. 'It's all right – she's not going to spring out of the bushes between here and London!'

She might, actually, as we drive past the track to the cottage. But she doesn't.

'I don't suppose he'll notice I'm not there till he wonders why there's no sign of dinner,' she says. 'I guessed what had happened when you went and you hadn't got the other pictures with you. Then when that awful grinning little man came through the door looking so pleased with himself I thought, "Right! Enough's enough!"'

The lake by the wood where the dead tramp was has dried to a scattering of dust. We turn out on to the Lavenage road . . . Pass Busy Bee Honey . . . Strike south into the unreal country . . .

I suppose I've won after all. Not that I feel the slightest sense of it. The only thing I actually feel is that I've nothing more to lose. It's gone already . . . It hasn't, though, it hasn't! She doesn't mean *ever*. No one means *ever*.

And Laura's right. We're not committing any crime. We're not stealing Menelaus's treasure. I'll send him the money. Every penny I was going to give him anyway. Though since he owns those three pictures no more than I do . . . Since *no one* owns them . . . Since no one's in control of anything any longer . . . Yes, what I feel like isn't Paris or Dicky – it's the man in my picture in the boot who's falling helpless into the water. Falling, falling, into the depths, where the waters will close above him for ever.

I stop the car with clumsy suddenness in the middle of nowhere, and crash over a kerbstone on to the verge. A terrible thought has just come to me. Not a thought – a certainty, as icy and final as the waters in the millpool.

I slowly turn to look at Laura. She's already looking at me, smiling. 'Don't look so grim about it, then,' she says. 'You don't *have* to go through the motions. I know you really don't want to . . .'

I just go on gazing at her, unable to take in what she's saying, frozen by the freezing certainty that's come to me.

'Well,' she says, 'one kiss, then.'

She stops smiling. She brings her face slowly and seriously closer to mine. I get out of the car and open the boot.

The picture on top is the cavalrymen. The next one's the skaters. I throw them aside and pull out the bottom one.

But I know already. It's not mine – it *can't* be mine, because mine's solid oak – it weighs twenty or thirty pounds – she couldn't have carried it to the end of the drive with her suitcase and the other two pictures – it's three foot nine by five foot three – there's no way it could be got into the car . . .

The one I've got in my hands now is in a frame, for a start. It's on canvas. It's about one foot by two foot. It's the dog.

'That *is* the one you really wanted, isn't it?' asks Laura. I look up from the picture. She's got out of the car, and she's watching me anxiously. 'It was supposed to be a surprise. I just suddenly thought of the way you looked at it, and I crept back in and took it off the wall.'

I look at her. I look at the dog. I look at her again. I thought there was nothing more to lose. But of course there was, there was. There always is.

I'd forgotten – I managed to deceive *her* about my intentions as well. As a deceiver I've been a success beyond all reasonable expectations.

'He's going to go into orbit when he notices,' she says. 'It's the only picture he really cares about . . . It *is* the one you've had your eye on?'

Well, at this point all the springs and shock absorbers inside me finally give way. They've carried me on a long journey over a very rough road, and now suddenly they've gone. I hurl the dog away into the darkness, sit down on a low ornamental wall in front of somebody's ornamental hedge, and burst into tears.

It's the Amalienburg Palace all over again. Then I was mourning the demise of four days' happiness. Now I'm weeping for the loss of everything I ever had. Of everything I ever hoped to have.

Laura sits down on the wall beside me, very close but not touching. I can't look at her, but she puts her hand on mine, and I can feel the patience and tenderness of her waiting. Surprising. I shouldn't have expected it of her. I'm wrong about her, as about everything else.

It's getting dark; the sun has definitely set. Every few seconds a passing car lights us up, and gets a brief glimpse of two figures engaged in some inexplicable emotional scene at the edge of the spring evening, as marginal to their world as Icarus or Saul.

'Sorry,' I manage finally. I take several deep breaths. 'Sorry.'

'It was the other one?' she says gently. 'The one in the bedroom?'

I say nothing. No point any longer in trying to conceal it. But then from her, as it's turned out, there never was.

'It's back in the bedroom,' she says. 'Otherwise I might have brought it anyway. He fetched it in from the hatchery to have another go at washing the corner. If only you'd told me! I thought it wasn't worth anything!'

I withdraw my hand and put it on top of hers to console her in my turn. I feel almost as sorry for her and her mortification as I do for myself and my ruin.

'And it really would have meant so much to you?' she says.

I translate my feelings about it into the simplest possible terms. 'I think it's worth a couple of million pounds or so.'

With her free hand she strokes the hand of mine that's holding hers.

'Wow,' she says finally.

I manage another wobbly laugh. 'You haven't said that for a long time. Everything used to be "wow". And once you called me a frightful little wet fish.'

'Did I? Sorry.'

'No, you said it very nicely. Anyway, it's true.'

I suppose Tony's a pretty wet fish as well. So, by the sound of it, is the husband he pinched her off. I'm her third wet fish in a row. Perhaps we're all really just the children she still hasn't had.

'A couple of million or so,' she repeats. She likes the sound of the words. 'He never suspected, you know. Not for a moment. Nor did I. What a sly little fish you are! A couple of million . . .! How much were you proposing to pay *him* for it?'

'I thought a couple of thousand.'

She laughs in sheer delight. 'How wonderful! I see why you're a philosopher.'

She jumps to her feet. 'Come on. It's getting cold now the sun's gone down.'

In the light from the passing cars she collects the dog and the two Dutchmen from the darkness I consigned them to.

'He keeps it hidden under the mattress,' she says. 'Killing two birds with one stone – he's got a bad back.'

We settle ourselves in the car again, and I start the engine to continue my now pointless odyssey.

'We'll never get it into this little car,' she says. 'We'll have to take his Land-Rover.'

I've turned my head to see if the road's clear behind us. I turn it back to look at my passenger. *What* did she say?

'I'll go in and make him dinner,' she says. 'Then as soon as I've got him and the dogs safely shut away in the kitchen, I'll open the front door for you. A couple of million? Maybe you *could* afford me.'

We park the car in the shadows, by Private Property, Keep Out.

'I don't know what you mean about *burglary*,' she says, because I haven't ceased to express my uneasiness and reluctance all the way back here. 'How can it be *burglary*? It's *my* house! Anyway, I simply brought the wrong one! We're taking it back and changing it. It's just the same as taking a sweater back to Marks and Spencer if it doesn't fit.'

And already she's out of the car and getting the dog picture out of the boot.

'Wait, listen . . .' I whisper desperately.

'Leave the key in,' she says quietly. 'Then when we come back in the Land-Rover you can drop me, and I'll take your car and follow you . . . Martin, he'd be *pleased* if he knew. He'd much rather have the dog one.'

She vanishes into the darkness of the drive. I run after her, stumbling in and out of the potholes.

'Stop!' I whisper. 'Wait! I don't want it!'

'Of course you want it.'

'I don't, I don't! I just want to get out of here! I just want to go!'

'Don't be *too* much of a wet fish, darling. We'll manage it between us. He may not even *be* there.'

No, quite – he may have gone rushing down the hill to call on Kate for some mutual consolation.

Apparently not, though. When we emerge from the trees,

there's the Land-Rover, dimly silhouetted against the muted light from some of the downstairs windows. I stop. So does Laura.

'I thought I'd never have to see him again,' she says in a different voice. 'I can't tell you what it's been like these last few weeks . . .'

Now *her* courage has gone. I'm shamefully relieved. I pluck at the sleeve of her sweater. I just want to be away from here before the dogs find us.

She takes my hand and squeezes it. 'Keep watching the front door,' she says. 'The moment it opens – in you go. He won't come out of the kitchen. We'll almost certainly be in the middle of a row by then.'

She gives my hand another squeeze, painfully hard this time, and moves forward into the darkness. I grab at her sleeve again. 'Laura! Please, please, please!'

She stops.

'Please, Laura,' I whisper abjectly. 'For my sake! Please!'

'A couple of million?' she whispers.

'I don't know! I'm not sure! I think I'm wrong!'

But she's gone, swallowed up into the night. A moment later a pale rectangle of light shows in the porch, and she's briefly a dark shape against it. Then the rectangle's wiped away again.

I find a place at the edge of the woods to wait. I think it's roughly where I waited to watch the door one damp morning all those weeks ago . . . No, *one* week – less than a week – five days ago. It seems like a lifetime. A *second* lifetime, because I remember I felt then that I'd already spent my entire life waiting outside that same front door.

I try to imagine what's going on inside, then on second thoughts try not to. This little charade is somehow the worst yet. Perhaps he'll talk her round, as he did before when she was married to the first of her three wet fishes. Perhaps she'll feel sorry for him, as she did for me, and go back to him. Perhaps I'm going to spend a third lifetime where I've spent the first two, waiting outside their great oak door.

The whole enterprise has now become completely insane in any case, I understand that perfectly clearly. Even if we manage to lay our hands on it now, the picture and I are very shortly going to be going our separate ways, the picture into a bank vault, me into a prison cell.

In the meanwhile the year goes slowly by. My anxiety subsides; I surrender to my destiny. Through the young leaves of the trees above me I can see the Plough on one side of the Pole Star and Cassiopeia on the other, revolving around each other as they've always revolved. It's a rather idyllic scene, it occurs to me. A solid country house beneath the stars on a serene spring evening. Yet unseen in the shadows outside waits the intruder. The Manichaeans are right: the darkness balances out the light, the evil balances out the good. The light shines on the happy year in Bruegel's panels; around them the darkness gathers.

How would Bruegel, who painted so much that can't be painted, paint the evil in the darkness, Death lurking in Arcadia?

I focus my eyes once again on the darkness of the front door. There's something strange about it. There *is* no front door. Where the front door was, the pale rectangle of light has returned. Laura's opened it again.

And in I go. It's like diving from a high board, or going into hospital for an operation. When the moment comes, you do it. How do you do it? You just do.

In the hall – silence. And only a dim, oblique light coming from somewhere in the heart of the house. I creep towards the great staircase, then stop. I begin to make out faints sounds, presumably from the kitchen – a muffled thud, a barely audible skein of voices. One of the voices, the higher one, is briefly raised, then the lower one raised to overwhelm it. The words are still indistinguishable, but the sense is plain enough – Tony and Laura are occupied with the row that she predicted. The voices fall away again, but I force myself to move forwards. As I start up the stairs I stumble over something hard. It's the dog picture, returned from its little outing. I pick it up and hang it on its hook on the landing as I pass. Yes, I'm just making a simple exchange, the size 34 for the size 32.

The bedroom's in darkness, and I don't turn the light on. The bed itself is as tumbled as it was five days ago. I have to put my face right down into the rank confusion, as I did with such delight on our bed in Oswald Road, to locate the panel. I have a great struggle to work the heavy oak free of the bedding, doing heaven knows what to the painted surface in the process, then bash it on the door handle as I get it out of the bedroom, and scrape it yet again at the turn on the landing. Half-way down the stairs, in the first reasonable glimmer of light, I stop and rest it against the banisters while I edge round to the front and examine it. Yes, no mistake this time. Shimmer – dance – ship – crags. The whole panorama of late spring; it's all there. I feel a sudden wild surge of terrified joy. The fucker's mine!

And then the silence of the house cracks apart. There's the crash of a door being flung violently open, and a lava of sound comes flowing out of the back corridors into the hall beneath me: Tony shouting, Laura shouting after him, the dogs barking and frolicking in delight at this sudden eruption of fun. I freeze, balancing the picture against the banisters, not daring to turn my head to look for fear of the faint light catching my face. The dogs don't need light to find me, of course, and already I'm waist-deep in smelly dog breath, wet tongues and joyously thrashing tails. Still I keep my face averted. Tony seems to have come to a halt in the middle of the hall, with Laura somewhere beyond him. I can feel his gaze on the back of my neck. I can feel hers.

I wait for him to cry out. But he doesn't. 'I'm sick of it!' he's still repeating, with a blind mechanical fury.

'Raspberry sponge,' she repeats pleadingly in her turn. 'In the kitchen. Raspberry sponge.'

'Sick of it!' he insists, and not just of the raspberry sponge, by the sound of it. 'Sick of it! Sick of it! Sick of it!'

He's very drunk, I realize. I can sense behind my back the difficulty he has in keeping his balance. Or in focusing his eyes on the still and silent intruder among the jostling dogs.

And then suddenly the dogs have gone. They've followed their drunken master out of the hall and on into the depths of the house. At last I dare to turn my head. Laura's running across the hall towards me.

'Get out!' she whispers, and now there's real fear in her voice.

I bend to lift the picture again, only too eager to obey.

'Leave it!' she says. 'Quick! Just get out!'

Leave it? Now?

'He's in the gun-room!'

And before I can make up my mind whether to drop the picture or not, he's back, escorted by an exultation of wild anticipatory barking. He shouts at the dogs to be quiet, and as they fall silent I hear behind my motionless back the reason for their excitement: he's going shooting – he's breaking open his gun and cramming in the cartridges.

'Give that thing to me,' commands Laura.

'You'll never forget the sight,' he says. 'I'll tell you that.'

'I said give it to me.'

'I found my uncle. When I was a boy. I still dream about it.'

The gun clicks softly closed. I remain half-stooped, the picture half up and half down, as I wait for the terrible noise that will end his side of the story for good and all. I should move to stop him – of course I should. But I know that if I give the slightest indication of my presence, the gun will jump of its own accord from him to me, and it will be *my* story that ends.

'Please,' says Laura. 'Please, Tony.'

Nothing. Even the dogs have become still. The stream of time has frozen motionless.

And then the phone rings.

Still none of us moves. It goes on ringing, on the great oak sideboard just below me, an event at last in the great eventlessness. We all ignore it, just as Kate and I did the earlier phone call this evening. It won't let itself be ignored, though, any more than the earlier one would. Slowly time resumes its flow. Tony makes a little sound like a sigh.

'Answer it,' he says softly. 'It'll be your friend again.'

'Give me that thing first.'

'Answer it!' he shouts, and the gun cracks wildly against the edge of the table as he swings it towards her. She moves to obey. Before she can reach it, though, he evidently changes his mind. I hear him barge in front of her and fumble with the receiver himself.

'Listen, you cunt . . .' he begins, and then stops, because whoever in this world it is at the other end of the line, I realize with a brief spasm of relief, at least it's not me. A pause while the caller presumably makes this clear. A worse possibility occurs to me: it's Kate, looking for me, wanting to convey some painful message of reproach or appeal.

'*Not* in the boot?' cries Tony. 'What do you mean, they're not in the boot? Is this some sort of stunt . . .?'

Quiss. Of course.

'It was *you*,' says Tony suddenly, in a terrible voice, and at last I turn to look at him, because he's not talking to Quiss now. '*You* took them.'

But it's not me, either. He's dropped the phone, and he's advancing on Laura, still holding the gun.

'You and that little rat in the cottage,' he says, with a sudden flash of drunken perception. 'That filthy little teacher. Of course! He's the one you're fucking!'

Laura snatches the gun out of his hands, and hurls it away across the hall. Whether it's because of her supposed infidelity or the sight of his precious Purdey skating across the flagstones, he finally loses all control. He puts his hands round her throat, and begins to slam her against the banister. She tries to say something to me, but no words emerge. I let go of the *Merrymakers* and put my hands out to do something, I'm not sure what, and the picture goes tumbling end over end down the stairs. Tony turns at the noise and at last sees me. He gazes at me with his mouth hanging stupidly open, still holding Laura by the neck.

For a moment we all stand there, frozen once again. Then he throws Laura down and whirls around, presumably to see where his gun went, though I don't wait to be certain. I come down the rest of the stairs almost as fast as the picture did, then grab hold of Laura with one hand and the picture with the other. Somehow the three of us, picture, Laura and I, are through the front door and out into the night, and I'm unpicking the knot in the baler twine on the tailgate of the Land-Rover. Laura makes some sort of warning noise, her voice still choked from his fingers. And there he is again, gun in both hands, stumbling over the dogs on the threshold, which may be what both fills the night with explosion and sends this first barrel wide. I throw the picture into the car and slam the tailgate across, then bend down to scramble some kind of knot in the twine to hold it. Out of the corner of my eye I can see Tony getting to his feet and steadying himself. I flinch away blindly as he fires again, and a searing hot whip passes across the back of my head.

'Quick!' croaks Laura. 'He's reloading!'

By the time he fires again, though, we're in and away. The window beside me crazes over, but we're bounding down the drive, our heads cracking against the roof, safe in the familiar reek of dirt and petrol, and the wildly barking escort on either side. There's one last tremendous thump as we turn out on to the road, and I see one of the dogs go rolling away like a circus tumbler into the darkness. But I'm too busy feeling the tender wetness at the back of my head to pay much attention.

'A couple of inches to the left . . .' I say, looking at the blood on my hand.

'A couple more seconds . . .' whispers Laura, feeling her throat.

We seem to be alive, though. We seem to have the picture. For the second time tonight we seem to be driving very fast down the hill to happiness.

Tramp wood . . . Lavenage road . . . Busy Bee . . .

Laura's voice begins to return.

'I should never have left that gin out,' she croaks.

She feels her neck, then pulls up her sweater to inspect her ribs. But I can't really look, because I'm at last beginning to put two and two together.

What I'm putting together is baler twine and suffocation. To avoid giving heretics the opportunity of public martyrdom, decreed Philip II in that idyllic, shimmering late spring of 1565, they were henceforth to be executed at midnight in their dungeons. They were to have their heads bound between their knees, and then they were to be slowly suffocated in tubs of water.

'Never mind,' she says. 'We've won. We've got it.'

But I'm not thinking about our triumph. I'm looking in the mirror at the heavy panel wedged across the back of the Land-Rover in the darkness. Not a single detail of it can I see from here, of course. But I think I know what I shall see when I examine it again.

I shall see that the little man tumbling into the millpool has his head bound between his knees.

That they're not ducking him. Not saving him. They're drowning him.

Way off in the middle distance, unnoticed by anyone around, remarked only by an eye outside the world of the picture, a secular martyrdom is taking place. The small event at the edge of things that gives the scene its significance, just like the fall of Icarus and the blinding of Saul and the unnoticed arrival of that pregnant woman among the crowds in Bethlehem. The busy year revolves, but before the first season's out the small concealed murder has occurred that turns the whole idyll into an irony.

'You're very quiet,' says Laura.

'Thinking.'

What I'm thinking is: *Multa pinxit, hic Brugelius, quae pingi non possunt*. What we have here is one of those many things that can't be painted – the invisible execution in the darkness, the judicial murder hidden from the eyes of men. Here it is, exposed to the light of day, and to the eye of every Netherlander who might suffer the same fate, of every Spaniard who might inflict it. Here once again is the more that's always understood, the more than is painted.

The thunder and the thunderbolt. The whole brutal regime, indicted and mocked in one sustained flight of irony. No wonder he was frightened. No wonder my precious burden was removed from the conqueror's baggage.

'Something nice?' asks Laura. 'That you're thinking about? The couple of million? Me? Us? All three together?'

I put my hand on hers. But what I'm thinking is: I have to stop for a moment and check. I have to see whether the man's head is indeed bound between his knees. If it is, then I've done what I said I'd do. I've fulfilled my pledge. I've found the detail that identifies the picture. That locks into place my reading of *all* the pictures. Who owns that piece of oak in law may take some sorting out. I'll have established my moral right, though, to be its temporal guardian. If the binding is there. I look in the mirror to see if it's all right to stop. No, not yet – there's a car coming up fast behind me.

The headlights come rapidly closer and closer, undipped and dazzling, lighting up the picture as if the driver were trying to see inside my tailgate and check the detail himself. I move my head out of line with the mirror, and catch sight of Laura's face shining as she turns round to look at the source of all this sudden light.

'Your car!' she cries. 'We forgot to collect your car!'

The implications dawn on me rather slowly. Not possible! Is it? I look in the mirror again, my eyes screwed up against the dazzle. Unnecessarily, though, because the headlights are now so insanely close that they've vanished below the bottom of the tailgate window.

'Quick!' screams Laura. 'He's going to ram us!'

The story's not over, after all.

I speed up, feeling nothing but despair. The headlights briefly reappear, then disappear as the car behind comes bounding forward to within touching distance again. I slow down, terrified. The Land-Rover lurches as the car behind actually nudges it.

'Get away from him!' screams Laura. 'He's hopelessly drunk!'

I try speeding up again. But now the headlights have adopted a different policy. They go swinging wildly out into the centre of the road.

'No, no – don't let him overtake!'

I put my foot down harder, and now we're running side by side in mad parallel.

'Faster!' cries Laura. 'Faster! Faster!'

Characteristic advice, I realize even in the midst of my terror, and almost certain to be characteristically wrong, but I can't think of any better policy. The whole accelerating, headlong rush of events has been focused into this one final insane fugue, which will only be ended by a vehicle coming in the opposite direction.

But no vehicle does. We're on the emptiest road in England. For second after second, for year after year, we race on together. Come on! Someone! Please! End it, end it! Kill him!

We soar, almost airborne, over the crest of a hill – and there at last it is. A pair of headlights closing us at a combined speed which must be at least 150 miles an hour.

It's not Tony who gives way – it's me. I flinch at the last, characteristically, from delivering him to his death – my foot's down on the brake before I can even consider the question. What Tony does, even more characteristically, is simply to pull back into the left-hand lane, across the front of me, as if I weren't there at all. I think the first colossal bang, and the first colossal jolt, comes as he catches the front wing of the Land-Rover, and sets the wheel spinning uselessly through my hands. A whole fusillade of bangs and jolts follows as we mount the grass verge and take off once again across the great unpathed lands. There's another noise filling the car, too – someone screaming, either Laura or me, or both of us, because there in front of us, inexplicably, in the middle of the trackless waste, is the abandoned hulk of a broken-down ice-cream van.

I jam my foot down on the brake even harder, but it has no very decisive effect on events; they continue to unroll with the same kind of leisurely inevitability. The approach of windscreen and stationary van to my face. The escalation of the noise. The sudden darkness as the headlights shatter. The surprisingly long distance that we and the no longer stationary van travel together until everything stops happening. The silence. The strange new lack of space inside the car. The weary familiarity of its old-car smell. The oddity of Laura's voice as she explains about some problem with her arm. The difficulty of getting the door open. The oddity of *my* voice as I explain that I'm going to see if the picture's all right. The shakiness of my hands as I try to undo the twine in the dark. The sudden burst of flickering but helpful illumination from somewhere at the front of the car. The repetitiveness with which Laura asks me to get her out.

I'm buoyed up by one clear conviction: that I'm in control of the situation. I've been in worse situations than this in the past few weeks and I've triumphed. I know there'll be time to do everything I have to do before the flames take hold. Time to get the twine untied, and the picture out. Time to get the nearside door open, and Laura free. The only thing that's holding me up is the shake in my hands, and the difficulty I still have in seeing how the knot works. Laura begins to scream. 'Martin! Martin! Martin! Martin!' It's as if the crash has set off an alarm. It's a logical idea, though, I realize: Laura first, twine afterwards, when my hands are steadier and there's more light from the fire. No rush.

But the complications of jammed door and stuck seat belt and the angle of Laura's left forearm and her screaming and the heat seem insurmountable. I find someone alongside me, fortunately, shoving me out of the way and dragging Laura's broken arm through the tangle of seat belt regardless. I move aside and let him get on with it, frightened that the stinking haze of alcohol on his breath will catch fire. Which gives me the opportunity to return to my original task with the twine.

My order of doing things, I find, has been more than justified by events. The plastic strands of the twine suddenly melt and shrivel away in front of my eyes, and the tailgate swings open.

I start to pull the picture out. It's difficult because of the heat, but I'm still thinking very clearly. My first priority is obviously to do what I was intending to do before all this trouble started – to see whether there is in fact some binding between the man's head and his knees. In the bright, unsteady orange light I can make out the snowy crags clearly enough, and the shimmer of the new leaves on the trees. But as my eyes find their way to the party by the millpond the whole valley begins to darken and blister. A yellow veil's drawn smoothly down from the top of the picture, over the mountain blue and the tender green. The yellow veil's closely followed by a brown one, and then a black one.

My eyes reach the man just as the blackness does.

And he's gone.

I suddenly become aware of the pain in my hands, and drop the charring wood.

Man, trees, mountains, sky – they've all vanished into the blackness for ever.

Results and Conclusions

The year rolls round. Late spring gives way to early summer, early summer to high summer, autumn to winter, winter to the first muddy brown signs of another spring. The trees grow green, the sun grows warm, the peasants dance. My burns have long since healed.

Tilda's walking and beginning to talk. She pulls Kate's books off the kitchen table and sits down on the floor with them, turning over the pictures and making little critical noises. So maybe she's another art historian in the making. Another specialist in Christian iconography, even – Kate's just had her baptized, to set her on the road, and started taking her to mass each Sunday. I don't approve, of course, but I say nothing.

It's just after Easter, and we're back in the cottage again for the beginning of the old Julian year. Kate's started doing a little more work on her book, though no progress is visible to the outside eye, but then it's almost certainly going to take her entire working life to finish; it's that kind of book. She got very gaunt and bony last summer – it didn't look right at all. Now she's fattening up again, and we're beginning to think about another baby.

'Ever' didn't, in this case, in the end mean ever. First she came back to London to feed and bath me while my hands were bandaged, and then, I suspect, her confessor got at her. Because of course she has to go to confession before she receives communion. It's a little humiliating, I suppose, to be taken back as a Christian duty, to find oneself used as the instrument of her uplifting self-sacrifice. But I didn't have much choice until I could feed myself. And it could be worse – he might have suggested that it was also her Christian duty to tie my heretical head between my knees while she was washing my back and hold it under the bath water.

I look up now from my writing, and see her watching me from the other end of the kitchen table. She smiles at me. What her smile means is that whatever I'm writing when I write, whatever I'm going to say the next time I open my mouth, whatever I'm thinking now that I've looked up and smiled back at her, she doesn't believe a word of it. Not a syllable of it.

What my smile means is that I'm not sure I do, either.

We're normalizing.

What I'm thinking at the moment, as a matter of fact, is that one of these days I might try to write something about normalism. I believe it's a rather important concept, and I seem to have given up on nominalism; my sabbatical ended without another word on the subject uttering itself. I tried to explain my ideas to Laura, since normalism was her invention, but she said, 'You're Irving again.' It took me a moment or two to translate this into some generally recognized language. 'Oh, *Erwin*,' I couldn't stop myself saying, when I finally got there. She was delighted. 'Every time you do it,' she said, 'you have this same funny solemn look on your face.'

Her father rallied round, as soon as he heard she was in hospital and out of Upwood, and so did the family trust. While she was recuperating on someone's estate in the West Indies, she met Roland Kofos, an apparently much-admired figure in the London financial world, and began a discreet relationship with him, which seemed like a sensi-

ble arrangement, until his wife shopped him to the Serious
Fraud Office, and he was rather dramatically remanded in
custody. So I'm trying to be supportive, which means
mostly lunch when she's at a loose end, paid for I'm afraid
by either the absent Kofos or the family trust. We're friends,
just as she said we should be. Each time I smile at her I'm
remembering that it could be the picture instead of her that
I'm looking at. Each time she smiles back at me she's
remembering that I could have exchanged her for a figure
seven digits long in my bank account. She feels sorry for
me. She's long since forgiven me for the brief moment of
uncertainty I suffered in my state of shock about which of
them I was rescuing from the flames first. Whether I've forgiven myself I'm not sure.

She looks almost as unsettling as she did before. A slight
limp, which I feel in my own bones at every step, but the
plastic surgery's been a total success. And she's still not
smoking, which may be the most positive result to come
out of the whole enterprise.

The dog that I hit, I'm sad to say, had to be put down. It
was this that exacerbated my negotiations with Tony most
of all. My departure with his car, picture and wife always
figured below it in the list of grievances he presented to the
police. His first idea was to have me charged not only with
burglary, motor theft and enticement, but with causing
unnecessary suffering to a domestic animal. Laura's very
tough and efficient lawyers at once threatened to bring a
counter-charge of attempted murder, however, and in the
end we came to a reasonable arrangement. I was driving
the Land-Rover with his consent; he contented himself
with recovering the two Dutch pictures that we'd left in my
car, and agreed to forget about the third; and no gun came
into the story at all. It wasn't as good as the deal I thought

I'd done with him, but it could have been a lot worse, like everything else.

One minor mystery is what happened to the Sainsbury's carrier bag, and the £3,150 inside it. Was it stolen out of my abandoned car at some point? I have a feeling that I may have taken it with me in my confusion, either for safety or with some vague idea of paying Tony spot cash. If I did, I presumably dropped it somewhere in the darkness, or left it in the house, or took it into the Land-Rover with me and incinerated it, because no one's seen it since. Well, fairly small change, in the scale of things, though it would have helped. Kate and Laura both insist that they've written off their loans, but I haven't. Kate will get her six thousand, Laura her seven, even if I have to take that job in the petrol station to do it. I'll repay them in the end just as surely as we're already month by month repaying the bank its fifteen thousand and its interest – mainly so far, I have to admit, by Kate's finding extra work lecturing American cultural tours, which of course is one of the things delaying progress on her book.

Tony's legal battles continue with Laura over the divorce settlement, and with his brother over everything else. He can afford them, fortunately, even though his pheasants are dying of every unnatural cause except gunshot wounds, because when the admirably percipient and unnervingly straightforward Mr Quiss took those two Dutch paintings to Christie's for him, the cavalrymen turned out to be a genuine Philips Wouwerman after all, and fetched £162,000. The chocolate-box skaters they identified as an Aert van der Neer. Not someone I've ever heard of, but other people in the world must have done, because it went for almost one and a half million.

Well, I was plainly not put into this world to be an art dealer.

So the year's rolled round, and the one question that remains is what it was that I discovered.

My view on this has changed with the passing seasons. In early summer I began to believe that the picture hadn't been what I thought it was at all – the entire trail of confusion and destruction had been over nothing. In high summer I was certain of it, and almost serene in the knowledge that nothing of any great value had been lost to anyone except myself.

In the autumn, though, as I returned to work from the summer pastures, my feelings began to change. Now it seemed to me just possible that it *had* been what I thought it was. By deep midwinter I knew it for certain – knew that I should have to live with the consequences of my action until the end of my life – and that the world would have to live with them until the end of time.

Then in the gloomy days of early spring my feelings changed again – changed back and forth between one view and the other with each shift in the weather. And I realized that what I and the world would have to live with was something worse than the certainty that the picture was lost for ever. It was the uncertainty. It was the anguish of the doubt that could never be resolved, of an endless shifting back and forth between light and darkness.

And now, in late spring, as the trees grow green and I pick daffodils to give my nice fat wife, as Tilda and I dance round the broken kitchen chair that's still waiting for the bonfire we still haven't had, and the old New Year begins again, I'm wondering what else has slipped through my fingers since that unremarkable day at the beginning of last spring. What else since I was born, for that matter. Do I know for sure the identity or value of any of it?

Round and round the wheel rolls, and I come back to

where I started out. I've done what I said I would, in this instance at any rate. I've reported my findings to the world. I've set out my claim to any credit that may be going, and taken upon myself whatever shame and opprobrium may seem proper. I've made my deposition, as fully and honestly as I can, mentioning every possible circumstance that might assist the court in its deliberations.

And now I shall rest from my labours, and sit as quietly as I can for whatever of my life remains, doing nothing further of any note at all, I imagine, as the years roll by.

Except await judgement. A judgement that can in the nature of things almost certainly never be delivered.

Author's Note

I had to have a lot of help with this book. I should particularly like to thank Charles Saumarez-Smith, Nicholas Penny and Michael Baxandall for their suggestions about where to look for the information I needed; Robert Erskine and William Mostyn-Owen for their guidance on the art market; a great many librarians, particularly the patient and helpful staff of the National Art Library in the Victoria & Albert Museum, and Frances Carey, Deputy Keeper in the Print Room of the British Library, who drew my attention to Jean-Michel Massing's book *La Calomnie d'Apelles*; to Ashok Roy in the Scientific Department of the National Gallery and Catherine McLeod at the National Portrait Gallery for their advice on painting materials and techniques of the period; to Professor M. G. L. Baillie at the Paleo-Ecology Centre of the School of Geo-Sciences in Queen's University, Belfast, for his advice on dendrochronology (though in the end I decided not to pursue this line of inquiry); to three old friends for their help with languages: Gerda Rubinstein with the Dutch, Sarah Haffner with the German, and Nicholas Monck with the Latin; to the Librarian of Pembroke College, Cambridge, for supplying a copy of the Ortelius epitaph; to Victoria Glendinning for sharing the assistance that David Singmaster had given her with his account of the mediaeval calendar; to my accountant Darrell Nightingirl and my solicitor Michael Wood for their advice on the financial and legal aspects of the deal; to an American reader, Rudy Rucker (also writing a novel about Bruegel), for reminding me of the gibbet in *The Return of the Herd* and pointing out the false perspective in *The Magpie on the Gallows*; to Bamber Gascoigne, for noticing that I was six popes out on the rebuilding of St Peters; and to all the art historians and others whose published researches my character and I have so freely plundered.